Hidden Away in a Paradise— They Found Each Other. . . .

The penetrating moonlight lit her path, and she passed the small slope that hid the hotel from view. She was just a few feet from the private place she'd found that afternoon, when she discerned the figure of a man standing about twenty feet in front of her.

Silently, she glided up to him and murmured, "Hello again."

"I thought you'd come," he said. He was barefoot, the business suit exchanged for faded dungarees and a T-shirt. They faced each other as man and woman, all other roles stripped away.

"You're a very beautiful woman, Tracy," Wes said quietly.

She said nothing, her eyes shining like two golden jewels in the clear night. As she looked into his blue eyes, she saw that his face was etched with desire, and she wanted him suddenly, wanted him urgently, fiercely, with an ardor she did not quite understand. They had waited a long, long time for this moment, and now that it had finally come, it was irrevocable. . . .

Dear Reader:

We trust you will enjoy this Richard Gallen romance. We plan to bring you more of the best in both contemporary and historical romantic fiction with four exciting new titles each month.

We'd like your help.

We value your suggestions and opinions. They will help us to publish the kind of romances you want to read. Please send us your comments, or just let us know which Richard Gallen romances you have especially enjoyed. Write to the address below. We're looking forward to hearing from you!

Happy reading!

Judy Sullivan
Richard Gallen Books
8-10 West 36th St.
New York, N.Y. 10018

Trade Secrets

DIANA MORGAN

PUBLISHED BY RICHARD GALLEN BOOKS
Distributed by POCKET BOOKS

A RICHARD GALLEN BOOKS *Original* publication

Distributed by
POCKET BOOKS, a Simon & Schuster division of
GULF & WESTERN CORPORATION
1230 Avenue of the Americas, New York, N.Y. 10020

ISBN: 0-671-43540-X

First Pocket Books printing November, 1981

10 9 8 7 6 5 4 3 2 1

RICHARD GALLEN and colophon are trademarks of Simon & Schuster and Richard Gallen & Co., Inc.

Printed in the U.S.A.

To Ruth Kamzan,
who knew all along

Chapter 1

THE LONG, BLACK LIMOUSINE CAME TO A HALT IN front of the Beverly Hills Hotel. The doorman opened the back door, and bowed slightly as the young woman emerged from inside the luxurious vehicle. She was dressed in shimmering off-white silk, and the folds of her dress clung to her slim but shapely form. Her dark, glossy hair, sparkling with red and gold highlights, cascaded over her shoulders with measured abundance, for it had been cut and arranged to fall exactly where she wanted it to. The large, golden-brown eyes widened as she greeted the exquisitely groomed young man who had come to meet her.

"Miss Bouchard?" he inquired, extending a hand.

"You must be Tony Amato," she replied.

"Welcome to California," he said smoothly, as the doors were held open and they glided into the hotel. He was dressed in a cream-colored suit, a blue shirt open halfway down and no tie. "I hope you had a pleasant flight."

Tracy Bouchard looked around the elegant lobby and wondered how she had got there. How was it possible, she thought, how could this be happening? Then she drew herself up sharply. Cool it, Bouchard, she commanded herself. You're in the big time now. Don't blow it.

As they went up to the front desk, eyes turned toward her and then looked casually away. She wondered how she was doing. Did she fit in? Was she now a part of the glamor and hustle that went along with her new position? She wasn't sure, but she couldn't suppress the excitement that welled up within her.

What if this Tony Amato could guess the truth? He had greeted her like a princess, but what would he say if he knew that only the day before she had been a lowly editorial assistant to a senior editor at Robert Carey & Sons, one of the most distinguished book publishers in New York?

Waiting for the maître d' to seat them in the cool, dark Polo Lounge, her suave companion waved to a couple in the corner. With a start, Tracy realized that the woman was Faye Dunaway. If only Kramer could see her now, that louse. He'd probably want to break her neck. She had turned the tables on him, to say the least. Tracy pictured him as he had looked yesterday when he lowered the boom on her.

". . . and I'm afraid we're going to have to let you go."

Fired?!

A flash of heat shot through Tracy's body and exploded in her head as she fell back in the chair. I can't believe it, she thought. Then came panic, short circuits. Where am I going to get another job? What about the rent, the bills? She stared down at the new dress she had just charged at Bloomingdale's, and wondered desperately how she was going to pay for it. Then she looked up.

"But *why?*" she demanded.

The short, dapper man behind the desk tensed a little. He pushed a stack of manuscripts to one side and found the ashtray he was looking for.

Then he lit up a cigarette and said, "Look, Tracy. I like you. I really do. You're a good kid. But there are a few things you have to learn. You've rocked the boat around here."

Tracy struggled not to show any sign of her distress. She was not about to make this any easier for Kramer. Not after the condescending way he had treated her.

Kramer took a long drag on his cigarette and went on. "We're a nice, easy-going publisher, you know? You've been—well, too pushy. Some of the editors have made comments. And—"

2

"Like who?" she asked.

"Well, let's not name any names. But there have been a few incidents," he oozed.

"I want to name some names. And tell me what incidents." Her poise had changed to anger. That tone of voice of his. Ugh! Why did he always speak to her as if she were four years old? Tracy felt tears start to come. *Damn,* she thought. Don't cry! She ordered the tears back in place. I won't give this creep a show.

"Don't worry about it, Tracy. You'll find another job. You're smart and determined and you're a good editorial assistant, but you've got to slow down and be patient. You have to pay your dues. Some of the other girls have been here longer than you. You can't just barge into editorial meetings. Assistants aren't even supposed to be at them. What if my phone rang and you weren't here to answer it?"

Tracy thought bitterly about all the golden promises of advancement he'd made to her when she was hired eight months ago. She had found out fast that an editorial assistant was a glorified secretary, and for six of those eight months she had been straining to break out like a racehorse at the gate. She had been promised a chance to work on manuscripts, to work with authors, to learn contracts and book production, but Kramer kept her chained to the phone and the typewriter, with occasional trips to the coffee machine and the copying room.

It wasn't as if no one would pick up the phone if she were away from her desk for ten minutes. The receptionist would pick it up on her board and take a message. Kramer just didn't want anyone horning in on his preciously guarded territory. She had learned a lot in the past eight months, but only by keeping her eyes open and asking questions and taking on extra work on her own initiative. Kramer had not encouraged her at all.

"Look, Steve, when you hired me, I thought I was supposed to be your assistant. That's what *you* led me to believe. But it hasn't been that way at all. If you

3

wanted a secretary, you should have hired one," she told him as evenly as she could.

Kramer glanced at his watch. "Can we continue this discussion tomorrow, Tracy? I have an important meeting this afternoon."

"Let's continue it now. Surely, you can spare five minutes." Tracy looked him square in the eye.

"Okay. You want it? You're going to get it." He leaned forward and stubbed out his cigarette. "You were hired to assist me. That's your job. If I had needed an editor, I would have hired an editor. I should have fired you the first week you were working here, but I decided to give you a chance, and I'll tell you why. You are the sharpest, the smoothest, the fastest learner I've ever had. But you don't know when to shut your mouth. The last straw was barging into the editorial meeting last week—which you had no business doing— to present a book proposal we had already turned down! The other assistants resent you and the editors don't want you trying to take over their jobs. You break the rules, Tracy. And that makes waves. We've got to let you go."

Tracy's eyes were flashing, but she heard him out.

"I've got an important deal coming up," he said. "And I don't want you around to ruin it for me." He realized that he was being very hard on her, so he relaxed a little and added, "Hey, I'm sure you'll get another job. Let's face it, turnover in publishing is pretty high. You're not the first and you won't be the last."

She had many things she wanted to say to him to defend herself, but her anger and frustration got the best of her.

"Go to hell!" she snapped, and before he could reply, she got up and stalked out of his office. She walked to the ladies' room, and collapsed on a sofa in the deserted lounge. At last, she could let the tears come, and she dropped her head onto the arm of the sofa, letting the sobs overtake her. Someone came in, so she turned her face to the wall and composed herself. Then she went over to the sink and splashed her face with

4

cold water. Taking a deep breath, she went back out into the hall. What should she do now? Go back to her desk as if nothing had happened and finish out the day? How could she sit there, answering the phone with a cool "Mr. Kramer's office"? Perhaps she should attack the huge, sloppy pile of unsolicited manuscripts that sat on the bookcase behind her desk. She usually faced the slush pile when she felt like taking her hostilities out on something, but now she didn't feel like doing anything. She walked automatically back to her desk, and to her dismay, Steve Kramer was standing in the hall in front of his office.

"Well, Tracy," he said tentatively.

If he was waiting for an apology, she thought fiercely, he wasn't going to get it. As she looked over her small working space, cluttered with personal knick-knacks, a large Boston fern, and piles of manuscripts and papers to be filed, a wave of self-pity swept over her. For eight months, this had been her home away from home, and now she was going to have to leave it all behind her. She faced Kramer.

"When would you like me to leave?"

"Oh, yes. We didn't have a chance to get to that before you, uh—left. Let's see—today is Thursday, so let's say two weeks from tomorrow? How's that?"

"Oh, just fine," she answered. "Just great." She knew he couldn't handle sarcasm, and she wished he'd go away.

"We'll talk some more later, okay?" he said. "I might even be able to give you a few leads, help you find something else."

She looked at him and she knew he didn't mean it, that he wouldn't help her any more than he had in the last eight months. But she decided to take advantage of the opportunity.

"Sure," she said. "How about after lunch?"

"I've got that meeting at three, but we'll talk soon, okay?" He looked at his watch.

She didn't even answer.

"Say, did you make that reservation for me at Rendezvous?"

"No, I didn't," she answered sullenly. "I didn't have time. I was in your office talking to you."

"Oh. Well, call them now, will you? I already told the agent I'm having lunch with to meet me there."

Howard Collins, the sales manager, came down the hall and slapped Steve Kramer on the back. There was a glint of anticipation in his eye.

"See you at the meeting later, Steve," he said.

Kramer straightened up. "Right." Then he asked in a lower voice, "Any word from Zwerdlow?"

Collins nodded intently, and both men looked at Tracy. They went into Kramer's office and closed the door.

She sat at her desk and typed routinely, letting her mind bubble down to rational, orderly thoughts. The repetitious chore calmed her, and when the two men emerged from the office, she was able to greet them with a polite smile. They went their separate ways, and she stopped typing.

There was something going on. Tracy could tell. Kramer was as jumpy and wide-eyed as a cat. What could Steve Kramer be cooking up with the biggest agent in Hollywood? Max Zwerdlow, huh? Very big deal. Then again, maybe it *was* a big deal. She had taken a call from Zwerdlow's office yesterday. That made three in the last week. Her curiosity grew as she stared into the empty office. What the hell, she thought. I'm already fired. I have nothing to lose by snooping around.

Most of the people in her hall had already left the building for lunch. A few typewriters still clicked away from distant desks, but the phones had grown quiet, and the hallway was deserted. Tracy got up and walked into Kramer's office. She stood uncertainly in front of his desk, her heart pounding, and leafed through the tray of outgoing letters. Nothing there except the two letters she had typed the afternoon before, hastily scrawled with his signature and waiting to be mailed. The "In" box was full, crammed with memos and requisition slips and photocopies of reviews. The usual pile of tedium, much of which would eventually get dumped on her.

Casting a quick glance out into the hall, she went around to the back of the desk and tried the top drawer. It was surprisingly empty. There was nothing there except a box of pens, a few rubber bands and a small snapshot of Kramer taken in a dimestore photo-booth. Tracy resisted the temptation to draw a mustache on it, and tried the drawers on the side. The top one on the left contained a stack of yellow legal pads and a thick bunch of plain, white paper. The second one held a few bills, expense account sheets, a pocket calculator and a memo pad. The bottom drawer was filled with paper napkins, plastic forks and spoons, and a collection of matchbooks and packets of sugar.

Tracy pushed the junk aside and reached into the back of the drawer. Oh, no, she groaned to herself as she pulled out a well-thumbed copy of *Penthouse,* opened to the centerfold. Ugh, ugh, ugh! Her already low opinion of Kramer plunged even deeper. She threw the offensive magazine back in the drawer, resisting the impulse to take it out and tear it to shreds.

Moving on, she found the bottom right-hand drawer held a single file folder, unmarked and unlabeled. She opened it cautiously, and flipped through the first few pieces of paper. Notes from an editorial meeting. A list of book ideas. A torn sheet of lined paper that held a few scribbled figures, and the underlined name Zwerdlow. Zwerdlow! She pulled out the scrap of paper and looked it over quickly. Her eyes widened at what she saw. The name "Fleming" was written in small block letters, and Kramer had etched them over and over again with a felt-tip pen so that they were embedded deeply into the paper. Under that he had written "Ceiling—1.2 mil." Tracy's mind raced. Jim Fleming, Zwerdlow's top client, was the biggest TV talk show host in America. Publishers had been trying to get him to write his memoirs for years, but he had refused adamantly time and time again. If Robert Carey & Sons were about to acquire his autobiography, a sure best-seller, then that was a very big deal indeed. She tried

7

to construe the other figures that were jotted down on the piece of paper. "Straight 15" probably meant the royalty rate, she reasoned. But what about "Wednesday, 4:00"? There had been no meeting on Wednesday, not at Carey & Sons. Maybe the meeting had been on Zwerdlow's end, in L.A. Tracy heard footsteps coming down the hall. Her stomach began to knot. Someone could take this the wrong way—like before, like in high school. She shoved the drawer shut with a bang.

"What are you up to, Tracy?"

Tracy looked up, her eyes wide with panic. "Oh, Janie, you startled me." It was only Janie Goldman, another editorial assistant. "Going out to lunch?"

"No, I'm on a diet. I'm just having some fruit and cheese at my desk."

She watched Janie's ample form move down the long hallway, and a plan started to form in the corners of her mind, a plan so outrageous that she thought she must be crazy. Then again, what did she have to lose? She had only to dare. She didn't want to end up like the Janie Goldmans, all the eager girls who came to New York to work for a dream that never came true. Adrenalin rushed through her body. *Dammit, why not?* She slammed her hand down on her desk and said out loud, "Right now!"

She glanced at her watch. Everyone in town was out to lunch. To make sure the coast was clear in the office, she went back to the ladies' room, taking a moment to run a comb through her wavy hair and apply cinnamon-colored lipstick to her mouth. Quiet as a church! Excitement banished all thoughts of food. She had more important things to do during this lunch hour than eat. Besides, the audacity of her plan was keeping her stomach in knots.

She walked quickly to Kramer's office, flipped through the Rolodex on his desk, and found the name she was looking for. Zwerdlow. She jotted down the number on a scrap of note paper, and folded it in half. Slipping it into her pocket, she went to the elevators and rode down to the lobby. Her heart was pounding as she strode out into the street.

Fifth Avenue was glutted with people, marching like a huge army down the sidewalks. The sun shone brilliantly in a bright blue sky, its rays bouncing off the tall buildings. Taking advantage of the fine late April weather, a flute and violin duo played Bach in front of Tracy's building. From the small crowd of onlookers, a man with an enormous mustache threw a dollar bill into the open violin case on the pavement, and the young violinist bowed ceremoniously. Tracy hurried past them and crossed the avenue.

Her plan was percolating furiously in her mind. Cool it, she thought. Don't get crazy. Get a hold of yourself. It was only one o'clock, so she walked over to Bloomingdale's and looked in the windows. One of them featured a svelte mannequin wearing a black silk suit with a flowing burgundy silk scarf, and sleek, black, high-heeled shoes. She bunched up her dark red hair in one hand and looked down thoughtfully at her cotton dress. Then she marched into the store, rode up to the third floor, and in ten minutes was modeling the black suit in front of a three-way mirror.

"You look stunning," the saleswoman drawled.

She did look stunning. How much? Three hundred dollars. Tracy pulled out her charge card and asked the saleswoman to hold the suit while she went to the shoe department and then to the first floor to find the long burgundy scarf. She went back into the dressing room and took off all the price tags and put the new outfit on.

When she emerged, carrying her other clothes in the Bloomingdale's shopping bag, she drew stares from the well-groomed salespeople and customers. Her glossy hair bounced as she walked, and the excitement within her put an added zest into her stride. I think I am beginning to enjoy this, she said to herself. If only my stomach would, too.

Out on Lexington Avenue, the three o'clock crowd was thinner. It was time. All it took was nerve, and Tracy knew she had plenty of that. Kramer had told her as much this morning. Well, now she was going to put it to good use. She walked to Park Avenue and

9

went down to Fifty-seventh Street. On the corner stood the black and chrome Franklin & Fields Building, home of the most famous and influential book publisher in New York. She stood on the sidewalk looking up and up, squinting in the strong sun, as she eyed the top floor that held the executive offices. Then she took a deep breath, threw her head back and entered the lobby through the revolving doors. Her eyes ran quickly over the building directory. Executive offices. Wesley Canfield. Fortieth floor. She rubbed her stomach to soothe the aching sensation.

As she ascended to the top of the building, she realized she was still carrying the shopping bag with her other dress in one hand. The car came to a smooth halt, and she walked out onto a wide expanse of navy blue carpeting, in the middle of which sat a curved, mahogany desk. A receptionist was seated behind it, and Tracy approached her with a friendly smile.

"Hello, I'm Tracy Bouchard. Will you hold this for me?"

The receptionist regarded her coolly. "May I have your name, please?"

"Tracy Bouchard. I'm here to see Mr. Canfield."

"Do you have an appointment?"

"Yes."

"I see. Well, very well." She took the shopping bag that Tracy extended and tucked it under her desk. "His office is located at the end of that hallway. His secretary will announce you." She pointed with one long, red fingernail, and Tracy followed the direction. A young man in a pin-striped suit approached from the opposite hall, and gave Tracy a quick, appraising glance. She heard him say, "Who was *that?*" to the receptionist before she was out of earshot.

The hallway seemed very long to her, and she passed no other offices—nothing except a small alcove that held a potted palm. Her heart pounded wildly, and she thought, Okay, Bouchard, this is it. This was your idea, so make it work.

At last, the hall opened onto a small but very plush reception area. The deep navy blue carpeting here was bordered with gold. Tracy took a deep breath, squared her shoulders and marched up to the poised, middle-aged woman who sat guarding the fortress, and said, "Is Mr. Canfield in?"

The secretary looked up. Her hair was pulled back into a neat bun, and her makeup was flawless. She looked like a retired ballerina. "Your name, please?"

"Is he in?" Tracy repeated. Then she pouted a little. "He is in, isn't he? I was supposed to. . . ." She stopped and looked confused.

"Yes, he's in. But—"

"That's all I wanted to know." Tracy strode past the secretary and opened the oak door behind the desk.

Behind her, the secretary was fluttering. "Where are you going? You can't just. . . ."

Tracy wasn't listening. She wasn't looking back, only forward. She closed the door and confronted the man who was standing by the floor-to-ceiling bookcase that covered one entire wall of the office. He had a lean, compact build that was elegantly framed by a dark gray suit and black, curly hair. His face was vivacious, his blue eyes electric with energy. So this was Wesley Canfield, the *enfant terrible* of the publishing world. At age thirty-three, he was the industry's youngest company president. Tracy could almost feel the drive that had got him to the top in a few furious years. Canfield regarded Tracy with a curious but slightly arrogant air. He was clearly a man who ruled the kingdom in which he worked, and just as clearly she was trespassing in his domain.

"Who are you?" he asked sharply, one black eyebrow arching slightly.

She inhaled quickly. "My name is Tracy Bouchard. I—"

"What are you doing in my office, Tracy Bouchard?"

The door opened, and the secretary hovered there uncertainly.

"I'm sorry, Mr. Canfield. She just pushed right past me. . . ."

"It's all right, Margaret," he said smoothly. He

11

waved her away, and she backed doubtfully out of the office.

Tracy felt a small surge of triumph, and she came right to the point. "How much will you pay for a book by Jim Fleming?" She was just as brusque as he was, and her words brought a skeptical smile to his handsome face.

"Jim Fleming? I've talked to him already. He's not interested in doing a book."

"When was the last time you talked to him?"

He shrugged. "About a year ago. But I talked to Max Zwerdlow a few weeks ago, and he didn't mention anything."

"Maybe Jim Fleming's changed his mind and maybe Max Zwerdlow's been talking to another publisher." She kept her gaze fixed firmly on his face. "How much are you willing to pay for a book by Jim Fleming?"

His eyes, a startlingly clear blue, assessed her. Tracy did not flinch or betray her nervousness. A slight nod of his head indicated he was not going to throw her out of his office.

"Is he available?" he asked, feeling her out.

Her excitement turned to calculation. Round One, Bouchard. Her eyes narrowed, and she repeated, "How much?"

He laughed suddenly, and his laughter surprised her. It was the bold, hard laughter of a man who was not afraid of anything.

"How much? I don't know. How about a million dollars?"

He was teasing her, toying with her determination. She saw that he did not believe her, and she took a step forward.

"That's not enough," she said flatly, remembering Kramer's 1.2 million dollar ceiling.

His smile faded. "All right," he countered, gesturing. "How about *two* million?" Canfield was not a patient man, and his patience was beginning to wear thin. Tracy sailed past him, crossing the navy blue sea under her feet.

"May I use your phone?" It was not really a question. She had already reached the gleaming oak desk that stood solidly near the back of the huge office, and she reached over it to pick up the telephone. Nothing was going to stop her now. Her nervousness had vanished, and she reached into her pocket for that important scrap of paper. Canfield quickly traversed the space between them, and moved around to the other side of his desk. He sat down in his leather swivel chair and leaned back.

Tracy dialed Zwerdlow's office, and perched herself on the side of the desk, crossing her legs. The desk was practically bare, and she sat facing him, her legs crossed at the knees. While the call connected over the miles, Canfield looked at the shapely legs dangling over the side of his desk. His eyes traveled to the three pressed pleats in the side of the slim black skirt. The tightly fitted jacket outlined the smooth contours of her slender but full-breasted frame.

Out of the corner of her eye, she watched Canfield's frank appraisal of her. If Steve Kramer had done that she would have thrown a punch at him, but she found Canfield's stare exciting and unnerving. He was devastatingly attractive. A voice at the other end of the line brought her back to the important business at hand.

"Mr. Zwerdlow, please."

There was a pause, and she looked Canfield right in the eye. "Tracy Bouchard," she said. "I'm with Franklin & Fields."

Canfield met her stare and the eyebrow went up again. He waited.

"Tracy Bouchard, I'm with Franklin & Fields," she repeated. There was a longer pause. "An editor with Franklin & Fields."

Tracy's foot began to jiggle up and down impatiently. She listened to the person on the other end with increasing annoyance.

"I'm calling to make an offer on a book. I need to speak to Mr. Zwerdlow personally," she said firmly. A flash of anticipation crossed her face and she sat up straighter.

"Hello, Mr. Zwerdlow? Tracy Bouchard of Franklin & Fields. . . . Yes, that's right. . . . Certainly, I'll hold."

She leaned forward slightly, her fingers drumming on the desk top. "Hello? Yes, I'm still here. About the Jim Fleming book, Mr. Zwerdlow, we're prepared to offer you—" She cast a sidelong glance at Canfield, and her eyes registered a brief calculation. "—one and one-half million dollars."

Tracy bit her lower lip as she listened to Zwerdlow's response. Then she brightened and flashed a brilliant smile at Canfield. Zwerdlow was interested! She was almost home!

"Yes," she said. "As a matter of fact, he's right here. Would you like to talk to him?" She smiled triumphantly and put her hand over the receiver. "He wants to talk to you," she said in an excited whisper.

He took the receiver from her and their hands brushed for an instant. He winked at her and said into the phone, "Max? Wes Canfield here. Yes, that's right. . . . Well, Max, you know how it is. We have our ways. . . . Good. . . . Okay, fair enough. . . . You got it. . . . Can we wrap it up by early next week? . . . Well, I'm sure that can be arranged. Call me in the morning and we'll talk some more. . . . Well, I can't come out to the coast myself right now, but I'm sure we can find someone reliable to send. . . ." He laughed and looked at Tracy. "Okay, sure. . . . Talk to you then." He hung up without saying goodby. Then he looked at Tracy, who was now standing in front of his desk, watching him.

"What title did you give yourself, Miss . . . Bouchard?"

"Editor."

He stood up and extended his hand. "Welcome aboard."

Chapter 2

"THIS WAY, MADAME," SAID THE MAÎTRE D', AS TRACY and Tony Amato were shown to a table.

"Drink, Tracy?" Tony asked.

"White wine, please."

"Same for me," Tony said, and the man hurried away.

"Much as I'd like to spend the afternoon with a beautiful lady like yourself, I've got some business to attend to. I'd be heartbroken, but there's a party at Max's tonight, and it will be my pleasure to pick you up and introduce you around. I'll be counting the minutes until nine o'clock. Is nine all right?"

"That's fine." Tracy smiled at Tony. He was giving her a royal snow job, but he was so sincere it was hard to resist. "I'll need some time to freshen up. This whole trip was arranged on short notice."

"I know. Max had to pull the strings himself to get you a room here. Your timing is amazing. We were feeling out another publisher when your call came through yesterday. I like a lady with good timing."

Tracy thought back to Kramer's three o'clock meeting and smiled serenely. "It looks like what we have here is a case of fated intervention." She settled back into the leather banquette and looked at Tony, liking his dark good looks more and more.

"What we have here is a bestseller," Tony said bluntly. "And you made the better offer." He paused. "But you—and Franklin & Fields—still have to pass muster with Fleming."

"I know. Will he be there tonight?" Tracy tried not to sound too anxious, and Tony smiled.

"Of course." Tony touched her hand. "Relax, kid, you'll knock 'em dead. Trust me."

Tracy opened her mouth to laugh, but found herself yawning instead. "I guess I'd better finish my drink and catch a few winks before tonight."

"That jet lag will get you every time. I can't tell you how many times I've taken the red-eye to New York myself."

Tracy asked if he came to New York often.

"Every now and again," Tony replied. "But now that I know you're there, I may make it my business to get there more often." He took her hand, and Tracy found the feel of his warm fingers inviting.

"You don't beat around the bush, do you, Tony?"

He shrugged and smiled. "What for? When I see something I like, I say so. And you I like."

She hadn't expected to be swept off her feet the minute she stepped out of the plane. Something about the headiness of the past twenty-four hours made her feel very sexy. Maybe it had to do with meeting Wes Canfield—who was strictly off-limits now that he was her boss.

Tracy and Tony chatted for a while, comparing California and New York, and Tracy was grateful for his attention and his forthright admiration of her. So much had happened so fast, and it was hard to keep her head from spinning. Having Tony at her side was comforting and reassuring. Not to mention exciting. Despite her excitement, Tracy was bone-tired after her sleepless night and long plane ride. When Tony saw her stifle another yawn, he called for the check. But even in her haze of fatigue, Tracy was keenly aware of the tantalizing way his long, lean legs swung from his narrow hips as he walked out of the restaurant.

She took his arm as they strolled amiably back to the lobby. After they said their warm goodbys, Tracy threw him one more glance over her shoulder. Tony did the same and their eyes met. Knowing smiles crossed both their faces. "See you at nine, babe," Tony called across the lobby. Tracy waved her acknowledgment and headed happily to her room.

The whole suite was grand, but the bathroom was larger than her living room in New York! She filled the tub with hot water, adding several capfuls of bath oil and a handful of scented bubble bath. A leisurely soak in the fragrant water left her drowsy, and she crawled naked under the quilted blanket on the huge bed. The satin cover caressed her body, and as she fell asleep her thoughts drifted once more to the previous day.

Her hands had actually been shaking when she walked out of the glossy F & F building. She didn't feel jubilant or elated, and she didn't know why. What's wrong with me, she wondered, as she trotted up Park Avenue, ignoring the bustle of traffic and the hordes of people. It had all happened so fast. She had got up that morning and gone to work, just like any other morning. By noon, everything had exploded. For an instant, she wished that none of it had happened. She wished for her old desk, her old job, her familiar dreary chores, the security of the routine that had given her life an even keel. But she knew she could never turn back. Nor did she really want to. She had catapulted herself into a new world, one that she would have to master before it overpowered her completely.

She was so intent on her thoughts that she crossed against the light at Sixty-seventh Street, and a yellow cab swerved sharply to avoid her. "Hey, lady, you're gonna get yourself killed!" the driver screamed. She hurried on, feeling the pinch of the new high-heeled shoes as they struck the concrete again and again.

What have I done? she thought wildly. Why do I always act first and think later? Why can't I straighten up and fly right?

She walked for thirty blocks before she realized how far she had traveled. Stopping at Eighty-fifth Street, she let out a long breath, and looked around. Her feet were killing her. She was too close to her apartment to get on a bus now; she had walked all the way home. She turned right at the corner and headed for her favorite bar on Third Avenue.

"Hi, George," she said wearily, as she plopped onto

a tall bar stool. "Let me have a gin and tonic. A strong gin and tonic." She threw a five-dollar bill on the bar.

The bartender looked twice and then let out a long, slow whistle. "Say, don't you look spiffy today. What's the big occasion?"

Tracy gave him a weak smile. "Got a new job today, George."

"Oh, yeah? Well, congratulations." He mixed the drink deftly and placed it in front of her. "Cheers," he said, wiping his hands on a white towel.

Tracy picked up the glass and took a long swallow, closing her eyes briefly against the sting. A few hours ago, she had been so determined, so bent on getting her way. And now that she had it, she felt let down and confused. As she sat at the bar quietly nursing her drink, her tumbling thoughts began to take shape and sort themselves into patterns. She realized that her new job still seemed as unattainable, as out of reach, as before, and that she felt absolutely no sense of achievement. Maybe that's because I haven't achieved anything yet, she thought soberly. Nothing except a very nervy coup in the office of a powerful man. But how long could it last? Surely, he would see through her. She was sorely lacking in the skills and experience needed to be an editor at Franklin & Fields, and she knew it. She felt the terrifying weight of the new responsibility she had yearned for and finally seized. Tomorrow, she thought, panicking. I have to get my act together by tomorrow. One stupid mistake and I'm out. But I don't even know what I'm supposed to do next. We didn't talk about when I'm supposed to start, and what my salary will be. Salary? She laughed to herself. If I don't pull this off, there won't be any salary. I'll be out of another job. That's two in one day. Not bad, Bouchard.

She finished her drink and ordered another one, sipping it as she watched the sun recede behind the building across the street. She had no idea what she was going to do, and she had never felt more insecure in her life. The bartender threw her a curious glance when she asked for a third drink, and she told him to forget it. She usually didn't drink more than one, or stay this late, and there was no point making a spectacle of herself. Leaving George what was left of the five dollars, she stood up and walked gingerly into the gray twilight.

When Tracy let herself into her apartment on East Eighty-fifth Street and York Avenue, she noticed the usual pile of dishes in the kitchen, and she was in no mood to confront either one of her roommates. Ellen would be making excuses for the mess in the kitchen, and Barbara would be wanting to borrow Tracy's hair dryer or her cosmetics. She didn't need those petty hassles now; she needed time to think. Maybe, she thought with a glimmer of hope, I'll be able to afford my own apartment now. That idea was so pleasant that she clung to it for several minutes. No more noise, she thought. No more arguments. Peace and quiet. Privacy. She could get something small but comfortable. She knew that editors didn't command huge salaries; still, she was bound to get a substantial increase. The tangible rewards of what she had accomplished that day began to float appealingly in her imagination, and she decided that if she couldn't feel elated, she could at least feel proud. She had almost managed to lull herself into a soothing false complacence, when the sudden ring of the telephone jerked her back to reality.

"Hello?" she answered tiredly. Then she stiffened sharply as she recognized Wes Canfield's voice. "Tomorrow at four? Flight 405, Kennedy. Yes, that's fine. I'll be there."

A long silence ensued on her end as she hurriedly copied instructions, grabbing a pen from her dresser and knocking over the reading lamp as she switched it on. She was scribbling furiously when Ellen strolled in, jabbering energetically as the front door slammed behind her.

"Hey, Trace!" she yelled. "I'm home."

Tracy waved her hand commandingly and Ellen halted her chatter, watching Tracy impatiently.

"Yes, I understand," Tracy was saying. "Refer Mr. Zwerdlow to you on any questions about money or the contract. Fine. I'll see you then." Tracy hung up the phone and looked placidly at Ellen, who was now bursting with curiosity.

"What the hell was that all about?" Ellen demanded.

Tracy just stared into space. Her fingers drummed unconsciously on the night table. "What?" she asked distractedly.

"What's the matter with you? Didn't you hear me?"

Tracy broke into a careful but triumphant smile. "Ellen," she said quietly, "did you see all the teacups on the coffee table? The ones that have been there for three days? Did you see the stack of dishes from your little dinner party last night for what's his name? Bob?"

"Jim. And what does—"

"Yes. Jim. The one that keeps you up half the night complaining and waiting for him to call."

"Okay, stop right there, Tracy. You don't have to live here. Your standards are too high for us? Fine, then move."

Tracy said as nonchalantly as she could, "I have to go to Los Angeles on business tomorrow afternoon. When I return, I'll be looking for a new apartment. I should be out of here in about a month."

"You're going where? Are you kidding?"

Tracy's face clouded a little. "No, I'm not kidding. I—I got a new job today."

"Really? When? Where?" Ellen was sputtering, but she stopped abruptly when the phone rang. Tracy looked at it, and then picked it up and said hello in a low voice. She paused. "It's for you," she said, disappointed not to hear Wes Canfield's voice again. "It's Jim." Ellen turned and ran into the other room to pick up the extension. After clicking down the phone on her end, Tracy closed the door to her room.

She rubbed her palms against the sides of her skirt and went over to her closet. A hasty look assured her that she had nothing appropriate to wear on this all-important trip. She sighed. Well, she had tomorrow morning to shop. Maybe it would take her mind off her confusion. As her conversation with Canfield began to sink in, she was once again assailed with doubts. They had made reservations at the Beverly Hills Hotel for her, and an agent from Zwerdlow's office would be meeting her. Could she pull this off? She didn't know, but the call from Canfield left no alternative. She would have to try her damndest, and if she fell flat on her face, she would just have to pick herself up, dust herself off and try again somewhere else. Somehow.

The gin and tonics began to catch up with her. Her stomach cramped uncomfortably, and she fought to maintain control. Swallowing hard, she realized that she would never be able to hold down any food, and she might as well forget about dinner. Slowly, she let the one feeling she had suppressed all day rise to the surface.

It was guilt. Even as she remembered how angry she was at Kramer for firing her, she couldn't stop the pangs of remorse that were creeping up on her. She began to imagine how he would look when he found out what she had done. Oh, hell. He probably knows already, and he probably wants to kill me, she acknowledged grimly. Staring down the gloomy hallway, she entertained visions of him crashing through the door to come and get her. Then an even more frightening thought occurred to her. What if he goes out to California at the same time as I? What if I run into him out there? Oh, God, anything but that. She pictured him laughing at her in front of Fleming. Her? She's my secretary. Used to be, that is. I had to let her go.

She shuddered as the night deepened, and at last she stood up, sighing with resignation. What's done is done, she thought. I'll just have to make the best of it. Settling onto a wicker chair, she switched on the television but couldn't even concentrate on an old Darin McCane western. She wondered what she would do if she met him in L.A. He's probably as macho out of his cowboy outfit as he is in it, she laughed to herself.

At eleven-thirty, she realized with a slight shock that Fleming's show was on. With a feeling of frenzy and a great sense of forboding she turned the channel to watch it, but as the familiar strains of the theme song echoed in her quiet room, she found herself brimming with anticipation. This was one of the top stars in America. He was an impeccable entertainer, in a class by himself. And she was supposed to take him on! Tracy watched him as she had never watched him before. As always, the audience greeted him with unbridled enthusiasm, and he handled them with precision and finesse. How can I ever make an impression on him? she wondered nervously. He's in complete control. She sat mesmerized by the show until the last notes of music had faded, and she knew that she had to talk to someone before she went crazy. Turning the sound down on the small set, she leaned into the light and dialed the number of her best and oldest friend. She had known Kippy Martindale since childhood. Kippy had married young and lived with her lawyer husband and two small children in a Connecticut suburb. The two young women kept in close touch, and still turned to each other in times of crisis.

The phone clicked rapidly and then settled into a steady ring. Tracy looked guiltily at the clock. It was very late, but she kept on waiting for someone to answer.

"Hello?" It was Kippy. She didn't sound sleepy, thank goodness.

"Kippy? It's Tracy."

"Tracy! It's one o'clock in the morning! Are you all right?"

"Well . . . I don't know. I guess so."

"Something must be up if you're calling at this hour. What is it?"

Tracy let out a weak laugh of relief, and poured out her story. Kippy listened without comment, punctuating the narrative with an occasional "uh-huh," and when Tracy had finished, she gave a long, slow whistle.

"Sounds like you've had quite a day!"

"You're not kidding. Success doesn't agree with me."

"But how do you feel?"

"I don't know. Scared."

"I know, but what else?"

Tracy thought for a minute. "Well, guilty. Kramer must have been trying to get that book for a year. But there's no way to stop it now."

"That's true. The cat's out of the bag. Canfield knows the book is available, and he's going to stay with it, with you or without you. So it might as well be with you."

Tracy sighed. "But I'm not sure I can handle this. There's so much I don't even know. Canfield will find out, and I'll look like an idiot."

"But you've done pretty well already. Think about that. Don't try and fake anything. If you don't know something, ask. Just be yourself, but don't volunteer your ignorance."

"Oh, sure," Tracy retorted. "Be myself! The me that got fired today? God, it seems like a million years ago."

"No, not the you that got fired. The you that got the Fleming book in the first place."

Tracy was unconvinced.

"Look at it this way. You may be inexperienced, but obviously you did something right. This Canfield guy sounds like he has a lot on the ball."

"He does."

"Okay. So if he wants to take a chance on you, then maybe he knows what he's doing. Look." Her friend knew her well. "You always do too much. Don't go out to L.A. to impress anyone. Just be yourself. They're people, after all. Famous, but still people with feelings. If you treat them like they're some sort of gods, then they'll treat you like you're not."

Tracy listened, but couldn't believe her friend. Kippy's optimism seemed so naïve, and yet the advice was sound. What did Kippy Martindale, suburban mother, know about the publishing business? But then, how much more did Tracy Bouchard know?

"I don't know, Kip. My head is spinning, my stomach is doing flip-flops and my sixth sense predicts disaster. I don't know what I'm doing, or why they would like me, but I'll give it my best shot."

"Good. You're leaving tomorrow afternoon?"

"Yes."

"Maybe you should plan something to keep you busy in the morning."

"Oh, I've already got something in mind."

"What?"

"I'm going shopping."

"Tracy, take it easy. Don't do everything at once. Be patient. And call if you need me."

"Thanks, Kippy. I'm glad you were home."

Be patient, Tracy thought as she hung up the phone. People have been telling me that all my life. Not that it's done much good.

Chapter 3

PATIENCE WAS A VIRTUE TRACY HAD LEARNED TO LIVE without. She was the youngest of three daughters, and her two older sisters paved the way for her as she grew up. Kimberly was seven when Tracy was born, and Rosemary was five, and they treated her like a precious, new toy that had been brought home just for them. They shared everything with her, and Tracy's rate of growth was never far behind theirs. When they got two-wheeled bicycles, she had to have one. When they went skiing in Vermont, Tracy learned, too. She was smaller and clumsier than they were, but it never occurred to her that she would have to wait. If there was something to be learned, she wanted to learn it now. At the age of six, she was already taking piano lessons because Kimberly was, and the teacher had to wait for a year before her tiny pupil's fingers could reach all the keys.

Kimberly was an avid reader and encouraged Tracy to read all her books. She and Rosemary took turns reading fairy tales to their younger sister, and by the time Tracy was seven, she had read most of A.A. Milne and her first two Nancy Drews. The Bouchard house was well stocked with books of all kinds, and Tracy read everything she could get her hands on. She would curl up in her tiny rocker and read far into the night, until her mother had to come in to turn out the light.

When Tracy was ten, she developed a fascination with Marie Antoinette. She read children's biographies of the unfortunate queen and drew endless pictures of her trend-setting hairstyles. One day, when she was riding in the car with her mother, she asked, "How did Marie Antoinette's mother know that she would grow up to be a queen?"

Mrs. Bouchard smiled indulgently. "Well, dear, that's just how it was for a princess in those days. Just like you know that you will grow up and get married and have children."

Tracy understood. A husband and children were her birthright. She was not privileged or special. This was the natural goal and heritage of every girl, and she avidly watched her two sisters proceed through the rituals of young womanhood.

Kimberly married at the age of twenty-one, when Tracy was fourteen. She had met her husband in a college French class, and she taught French in a junior high school and paid the bills while he finished law school. Three months after he graduated, she became pregnant with her first child, and two years later she had twins.

Rosemary married almost exactly two years later. Her husband was the college roommate of her best friend's brother, and they met at a party during Christmas vacation.

Tracy knew her turn would come in time, and when she walked down the aisle as a bridesmaid at her sisters' weddings, she felt that she was rehearsing for her own rite of passage into the land of happily ever after.

Tracy blossomed the summer she was fourteen, turning into a shapely, slender beauty almost overnight. Until then, she had been the tallest girl in the class, with no hips and no bosom. She had always had her father's wavy hair, but it was kept short in a pixie cut until she rebelled and insisted on growing it long. When she walked into school the next fall, her classmates almost didn't recognize her. Her hair now flounced down to her shoulders, and a figure had developed where there was no figure before. The boys had shot up, relieving her of her Amazon status, and they began to buzz around her with ardent interest.

Tracy found herself looking at the boys with a new set of rules. Even at this early age, she was rating them as husband material, using guidelines that had been established from the time she was born. Was this one responsible? Did he treat her nicely? Did he have a part-time job after school? Did he know what profession he would choose? Did he like children? All of these criteria registered unconsciously, and she learned to spot danger signals as well as good traits. Her destiny had been made clear, and she had no intention of straying from that secure path. Although she toyed with the idea of law school or a business degree, she fully expected her male counterparts to think seriously about them, and most of them did.

In high school Tracy was popular and dated frequently, but she didn't have a steady boyfriend and didn't want one. She joined the school paper and the drama club; spent hours on the telephone with her girlfriends, agonizing over clothes and dates and schoolwork. She was spirited and had fun, eager to explore the world. Time enough in college to find Mr. Right.

Tracy set out to do everything she did as well as it could be done. The Bouchards had decided to have no more children after Tracy, and her father knew he would have no sons. So he lavished attention on Tracy and expected a lot from her. Tracy worked hard not to let her father down, and he returned her efforts with the full measure of his support.

There was one thing Tracy learned that her sisters never learned. Their father had been a captain in the Air Force during World War II, and he had retained his love of flying. Kimberly and Rosemary were already in high school when he first bought his Cessna 150 Commuter, but Tracy was only ten. While her sisters worried about dates and college and learning how to drive a car, Tracy decided that she wanted to fly a plane like her father. There was nothing more exciting or satisfying than flying high above the city with him. When she was very little, he would hold his hands over hers on the controls, and she would thrill for a few seconds when he lifted his hands and let her pretend to be the pilot. Later on, he let her fly the plane herself as he hovered near, watching for errors. Tracy loved the surge of energy as the plane rose in the air and gathered speed, and she loved the feeling of power it gave her when the small aircraft would sail off into the empty sky, carrying only the two of them. The roar of the engine would pierce the magnificent silence, announcing grandly to the heavens that Bouchard and daughter had arrived.

Tracy never forgot her first solo flight the summer before her senior year. When she pulled the throttle and guided the plane upward as she had done so many times before, she was seized with a feeling of incredible exhilaration. Here she was, entirely on her own, controlling a complex piece of machinery that lifted her above the earth. There was no one to help her, no one to stop her. She would do anything she had to, and she would never, never let the words "I can't" stand in her way.

She returned to high school more confident and independent than ever before. She was Tracy Bouchard, the flyer, the only student in the school who could offer to take her friends for a spin in her father's plane. She continued to be the impatient student who could never sit still. Her voracious and indiscriminate reading made her mind continually active. In class, her hand waved, questioning, challenging. And then it was Tracy who was challenged. The incident left her scarred for years to come.

Four months before graduation, she was sitting in her homeroom waiting to go to her first class, when her guidance counselor appeared at the door. He motioned for her to follow him, and as he led her back to his office, Tracy sensed something was wrong. He waited for a student to leave his front office before closing the door to his back room. She sat facing his grave countenance, and his expression upset her as she wiped her hands nervously on her skirt. He cleared his throat, and asked, "Were you in Mr. Gidry's room yesterday afternoon?" The question was put solemnly, and she shrugged.

"Well, yes—why, is something wrong?"

"I think you already know the answer to that."

She felt the first sting of accusation as his eyes regarded her sadly. Shaking his head, he said, "I'm very disappointed in you. At first, I didn't believe it, but one of the teachers—" He stopped, hoping she would fill in the blanks. He wanted her to admit to something, but she didn't know what it was.

"One of the faculty members saw you in Mr. Gidry's office after school."

She was still bewildered. "So?"

"Why were you there?"

"I went in to deposit the money from the prom collection. I'm on the prom committee." She laughed nervously. "I didn't want to walk home with that much money. Mr. Gidry said I could put it in the safe until the banks opened up tomorrow—I mean today. Kippy is going to drive me over to deposit it this afternoon at two." She shrugged once more, not knowing what else to say.

The man said nothing and the silence became unbearable.

"Is there something wrong?" she asked helplessly.

"Tracy." He paused once more and the suspense made her nearly frantic. "It's missing. The money— everything collected yesterday is gone."

"Gone? What do you mean, gone?"

He said nothing. Looking up at her, he shook his head. "One of the faculty members saw you putting a lot of money in your purse, but nothing in the safe."

"Oh," Tracy said with a rush of relief, "when I got there I thought it was locked, so I put the money in my purse to take it home, but then I decided to try the dial to make sure it was locked."

"What do you mean?" He looked skeptical.

She rushed her words in an attempt to explain. "You know, I turned the handle to see if maybe the safe was still open, and it was."

"Did you notice if any money was missing?"

"I just assumed that no one else put any money in because they also thought the safe was locked. So mine was the only deposit."

"Yes," he said, "we found your deposit in there this

morning, but nothing else. And incidentally, yours was the last deposit. Everyone else had deposited their money before Mr. Gidry went home."

She couldn't believe it. "Are you accusing me?"

"I'm only saying that one of the faculty saw you putting money in your purse, and—"

"I told you," she said, shaking. "I thought the safe was locked, and I gave it a tug just to make sure. It opened and the safe was already empty."

He said nothing more, but she knew what he was thinking. For the rest of the day, she was visibly upset. Rumors were already flying that something was fishy about the prom, and that Tracy had something to do with it, but no one knew what that something was. But the next morning during announcements, every eye in Tracy's homeroom turned toward her when they heard the principal's voice explain about the robbery. His words shot through the school like a lightning bolt, and Tracy felt sick as she listened.

"So," his voice crackled over the speaker, "because of all the missing money, there can be no prom this year unless the guilty party returns the money."

It was never the same after that. For the final months of her senior year, she was treated like a thief. Cold-shouldered and ostracized by her classmates, every day was agonizing for her. Her stomach hurt every day for four months but she never gave up hope that the real thief, whoever he or she was, would materialize before the end of school. It never happened. All her friends deserted her. Only Kippy and her family remained loyal.

During the difficult period, two things kept her from breaking down—flying, and looking forward to attending Tufts University. She received acceptances from Stanford, Wisconsin and Tufts, and chose Tufts because it was in Boston—far enough to put much-needed distance between her and her problem, but not thousands of miles away from her family.

Although Tufts was actually in Somerville, Massachusetts, the town bordered directly on both sides of Boston and Cambridge. Tracy spent her first year in a dormitory, but then she found an apartment in Cambridge, only a ten-minute walk from Harvard Square. It was during her second year that she met Robert Randolph III, and she knew when she first saw him that he would change her life.

She had got into the habit of studying at the Harvard libraries because they were so close to her apartment, and one sunny day in October she saw him crossing Harvard Yard, his wavy blond hair shining, his light blue eyes looking straight ahead. There was something about him that appealed to her instantly, and she took off after him. He had the Harvard look— scruffy, industrious and slightly arrogant—combined with a scowling expression and a brisk walk. This particular scowl shouted law student, and as Tracy followed him into the law library, she knew she had interpreted the scowl correctly.

Harvard Law School students had a right to scowl. They studied every night until midnight or later; they never had exams until the end of the year, so they never knew how they were doing; they were under tremendous pressure to find prestigious jobs even before they graduated. They said they detested Harvard, but they endured it willingly. They complained bitterly, but they would always be proud of their stint there, and would display their diplomas conspicuously in their law offices around the country. They deplored the "Harvard mystique," even as they encouraged its growth. When asked where they went to law school, they would whisper the revered name with affected casualness, but privately they reveled in the effect their words produced.

Robert Randolph III sat down at a long table in the painfully quiet room and opened a thick casebook. Tracy sat across from him and pretended to read a *Time* magazine. The first half-hour, he never took his head out of the book once. She was sure he had noticed her, but he was either very shy or very stubborn. As it turned out, he was both shy and desperately in need of several hours of study.

Finally, she brought him out of his trance. "How

31

long are you going to keep this up?" she asked brusquely.

"Huh?" He looked up, scrutinizing her foggily.

"You know what I'm talking about. Look, Perry Mason. I've already read this magazine three times from cover to cover."

He was still in a daze. "I'm sorry, my name's not Perry, it's Robert. Uh—what's yours?"

"Why do you want to know?" she teased him.

"I'm not sure I want to know. I mean, well, you're the one who started this."

"What do you mean *I* started this? You think I came here on purpose just to meet you?"

"Say, now, don't get upset."

"Who's upset? You're the one who's upset. What do you guys do, smoke your textbooks? You're all stoned from studying all the time."

"That's the way it is the first year. Can't be done any other way."

She smiled at him, and he relaxed enough to put two and two together.

"You come here often?" he whispered hoarsely.

"No, why should I? I'm not a law student."

"Well, then, what are you doing here now?"

"Leaving!" She got up to leave, hoping he'd take the hint and follow. As she walked out, she could feel his eyes on her back. Once outside, she turned around, but he hadn't followed her. She stomped back inside, walking straight up to the table where he was seated. He saw her and looked up quizzically.

"You want to take me out to dinner this Saturday, Perry Robert?"

"That's Robert Randolph."

"Okay, Robert Randolph, what will it be?"

"I'm not sure." Now he was teasing her.

"Fine, then I'll just wait until you make up your mind."

She sat down opposite him and put her chin in her hands.

He smiled for the first time. "I don't even know your name."

32

She was delighted he had asked. "It's Tracy. Tracy Bouchard." She extended her hand and he took it. "Does this mean we have a contract?"

"What's the quid pro quo?"

"If you have dinner with me this weekend, I'll have dinner with you. That way, we both end up with dinner."

She picked up a large black law book from the pile sitting next to him. "Is this your contracts book?"

He nodded. She grabbed the yellow highlighter he had been using and wrote her name and address on the inside cover. "What time will you be picking me up?"

"Is six all right with you?"

"Saturday at six. See you then."

This time he watched her closely as she left, blinking his eyes rapidly to make sure he had not hallucinated the entire incident. Confident there really was a Tracy Bouchard and that they had a date for dinner on Saturday, he plunged back into his studies.

Robert rang the bell promptly at six that Saturday, and Tracy was pleasantly surprised when she opened it. The law student look had disappeared, replaced by a tan corduroy suit. Although he would not wear corduroy when he was Robert Randolph III, Esquire, Tracy got a preview of the person he would become. He was exactly the kind of young man she had always expected to come into her life. Tracy's student look had disappeared, too, with the elegant green linen dress that contrasted dramatically with her dark red hair. They smiled with pleasure at one another and walked down the street to his car.

"I know a great little seafood place on the North Shore," he said. "They've got the best lobster Newburg on the coast."

She thought he was kidding, but when she saw his car, she knew he was no struggling student. She folded her long legs gracefully into his blue MGB. Robert drove up Route 1-A to Marblehead, a quaint seaside town about an hour out of Boston. Tracy's hair whipped in the wind and the roar of the engine and the salt air on her cheeks invigorated her. When they arrived, she was glowing with excitement.

Tracy feasted on lobster until she thought she couldn't hold another morsel, but Robert insisted she try the chocolate soufflé. She found him not only cultured and charming, but generous as well. He was obviously comfortable with his wealth, and he was happy to spend it on her. They talked about everything from law school to Tennessee Williams, from fishing to economics, and when they walked outside into the cool night, they both knew something had started. They drove in and out of the little towns around the bay, looking at the grand old houses and sailors' landmarks, and then they headed back to Cambridge. Tracy fingered her keys and leaned against her door, smiling up at him.

"I'm impressed, Robert Randolph. Impress me some more."

He leaned down and kissed her gently, and her hand moved up to curl around his neck. Then he stepped back, looked at her for a moment and said, "I'll call you."

"No."

"No?"

"Next week it's my turn. Let's go up to Maine for a picnic, and I'll do the driving."

He smiled gamely. "Fair enough." She winked at him and went inside.

What he hadn't counted on was what she would be driving. At the end of the week, she went home to borrow her father's plane, and on Saturday morning she called Robert from a small airfield near Concord.

"Hi, counselor. Can you meet me at Berman Airfield in half an hour?"

"What are we going to do there?"

"We're going on a picnic, remember?"

"Well, all right," he said dubiously.

She greeted him in the parking lot, and walked over to the Cessna that she had just landed.

"I told you last week, it's my turn to drive."

"Are you serious?"

34

"Sure. Hop in."

In a few minutes, they were high over the lush New England countryside, and Robert Randolph III was high on Tracy Bouchard. She wasn't like any other girl he had ever met—she was a free spirit, interested in him, not his wealth and social prominence. And she challenged him as no one else had.

Tracy was a virgin the first night she went to bed with Robert. He was barely more experienced than she, having spent most of his adolescence and college years being an overachiever. The two of them did the best they could under the circumstances, and they were both fast learners. Robert assumed he would excel in everything he tried, and Tracy believed that assumption. She was a naturally sensual creature, playful and curious beneath the sheets. Between them they managed very well, and Tracy's newfound discovery kept her happily occupied.

Robert Randolph III did not dabble lightly with women. After he had been dating Tracy for six months, he invited her to meet his parents, and they drove to Cos Cob, Connecticut in his MGB.

The family mansion was a huge stone fortress, decorated with the simplicity dictated by conservative tastes. Walking past the somber portraits on the hall landing, and the priceless silver tea service that had been made by Paul Revere, Tracy did not fully realize what kind of family this was, until she met Robert's parents in the library.

Mr. Randolph was a precise gentleman with clipped, gray hair and erect posture. His pale blue eyes had sunk behind folds of flesh, but they were shrewdly alert as he greeted Tracy. His slim wife was dressed modestly in pearl-gray, and her cool, modulated tones befitted her obvious social standing. Tracy was keenly aware she was under scrutiny, and she tried her best to please Robert's family. She had been brought up Episcopalian, and that helped. And being of French descent lent a touch of Continental elegance to her otherwise insufficient genealogy.

Tracy was impressed with Robert's family, but there

35

was something in this Puritan household that disturbed her. Robert was subtly different here. It was hard to put her finger on just what it was. Perhaps his spine was straighter or his diction more distinct and correct. Perhaps it was the way Robert deferred to his father. The visit proved that despite his youthful flings with marijuana and the campaign of a Democratic congressman, Robert was still every inch a Randolph.

After luncheon—Tracy could call it nothing else, for the formal meal was far different from the catch-as-catch-can Saturday lunch at the busy Bouchard home—Mrs. Bouchard took Tracy to see the conservatory and her prize-winning African violets. Mrs. Randolph spoke about her charity work and of the importance of the fact that members of a family like the Randolphs set an example and participate in such endeavors. She asked Tracy if she had plans for a career and how she felt about children. Tracy answered that as she was only a sophomore, she hadn't thought much about a career, but that she expected to work at something until she had a child to care for at home. "Now don't worry your pretty head about a career, my dear," Mrs. Randolph told her. "In the Randolph clan, we leave all that to the men. It works out very nicely." Tracy thought it a strikingly old-fashioned remark, but said nothing and followed Mrs. Randolph back into the drawing room, where coffee was being served.

The visit concluded with formal handshakes all around. Only Robert offered his mother a peck on the cheek during the leavetaking. When they turned out of the vast, circular drive onto the road, Tracy had an impulse to stick her head out the window and shout. She had been quiet and polite all morning and wanted to break loose. At the time, she attributed it to the tension in meeting Robert's parents for the first time, but she continued to feel that way after every visit to the Randolph mansion. But she was so in love with Robert that she put those feelings aside.

When they got back to her apartment in Cambridge,

Robert took a small, blue velvet box out of his pocket. "This is for you, Tracy."

She opened the lid slowly. Nestled on a field of royal-blue satin was a large, pear-shaped diamond. Tracy gasped.

"It belonged to my great-grandmother Randolph. Monday we can go into Boston and choose a setting. I asked father for it this afternoon while you and mother were in the conservatory. He was very pleased, Tracy."

"Oh, Robert. It's beautiful." Tracy ran to him and put her arms about him. "I love you. I love you so much." Tears of joy formed in her eyes.

"And I love you, Tracy. I always will."

Tracy spent the next year and a half in a state of confident serenity. For her, the great search was over, and she could relax, secure in the knowledge that she would soon be happily married. Robert did not always have time for her, but she had her own classes to attend, and there were many plans to make. There was the slightly nagging feeling that Robert had never actually proposed to her, that the whole thing had somehow been arranged and stamped with approval by his parents, but she brushed that off as a childish fear. Her own family accepted the turn of events with interest and joy. They found Robert pleasant and charming, and he would provide handsomely for their daughter. Her future was assured.

The engagement was officially announced in the fall of Robert's third year of law school. *The New York Times, The Boston Globe,* and *The Connecticut Register* all carried the article that had been carefully prepared by Mrs. Randolph.

MISS BOUCHARD TO WED A RANDOLPH

Mr. and Mrs. Daniel Bouchard of Huntington, Long Island, have announced the betrothal of their daughter, Tracy Elizabeth, to Robert James Randolph III, son of Robert Randolph II and Margery Babcock Randolph of Cos Cob, Connecticut. The wedding will take place at the home of the groom's parents in June.

Miss Bouchard, a student at Tufts University, will graduate in May.

Mr. Randolph, a graduate of the Brooks School and Harvard University, attends Harvard Law School. Next fall, he will join the New York law firm of Randolph & Winchester, founded by his grandfather.

His great-grandfather was ambassador to France under President Taft, and his maternal great-uncle, Joshua Babcock, served in the United States Senate. In 1752, his paternal ancestors established Randolph and Company, a ship-building concern which supplied vessels for the Revolutionary War effort.

The couple will reside in New York City after a honeymoon in Nice, France.

Tracy's mother was a bit surprised at this announcement, since she had planned to write it herself. But she put her doubts aside and prepared to welcome Robert into her family.

It was more the other way around. The Randolphs were cordial to the Bouchards, but it soon became clear that they intended to take complete control of the wedding. Dan Bouchard had expected to pay for it, and had in fact put aside a sum to cover the costs, but the Randolphs firmly and coolly took charge. There was very little Tracy's family could do, and they did not want to interfere with her happiness. They decided finally on an engagement party for the couple, to be held in their garden a month before the wedding. They invited most of the Randolphs, but only Robert's parents and two of his aunts attended.

The Bouchards lived in a comfortable three-bedroom house in the suburban town of Huntington. The informal open house buffet was held on a Sunday afternoon, and by three o'clock, the guests were busily chattering and sipping the champagne fruit punch that Tracy's sisters had made. Mr. and Mrs. Randolph sat regally on deck chairs on the lawn, and Tracy circulated easily among her old friends, introducing them proudly to her fiancé.

"We've looked at a lovely home in Westfield, and Robert thinks she'll just love it," Mrs. Randolph was saying. "Mr. Randolph has already ordered the decorator to start looking at furniture."

"Well, that's quite generous of you and your husband," Mrs. Bouchard said. She was more annoyed than she cared to let on. "Does your son approve of this?"

"Robert? Oh, of course. And I'm sure Tracy will adore the house when she sees it."

Tracy overheard this exchange and took Robert aside. He was genuinely surprised at her concern. Inside she felt a wall start to crumble. "Robert, where did you and I decide to live?"

Robert hesitated too long, and she saw clearly what had only been a shadow before. Tracy began to feel a sickening fear, and she grasped his hand frantically. "Robert?"

"Well, I know we had decided to live in New York, but well, I've been thinking it over." He tried to muster his usual confident composure.

"I see. And your parents have been thinking it over, too."

"Look, Tracy, they only want the best for us. They're just trying to help."

"But I don't *want* to be stranded out in the middle of Connecticut!"

"You won't be stranded. You can take the train into the city whenever you like."

"But I don't want to! And I don't want these decisions made for me. How could you go along with such a plan without telling me?"

"I—I wanted to surprise you. I was going to tell you, but I didn't know it was that important."

"Well, it is!"

"Look, why don't you come out and see the house

they found for us? You might just love it, and then you'll see how foolish you're being. What do you say, Tracy?"

Mr. and Mrs. Randolph had noticed the quarrel, and they approached the hedge where Tracy and Robert were standing.

"Anything wrong?"

"No, Mother. Tracy just wants to live in New York, as we had originally planned."

Mrs. Randolph's eyebrows went up, but her husband intervened. "If that's what you'd like, then the house can wait until next year or the year after. There's no rush, after all." He took his wife by the arm and led her away, not wishing to get mixed up in a lover's quarrel.

Robert turned back to Tracy. "You see? Whatever we want is all right with them. Didn't I tell you?"

But Tracy was not at all placated. She was beginning to see Robert in a new light, and it disturbed her more than she wanted to admit. It wasn't so much that his parents meddled, it was that he let them and even welcomed their intrusions. He didn't seem to have a mind of his own, wanting only to please them. But she still loved him, still believed in him, and decided that he would overcome these foolish weaknesses. No one was perfect, and he just needed time to be on his own long enough to stand on his own two feet. He had gone from prep shool to college to law school without much time to learn about the world. She wasn't any more experienced than he was, she reasoned. Maybe they could use a little well-meant guidance, after all. Tracy calmed herself and hid her qualms. The wedding was only a month away. Probably every bride gets nervous at this time, she thought. I'll get over it.

The Randolphs continued to make plans for Robert and Tracy, and Tracy let them. Mrs. Randolph went so far as to select Tracy's wedding dress, an imposing creation made by Priscilla of Boston. The day the dress was delivered, Tracy modeled it in front of the long mirror in her bedroom.

"Oh, Tracy, you look just beautiful. You're so lucky," her sister Rosemary exclaimed.

Mrs. Bouchard entered the room with the mantilla headpiece and the long veil. "Here you are, dear. Mrs. Randolph certainly has good taste. And it's wonderful that she's giving you the family pearls to wear at the wedding."

Tracy felt herself being carried along on a tide of propriety and decorum. Her life was proceeding according to a prescribed ritual, and she struggled to accept it and appreciate what was being done for her. The enormity of the step she was about to take confronted her at every turn. When she graduated from college in May, she walked out of the school auditorium with a diploma and a sense of isolation and confusion. Robert was her future, and she should trust in him. And yet she felt she was being pushed into a life she hadn't asked for. She had planned to look for a job after the wedding, but the Randolphs made it clear in their gently intimidating way that this was hardly necessary. Mrs. Randolph began to instruct Tracy about teas and formal dinners and executive social functions, and at last Tracy could not fail to see that she was being groomed for her new role as a horse is bred for public display. She would grow into a genteel country club member, staunch contributor to charitable organizations, a staid pillar of the Friends of the Museum and a perfect, gracious hostess who would support Robert and boost his career. Without realizing it, she had played right into the Randolphs' hands, and now it was too late. She would have to explain it all to Robert. She was sure he would understand. He loved her, after all, and surely her needs would come first. She was determined to be happy in her new life. It was impossible to believe that the dream would not come true. She was going to reap the best reward of the happily-ever-after promise that had been handed down to her so long ago.

On the morning of the wedding, she felt numb, and she watched the day progress as if it were a scene in a movie. The flowers arrived, her dress was laid out, her father dressed in his rented tuxedo, the limousine arrived. Her sisters dressed her, just as they had when she was a little girl, and they fastened the tiny seed pearl buttons and arranged the long veil of eighteenth-century Honiton lace with loving solicitude and pride. She stood motionless before the mirror, looking at a dark-haired, white-robed figure that seemed to have stepped out of a magazine. The Randolph pearls hung at her throat, and the magnificent charmeuse satin gown trimmed with hand-appliquéd Edwardian lace and Schiffli embroidery swept stunningly down to the floor. The chapel-length train was caught with silk ribbons, shirred to form soft scallops as it trailed gracefully behind her. A bouquet of white roses and satin ribbons rested on her arm, and her hands remained unadorned except for the ring that had been made from Great-grandmother Randolph's diamond.

As the wedding party assembled and the guests arrived, Tracy peeked through the elaborately carved double doors. Five hundred people had been invited, and she could hear the first strains of the twelve-piece orchestra as they began to play. The most socially prominent and indisputably wealthy families on the east coast were represented—there were Cabots, Peabodys, Winchesters and Bentleys. The hushed murmur of the guests confirmed the reality of what she was doing. They've all come here because of me, she thought. Me and Robert. A few of Mr. Randolph's business associates had come from as far away as Japan!

As more and more people arrived, the automobiles and limousines overflowed from the circular driveway in front of the house onto the road, and they parked on the grass in a two-mile radius around the estate. Extra maids had been hired to take the coats and see to the guests upon arrival, and scores of waiters, busboys and bartenders hovered in the wings, waiting to bear silver trays of caviar on toast points, lobster mousse and crystal champagne glasses.

The oval swimming pool had been filled with floating water lilies for the occasion, creating a fragrant pond.

Sixty round tables had been set up in the expansive garden area, covered with snowy linen and exquisite floral centerpieces of delicate orchids and ferns. In the center of the garden stood a carved marble fountain that spouted graduated tiers of water in a continual stream. A floral archway led to a white helicopter that would fly the newlyweds to the airport for their honeymoon in Europe.

The ceremony itself was to take place in the ballroom, and chairs had been arranged in neat rows in the gilt and white room. Tracy was closeted in the adjoining room, a wood-paneled anteroom with no windows. She stood motionless on a white sheet that had been spread out on the floor for her, clutching her bouquet and staring into space.

Tracy's palms were sweating. The strange queasiness she had been feeling for a month had given way to a terrible calm. Mrs. Randolph came in and inspected her, and she bore the scrutiny silently.

"You look beautiful, my dear. I'm very proud of you. I've waited so long for this day."

Tracy smiled her thanks, and her father entered the room.

"Would you—I mean, would it be all right if I spent a few minutes alone with my father? I'm just a little nervous."

"Of course." Mrs. Randolph smiled graciously and left the room.

Tracy looked at her father, and her face fell. He waited for her to tell him what was bothering her, and he had to restrain himself from folding her in his arms, just as he had done when she was a little girl.

"Daddy . . . I'm . . . I'm not sure any more." Her face was pale and her voice was that of a frightened child.

He took her hand and nodded bravely.

"Most people get cold feet right before the big moment."

"I know, but . . . I think this is different." She held up her hand. "Look, it's shaking."

"This wedding is rather frightening, I must admit.

You're the center of attention. No wonder you're afraid." He squeezed her hand encouragingly.

"It's not that. It's just that . . . I'm not sure if I want this." She said the last few words so softly that he almost didn't hear them.

He looked at her gravely. "Do you love him?"

She looked down, unable to face him. "I think so," she whispered.

"You're a big girl now, Tracy. This decision must be yours alone. Handle it the way you handle the Cessna when you're up in the clouds by yourself. You took off, but it's up to you whether you want to fly on or land."

"Or bail out." The words slipped out, and she was astonished at how easy they were to say.

"Bail out?"

She didn't answer.

"You're the pilot now. I have confidence in you. Just remember that your mother and I love you, and we want whatever is best for you." He kissed her on the cheek and they clung to each other for a long moment.

She was alone for the last time before facing the altar. It could all be so easy, she thought. Just walk down that aisle, say a few words, and it will all be over. The helicopter would take them to the airport, and they would fly to Paris after the reception. A life of luxury and ease awaited her.

The familiar strains of the wedding march reached her ears. Her heart jumped. Her hands were ice-cold and she felt her whole body trembling. My God, she thought. Not yet. A little more time. I need time to think. There was a knock at the door. "Tracy!" a voice called. "It's time!"

Too late. The double doors flew open, and she advanced shakily into the short hallway that led into the ballroom. The other members of the processional had grouped behind a screen at the back of the room, and were now moving one by one down the aisle. What am I doing here? Tracy thought. Here, in this strange place? Is this what I always wanted? Marriage. Her dream. In just a few moments, it would all be hers.

44

Then why was her head buzzing with confusion? She groped desperately for answers that were not there.

She wanted to call out to her father as he took her hand and wrapped it around his arm. She thought about what he had promised her all those years. How he had saved for her wedding. It was supposed to have taken place in the house where she had grown up. But, somehow, that had never happened. The Randolphs had seen to that. There was so many guests. Little by little, Tracy had lost control. Even now, she could hardly muster the strength to move her legs. Tracy tried to swallow, but couldn't. Everyone waited with silent anticipation, and Tracy stepped into the spotlight. She almost swooned. Five hundred people were looking at her, their heads craning to see her as she stared blankly into the sea of swimming faces. The lighted sconces on the walls of the ornate room began to blur as she stood there, and the long expanse of white carpet stretched endlessly in front of her.

Her face was whiter than her gown. She searched frantically for a familiar face, for a smile of encouragement. But she was surrounded on all sides by the venerable friends of the Randolphs. There was no one to help her. She was utterly, hopelessly alone at this moment, and she knew she would have to help herself. Her father's words came back to her, the words he had spoken when she was learning to fly. "I'm handing the controls over to you now, Tracy. You're the pilot now. Fly straight and stay level. Someday you'll be on your own."

Mechanically, she began the long, shaky walk toward her future. All she could think about as she made her way closer to the altar was flying. She remembered her first solo flight. Alone in the pilot's seat, the engine revving up, waiting for just the right moment as she taxied down the runway. "Don't be nervous," her father had told her. "Relax. You don't need me next to you any more. You can fly by yourself. Don't panic. If anything goes wrong, stay calm, otherwise the plane takes on a mind of its own. Soon you're out of control, and then you have to bail out."

"I'll never bail out, Dad," she remembered telling him. "I'll always take good care of the plane, I promise."

"Honey, if you ever have to, let it crash. Just keep the parachute under your seat."

The music had stopped. Somehow, they had reached the altar and she found herself at Robert's side. His hand felt limp in hers. The minister's voice rose over the quiet room, but she had trouble understanding what he was saying.

No, she thought. I'm not flying right. She tried to adjust. Easy, Bouchard. Calm down. Relax. The minister's words became clear. "As long as you both shall live."

This is it, she thought. Forever and ever. She was back on the runway. She pulled gently at the throttle and the plane lifted her off. Here she was, standing at her own wedding, and all she could think about was flying—the freedom, the wind, soaring into the air. It was so free up there with nothing but God and the clouds for companions. Tracy was gripped by a terrible fear that pierced her very soul. I'm not flying right, she thought, panicking. Something is wrong. I'm not level. I'm diving into oblivion. *When something goes wrong, don't panic. If you do, the plane takes on a mind of its own. You lose control and the next thing you know, you have to bail out.* She was numb, frozen at the wheel.

"Do you, Tracy, take this man to be your lawful wedded husband—"

She gasped. The minister paused and looked at her ghostly countenance. All at once, her raging mind focused on a single pinpoint of light. The minister continued speaking. She looked at Robert. He was like a puppet in a play. They were all characters in some grisly, contrived plot. None of this was real. Not for her. The plane was out of control. Spiraling downward. *Bail out. Bail out. Bail out.*

She turned abruptly and fled down the aisle. She flew recklessly past the Cabots and the Peabodys and the Winchesters, holding up her long skirt and running for her life.

She had no idea where she was going, but she ran out to the garden, where the round, white tables stood ready on the lawn. Up ahead she caught sight of the helicopter that was to have taken her off on her honeymoon. She reached it just as Robert appeared, looking angry and embarrassed as he followed her through the maze of decorated tables. The pilot of the helicopter gazed at her in astonishment, but instinctively he turned on the engine as she climbed on board. The props turned slowly and then picked up momentum, sending flowers, tablecloths and napkins into the whirlwind. As the 'copter rose into the air, Tracy collapsed against the seat and closed her eyes. At last, she had stopped trembling.

Tracy Bouchard was on her way to New York.

Chapter 4

TRACY ARRIVED IN NEW YORK CITY WITH A BROKEN dream and five hundred dollars that she had saved. But she was determined to make it on her own, and she knew when she walked out of her parents' house that she would never come back there to live. Within a month, she had rented a two-bedroom apartment on East Eighty-fifth Street with two other girls and had got a job as a clerk at the Barnes & Noble bookstore, where she earned one hundred and ten dollars a week. Although she could barely pay the rent and had no idea what she might be doing in a year's time, she had a sense of freedom and a chance to make her own mistakes.

She walked all over New York, and her travels took her to East Side bars, Village coffeehouses, SoHo art galleries, Madison Avenue boutiques and the riotous streets of the Lower East Side. As she learned her way around, she found that her ventures strengthened her independence and increased her solitude. She thought of picking up the phone and calling Robert countless times, but each time she stopped herself. It was difficult, but she convinced herself it would get better.

Her job took a great deal of energy, and she came home from work exhausted for the first few months. Robert gradually became a memory as she adjusted to the new schedule, but her spare hours remained empty. Her roommates were busy, disorganized and unpredictable. They kept crazy hours and stripped her privacy to the core, but she couldn't afford to move.

At last, she decided that it was time to find a new romance, but to her dismay, she found it was infinitely harder to meet men in the daily grind of city life than it had been in the comforting confines of school. There just didn't seem to be any nice men around, and she began to wonder where they were hiding.

The ice was finally broken when she met a flying student at the local airfield during a visit to her parents, and helped him learn the details of an instrument landing. They dated briefly, and then she met a graphics designer at an art gallery, an advertising copywriter during an intermission at the ballet and an unemployed actor on the crosstown bus. He was on his way to an audition and asked her to cue his lines.

In the meantime, the job at Barnes & Noble had taken some form, and little by little she began to learn. She read book reviews and *Publishers Weekly,* and learned what books sold and why. She saw how different covers made books more marketable, and how merchandising could make or break a title. One day, she tried an experiment. She took a second-rate thriller and stacked copies neatly in the window next to four bestsellers. By the end of the day, half the pile of books had been sold.

Her managers were impressed with her feel for the product, and promoted her to head clerk and then to assistant manager. She became involved in buying, and learned the retailing end of the business. After a year, she knew that her future was in books, but she did not want to stay in retailing.

Phil Monroe came into her life one summer evening as she was restocking the shelves. He was a writer, he said, working on a novel and waiting tables in an Italian restaurant to pay the rent. He lived in a studio apartment with a Siamese cat named Coco, and everything he owned could be packed into one small suitcase. Tracy liked him immediately. He was the most unmaterialistic person she had ever met, and although she did not realize it at the time, he was a marked contrast to Robert and the Randolph possessions. Phil never had enough money, but his dedication to his writing filled her with awe. Here was a person with a real purpose in life, and her respect for him grew daily.

49

She went home with him the night she met him, and stayed. She worked during the day and he worked at night, which gave them very little time together. But they had Sundays free, and they would go to the park with a bottle of wine and a basket of fruit and cheese, and he would tell her about the dreams and passions he was trying to capture in his novel. It was the focus of his life and had been for the last five years. She had asked to read it the first night she was with him, but Phil didn't want anyone to read it until it was finished.

She trusted him and was sure his talent would be recognized. In the meantime, she had become restless with her job at the bookstore and decided to look for something more interesting in publishing. Tracy saw an advertisement in *The New York Times* for an editorial assistant at Robert Carey & Sons, and she called for an appointment. Steve Kramer hired her immediately; she was the first person he'd interviewed who'd had any experience with books at all. Tracy made it clear she didn't want to stay on the bottom rung for long, and emphasized her rapid advancement at the bookstore. He assured her that hard work and diligence would move her up the ladder. But the phone never stopped ringing, the letters never stopped coming, and Tracy always had a mound of paperwork on her desk. However, on her very first day on the job, Tracy learned the most important lesson she was to learn in publishing. It was something she had seen in the bookstore, but Phil's influence had clouded her astute observation. Once she was sitting in the editorial department of Robert Carey & Sons, it became crystal clear to her, and it changed her perspective on books forever.

What Tracy accepted wholeheartedly was that book publishing is a business, that books are a product, and that the purpose of a business is to make money. She wanted to understand everything about the publishing business and she set about learning it with her customary zeal. She talked to everyone at Carey & Sons, asking questions about copy-editing, production, promotion, advertising, marketing and budgeting. She read everything she could get her hands on. Her self-education flourished as she strove to master her new field.

The only thorn in the plan was Phil. He came home after midnight, full of energy, eager to share his thoughts with her. If she were still awake, they would have a glass of wine and make love until they fell asleep, sprawled under the thin Indian bedspread. She would get up and go to work, and sometimes he would come uptown and meet her for lunch. Her new world was a glaring reality he didn't want to face. She talked about books in a way that frightened him, and he tried hard to pull her back to the long, reverent discussions they used to have. But it was too late. Her drive inspired him to put the finishing touches on his novel, and he presented it to her one evening, asking her to take it in and show it to Kramer.

She sat down to read it, and was dismayed and upset by what she read. Phil's novel was boring, filled with pompous displays of self-styled philosophy, personal revelations and great truths that had meaning only to him. After her crash course in commercial book publishing, she knew his great effort was a disaster. She didn't want to show it to Kramer; it would make her look like a fool. When she had read the last page, she breathed a sigh of relief and looked up. Phil was hovering in the doorway, watching her with hopeful, searching eyes. When he saw that she had finished, he came over and sat down on the rug at her feet.

Although it broke her heart, she could do nothing but tell him the truth. She told him calmly and without apology, and he listened stonily, refusing to believe her. Then he stood up and faced her.

"What do you know about it, anyway?" he cried bitterly. "All you care about is crap that sells a million copies and makes a pile of money."

She sighed. "That's not true, Phil, and you know it. I'm just talking about something that more than a few people would want to read."

He picked up the manuscript and flourished it in her

face. "And how do you know that no one wants to read this?"

She gave up. "I don't. It's just my opinion. Please, Phil, I didn't mean to—"

His face was red with anger. "Well, the hell with you. Ever since you started that damn job, you've changed for the worse. You don't have standards any more. All you care about is money."

"Stop it! You know that's not true!"

"Five years of my life, and what do you care? Well, I've got news for you, Bouchard. I'm going on, and I don't need you. I have something to say, and I'm going to say it, and people are going to listen."

She didn't look up. Tears were running down her cheeks, and she didn't want him to see them. Not because she was afraid to show her feelings, but because it was too late for a reconciliation. It was over, and she knew it. She wiped the tears off her cheeks as he turned to the window.

"Goodby, Phil," she said quietly.

He wheeled, his face collapsing with surprise and disappointment. "Where are you going?"

"I'm going back. To my own apartment. To the real world."

He advanced, trembling with suppressed anger. "Go on, then. Go back where you came from. Go hide yourself in a plastic world made of money. Or do what you almost did before. Marry into it!" He spat out the last three words with venom, and she regarded him with quiet determination.

"No," she said. "This time I'll get it myself."

Chapter 5

WITH ONLY A FEW HOURS FOR SHOPPING, TRACY'S last-minute spree had been frenzied. She had stormed through Bloomingdale's and Bergdorf's with relentless energy, and by lunchtime she had bought a sensational black and gold off-the-shoulder evening dress, high-heeled gold sandals, a shimmering off-white silk dress to wear on the plane, a new pair of designer jeans, a raspberry satin blouse and a scanty ice-blue negligée.

Now, in the suite at the Beverly Hills Hotel, the new clothes hung neatly in the closet. She climbed out of bed at eight o'clock and selected the black and gold gown to wear to Zwerdlow's party. She hoped it would not be too formal and wished she had asked Tony Amato's advice. Oh, well, better to be overdressed than underdressed, she thought nervously.

An hour later, she was speeding along the freeway in Tony's silver Porsche. Tracy watched him out of the corner of her eye. She still wasn't sure if he was a guy with real clout, or just a smoothie Zwerdlow hired to run errands. But she didn't really care. His undisguised interest in her was having its effect, and her breathing deepened when she noticed the way his leg muscles tensed as he braked for a passing police car. He looked like a model in an advertisement for California living—the casual, elegant clothes, the gold chain bouncing off the bare chest.

The car left the freeway, and began a lazy, winding drive through a fabulously wealthy neighborhood. Tracy looked at the enormous, opulent houses with their acres of manicured lawns. I may be a newcomer, she thought, but I could belong here. I could fit right in. If only I don't make a fool of myself first. After all, who was Tony but a street-smart guy who had used his wits and nerve to get ahead? Only a trace of a Brooklyn accent lingered in his speech, but it was there. The alligator shoes and the carefully styled hair could not entirely erase Tony's background. Tony belonged here, though; he knew it and he acted like it. Tracy wondered how long it had taken him to get comfortable, to be accepted. She put her worries out of her head and turned to the passing scenery.

The huge houses were more often than not hidden behind groves of artfully planted trees, and the road took on a countrified air.

"No sidewalks out here, huh?" Tracy asked.

Tony threw her a quick, easy smile. "We don't need 'em," he said.

They drove for a while in silence. Then, as the car glided noiselessly around a shaded glen, Tony said, "Just remember, this isn't New York."

"What do you mean?"

"I have a feeling that the people at this party are going to be different from what you're used to."

"Oh, come on. They're just people. I'm sure I can handle it." She wondered if he could see through her, and had the distinct feeling that he could. But she was afraid to fully confess her ignorance—even to Tony. She would just have to play along and learn fast.

"These aren't just people," he went on. "They're filthy, dripping, disgustingly rich—and they have the power to take a nobody and turn him into a somebody." He paused. "Or vice versa. You remember a guy named Elton Hansen?"

"Sure. He was a big star. I used to see all his detective movies with my girlfriends." She smiled, remembering. "Whatever happened to him?"

Tony laughed grimly. "Hansen wasn't smart, that's what happened. He asked for it. Does the name Heather Gentree ring a bell?"

Tracy shook her head.

"She's one of the older rocks in this business," Tony said simply. "She took her father's money out west with her and bought up a studio and a few thousand people. Elton used to fill in as an extra. He came out from Idaho or someplace. While he was waiting for a break, he got a job driving Heather Gentree around town. He must have made her feel young and wanted. He's good at that—after all, he's an actor. She put him on top, and in return for helping him, she got a slap in the face. He signed with another company, and then, to add insult to injury, he shacked up with her niece in the girl's Beverly Hills home that had been a gift from her aunt."

"So she axed him out."

"Right. In those days she had a blacklist that was longer than Joe McCarthy's."

Tracy frowned. "Maybe she doesn't go for young, female competition."

"No. You got it wrong. She doesn't *have* any competition. Half the people in town owe her favors, and the other half would like to."

"Whew! Is there anyone else I should know about?"

"Look," he said emphatically, "the party will be made up of four types of people. Those who always had, those who didn't and now they do, those who don't but will and those that never had and never will. Heather Gentree falls into the first category. Max Zwerdlow and Jim Fleming fall into the second."

"And you fall into the third," Tracy said.

"So do you."

They smiled at each other, and Tracy felt a real rapport with him. He was more than just a terrific-looking guy or a host doing his job. He was her friend, and it had happened in just a few short hours. Whatever else happened between them—Tracy tingled at the thought of being alone with Tony—she knew she had an ally here in L.A. She had felt so nervous and alone when she left New York, but Tony had responded to her almost immediately, and here she was driving in his Porsche, enjoying the night air, breathing in the smell of success. Everything's going to be just fine, she thought to herself.

"Zwerdlow only gives these parties every few

months," Tony was saying. "You arrived at the right time. You're a lucky lady, Tracy Bouchard. And that's what this town is all about. But being in the right place at the right time isn't all that matters. It's what you make of your lucky breaks that counts. One false step can eliminate you from the scene. The right steps can put you on a rocket to the stars. So take your time tonight, Tracy. Relax. Enjoy yourself."

He slowed the car as they approached their destination, and at first Tracy couldn't see where they were going at all. They seemed to be entering a forest, until the trees parted suddenly and she caught a breathtaking view of a sprawling, Spanish-style house centered in a small valley. The car glided smoothly down the hill, passing elevated tennis courts and a magnificently landscaped swimming pool. They pulled up beside the house, parking in back of a white Rolls Royce.

The party was already in full swing when they walked inside. The large room glowed from rows of precisely aimed track lighting. The walls were white, and thick Persian rugs partly covered the oak floor. Although several armchairs and plush sofas were arranged in the center of the room, the overall impression was one of light and space. An enormous window looked out over the grounds, and the pool, illuminated by Japanese lanterns, glittered like a turquoise gem.

Tony led Tracy into the room, and she stood for a moment watching the fifty-odd people milling about, all with drinks in their hands. She knew at one glance that Tony was right. These were not ordinary people. There was something different about them, something subtle yet powerful. They were all beautiful, all perfectly groomed, elegantly dressed, not one hair out of place. The women all looked as if they had just walked out of the beauty salon; the men looked like the models in *GQ*. Yet there was no feeling of effort, no sense of struggle or achievement. These people always looked like this; they could afford to. That was it. The flawless skins, the lack of wrinkles, the even muscle tone and firm limbs had all been bought. These people had bought their very bodies, and they had done so without pride or shame. It was simply their way of life. No one in the room looked over forty, although many of them were. It was a modern day Never-Never Land that Tracy stared at. And I have to conquer this, she thought nervously.

Tony took her hand and led her over to a short, silver-haired man in the corner who was talking to a stunning blonde. The man turned and Tony said, "Max, this is Tracy Bouchard."

Zwerdlow extended a well-manicured hand, and she took it.

"Tracy! So good to see you. Welcome to L.A."

"It's my pleasure," Tracy said with genuine enthusiasm. "Your house is beautiful."

"Thank you, thank you. Tony will show you around. You might go for a swim in the pool later on."

"Thanks, I might just do that."

Underneath the California tan and the polished smile, she could see that he was all business. The handshake was firm, and the voice betrayed his New York origins. The dark brown eyes scanned her quickly, not with masculine appreciation, but with the practiced eye of a seasoned negotiator. He was sizing her up. Tracy fidgeted under his gaze.

"I'd love to see the rest of the house," she said.

"Good. Tony, why don't you get Tracy a drink, and we'll talk some more later. Jim will be here soon, and of course I'd like you to meet him. In the meantime, relax, have a good time."

She breathed a private sigh of relief, thankful for the chance to get her bearings.

Zwerdlow turned back to the blonde, who looked vaguely familiar to Tracy, and Tracy heard him say, "Now, look, Cheryl, sweetheart. A contract's a contract. You can't start backing out yet. . . ."

It was exactly the sort of conversation she would have loved to overhear, but Tony, an amused grin on his face, was taking her over to the bar.

"What'll it be?" he asked.

"Perrier."

"That's all?"

"Yes. I want to be on my toes tonight."

He flashed her a knowing look and poured her mineral water. He fixed a scotch and water for himself, and nodded toward the hall at the far end of the room.

"I'll take you out back and show you the rest of the house. Then I'll introduce you around."

He was giving her time, giving her a chance to get used to all this, and she was grateful. They sauntered down the long hall, which opened onto a large, square room with a sun roof. A palm tree was planted in the exact center of the tiled floor, surrounded by a neat circle of gravel. There was no furniture, only a series of Indian mats, and a large picture window that overlooked the trees.

"What's this?" she asked.

"Meditation room."

"Oh. And who's that?"

A tiny figure sat in the lotus position on a mat under the picture window, barely visible in the shadows of the dimly lit room. Her eyes were closed, and she seemed unaware of Tony and Tracy.

"It's just me," Tracy heard a thin, breathy voice reply.

Tony grinned. "It's Ambrosia," he told Tracy. "And how's my favorite jewel?"

"I'm fine today. Who is that with you?" The woman had not moved an inch or opened her eyes.

"This is Tracy Bouchard. She's an editor with Franklin & Fields." Tony took Tracy's arm and guided her to Ambrosia's mat. "Tracy, this is Ambrosia Jewell."

Tracy extended her hand, but Ambrosia still did not open her eyes.

"Wesley Canfield is my dearest friend," said Ambrosia in her childlike voice.

Tracy dropped her hand, unsure what to make of this strange greeting. "It's good to meet you. Of course, I've seen your picture so many times I almost feel I know you."

It was hardly possible to walk past a newsstand without seeing Ambrosia Jewell on the cover of *Vogue* or *Mademoiselle.* She was shockingly beautiful. Her face seemed to be chiseled from shining ivory, and her skin had a radiance that looked like moonlight. Her soft, jet-black hair flowed like the wings of a bird down to her waist. Her eyes were shaped like piquant apricots and framed by long, graceful lashes. Their deep violet color was hidden tonight under pure white eyelids. She seemed like a talking statue to Tracy. And did the statue come to life in the arms of Wes Canfield? Tracy wondered. Ambrosia's exquisite beauty made her the object of desire, but she held herself remote and untouchable. It was the kind of challenge a man couldn't turn down, especially a man like Canfield, who thrived on challenge.

"Why don't you come out and join the party, Ambrosia?" Tony asked gently. "I'm sure Max would like to see you, and Jim Fleming will be here soon. I know you like Jim."

"I will, Tony. I promise." Ambrosia answered Tony like a little girl trying to get on daddy's good side. "Goodby, Tracy."

"Goodby. I hope we'll get to talk more later." Tracy looked at Tony, wondering if she'd said the right thing. California was full of surprises. How many New York apartments had meditation rooms? You'd never meet someone at a party there who kept their eyes closed the whole time.

"Ambrosia's a rare flower," Tony explained as he led Tracy through the beaded curtain at the other end of the room. "Everyone thinks she lives in the fast lane because she's a cover girl, but she keeps to herself. There aren't too many people she's not scared of."

"She didn't sound like she's scared of Wes Canfield," Tracy probed.

"No. She and Canfield have a really special relationship. He's the only person in the world she trusts. Besides me, that is."

"It's hard to build trust if you can't look people in the eye. She never opened her eyes to take a look at me. She won't even know me if we meet again."

Tony pulled her close, taking her face between his

hands. "Don't be so hard on her, Tracy. She's been through a lot." He looked at her with his soulful eyes and Tracy felt herself begin to melt as she met his gaze. He leaned in and kissed her gently on the lips.

"Mmm. That was nice. Think I'll have another." This time the kiss was longer and deeper, and Tracy wrapped her arms around his neck, pulling him closer. His lips were warm and soft and they parted slowly, sizing up each other and this surge of new feeling.

"So why don't we see the rest of the house and get back to the party? You've got more important things to do than kiss me in the hallway," Tony said, bringing them both back to reality.

"Okay. Back to the party. But only if you promise we can continue this discussion later," Tracy challenged.

"I think that can be arranged. In fact, I'm sure it can."

They continued down the short hallway that gave access to four bedrooms and Zwerdlow's office, huge and imposing and flanked by two smaller secretaries' rooms. The walls were covered with signed photos and awards, and Tracy noticed a large, autographed photo of Jim Fleming, taken just after he had won his fourth Emmy. The furniture was covered in burnished brown leather, and a deep burgundy carpet adorned the floor.

Tony led her down another hallway that opened into the kitchen, and Tracy could not help laughing at the sight of it. It was immense, equipped with every imaginable appliance, and it was larger than her whole apartment. Adjacent to it was the dining room, comfortable but elegant, and then they were back in the living room. As they stood surveying the scene for a moment, Tracy heard a voice at her side.

"You know something? If you're not the classiest lady at this party, then I'm not the toughest guy."

She turned and found herself face to face with Darin McCane. It was funny seeing him in the flesh after watching him on TV just last night. He wore a pale blue leisure suit that contrasted sharply with his deep tan, and she wondered if he packed a six-shooter underneath it. She wasn't at all sure what to say to him, but she smiled with friendly interest.

"Careful, Darin." It was Tony Amato. "This girl packs a pen and a contract."

"Hell, I should have figured you for an agent."

"You figured wrong." Tracy smiled up at him.

"Actress?"

"Wrong again. I'm an editor at Franklin & Fields."

"No kidding." He winked slyly. "A literary type! Hey, you wanna buy my life story?"

She was so surprised that she missed a beat, but then she quickly offered her hand and said, "Sure. I'll give you a hundred thousand dollars for it."

He reached out to take her hand, but Tony cut in quickly.

"Hold on there, partner, before you shake on anything. Verbal agreements are just as binding in her business as they are in ours. Don't let those gorgeous eyes fool you."

"Oh, Tony," she said, trying to laugh. "I was just kidding."

Darin McCane slid his arm too tightly around her waist, and drew her over to the side with mock secrecy. Tony came to her rescue, making light of it, and she turned to join another group. To her delight, she found herself talking to Marilyn Mullaney, star of a new hit TV series. Marilyn Mullaney had been a New Yorker only a year ago, going to auditions and looking for the big break. It came in the form of an audition for MTM Productions, and she was floored when they offered her a series of her own. Marilyn was now the star of a show about a very rich young widow, and had become an overnight sensation. Tracy found she was as charming off-screen as on. They chatted about the effects of success for a while before parting, and Tracy struggled to understand. She knew instinctively that every contact, every person, was a valuable source that might come in handy one day. She knew it was important to build an arsenal of powerful people, to form a network that would establish her own power base, but it was obvious that she needed them much more than they needed her.

An hour later, she had met songwriters, TV anchormen, last year's Oscar winner for Best Actress and the director of *Four Letter Words,* the movie that had set Hollywood on its ear last month. When she finally ran into Tony again, she was confused and flustered, still trying to find a formula that worked.

"You look like you're working hard, babe," he said, slipping a muscular arm around her waist.

"I am," she replied, with a small sigh.

"Well, you shouldn't be. Have you met Heather Gentree yet?"

"No, where is she?"

"Right here, darling," said a low, throaty voice.

Tracy turned to acknowledge an impeccably groomed woman under a halo of silver-blonde hair. She was petite, ladylike and razor sharp.

"How do you do? I'm Tracy Bouchard."

Heather Gentree took her hand briefly, but did not take her eyes off Tracy's face.

"I know," she said. "Max told me all about you."

"In a favorable context, I hope."

There was an inscrutable pause as Heather's gray eyes twinkled. "I think your mission here will be successfully accomplished."

"I certainly hope so," Tracy replied cautiously. Heather's eyes were shrewd, but her smile remained pleasantly neutral.

"Book publishing is a new interest of mine. You're with Franklin & Fields now, isn't that right?"

"Yes, I am."

"We'll see how long that lasts."

Tracy was taken aback by this abrupt statement. Heather seemed to know something Tracy didn't.

"Don't worry, my dear. It will all be for the best. We'll be meeting again, I'm sure." She turned away as quickly as she had appeared, and Tracy watched her with a puzzled smile on her face, not knowing if she should be flattered or afraid.

Tony had witnessed this unusual exchange wordlessly, and he put a hand on Tracy's shoulder. "Well—that's Heather," he said simply. "She's quite a dame, isn't she?"

"I'm not sure," Tracy said, dumbfounded. "But I believe she's right about one thing. I think I'll be meeting her again."

"If that's what she said, then there's no doubt about it."

The party swirled on around them, and Tracy heard a man's voice nearby saying, "Hell, I don't know where it should take place. Frankly, my editor and I don't get along, and I think that's why she rejected the idea. The world doesn't need another family saga, she told me. Stick to what you know best. So, she wants another Hollywood sex-podge."

"Why not do both?" Tracy broke in earnestly.

The writer turned, and looked at her.

"Do a Hollywood dynasty," she continued. "Then send it to me, Tracy Bouchard, at Franklin & Fields."

He looked her over, unimpressed. "My books *are* Hollywood dynasties," he said with exaggerated patience. "They're exactly what I'm trying to get out of doing."

She flushed, and he turned back to his friend. Her glass was empty, and it was definitely time for a breather. She knew she was doing something wrong, but she couldn't figure out what it was. Kippy's words about being herself came back to her, but they seemed hollow and inadequate in the face of the high stakes and immediacy of this top-level challenge. Driving here with Tony she had felt she belonged, but now she saw how arrogant she had been.

Pouring herself another Perrier, she stood quietly in a corner and tried to calm herself. She was trying too hard. Perhaps the best thing was to sit back and observe. It was worth a try. Things could only improve.

Tony sauntered over and smiled encouragingly. His affection had a wonderfully soothing effect on her jittery nerves. He chatted with her in a soft, offhand way, gently washing away her anxiety. He knew exactly what he was doing. She stole a glance at the people around them, and saw for the first time that not all of them were wheeling and dealing at every moment. They were chatting just as she and Tony were. All she had to do was relax and stop acting as if her entire future depended on whom she met at this party.

Then she noticed heads turning, and swung to see what was causing the distraction. Jim Fleming was framed in the archway that opened onto the living room. Tracy could see at once that he had a quality that set him apart from even these polished, accomplished people. He moved with the easy confidence of a man who feels comfortable everywhere he goes. By God, Tracy thought, he's electrifying.

His dark brown hair was sprinkled liberally with salt-and-pepper gray, giving him a lively, distinguished air. His broad smile was charming and completely genuine. It was clear he liked the company and was looking forward to an enjoyable evening. There was nothing phony about this man. Fleming's open demeanor put Tracy at ease immediately. She wouldn't have to trade schmaltzy Hollywood jargon with him. All she had to do was be herself.

Tracy glanced at Tony, who gave her a go-ahead nod. Fleming had made his way across the room and paused to gaze out at the pool.

"Mr. Fleming?"

Fleming turned and acknowledged her.

"I'm Tracy Bouchard. It's a pleasure to meet you."

She meant it and said it with quiet, genuine warmth. There was no need to hustle a man like Fleming. He could size up anyone in a single glance, and had interviewed thousands of people on live television without ever being at a loss for words. Tracy could tell he liked what he saw. So far, so good.

"How do you do?" he replied, extending his hand. "The pleasure is mutual."

Tracy thrilled to the voice she had heard countless times on television. Only now, the voice was addressing her.

"You seem rather young for your position, Ms. Bouchard. I had expected someone, well, tougher, if I can be frank." The interviewer in Fleming never took a rest.

"I've only been with Franklin & Fields a short time." If he only knew how short! she thought. "I haven't had time to develop a thick skin." She laughed.

"And I hope you never do. Your skin is far too lovely," he complimented her.

Tracy changed the subject and asked questions about the pressures of his special brand of entertaining before she broached the subject of the book.

"Does your schedule allow much time for other activities?"

"Sure. I run three or four times a week. I read and relax at home. I need time to unwind. Live television is grueling. You can't let your concentration slip for a moment."

"Are you sure you have time to write a book?"

Now he was truly surprised. What was she going to do, try to talk him out of it?"

"Well, I assume I'd have some help. I've never written a book, you know."

"You don't mean a ghost writer? Oh, I don't think that's a good idea."

"You don't?"

"No. For some people, it's a necessity, but not for you. If you just write the way you talk, you won't need a ghost writer. Don't you think you have a lot to say?"

"That depends on what people want to know."

"They'll know whatever you decide to tell them."

"Not my life story?"

"Sure, if you want to tell it. But your private life is your own. People don't tune in every night to watch your personal life. They tune in to see a master of timing and conversation, with a sense of humor to boot. And they tune in to see the people you have on your show. What you have to offer is a unique perspective on American television and show business today. You can tell juicy stories or not—that's up to you. They'll probably creep in anyway. But it's your book. Don't let anyone tell you how to write it."

Fleming smiled. "That's a rather unusual approach, don't you think?"

Tracy shrugged. "It's how I feel. And it's the way I think the book should be done. I don't want to work with ten different puppets pretending to be you. I want to work with you."

Fleming was surprised by the strength of her conviction, but regarded her quietly and said nothing. She gazed back at him steadily, letting him know that she meant what she said. Then she heard a familiar voice behind her.

"I see you two have met. How's it going?" It was Zwerdlow, and he was addressing himself to Fleming, not to her.

"Interesting," Fleming answered. "Very interesting. Tracy thinks I should write the book myself."

Zwerdlow looked at her, eyebrows raised. "Does that make such a difference?"

"Yes," she answered. "I think it does. He's too intelligent and too articulate not to. I think it's the only way to do it. You have a choice between another glitzy celebrity book, or a witty, perceptive narrative that will be a one-of-a-kind comment on American television and the entertainment business. The choice is yours."

Zwerdlow's eyes twinkled, and Fleming continued to smile noncommitally. She could not tell what he thought. Then he changed the subject.

"I hope it's not too late for a swim, Max."

"No, no, not at all. Oh, look, there's Juno."

"Oh. Well, forget it. I'm not getting into the pool with him around."

They all looked out at the pool and saw Wade Juno, a notorious stunt man, standing on the diving board wearing a complete scuba diving outfit. They watched as he dove into the pool and sank into its watery depths.

"There's something you'd never see in New York," Tracy said. "What in the world is he up to?"

"You never know with Juno." Zwerdlow shook his head and started for the pool.

"Max," Fleming called, "if he finds a mermaid, book her for the show next Tuesday. I think we have a cancellation. So much for the pool, Tracy. Why don't we sit on the patio? I'd like to talk to you some more."

"Of course." Tracy beamed.

The patio was bathed in pale pink light, giving it a peaceful feeling. Tracy felt far from the party and the pressures she had felt earlier in the evening. Here she was, sitting on a chaise longue talking with Jim Fleming. I may wake up tomorrow and find this was all a dream, she thought. But tonight I'm going to enjoy it.

They talked about books and writers and found they both enjoyed the same authors. Books had always been Tracy's passion, and her natural enthusiasm for the subject made for a lively discussion with Fleming. The discussion moved toward Fleming's book, and Tracy felt herself more and more in control of the conversation. Fleming was impressed with her knowledge and she found herself giving confident, ready answers to his questions. By the end of a half-hour, they had established a solid rapport. The groundwork of an author-editor relationship had been laid.

"It's been a real pleasure, Tracy," Fleming said. "We'll be in touch soon."

"Good. I'll look forward to talking to you again. And thank you. I have to admit I was nervous about meeting you, but you do know how to put people at ease." Then she laughed. "You have to. It's your job."

Fleming grinned. "I know you won't believe this, but I was nervous about meeting you, too. I've never written a book before."

"Don't worry. You'll do just fine," Tracy answered.

"Thanks, coach." He flashed her his world-famous smile, and then he was gone.

Tracy lay back on the chaise longue and looked at the stars that were spread across the sky like a glittering rash. She closed her eyes and took in a long, contented breath of air. Then she coughed. Los Angeles air was living up to its reputation.

Wade Juno emerged from the pool and treaded over to her, looking like a creature from another planet.

"Hey, foxy lady!" he yelled and padded right into the house. Tracy was too lost in her own thoughts to pay attention to Juno's antics. She stared at the stars for a long moment before she went inside.

An hour later, she and Tony were speeding along the freeway, her hair whipping against her shoulders.

"Zwerdlow liked you," he said as soon as they got in the car. "I can tell."

"How?"

"Because Fleming did. That was Max's main concern. Fleming was uptight about getting ripped off. He didn't want to have to spill his guts for everyone in the world."

"I know that. That's what I told him."

"Well, whatever your act was, it worked. I think you've got him."

What makes you think it was an act?"

"Baby, everything out here is an act."

"Show biz, right?"

"Right."

"Then how do I know that you're not an act?"

"You don't. But what you see is what you get." He smiled. "And what about your act?"

She stiffened. "What do you mean?"

"You really knocked yourself out trying to impress people tonight. Did it work?"

She didn't answer his question, not because the answer was a salty bit of reality, but because she had a better question of her own. "Aren't you trying hard to impress people?"

He grinned. "Maybe. But if I am, it doesn't show."

"Then what's with the gold chains and the unbuttoned shirt? Are those the real Tony Amato or are they today's costume?"

The car swerved sharply as he pulled over to one side of the road and switched the motor off. Facing her solemnly, he slowly lifted the gold chain from his neck and tossed it over his shoulder so that it fell behind his seat. Then, without taking his eyes from hers, he buttoned his shirt up to the very top.

"What you see is what you get," he said, a smile starting to dance at the corners of his mouth.

"What do I get?"

"Whatever you want."

"Tony. . . ."

"Yeah?"

"I want."

"I know that, babe. And you got it."

They said very little after that. The car pulled back onto the road, and Tony's hand dropped from the steering wheel and moved on top of Tracy's, caressing her fingers gently. He drove swiftly to his house in Santa Monica, and led her inside. The night was very still.

"Would you like a drink?" he asked.

"No," she whispered.

They stood facing each other in front of the fireplace, and his hands traced delicate lines up and down her bare arms. He bent and kissed her quickly, tenderly. Her eyes closed and her mouth opened to take him in. Her head began to swirl as his tongue found hers, and they held each other tightly and with increasing need.

At last, he picked her up in his strong arms and carried her to the plush velvet sofa. Before he let her lie back on the sumptuous burgundy material, he deftly unhooked her dress so that it slid off her body quickly. She was wearing nothing underneath except a pair of black lace panties, and Tony's pulse quickened at the sight of her firm, sloping breasts, and long, slender legs. A shock of black hair fell across his forehead as he knelt by her side and took her pink nipples in his mouth, one by one. They stiffened at his touch, and she began to move beneath him and moan softly with delight.

He stood up, and her hands tugged at his shirt buttons and his belt. She explored his lean, naked body hungrily while he kissed her deeply and stroked the insides of her thighs. When they were straining toward each other, unable to bear it any longer, he lay forward on his elbows and pushed himself inside of her. She

69

arched her body up to meet him and matched each powerful thrust with eager movements of her own. Everything began to whirl as they pounded against each other, and at last they reached the peak of intensity and fell back, exhausted.

"Oh, Tony. . . ." Tracy breathed, opening her eyes. The easy-going grin on his face told her the evening was far from over.

"Hey," he said with a weak laugh.

"What?"

"I'm not sure if. . . ."

"If what?"

"If you're my conquest, or if I'm yours."

Tracy chuckled softly.

"I'll tell you what," she said as his hand moved to her breast. "We'll call it a draw."

Chapter 6

As Tracy walked down Park Avenue on Monday morning, everything looked different to her. The silver façade of the Franklin & Fields Building didn't look quite so imposing now, and she rode up to the fortieth floor with a mixture of newfound confidence and left-over fear. She knew she had clinched the Fleming book, even if no one had said so in so many words. That, as before, would be her shield with Canfield. Her trip to L.A. had been an audition, and even though she had passed it with flying colors, she knew she still had a long way to go. Passing muster under Canfield's shrewd eyes would be no easy matter.

She would have to proceed with caution. Her new colleagues would probably resent the way she had got her job. People always thought she was pushy. She didn't mean to be, but her determination and impatience often got the better of her. Her instincts were usually right, as she had discovered with Jim Fleming, but she knew there were gaps in her knowledge and expertise and she would have to learn a great deal in a short time.

The car stopped at the fortieth floor, and she faced the now-familiar blue carpeting of the reception area. As she headed down the hall to Canfield's office, she noticed that it didn't seem quite as long as it had only a few days ago. His secretary greeted her with cool politeness and waved her inside.

Wes Canfield was sitting at his desk, and he was not alone. Seated across from him was a pleasant-looking man with sandy hair and kind, brown eyes. With an impatient gesture, Canfield motioned her into a chair.

71

"Well," he said. "Let's hear all about it."

He wasn't going to bother with any preliminaries. The ball was in her court. She had a feeling he already knew what had transpired in L.A. He was just testing her, goading her.

Tracy was wearing her new off-white silk dress, and she couldn't help but notice Canfield's eyes on her legs. She crossed them deliberately, and the side slit opened wider, revealing most of her left thigh.

"It turned out better than I could have imagined," she began coolly. "I ran into Darin McCane at Max Zwerdlow's. We talked about an autobiography and I think he might go for it."

The stranger laughed out loud, a big, boisterous laugh, but Canfield was unimpressed.

"I didn't send you out there to chase celebrities. Your job was to move ahead on the Fleming book. So what happened?"

Tracy was taken aback by his attitude. She didn't like being treated this way in front of a stranger. "I'll tell you after you've introduced us."

"Look, Tracy," Canfield said, pointedly. "I had you checked out while you were away. Besides being an aggravation to Steve Kramer, the closest you ever came to a publishing firm was a job in a bookstore." He opened his mouth to continue, but Tracy interrupted with controlled fury.

"I was an aggravation to Steve Kramer because he didn't want me do anything except type letters and answer the phone. And I started as a clerk at that bookstore and was assistant manager within six months. I can do the unusual, get the impossible and boost sales figures. How I do that is my business. If I don't do that, then it becomes your business."

Canfield blew up. "You are without a doubt the most conceited woman that ever walked through this door! How would you like the shortest employment on record with this company?"

"How would you like to lose the number-one best-seller of the decade?" Tracy countered.

"Hi," the silent third party interrupted, extending

his hand. "I'm John Noble, editor-in-chief. Don't mind me, I just came by to see if I could introduce you around, show you your office and help you get started. Looks as though the only help you need is a lesson in diplomacy."

Chastened, Tracy sighed. "I'm sorry, I must be a little jet-lagged. I'm Tracy Bouchard." They shook hands.

"How did you fare with Mr. Fleming?" Noble asked.

Tracy looked at Canfield, who gave her an impatient wave of his hand and settled back in his chair. "We got along extremely well. He liked my ideas and wants to get started as soon as the contract is signed. He was nervous about doing a book, but now he seems eager and excited." She looked at Canfield again, but got only a blank stare. If he was pleased, he was determined not to let her know it.

"That's great! Fantastic!" Noble said enthusiastically.

Tracy gave a detailed account of her conversations with Jim Fleming. Noble seemed favorably impressed, but the company president remained silent. Now and then he jotted a word or two on the notepad on his desk.

"That sounds good, Tracy," Noble complimented. "Now, just two more questions. Who are the other celebs you might have and how much do they want?"

She told them about her experiences in L.A., glossing over her initial insecurity. The two men listened quietly and Tracy felt herself beginning to shake inside. It was true she had met a lot of celebrities and had approached them about book projects, but only Jim Fleming had taken her seriously. Because she had taken him seriously. As she kept talking, she felt she was sinking slowly. Noble nodded pleasantly, and Canfield tilted his chair back, looking at her with narrow eyes. At last, her story came to an end, and Canfield leaned forward, flipping his pen onto the desk.

"Well," he said matter-of-factly, "these projects should keep you busy for a while. Just don't talk price until you've discussed it with me." Canfield looked at Noble. "John, why don't you show our new editor around?" He said "editor" as though it were some kind of joke.

Tracy was nettled as she and Noble got up to leave. What was eating Canfield? He might not like her style, but she had accomplished what she had been sent to accomplish: she had convinced Jim Fleming that Franklin & Fields was the right house to do his book. Couldn't he at least be polite?

"Thank you, Mr. Canfield," she said, hiding her anger under a cool veneer.

A smile broke across his face as she and Noble reached the door. "Hey, Bouchard," he said.

She turned slowly to see what he wanted.

His right thumb was pointing up at the ceiling. "Good work."

She smiled back. "Thanks, Canfield." Maybe things were going to be all right after all.

Wes Canfield shook his head and laughed quietly to himself.

The walk down the hall led Tracy past the main reception area. As the woman behind the curved desk looked up, she recognized Tracy and lifted a black Bloomingdale's shopping bag from under the desk. "I believe this is yours."

"Oh, thank you. I was so rushed last Thursday, I'd forgotten all about it." She took the bag and followed Noble down the corridor to the elevators. They rode down two floors to the editorial offices, and John showed her into a small but comfortable room. It was furnished with a desk, some chairs, and several empty bookshelves. The room's single window looked down thirty-eight floors to Park Avenue. Tracy stowed the Bloomingdale's bag under the desk. "I guess my work is cut out for me," she said, looking around the empty office.

"Come on, I'll introduce you around."

They walked to an office at the far end of the hall and John introduced her to Martha Hauptmann. Martha was in her early thirties, tall and thin with long, black hair that was coiled on top of her head and secured with a Chinese lacquer comb. The Chinese motif was continued in her emerald green silk shirt with a Mandarin collar and black pajama trousers. Martha put down the manuscript she was reading and took off her oversize tortoise-shell glasses. She extended a well-manicured hand to Tracy.

"I've been waiting to meet the person who whisked Steve Kramer's book out from under his nose," she said, giving Tracy a frank once-over.

Tracy's stomach knotted. If there had been a carpet in the orderly office, she would have tried to crawl under it. She had expected to be resented, but was everyone at Franklin & Fields going to treat her like a common thief? This can't be happening again. It isn't fair. If only I could explain, she thought desperately.

Martha noticed Tracy's pallor. "Don't take that the wrong way, Tracy. I only meant it took some guts to do what you did."

"Well, I did it without thinking too much. I suppose if I'd thought about it. . . ."

Martha laughed. "I know what you mean. Come and talk to me when you get settled. We'll have lunch, okay?"

The knot in Tracy's middle began to loosen. She smiled wanly. "Thanks, Martha. I'd appreciate that."

"Shall we move on, Tracy?" Noble asked.

"Yes, please. It was good to meet you, Martha."

Tracy's step was unsteady as they left the room. The encounter had reminded her of the prom incident. That horrible misunderstanding had happened years ago, and she had struggled so hard to overcome it. But even now it took only a glance or a few words for the sickening feeling to return. Tracy took a deep breath and followed Noble into the next office.

It was occupied by Jeff Conway, a slick young man who sat behind a cluttered desk. The phone he was holding looked like it had been glued to his ear.

"Sure, Dirk. Sure. I know how it is. Look, it's a legitimate offer. I can't go any higher. My hands are tied. You know how it is." He paused and listened for a moment, his eyes narrowing into competitive slits. "Well, that's the best I can do. Think about it." He held the receiver away from his ear and cringed mockingly as the agent on the other end sounded off about the obviously low offer. Tracy's interest in the conversation caught his eye, and he winked. "Well," he said into the phone, "let me know." He hung up confidently.

"Will he go for it?" Noble asked.

"He'll go for it. It's the only offer he's got. He'll go down."

"I'd like you to meet Tracy Bouchard, our new editor," Noble said obligingly.

Jeff Conway regarded her with the unconcealed approval of one shark for another. "Oh, yeah, I've heard all about you."

Tracy cringed.

He softened a little, and smiled. "I saw you upstairs last week when you were going into Wes's office. Jim Fleming, huh? Not bad."

"Thank you," she said faintly.

"Say, listen, Tracy," he went on. "You got any questions, just ask me. I know how it is."

"I'll do that. Thanks."

He was friendly enough, but she couldn't help but think he was a left-handed ally. Still, a left-handed ally was better than none. Perhaps in time she could explain the full circumstances of her new job, but for now she would just have to hope they would all give her the benefit of the doubt.

"He's a little overwhelming," she ventured as she and Noble headed around the corner.

"Conway? He's a hustler, all right, but he can be a nice guy when he wants to be. He can also be very generous. Taking your questions to him is not a bad idea."

Tracy had a feeling she'd be seeing a lot of Conway in the next few weeks. The prospect of actually sitting down and working as an editor was becoming a hard reality, and it was not altogether comforting. As Noble led her into the next office, she was face to face with

Stephen Marcus. He was well known throughout the industry as an editor of the highest caliber. Many of his authors had won Nobel and Pulitzer prizes. He never got mixed up in office politics; he didn't have to. He spent the bulk of his time working with his authors, some of the most important writers of the day. Although he had been given a large, sunny office with a tremendous view of Park Avenue, the room was not elegantly furnished. His large, wooden desk was stacked with piles of paperwork and manuscripts, and a group of armchairs at the other end circled a low coffee table. The side wall harbored a long table at which a lot of nitty-gritty editing was done. Tracy noticed the scissors, scotch tape, glue, rulers and canisters of sharpened pencils.

Stephen Marcus rose politely as they entered the room, and his lined face broke into a gentle smile. "Hello, John," he said. "Who have we here?"

"This is a new member of our staff—Tracy Bouchard," Noble answered.

"I see. It's good to have you with us, Tracy."

"Thank you," she replied with quiet admiration. Her eyes strayed to the back wall, which was completely covered with books, some of them quite old. Marcus had been an editor for more than thirty years. "I'm glad to be here."

"Tracy just returned from Los Angeles," Noble announced. "She's been working on getting Jim Fleming to do a book for us."

Marcus was impressed. His gray eyebrows went up, and he asked in mock conspiratorial fashion, "How'd you get him to do that?"

"She works fast, Steve," Noble punted for her.

"Well, I'm sure we can use some speed around here."

She couldn't believe it. He didn't know. Was he really that sheltered? His gray eyes met hers with amiable sincerity. Did he know the whole story, or was he just being polite? She realized in a flash that she would never know, and she was suddenly very grateful that one person in the company didn't care how she had snagged the Fleming book or even that she had done it. She understood now why he was so universally liked: Stephen Marcus minded his own business.

"I guess it can be a little confusing around here at first," he continued. "If you need any advice, I'll be glad to help out if I can."

She felt suddenly near tears, and she choked out, "Oh, thank you. I—"

"Well," he interrupted modestly. "I'm just an old book doctor."

Tracy left his office feeling very humble and small.

The next office belonged to Kenneth Maguire. Blond, thin to the point of emaciation, groomed to the hilt and obviously gay, he had brought in some of the biggest, trashiest novels of the past five years. Tracy was nearly overwhelmed by his heavy cologne as she admired the glossy book jackets that adorned his walls. Ken jumped up and flitted back and forth across the room as he talked about his books with bitchy candor. "This one is absolutely the pits," he drawled. "Utter garbage. I just *love* it."

They left him quickly, and Tracy sensed that Noble felt uncomfortable with him. She wasn't surprised. Ken's almost manic energy made her uncomfortable, too. It had been exhausting just to meet him.

They peeked into the last office, but no one was there. It was the total opposite of Martha's neat room —extremely messy and disorganized, every available surface piled high with manuscripts. A file drawer looked as though it had regurgitated paper. The chaos irritated her and Tracy tried to maintain a neutral expression as a young woman entered the room and placed some letters on the desk.

"Jill," John said quickly, "this is Tracy Bouchard, our new editor. Tracy, this is Jill Clement, Sheila's assistant."

The girl's eyes met Tracy's for a brief instant. They carried an unspoken challenge. "Hello," she said simply, as Tracy smiled politely.

John was not interested in the implicit resentment

between these two. "Have you seen Sheila?" he asked Jill.

"I believe she went to the ladies' room. She has a lunch this afternoon," Jill replied. Her eyes traveled slowly over Tracy's form, taking in the healthy, well-styled hair, the trim figure under the shimmery silk and the slender legs that stood neatly poised in a pair of Jourdan shoes.

"I see," Noble answered. "Well, you can meet her later, Tracy. Just drop in and introduce yourself. I'm sure she's anxious to meet you. Oh, and Tracy. Call Personnel and tell them you'll be needing an assistant. They should be sending some candidates up to see you by the end of the week."

"Oh, that's good," she said. "But what about until then? I'll be making a lot of contacts and getting a lot of letters out."

He frowned thoughtfully, as Jill started to back away. "That's true," he said, nodding approvingly. "Jill, when does Sheila go on vacation?"

"Wednesday," the girl answered sullenly.

"Perfect. How'd you like to fill in for Tracy for a few days, show her around, help her get started?" he asked. It was a rhetorical question, and they all knew it.

"Okay," said Jill, trying to sound enthusiastic.

"Good," John said, slapping his hands together. "Then that's taken care of. You two can get together later."

She nodded, and he turned to go. "Thanks, John. I—I guess I'll see you later."

"Right." He checked his watch and left.

Tracy returned to her office. Well, she thought, as she looked around the spare room, it is a strong staff, and I'm proud to be a part of it. She only hoped she would live up to the standards at Franklin & Fields.

What to do first? She wasn't sure. She sat down slowly at the desk and looked around. Everything was so empty. It was her job to fill this office with new books and new authors. The only author she had so far was Jim Fleming. Not bad for a start, in fact it was quite a coup, but she couldn't rest on her laurels for too long. And how could she ever top an act like that? She had never bought a book in her life. All she had done on the Fleming book was place the call to Zwerdlow at the crucial moment. He and Canfield were negotiating the complicated contract. Canfield had outlined its terms before she went to California, but only for her own information.

Her stomach told her it was nearly lunchtime. Lunch. Right. That's what you do every day with agents. She got up and walked out into the hallway. "Oh, Jill?"

Jill hesitated and then looked up, visibly perturbed. "Can you get me a copy of the *Literary Market Place?*"

"There's one on everybody's desk."

Tracy could feel the girl's hostility, and it riled her. "Fine. Would you bring me one, please?" she asked icily.

Jill threw her pen down in exasperation and got up with a jerk to head into a nearby office. She emerged with the thick directory, handing it to Tracy without a word. Tracy thanked her, sorry she had made Jill get a reference book for her. It was the kind of request that had made her furious when she was working for Kramer. She would be more considerate from now on. Why did she always do things like that? Fly off the handle that way? All it did was alienate people. Slow down, Bouchard, she told herself firmly. Think first. Think.

Back at her desk, Tracy turned to the agents section. Whom to call first? There were over a hundred names listed. She spotted some names she knew, and picked one at random. Joe Shane. The phone rang several times, and the agent answered just as Tracy was ready to hang up and try someone else.

"Joe Shane."

"Hello. This is Tracy Bouchard. I'm a new editor at Franklin & Fields, and I was wondering if we could get together for lunch one day soon."

"Tracy Bouchard? Oh, I've heard of you."

There it was again. News certainly traveled fast in this business.

"Let me get out my calendar. How about the week of the fifteenth?"

This was going to be easier than she thought. By noon, she had set up three lunch dates, and was beginning to drum up a little confidence. She was going to put her expense account to good use.

Well, she thought, so that's a start. She still didn't have the faintest idea of how to negotiate for a book, or how to get a book the attention it deserved, but she had had a few small successes that morning, and that was enough for now. She figured she would just have to cross those bridges when she came to them. At least she did know how to edit a book and how to work with authors. That was something she had learned at Carey, mostly through her own initiative, and she knew she could do a good job once she had the chance. Of course, the only editorial meeting she had ever attended was one she had not been invited to.

It was a little nerve-wracking, sitting at an empty desk with nothing to do. She fished through her purse and pulled out her address book, turning to the Ms. The number of Darin McCane's agent was listed there, and she decided to try him. It was now 12:30 in New York, so the California agent would just be arriving at his office.

As she listened to the telephone ring across the continent, she planned what to say to him. McCane had seemed interested in doing a book, she thought. She would have to see how much money he wanted. Surprisingly, the agent was easy to reach. His secretary put the call through with no questions. A good sign.

"I met Darin McCane at Max Zwerdlow's last Friday, and we discussed the possibility of his doing a book for Franklin & Fields. I'm calling now to tell you of our interest, and to learn of the interest on your end."

The agent was polite in the California style. "Say, it's nice to hear from you, Tracy. Darin mentioned meeting you at Max's party."

"That's good. I hope the idea of a book still appeals to him."

"Well, he may be interested. I'll have to talk to him. He's been approached by book publishers in the past, you know, and he's never really committed to anything. We're not firming up any deals for him at this time."

"I see. When might I expect to hear something more definite?"

"Darin has a very tight schedule this year. He'll be shooting on location in Arizona next month, and he's due in Italy for another picture after that. But I'll try and bring it up."

Tracy realized that she was being given a royal brush-off. "That sounds great," she said bravely. "Give him my best. And let him know that any time he's ready, we're here."

"I'll do that, Tracy. Thanks for calling."

Tracy let out a huge sigh. The creep. All McCane had wanted was to get laid. The revelation made her blush with embarrassment. Maybe that's why Canfield was so uppity this morning, she thought. He knew all along that most of these guys were just handing me a line. I must have looked no naïve! Her thoughts were interrupted by a braying voice.

"Soooo, you're Tracy Bouchard. I heard about you." The woman marched in and settled herself in the nearest chair.

"Hi," she said in a heavy Bronx accent. "I'm Sheila Zimmerman." Tracy had heard about Sheila from one of the assistants at Carey who used to work with her. She was a thirty-seven-year-old divorcée with three children and a hundred boyfriends, and she greeted Tracy with haggard eyes and a voice like a buzz saw. "We must have lunch sometime. But not this week. I'm too busy. I have to run—I'm late for my lunch. I just wanted to drop in and say hello."

Tracy smiled politely, and said, "It's good to meet you, Sheila. Have a pleasant lunch."

Sheila snorted. "With Dennis Atkinson? Forget it. He's a good agent, but he's positively asexual. Well,

I'll see you later." She sashayed out of the room just as Martha Hauptmann entered, carrying a pile of manuscripts.

"How are you doing, Tracy? John and I wondered if you would take care of some of the things we've been too busy to handle. I know you won't have time once you get your own projects started."

Martha put the pile on Tracy's desk and sat down.

"These are the best of the slush pile. We need an editor to go over them. The assistants routinely screen the unsolicited material, and this is the cream of the crop."

"I see." Tracy tried to hide her lack of enthusiasm for this dreary chore.

"I know it's not the most exciting job in the world, but I like to do it myself when I have the time. It makes me feel like an explorer. You know, Henry Hudson looking for the Northwest Passage."

Tracy laughed, ashamed of herself for her reaction to the pile of manuscripts. "That's a good way to look at it," Tracy said to Martha.

"Actually, the one on top isn't the slush pile. It's a first novel that came from an agent. I like it but it's risky, and I'd like a second opinion. Could you take a look at it? There's no hurry. Early next week is fine."

"I'll be glad to, Martha."

"Good. Talk to you later." Martha rose and moved to the door.

"Martha," Tracy called to her. "Thanks."

"You're welcome, Tracy. If you need to talk, I'm available."

I have a lot to learn, Tracy thought. I've been sitting here wondering what to do and when someone walks in with something I act like I was asked to empty the trash. Fleming or no Fleming, I'm a greenhorn, and that's the way I'll be treated until I have a track record. Instead of resenting it and pretending I know everything, I should take it easy and learn like crazy.

Tracy picked up the manuscript on the top of the pile eagerly and hadn't finished the first page when the phone rang.

"Tracy Bouchard."

"How's it going, Bouchard? Your office okay?" It was Canfield.

"Oh, it's fine. It's great to have a window and a view instead of a cubbyhole in the hall."

"Listen, Tracy, about this morning. I'm sorry I blew up at you."

"Oh, please don't apologize," she broke in. "I was way out of line and I know it. It's just that I was nervous and I'm new at this and I want to do everything right."

"Good. I didn't want to start out on such bad footing. The draft of the Fleming contract is almost finished. I'll have my secretary send it down so you can see what we agreed on. Zwerdlow is a tough negotiator." He paused briefly. "But, then, so am I." Tracy could hear the satisfaction in his voice.

"That's great—about the contract I mean. I'm looking forward to seeing it."

There was a pause, and then he said, "We'll have to have lunch soon. I'll give you a call."

Tracy tried to keep her sudden excitement out of her voice. "Thank you. That would be lovely."

"Good. Take care."

"Bye."

Tracy set the receiver down gently. What made him so concerned all of a sudden? Was her office okay? Could she have lunch? It was quite a turnaround from this morning. Oh, heavens, she thought, impatient with herself. It's no big deal. He probably takes all new editors out to lunch. Tracy turned back to the manuscript she was reading, but found herself reading the same line over and over. Her thoughts kept straying to Wes Canfield. She imagined them sitting across the table from one another in a quiet restaurant. He would reach across and hold her hand, playing gently with her fingertips. After the meal, they would get in a taxi and ride uptown to his apartment. His hand would slip casually onto her knee. Their thighs would touch and she would feel the heat of his body next to hers. He would gaze at her with his wicked blue eyes. He might even kiss her, gently at first, and then passionately, oblivious to the driver. . . .

What are you thinking about, Bouchard? Are you crazy ?!?!!?? You'd better drive these adolescent notions right out of your head. The man is your boss, and your relationship with him is *strictly* business.

Tracy picked up her manuscript and read a few more pages before the phone jangled again. She picked it up, but before she could even say hello, someone shouted in her ear.

"Listen, and listen up good, Bouchard!" She immediately recognized the angry voice on the other end, and she was jolted out of her reverie. Her stomach twisted into a double knot and her hands began to sweat as Steve Kramer's livid voice lashed out at her. He called her a vile name, and she gripped the phone, paralyzed with fear. She sat immobile as a statue, waiting for him to finish. Her throat constricted and went dry. Finally, the tirade ended with, "You'll be hearing from my lawyers!", and the line went dead.

Tracy held the receiver away from her and stared at it blankly; then, she replaced it in its cradle and tiptoed to the door. She closed it quietly and sank down at her desk with her head in her hands. She had a sudden urge to call Wes, to tell him everything. He would take care of her. He would know what to do.

No, she had to take care of herself. She imagined Canfield's response to the situation. He would tell her Kramer's threats were useless, that he was just blowing off steam. The Fleming book had been up for grabs. No deal had been made when she placed the call to Zwerdlow. Kramer was furious she had stolen his thunder. It must have been humiliating for him.

Tracy looked at the door and realized it had been unnecessary to close it, but she knew why she had done it. She was afraid everyone could hear what Kramer had said, as if her telephone were linked up to a public address system that could broadcast the call to the entire company. But, of course, no one had heard.

It had been foolish and unprofessional of Kramer to

call her like that, exposing his feelings so openly. But in a way, the phonecall had made Kramer seem less dangerous, in spite of his threats. He had treated her with the kind of angry respect one enemy gives to another. She was his peer now, and she had to be able to deal with Kramer and people like him on her own. No running to Canfield or John Noble or anyone.

Tracy smiled grimly and picked up the manuscript yet another time. Steve Kramer could blow off all the steam he wanted, but she was still Fleming's editor. She smiled again, more confidently. The phonecall had taught her something. Kramer had made a tactical error. It was something Wes Canfield would never have done. Canfield was too smart. I have a lot to learn, she thought. But I've got some good teachers here. If I can be patient and hang on, I'll be all right.

She picked up a pencil and began to read, making notes on a yellow pad as she went along.

Chapter 7

THREE WEEKS FLEW BY, AND TRACY BARELY HAD TIME to think of anything except work. Then, one morning, there was a small box on top of the pile of mail on her desk—mostly manuscripts she was beginning to receive from agents she had contacted. She picked it up and shook it, hearing a faint jingle. Curiosity aroused, she ripped the outer cardboard covering, finding a small white box tied with a now-crushed red bow. Inside the box she found a card: "Charms for a charming lady. Love, Tony." Nestled on soft, white cotton padding was a silver charm bracelet. Tracy picked it up and examined the trinkets dangling from the delicate loops. There was a book that opened and closed, a bicycle whose wheels spun, a replica of a Porsche and a crescent-shaped moon. How like Tony, she thought. He may be a sophisticated Hollywood agent, but he's a Brooklyn boy at heart.

A wave of sadness washed over Tracy. Tony had been so wonderful when she was in California, gently helping her over the rough spots, and she'd hardly given him a thought since she'd been back in New York. The bracelet reminded her of the things they'd done together—bicycling to the beach, seeing L.A. in Tony's Porsche, a moonlight swim. She'd been so intent on making a good impression with everyone at Franklin & Fields that all the romance and fun had gone out of her life.

Tracy reached in her desk drawer and pulled out a box of notecards.

Dear Tony,

I just received the charming bracelet and it's reminded me of our three terrific days together. It's been all work and no play for me since I got back to New York, and I'm afraid Tracy is becoming a dull girl. The job is still bewildering and I have a lot to learn, but I'm a fast learner. I'm sure we'll be in touch about the Fleming book, but give me a call if you're in town. I'd love to see you. Don't worry, lover. I know you're not the going steady type. Neither am I these days. But I do miss you.

Love,
Tracy

Tracy read the note over, not entirely pleased with what she'd written. She wanted Tony to know she didn't think of him as a one-night stand, but a long-distance relationship was not what she had in mind right now. She sealed the note and put it in her "Out" box.

The pile of manuscripts stared up at her and she attacked it vigorously. This was one Friday she didn't want to leave the office laden with manuscript boxes. Tomorrow Kippy was coming to visit and they were going to go apartment hunting. She was finally going to get her own place.

Saturday morning was dull and gray, threatening rain, but Tracy was up and about by nine o'clock. She wanted to check through the real estate ads before Kippy picked her up. She could map out a route for them to follow, and that would at least save them some time. Unless she were awfully lucky, today could be a grueling experience. Good apartments in Manhattan were scarcer than hen's teeth.

Gulping down a fast cup of coffee, she made some last-minute notes on a pad, figuring how much rent she could pay. Canfield had not hired her officially until after he was sure of the Fleming book, and then he had named a figure that was much lower than what she had expected. She could see that he meant what he said, and hadn't given him an argument for once. Even though it was a huge improvement from her former salary, she would not have money to burn. Today's apartment-hunting excursion was going to cost a pretty penny, and it was going to take her months to pay for her two shopping sprees.

At 9:30, she went down and got the paper, and brought it back upstairs. After underlining the ads that fit her price range, she put on her raincoat and prepared to meet Kippy's car in front of the building. She took a last look around the living room, and the sight of it convinced her more than ever that she had to have her own space. The usual supply of dirty tea cups and the overflowing ashtrays were all she needed to see. I will not live like a slob ever again, she told herself firmly.

Kippy pulled up at 10:15 in her blue Datsun, and she greeted Tracy cheerfully. Her chestnut brown hair was pulled back into a loose tail, and she was dressed in a denim skirt and a plaid blouse under her raincoat. The mother of two at twenty-five, she didn't always look glamorous, but she was organized and practical. Kippy had the ability to find the root of any problem, so her advice was usually sound. Now she gave Tracy a fast hug and pulled the car back into traffic.

"So how's it going, Tracy?"

"Well, fine. I guess." Tracy sighed involuntarily.

"That doesn't sound too fine, Trace."

"It's hard to explain, Kip. It's nothing I can put my finger on. I'm working hard and no one tells me I'm doing anything wrong, but I feel like people resent me, like they're just waiting for me to make a colossal mistake so they can say, 'I told you so.' They think I've come too far too fast. I haven't paid my dues."

Kippy turned the corner, and they headed over toward the West Side. "Don't be so tough on yourself. People who have paid their dues will always resent those who rise farther and faster. What they don't understand is that you're paying your dues, too. It's not easy to go to work every day and feel all your colleagues are waiting to laugh if you fall flat on your face. Take it one day at a time, Trace. You'll be okay."

"I suppose you're right but . . . hey, slow down. That's the one, the white brownstone with the tree in front." She looked down at the ad. One BR, f/p, a/c, see super, no fee."

"But what?" Kippy's gentle voice questioned.

Tracy shrugged. "But I always feel like a hundred pairs of eyes are waiting for me to slip. It's like walking a tightrope with no net. Why can't they give me a chance? They act like I stole some top-secret military plans and sold them to the Russians." She smiled ruefully. "Martha Hauptmann is nice, but she's so aloof. The only one who seems to be on my side at all is Jeff Conway."

"The hustler?"

Tracy nodded. "But that only makes it worse. He's a real smoothie, and no one trusts him, either. He's the only one who's not afraid of me."

"Except for the president."

"Canfield. No, he's certainly not afraid of me. But I don't see that much of him, although I'd like to. He's gorgeous, Kippy. Unfortunately, he's the boss. The editor-in-chief is nice enough, but he's that way with everyone."

Kippy nodded, understanding. "Darn," she said. "There doesn't seem to be a parking space. Why don't you go inside and take a look at the apartment, and I'll stay here with the car."

Tracy came out five minutes later. "I knew there had to be a catch," she fumed. "The ad was too good to be true. It was a beautiful apartment, with a brand-new air conditioner and the original fireplace in the bedroom."

"So what was wrong?"

There isn't any real estate agent's fee, but the super won't tell me who the hell the landlord is unless I pay *him* off."

"How much?"

"A thousand dollars."

"Forget it."

"You're not kidding. Someone else will pay it, though. Those crooks!"

"Where to next?"

Tracy consulted the newspaper on her lap. "Let's try this place on West Sixty-eighth Street near the park. It's a studio and it's cheap."

Kippy started the car and turned onto Central Park West. As they came to a halt at a red light, she resumed their earlier conversation. "I've been thinking about your job, Trace."

Tracy sighed. "So what can I do, O practical one?"

"Well, you can start by keeping a low profile. You don't have to show off. Everyone knows about the Fleming book, and there's no need to rub it in. And the other thing is to ask them for help."

"What!" Tracy cried in surprise. "But I don't want to show them how little I really know!"

"Then ask intelligent questions. They don't expect you to know everything. You might look dumber by not asking and doing something stupid later on."

"Maybe you're right." Tracy admitted.

"People love to give advice. So let them. And in the meantime, you'll find out what they're thinking and where they stand in the company."

"Very true. You're terrific."

Kippy grinned. "Just common sense."

She pulled the Datsun up in front of a building that cornered on the park, with the entrance on Sixty-eight Street. "Here we are. This looks like a great place."

"It sure does. I hope it isn't already taken." Tracy jumped out of the car and ran up the steps to the door. A uniformed doorman held it open for her and she dashed inside. The lobby was clean and pleasant, and the elevator arrived promptly when she pressed the button.

The apartment was at the end of a long, narrow hallway, and she found the door ajar. The living room was crowded with people who had come to see it, and they milled around the loft bed that was built onto

91

four stilts in the middle of the room. As Tracy edged her way inside, past a tiny bathroom to the left and a tinier kitchenette that was squeezed into the wall, she realized that this one room was the entire apartment. The whole thing measured about ten by ten, bed and all. The building was well maintained and in a lovely neighborhood, and the apartment was within her budget. But who could stand to live in it? Tracy wormed her way out the door and ran down to the car.

"How was it?" Kippy asked.

"Nice. Cheap. But it was about the size of this car."

Kippy laughed, and they drove on.

By the end of the day, Tracy had looked at seven apartments, and there was something wrong with all of them. The one on East Seventy-ninth Street was too expensive for its two rooms, and the one on East Ninety-third was large and sunny, but it was in a crumbling building on a dingy, deserted block. The four-room walk-up on East Eighty-fourth had peeling walls and a bathtub in the kitchen. The "charming studio" on West Seventy-sixth was up six flights of rickety stairs. At last, they pulled up in front of a large building on Riverside Drive. The ad promised a "Lge studio, wbf, a/c, pre-war, drmn bldg riv vu." Tracy read it out loud.

"Large studio, wood-burning fireplace, air conditioning, pre-war, doorman building, river view."

"It sounds very nice, but it has to be expensive."

"Well, there's only one way to find out." She climbed the steps and located the doorman, who informed her that Number 17-A was still available. The elevator was old but in good condition, and it smelled like home-made chicken soup. The doors clunked open, and she found the vacant apartment. It was unlocked and she stepped inside.

Her first impression was of clean, white walls. The sound of her footsteps echoed on the shiny parquet floor. The pungent smell of fresh paint tickled her nose and Tracy noticed two empty, drippy cans sitting in the open closet. As she walked further into the apartment, the expansive view caught her eye and she rushed to the windows. Directly below her, Riverside Park was a slender, horizontal line of trees laden with delicate green buds. Beyond the park lay the restless, gray Hudson River, choppy and beautiful in the fading afternoon light. Beyond the small façades and rooftops on the New Jersey side, she could discern the rolling green of the Palisades, and to the extreme right, the lacy, steely points of the George Washington Bridge rose in a ghostly arc across the river. She sighed longingly as she turned from the window and gazed around the room. The view alone probably upped the price by a hundred dollars a month. But even without the view, the apartment was elegant and livable. There was only the one room, aside from the tiny kitchen and bathroom, but it was spacious, framed by a large, mahogany arch. The fireplace was small, but it worked, and it was built into the brick that lined one whole wall. There were three high, narrow windows facing west, and these were flanked by sturdy window seats. The apartment was a dream, but it would undoubtedly be out of her range. She sat down on a window seat and looked out over the park. It looked so peaceful from up here, so remote and unhurried.

"You want the apartment, miss?" a voice said from behind.

Tracy jumped up. A small man in green overalls was standing behind her, and he repeated the question without a smile. She asked the price and tried to mask her surprise when the man named a figure that was just a few dollars over her budget. "Who do I pay?" she asked eagerly.

After writing out a check for a month's rent and a month's security to Riverside Realty, she tipped the man in the green overalls, who had hedged on the name of the landlord until she hinted she would "take care of him." Tracy found herself down to $18.32 in her bank account, but it was worth it. Of course, she wouldn't be able to buy any furniture for at least another month, but she could shop around in the meantime and use her footlocker for a table and the floor for a chair. She already owned a double bed, but she would probably get rid of it and use a convertible sofa instead. A round oak table would look good by the windows, and perhaps she could find a second-hand dresser small enough to fit into the one large closet. Her thoughts raced as she began to plan her new home, and she was bursting with excitement as she ran outside the building to tell Kippy the good news.

They found a parking space and Tracy took Kippy back upstairs to show her the apartment and sign the lease. Then they drove down Columbus Avenue to Ruskay's, a dark, cavernous restaurant with an art deco look, mirror-topped tables aglow with white taper candles and a young man on the balcony playing a Mozart piano sonata. Since Kippy had to drive, they decided to celebrate with a pot of fragrant Earl Grey tea and a sampling from the pastry cart—a strawberry tart for Tracy and a chocolate napoleon for Kippy.

When the tea arrived, Kippy made a ceremony of pouring it into the fluted crystal cups. "Kippy Martindale poured at a celebration for Miss Tracy Bouchard's acquisition of the most fantastic apartment on the West Side of Manhattan," Kippy joked in her best Connecticut-matron accent.

They clinked cups, punctuating the final notes of the sonata and giggled with excitement and exhaustion.

"I think I'm in chocolate heaven," Kippy said as she savored a mouthful of napoleon. "The kids would die if they saw me eating this. I'm always telling them how bad sugar and chocolate are, and singing the praises of green vegetables and raw carrot sticks. The joys of motherhood, you know."

They chatted about Kippy's family for a while, and Kippy leaned back in her chair and sighed. "This is a real treat for me. It must be fun to go to places like this all the time with literary agents."

Tracy smiled. "I know it sounds glamorous, and I guess it is, in a way. But after a while, it just seems like an endless parade of chef's salads and filet of sole."

"But what's it like?" Kippy prodded.

Tracy explained. "Well, you eat lunch, and you talk

94

about books, usually with an agent who has a lot of them to sell. They tell you what they've got, and you tell them what you're looking for."

"And then what happens?"

"Then you go back to the office, and they send you the manuscripts you wanted to see. If you find something you like, you take it to the editorial meeting, and try to get the support of the other editors."

"My God, it sounds like a fraternity."

"It is, in a way. The agents want to send only their best books to editors with clout, and terrific books aren't hard to sell." Tracy paused. "Oh, Kippy, I'm never going to get anywhere if I don't get over this feeling of being watched."

"Are you sure you're not over-reacting?"

"I don't know. That's the problem. It's like that incident in high school. You remember?"

Kippy said nothing, but her eyes expressed compassion.

"Well, it's happening again. Guilty without a trial."

"Hey." Kippy reached out and touched Tracy's hand. "It can't be as bad as all that. You still have the Fleming book. That alone should make you proud."

"Well, I don't feel proud. It's just like before." Her stomach knotted suddenly, and she tried to push the past out of her mind, but it was too late. The faces of former high school acquaintances came floating into her mind, renewing the frustration and humiliation.

"This is nothing like that," Kippy said reassuringly. But even she didn't sound convinced. They changed the subject and talked about other things, but the sour, anxious helplessness that haunted her whenever she remembered her last year in high school stayed with Tracy. The thing that hurt the most was that it had never been resolved. She hoped fervently that her hand in acquiring the Jim Fleming book would not come to plague her. That's why it was so important for her to make it on her own, to be irreproachable.

Chapter 8

Jim Fleming was in town this week with his agent, Max Zwerdlow, to sign a contract with Franklin & Fields, who acquired his book for a hefty six figures. Pictured above: Fleming's editor, Tracy Bouchard, and Zwerdlow. Wesley Canfield, president of F & F (lower left), says this is "the book of the decade."

WES CANFIELD STUDIED THE ANNOUNCEMENT IN *Publishers Weekly,* and tapped his fingers nervously on the desk. The timing was perfect. Surely, they would have seen it by now. The group of men who held his future in their hands were halfway around the world, and he wanted them to see him in the best possible light. The glow from Jim Fleming's spotlight was one they could hardly miss. The phonecall that would come through at any moment could change the course of his life. He was only a few steps away from achieving his dream of heading his own publishing company. The Fleming deal had given him the edge he needed.

And if Tracy Bouchard hadn't stormed into his office that day, there might not have been a deal. He hadn't been courting Zwerdlow the way he should have been, and he hadn't realized Kramer had made a bona fide offer. That's not the way to stay ahead in this business.

Canfield smiled as he thought of Tracy. She was difficult and headstrong, but she had spunk. And those legs. . . . He should arrange that lunch soon. His reverie was broken by the ringing of his private line.

"Long distance calling from Paris," Margaret announced over the intercom.

He walked to the door and closed it—something he rarely did.

Margaret caught the tension in his face as he disappeared behind the door. These transatlantic phonecalls had been going on for months, and she hadn't a clue as to what was going on. Well, she thought reasonably, even a secretary can't know everything. But her radar, keenly developed over the years, told her that something enormous was afoot. This much secrecy could only mean that large sums of money were involved. If it works out, I'll know soon enough. It if falls through, I'll never know. Margaret shrugged and returned to her letter.

Two floors below, a delivery man arrived with a huge bouquet of yellow roses and a card addressed to Tracy Bouchard. Jeff Conway followed the fragrant bundle down the hall and hovered about as Tracy's assistant signed for it. Then Conway swooped up the bundle and presented it to Tracy with a flourish.

"What's all this?" she asked.

"That's what I'd like to know." Conway smirked.

His face lit up as she read the card aloud: "Thanks for everything. I'm looking forward to a great partnership. Best, Jim Fleming."

"Want me to get something to put them in?" Dennis Jordan, her new assistant, was eager to be of service. He was fresh out of college and frankly ambitious.

"Thanks, Dennis," Tracy replied, but he was already out the door.

Tracy was putting the vase on the window sill in back of her when her phone rang. Outside in his hallway cubicle, Dennis answered it crisply.

"Tracy! Mr. Canfield is on line twenty-three."

She picked up the receiver as she sniffed the roses again. "Hello? . . . Lunch? . . . Today? . . . Uh, yes, I can make it. . . . No, no. That's all right." She hung up with a surprised look on her face.

"Short notice," Dennis observed.

Tracy smiled gamely. "Out of the blue. We're going to the Four Seasons. Thank God I dressed up today."

She was wearing the black suit she had worn the first day she came to Franklin & Fields. "Something must be up. Canfield seemed incredibly happy about something."

"It's probably the Fleming thing. I could retire on a tenth of what the company's going to make on that book."

"You and me both, Dennis," Tracy agreed. She looked up and saw Jeff Conway walking toward them, eyeing her aggressively.

Conway sidled up to Dennis, elbowing him with mock conspiracy. "Hey, Jordan," he said, winking expansively, "how does it feel to work for a star? Roses from Jim Fleming. Lunch with the big boss. Some day."

Tracy's mouth fell open. "Conway, how come you know everything?"

Conway gave her an impudent grin and sauntered off. Tracy sighed and went to the ladies' room to fix her hair and makeup. She had seen little of Canfield since the meeting with Noble in his office. Tracy brushed her hair until the reddish gold highlights shone softly. She retouched her pearl gray eye shadow and added another layer of black mascara, giving her eyes a dramatic look. Carefully, she outlined her lips with cinnamon-colored lipstick, and was surprised to find her hand shaking ever so slightly. This is lunch with the boss, she reminded herself. Strictly business.

When she got back to her office, Canfield was waiting for her. He sat perched on the window sill next to the yellow roses, wearing a navy blue suit and a paisley tie with a swirl of colors that emphasized the electric blue of his eyes. His curly, black hair shone in the light of the midday sun that streamed through the window.

He smiled at her as she appeared in the doorway. "All set?" he asked, hopping up from the sill. "Nice flowers, Bouchard."

"Thanks. I hope you weren't waiting long. I. . . . "

"Just got here. Shall we go? I've got a cab waiting downstairs."

When they reached the street, Park Avenue was already bustling with the lunch crowd. Canfield guided her through the pedestrian traffic to the cab, which stood ready at curbside. He opened the door and handed her in.

"How are you, Mr. Canfield?" the driver asked politely.

"Fine, Bob. The Four Seasons, please."

Canfield turned to Tracy, surveying her from head to toes. He nodded his head slowly up and down. "You look good, Bouchard. Hard work must agree with you."

"Thanks, Canfield. You don't look bad yourself. Working hard?"

Canfield threw back his head and laughed heartily. "That's what I like about you, Tracy. You give as good as you get."

What is going on here? Tracy wondered. Compliments. Good humor. Something more than the Fleming deal must be going on.

The cab pulled up in front of the restaurant and a uniformed doorman helped Tracy out of the taxi.

"Good afternoon, Mr. Canfield."

Canfield nodded a polite hello.

Inside the plush room, the maître d' guided them to their table. Tracy felt as if she were making a dramatic late entrance to a formal party as she paraded past the Four Seasons regulars holding court at their assigned tables. Some of the guests turned to throw a quick glance at Canfield, wondering who his companion was.

The answer came when a low but demanding voice called out Tracy's name from across the room. Heads turned toward a table near the sparkling fountain. Heather Gentree was waving at them. Tracy could hear the buzzing increase, and her name was muttered once or twice by people as she passed by. She took Canfield by the arm and gracefully escorted him to greet Heather. The petite lady was seated next to a large, disheveled man in a rumpled, brown suit.

"Hello, Tracy, Wes. Tracy, this is Carl Bendex." The man rose and took Tracy's hand gruffly. Then, as he sat down, he acknowledged Canfield.

"I won't bother to ask how you're doing, Wes. Heather just filled me in on the escapades of your new editor here. Fleming, huh? Can't say I'm not jealous, but then I had my day."

Canfield was testy. "Yes, I remember a few good ones."

Bendex looked uneasy. But Heather Gentree interrupted, putting a stop to the caustic exchange between Bendex and Canfield. It was Tracy she was interested in.

"If he," indicating Canfield with a toss of her silver-blond head, "ever mistreats you, give me a call." She took out a business card on which she wrote a number, and handed it to Tracy while Canfield waited impatiently. "That's my private number. I want you to call me when you come out to L.A. next month."

"If she goes," Canfield added.

"She'll go."

Heather turned back to her lunch guest, ending the encounter as abruptly as she had the first time Tracy met her. The maître d', who had waited at a discreet distance, ushered them to their table. Canfield looked back at Gentree's table, perturbed.

"How do you know Heather?" he asked.

"Zwerdlow's party," she reminded him. "Who's this Bendex fellow?"

"A true s.o.b.," Canfield answered shortly. He told Tracy about the famous "Christmas Massacre" at Duchess House. Bendex had been president at the time, and he fired his entire staff just before the holidays. Then he hired new people at lower salaries and worked them to the bone. His new line was movie options, moving in on unsuspecting first authors and cheating them out of thousands of dollars. Canfield hoped Heather Gentree was trying to buy the louse out. "Hell," he told Tracy, "if I had the money, I'd buy him out just to be rid of him."

"Those are strong words, Wes." Tracy pressed her slender fingers gently but firmly on his arm, her golden brown eyes locked into his. With a start, she realized she was touching him intimately, in public, and pulled her hand back. They both looked away.

"Stay away from him," Wes warned. His whole demeanor had changed since the encounter with Gentree and Bendex.

"Let's have a drink," Tracy suggested, trying to ease the tension. A waiter appeared miraculously to take their order.

"Do you think we can have the Fleming book out in time for the Christmas list next year?" she asked as the waiter set down a Perrier for her and a martini for Canfield.

"If he delivers on time, we can. Feel free to encourage him."

She smiled. "I will. He's going to be all right. Fleming tells great stories and all he has to do is write them down the way he tells them, without trying to be literary about it."

"God forbid."

"He'll come around. He's a very bright, adaptable guy."

"So I've heard," Canfield answered dryly.

Tracy got the point. Here she was telling Canfield that America's top television talk show host was a bright guy. She remembered Kippy's advice. Take it slowly. Don't pretend to know it all. Ask questions. She had a lot to learn from a man like Wes Canfield. He knew about getting to the top quickly. It didn't seem to bother him that he was the youngest company president in the publishing industry.

Just as she was about to ask him a question along these lines, the waiter came to take their order, and both men turned to Tracy.

"I'll have the Crabmeat Casanova," she said. "With the iced shrimp to start."

"And for *monsieur?*"

"Shrimp and scallops with dill, please. And a mousse of trout to begin."

"Very good, *monsieur.*"

Canfield chose a bottle of Pouilly-Fuissé to go with the meal, and they were left alone.

There was a pause, during which Tracy ran her finger around the rim of her glass, and Canfield watched her, his shrewd eyes boring into her.

Finally, she looked up, surprised to see a mocking glint on his handsome face. She felt a sudden need to pick up the conversation once again.

"Are you looking forward to the sales conference?" she asked. She felt that she had slipped a notch somehow, but he wasn't letting her off the hook. He stared at her bluntly.

"Oh, I suppose so. It will be a hectic few weeks. I have to fly to Paris immediately afterwards," he answered carelessly.

"What's in Paris?"

There was a long pause as he considered his answer. He looked at her for a moment and opened his mouth to speak, but stopped himself. Finally, he said, "Business," and turned back to his drink.

Tracy could sense his vacillation and decided not to pursue the matter. If he wanted to tell her about it, he would.

"Does the company always hold its sales conferences in Bermuda?"

"No, not always. Sometimes, we have them in the Bahamas. Once, in Jamaica, but never again." He didn't offer an explanation, and again she didn't ask. This conversation was one dead end after another.

Suddenly, he asked, "How old are you, Tracy?"

She blinked her surprise. "Twenty-five."

His eyes traveled frankly from her face to her bare throat, and then rested briefly on the outline of her breasts. She tried to meet his stare boldly, but found herself shifting in her seat. Damn him! Despite her best efforts, he was making her feel unraveled, and she tried frantically to control the flush of red that was creeping up her neck.

Then he smiled—a smile that sent a warm glow through her body. Would she ever understand this man? His changing moods unnerved her. He could make her suddenly furious, filled with ice-cold anger, and just as suddenly he could melt the anger into a honey-glow of longing. What did she want from him? An ally in the company? Or something more?

"Let's hold the business talk for the office, Tracy. Why don't you tell me about yourself so we can get acquainted?"

"Sounds like a good idea, Wes."

"I hope Heather Gentree knows what she's getting into, trying to steal you away from Franklin & Fields. You might be a match for Heather herself. Where did you grow up and learn not to pull any punches?"

Before the espresso and the plate of Godiva chocolates arrived, Tracy had told Wes about growing up on Long Island, learning to fly her father's plane, her years at Tufts and her stint at the bookstore.

As they sipped the dark coffee and nibbled the exquisite, hand-made chocolates, Wes spoke about his years at Columbia University and his meteoric rise in the publishing business.

Time flew and it was nearly three o'clock before Tracy and Wes descended the marble staircase and emerged on East Fifty-second Street. It was a beautiful spring day, and Wes suggested they walk the few blocks back to the Franklin & Fields building.

"I'm glad we did this, Tracy. Now maybe we can talk to one another instead of barking."

"I won't bark if you won't," Tracy replied.

When the elevator stopped at the thirty-eighth floor, Tracy held out her hand. "Thanks for a lovely lunch, Wes." He took her hand in his and she liked the strength she felt in his firm grasp. For an instant, they looked at one another, each trying to read the other's thoughts.

"You're quite welcome, Tracy."

Tracy stepped outside the elevator and watched the doors close, whisking him away from her. She turned and walked slowly to her office. Canfield was an intriguing man. He had seemed so happy at the beginning of the lunch, but meeting Heather and that Bendex character left him moody and preoccupied. She had tried to stick to business, all too aware of her strong attraction for him, but he had waved business aside and treated her like a woman. Tracy found herself wondering what he was like at home. Where did he live? Who were the women in his life? How did he treat the fragile Ambrosia Jewell? It was hard to imagine a man with Wes Canfield's energy being comfortable with a vapid creature like Ambrosia. Tracy sighed. There was so much she wanted to know about him. But as long as he was her boss, it was unlikely she would learn much about his personal life.

Chapter 9

TRACY SETTLED BACK IN HER WINDOW SEAT, WATCHing the green and white dot that was the island of Bermuda grow larger and more distinct in the turquoise sea below her. She was excited and nervous about attending her first sales conference.

Twice a year, Franklin & Fields' editors and salesmen met for four days to talk about upcoming books. It was the responsibility of the editors to present each book in such a delightfully tantalizing way that the salesmen would go out and push it to the hilt. The sales conference could make or break a book, and the editors worked hard on their presentations.

Tracy would present only the Jim Fleming book, and she would have no trouble selling it to the sales force. A book like Fleming's sold itself. However, she wanted to make a good impression so that next season, when she had her own list, her books would be received favorably.

Ken Maguire sat across the aisle from Tracy, mouthing his speech silently, gesturing flamboyantly with his hands, making an occasional note on the yellow legal pad he held on his lap.

Jeff Conway had taken the seat next to Mark Kagan, the sales manager, treating Mark to an enthusiastic preview of Conway's presentation. The important thing at a sales conference was to get everyone's attention, and there were no holds barred on how to get it. Tracy slipped into the seat next to Jeff when Mark excused himself to speak to someone else.

"Hi, killer, how's it going?"

"Just great, Tracy."

"All set for tomorrow?"

"You bet. Tracy, I'm going to do something that's never been done at any sales conference before."

"Oh, what's that?"

He smiled wickedly. "I'll never tell. But you'll find out tomorrow. It's going to be big, Tracy. I promise you that."

"You don't have to promise. I'll take your word."

Sheila Zimmerman stopped by to say a few words to Jeff, making it clear that what she had to say was for his ears only. Annoyed, Tracy returned to her seat. It was just like Sheila to butt in when an eligible man was talking to a single woman—even if it were only business being discussed. She had hoped to see Canfield on the flight, but he was noticeably absent. Everyone else from the New York office was on this flight, and she couldn't help but wonder where he was. They couldn't very well hold the sales conference without him.

The sun was low in the sky as the plane curved gracefully around the airport and made a smooth landing, stopping just short of the terminal. As she stepped out of the plane onto the metal stairway, Tracy was hit with a blast of humid tropical air, so different from the still-chilly spring air of New York. A languid breeze ruffled her hair as she walked the short distance to the terminal.

A mini-bus waited to transport the Franklin & Fields people to the hotel. Tracy was assigned to share a room with Sheila Zimmerman but, fortunately, Sheila took off for the hotel hairdresser as soon as she unpacked, giving Tracy a few moments alone to get her bearings. She looked about at the spacious, white room with its bright green and white floral print drapes and bedspread. The room was relentlessly cheerful, commanding her to have a good time. Tracy drew the drapes and the calm, inviting coolness of the sea beckoned.

Quickly, she unpacked and donned a white bikini, throwing a red and white cotton sarong over her suit. With the first blast of tropical air through the plane door, Tracy had realized she would be on trial again at the sales conference. She had just got used to working with the other editors, and now she had to face a group of tough and seasoned salespeople. It would be four days in a goldfish bowl. She had been looking for Canfield on the plane because she needed a life preserver. No doubt her reputation had preceded her.

The hotel hallways were cool and empty, and she was grateful that no one entered the elevator with her as she rode down. The back of the hotel opened onto a broad terrace, flanked by pink stucco walls and rows of palm trees. The sky was flawlessly clear, and there were several round tables on the patio with umbrellas that flapped gently in the balmy breeze.

"Mmm, heaven," Tracy sighed to herself. She could already feel herself unwinding from the pressures of the city, forgetting the challenges that awaited her here. She ran lightly across the gravel path that led down to the beach, and threw her towel down on the gleaming white sand. Then she unhooked the clasp of her sarong and let it drop. She stepped out of it and ran into the water.

The waves caressed the shore gently, and Tracy sank slowly under the water with a sigh of relief. She surfaced, blinking water out of her eyes, and turned on her back to float. The beach was empty except for two small boys building a sand castle, and she had the water to herself. For twenty minutes, she swam and floated, allowing the water to restore her spirits. Dripping and refreshed, she returned to the shore, dried herself off with the large bath towel and headed back up the slope to the hotel terrace, draping the sarong around her. It clung to her still-damp body, and her wet hair gathered around her long neck in thick, dark reddish curls.

There were a few people sipping drinks on the terrace, but no one from Franklin & Fields was there, so she sat down alone and signaled the waiter. She ordered a Piña Colada, which was served in a hollowed pineapple. Before too long, she had another one. She put her feet up on the empty chair next to her and sipped lazily, staring out at the luscious, blue sea.

"Well, I see you've wasted no time availing yourself of the recreational facilities," a voice behind her said.

She squinted up through the sunlight into a familiar pair of crackling, blue eyes.

"Oh! I didn't see you!"

"Evidently not." His eyes focused on the length of sleek leg that was visible through the hip-high opening in the sarong, and she hastily lowered her foot.

"Uh—would you like to sit down?"

"Thank you." He took the offered seat and tilted his head slightly at the waiter, who immediately approached.

"Yes, sir?"

"Bourbon on the rocks, please. And another—good God, what is that?"

"A Piña Colada. Much more appropriate to Bermuda than bourbon," she pointed out.

"Right. Make it two of those, waiter."

"When did you get in?" Tracy asked. "I missed you on the plane." She ran her fingers through her hair hastily to smooth it, and droplets flew like sparks from her head.

Canfield wiped his face gingerly with the back of his hand. "Hey, take it easy, Bouchard. I'm not wearing my rain slicker. I got in last night. These conferences don't run themselves, you know."

"Well, you don't have to bite my head off. I thought barking was off-limits."

The eyebrow went up, and she felt his eyes boring into her. The flimsy sarong seemed like no protection at all as his gaze traveled aggressively down her body.

"Sorry, Bouchard," he said abruptly.

An uneasy truce was established.

"Isn't the beach gorgeous?" she asked.

His eyes twinkled. "It looks even better at night. There's nothing like a midnight stroll on the beach after a hard day at work here. But I see you've had a head start on leisure activities. I won't have to remind you to take it easy and have some fun, will I?"

Damn him! Why couldn't he be cordial?

"No, you won't," she said with forced sweetness. "In fact, I think I'll take another quick dip before I dress for the cocktail party." Tracy stood up and took a few steps toward the water, then stopped and looked back at Canfield. "Care to join me?"

He glanced down at his business suit and chuckled. "No, thanks. I'm not quite as spontaneous as you are."

"No," she said evenly. "You're not."

Canfield threw back his head and roared with laughter. Tracy was furious. She had meant what she said and now she had a sudden desire to stifle his laughter, to make him look at her seriously without that teasing glint of superiority in his eye.

Tracy tossed her head and ran down to the water, flinging her sarong onto the sand and diving head first into the gentle surf. She swam toward the horizon with a strong crawl stroke.

From the terrace, Canfield watched her thoughtfully, warning himself not to underestimate her. They had gotten along so well at the Four Seasons—after agreeing to a cease-fire. He knew it was the pressure that was making him behave like a two-bit actor in a late-night movie. He was inches aways from closing the deal with the French investors. He had hoped to have everything wrapped up before coming to Bermuda, but there were a few loose ends dangling. He was expecting a phonecall from Paris in the morning that would make Canfield Books a reality. Then he could relax.

He watched Tracy's dark curls moving through the water, her slender, white arms pumping, putting distance between them. In a few hours, he would no longer be her boss. What would happen then? Canfield took a long pull on the straw in his pineapple shell, wincing at the sweet taste of the concoction. He scrawled his name on the check the waiter had left on the table and strode off into the hotel.

When Tracy came out of the water, she saw he was gone. Clutching her sarong in front of her, she looked for him impatiently and finally went back to her room. The next time she saw him she would have to be the cool, polite employee, pretending nothing was going on between them.

Tracy showered, washed and dried her hair and slipped into a simple black silk jersey dress. It was cut straight across the bodice, with thin straps across the shoulders. The waist was gathered so that the knee-length skirt fell in gentle folds. With a thin patent leather belt and black high-heeled sandals, she was all set.

As Tracy was putting on her makeup, Sheila came in, her hair elaborately coiffed in an Edwardian up-sweep.

She greeted Tracy with an icy smile. "Almost ready?"

"Just about. Your hair looks—uh, nice."

"Thanks." Sheila stepped out of her jeans and threw them on her bed. Her blouse landed on the floor in front of the dresser. Then she put on a pair of tight, lavender satin pants, a silver metallic tank top and silver mules with heels so high she could hardly walk. Tracy thought the outfit would have been more appropriate at a costume party than a company cocktail party, but said nothing. They left the room together, locking the door behind them.

The cocktail party was held in a small lounge off of the dining room, and most of the editorial staff were already there. The salespeople had flown in from every corner of the country, and they mingled with the editors, putting names and faces and books together. Tracy went to the bar for a white wine spritzer, and strolled over to a group of new arrivals.

She mingled for over an hour, talking with the sales force and making the rounds. She was listening to two of the western salesmen exchanging notes on their Jacuzzis, when she felt a strong hand on her shoulder.

"Tracy?"

She looked down as Canfield's arm wrapped around her hip, pulling her in tightly for a moment.

"Come over here. I want you to meet someone."

She excused herself hastily and followed him as he

led her by the hand to a middle-aged man in a blue blazer and gray slacks.

"Sam, this is our new editor, Tracy Bouchard. Tracy, this is Sam Baxter, our number-one salesman."

He shook her hand firmly for a long moment.

"Well," he said, "I've already heard a lot about you."

"And I've been reading your reports from the field," she replied. "They're very informative."

Canfield shrugged impatiently. "Enough of this shop talk. Save it for tomorrow. Did you fly your own plane out here or take a commercial flight?" he asked Sam.

"You know me by now, Wes. I never let anyone else fly me around."

Tracy interrupted eagerly. "You flew here yourself?"

"That's right. Just got in here an hour ago. I flew right over the hotel before landing."

"Was that your Cessna Skyhawk I saw coming in?"

Sam's eyes lit up. "Yes, it was. You must know your planes!"

"Well, I should. My father has a Cessna 150. It's not as big as yours, but it flies like an angel. I've been flying it for over ten years. In fact, I knew how to fly before I knew how to drive."

"That's why I wanted you two to meet," Wes interrupted.

Sam turned to Tracy. "Say, if we have time tomorrow, maybe I'll take you up and you can try her out."

"That would be fantastic," Tracy exclaimed.

"How about it, Wes, want to come along?" Sam asked.

"Only if the plane has dual controls."

"Don't you trust me?" Tracy challenged.

"It's not that," Wes hedged. "It's . . . oh, what the hell. If Sam is willing to let you fly his plane, I'm willing to ride in it."

"Shall we say six o'clock, then? I'm a morning person myself. Wes? Tracy?"

"Fine with me, Sam. If it's not too early for Mr. Canfield."

"Oh, it's not too early for me. I'll be there."

Sam looked back and forth at them, like a spectator at a tennis match. "Looks like we're all set then. The lobby at six. Now if you'll excuse me I'd like to have a word with Mark Kagan. See you two in the morning." Sam called out to Mark and hurried away.

"And if you'll excuse me, I'd like to get back to the party. Six sharp, Canfield." Tracy moved off and joined a group listening to Ken Maguire spout the latest Hollywood gossip.

The alarm went off at five-thirty the next morning. She jumped out of bed and went in to take a fast shower. She bounced out of the bathroom fifteen minutes later, her face glowing with excitement. Sheila awoke as she was putting on a pair of jeans and a silk shirt.

"Where are you going at this ungodly hour?" Sheila mumbled, her drooping coiffure peeking through the rumpled bedclothes.

"Out flying!" Tracy called over her shoulder, laughing as Sheila groaned and pulled the covers up over her head.

The hotel lobby was almost empty at that hour, but Sam Baxter was waiting on a small sofa near the desk. He got up to greet her just as Wes Canfield stepped out of the elevator. Canfield was wearing a pair of form-fitting tailored jeans and a white cotton turtleneck. The casual clothes showed off his physique as a business suit never could, and Tracy was frank in her appraisal of this new look. Canfield smiled mischievously as he caught her stare.

"You look like you're raring to go, Miss Bouchard," he said.

"No doubt about it. I haven't flown in a long time. Is this your first time in a small plane, Mr. Canfield?"

"He's never been up with me," Sam commented. "Though God knows I've asked him often enough."

"I think you'll find it very interesting. Ready to go, gentlemen?" Tracy wondered what kind of a passenger Canfield would be. People sometimes had strange reactions to small planes. Even the most seasoned traveler could be unnerved by the sensation of flight without the buffers provided by commercial airlines.

They piled into Canfield's rented Austin Healy and drove two miles to a tiny airstrip reserved for private planes. Tracy got out and pointed to a silver, twin-engine propjet, decorated with royal-blue stripes.

"She's a beauty," Tracy breathed.

"Yep," Sam agreed. "I'm sure proud of her."

Canfield stared at the Cessna and said nothing.

They boarded the tiny aircraft, Tracy at the controls, Sam next to her and Canfield behind them in the minuscule passenger seat. Sam directed her briefly, but relaxed when he saw she was in full command. She took off easily, guiding the plane down the runway and up over the ocean. They flew over the length of the island, peering down at their hotel and the adjacent golf course. Canfield remained quiet, as she and Sam chattered away about planes and their flight experiences. It was unlike him to be so reticent, and she decided to liven up the outing. She smiled mischievously at her fellow pilot, who gave her the high sign. The plane took a sudden dive and swerved sharply to the right. Tracy leveled the plane out over the shoreline and rose gracefully into a cloud.

"Hey! What the hell was that?" Canfield demanded.

Sam laughed. "Aw, she's just showing off, Wes. You don't get airsick, do you?"

Canfield drew back into his cramped seat. "No," he mumbled.

"Oh, good," Tracy remarked, as the small plane made an arc around a village, one wing dipping down toward the ground thousands of feet below. She caught sight of his scowling face in the mirror. He was glaring directly at her reflection, his gaze riveting hers. Their eyes locked for a brief instant, hers glinting with amusement and his flashing with annoyance.

Tracy looked away quickly. Why was she always baiting him? What was she trying to prove? She straightened out the plane and flew quietly, concentrating on what she was doing. No more shenanigans, she told herself.

After a while, Sam glanced at his watch. "It's almost eight-thirty, Tracy. I think we'd better head back."

"Okay." Tracy turned the aircraft around and they flew back to the landing strip. She made a careful, measured descent and landed the plane evenly, stopping it exactly at the tip of the white line at the end of the runway.

"Perfect landing!" Sam cried. "Tracy, it's been a pleasure to be your passenger. I don't get to sit in this seat too often."

"Thank you," she answered, knowing Sam's praise was not given lightly. "I hope you enjoyed it, Wes."

He looked at her sharply. "Not bad."

They clambered down, walked over to Canfield's car, and got in. He drove the way he walked—fast and direct, making the little foreign car do what he wanted without any coaxing or stress. He'd like to control me the way he controls this car, Tracy thought. They arrived back at the hotel and, after a curt goodby to her and Sam, Canfield disappeared into the lobby.

Tracy turned to Sam. "I guess he didn't appreciate my flying." She sighed. "He's a tough one to figure out. He never lets anyone know what he's thinking. I wish I could read his mind. It would make my life a lot easier."

"It's not as hard as you think," Sam told her. "Just watch his face. It's all there, Tracy."

"I see." Studying Canfield's face might reveal more than she wanted to know, she thought. "Thanks, Sam. And thanks for the ride. It was great to be in the pilot's seat."

"My pleasure. Take it easy, Tracy. See you at the meeting."

Tracy returned to her room and changed into a white cotton dress with a halter top. She headed for the dining room, where a buffet breakfast had been set up. After filling her plate with scrambled eggs, bacon and two freshly baked rolls, Tracy saw Martha Hauptmann seated alone at a corner table and asked if she could join her.

"Please do." Martha looked up from the notes she was studying and eyed Tracy's full plate. "How do you stay so thin if you eat like that?"

"I'm starved. Been up since five-thirty. I went flying with Sam Baxter and Wes Canfield in Sam's Cessna. I haven't piloted in months. It was great—except that I started showing off and I don't think Canfield liked it."

Martha took a small nibble of the half-eaten croissant on her plate. "It's been my experience that he doesn't like to be thrown too many curves. He likes to be in the driver's seat. I'd go easy with him. He took a chance with you once. He may not take any more." She tidied the pile of colored notecards and wrapped a rubber band around them. "I've done all I can for this presentation. Are you all set, Tracy?"

"I think so. I only have the Jim Fleming book to present, and I don't think I'll have any trouble. I am a little nervous, though. You're so well prepared— all those notecards, different colors. I have my presentation worked out in my head, but I didn't make any notes. Do you think I should?"

"I find it's easier. There's a lot of pressure when you get up in front of the group, and I like to have something to hold onto and refer to in case I get tongue-tied." Martha glanced at her watch. "You'd better finish up. We're due in the conference room in ten minutes and I need to freshen up. I'll see you later, Tracy."

Martha stood up and Tracy admired her gracious appearance. Her hair was arranged in a bun at the nape of her neck, but she wore a fresh gardenia in it, giving the plain style a unique twist. She wore a teal-blue linen dress, crisp and fresh but feminine. Martha was successful without being pushy or brash. And of all the people at Franklin & Fields, she had been the most helpful to Tracy, the one most genuinely interested in her. Tracy wondered if Martha had always been so self-possessed, or if it were a skill she had cultivated. In any case, she thought, it's a skill I should cultivate, instead of being so impulsive and contentious. Tracy looked down at her food and found she had no appetite left. She put her napkin on the table and left for the conference room.

The conference room had an open patio that overlooked the beach. The room was filled with an excited buzz as people filed in and seated themselves around the large table that was soon covered with notebooks, pens, styrofoam cups, and cassette tape recorders. Tracy noticed that Jeff Conway was not in the room. Neither was Canfield.

A sudden hush fell over the large room as the door opened and Canfield entered briskly, nodding briefly to the assembled group. He strode across the expanse of carpet to the head of the long table and everyone turned toward him expectantly.

"Good morning," he said in a crisp, businesslike tone.

Papers rustled, people settled themselves in their chairs, and the business of the day began. Canfield introduced John Noble, who chaired the meeting from that point on. Canfield sat at Noble's left, occasionally jotting notes on a yellow pad.

Tracy listened with interest as the first few books were presented, but it was hard to stay riveted to the proceedings. So many books were presented in such a short time, and she understood now why it was important to think up something exciting to get the salespeople's attention. She wondered what it was that Conway had in store, and looked around the room for clues. Finding nothing, she returned her attention to Sheila Zimmerman as she finished up her presentation of a gourmet diet book.

"And the introduction, of course, was written by James Beard," Sheila was saying. "There will be a first printing of twenty thousand copies, and the author will tour in twelve cities."

There was a murmur of approval as Sheila sat down. John Noble stood up and said, "Ladies and gentlemen, I have a short announcement. The next book on the list is *Parachuting for Beginners,* and the editor is Jeffrey Conway. You may have noticed that Mr. Conway is not with us this morning, but if you will just look out toward the beach, you'll see him soon."

Everyone turned and watched as Noble pointed up toward the sky. People began to whisper and giggle as a tiny dot came into view high above the shoreline. They stared, fascinated, as it grew larger, and they made out a large, orange glider parachute that was sailing down from the clouds. Conway steered it slowly into their range of vision, and after a few minutes, he landed safely on the beach, about thirty yards from the water and fifty feet from the assembled audience. They all laughed and applauded as he disengaged himself from the parachute and marched over to the patio. He bowed ceremoniously and waited for the response to die down. Then he addressed the group with cheerful pride, explaining that anyone could learn to sky dive, and that it was destined to become the next sports craze in America. He added that they would be publishing both a hardcover and a quality paperback edition, and that the authors would perform several diving stunts in major cities to promote the book. His presentation was met with an enthusiastic round of applause, and he sat down looking well pleased with himself. He knew that the sales force would remember his book with no trouble at all.

There was no doubt that Conway's stunt dominated the morning's events, and Tracy began to wait impatiently for lunchtime. Several more books were presented, and at last Canfield stood up.

"I think we can just about wrap it up for the morning," he said. Everyone sighed with relief, and threw their pens down. "We'll meet back here at two-thirty." People began to stretch and scrape their chairs back. "But first," he said, quieting the noise, "I'd like to introduce our new editor, and ask her to tell you just a little bit about the new book she's brought in for us. Her name is Tracy Bouchard. Tracy?"

Tracy's stomach took a nosedive. Now she knew how Canfield had felt in the plane this morning. The group was tired and hungry and Conway's antics had already stolen the show. She had planned on preparing her notes during the lunch break, but now she would have to wing it. Tracy took a deep breath and faced the group squarely.

"I know you've all been waiting to hear about the Jim Fleming book." She began uncertainly, looking around the room for a friendly face. All she saw was a pencil tapping here, a foot jiggling there. "I don't know what to say, uh, except that it's going to, uh, knock your socks off." Tracy heard a few scattered chuckles throughout the room and continued with more assurance. "I got the completed outline and the first two chapters from Jim the other day, and they're better than anyone could have imagined. This is not going to be just another show business autobiography. Jim Fleming's book is going to be an eagle's eye view of the very guts of American television and the entertainment business. It will be an important book as well as a commercial one. Jim Fleming is as facile at the typewriter as he is in front of the camera."

Tracy spoke faster as she warmed to her task and the audience warmed to her. "Of course, we expect a record paperback sale and there will be a half-million copy first printing. Jim has agreed to do a major publicity tour for the book and Wes is negotiating with Fleming's network to allow him to plug the book on his own show." Tracy's face glowed with excitement and everyone in the room caught up her enthusiasm. Even Wes Canfield was smiling happily. "I think that's all I have to say about the book except," Tracy grinned broadly, "I'm so excited I think I'm going to burst!"

She finished so abruptly no one said anything for a moment. Then Wes Canfield let out a loud laugh and everyone joined him. There was a short round of applause and even some foot-stamping from some of the salespeople. Flushed and happy, Tracy sat down. Across the room, she caught Wes's eyes on her.

"Thank you, Tracy," he said over the buzz.

"You're welcome," she called back.

Wes rapped on the table to get the attention of the animated group. "Please limit yourselves to four martinis at lunch. We may have the Fleming book to celebrate, but we have a lot more good books to discuss this afternoon. We'll reconvene at two-thirty."

Everyone stood up and began to collect notebooks and equipment. Several people had questions for Tracy, and she walked from the room surrounded by a small crowd of excited co-workers.

"Well, Tracy," Sam Baxter said, "I don't think I'll have any trouble selling that one."

The group moved into the hallway, still laughing as they entered the dining room for lunch. The meal was festive and congenial, and the tensions of the morning melted away.

The afternoon session held no surprises. No parachuting editors. No blockbuster bestsellers. Tracy found her eyes and mind wandering in Wes Canfield's direction more than once. To her dismay, he always managed to catch her staring at him. It was impossible to tell what he was thinking, despite Sam Baxter's advice. Sam evidently did not melt under the scrutiny of those blue eyes.

The meeting broke up at five, and Tracy decided to go for a swim before dinner. She changed into her white bikini and ran down to the beach, her auburn hair flying behind her in the gentle breeze. The turquoise waves were soothing after her long day, and she let them lull her into a state of benign contentment. Her short swim left her refreshed and energetic and she went off to explore the beach. As she strolled along, her feet made hard, compact prints in the wet sand, and soon the hotel was hidden from the view behind a bend. No one else was on the beach and she had this seductive paradise all to herself, even though she was only a short distance from the hotel. It was an exhilarating illusion. She was queen of her own tropical island. Sitting down on the sand with her toes in the water, she stared out to sea, leaning her chin on her knees, surveying her domain.

"Well, I should have known."

The voice scared her half out of her wits. "Wes!" she sputtered. "What are you doing here?"

"I should be asking you the same question," Canfield retorted. "Franklin & Fields is not responsible if you get lost or eaten by a shark." He smiled wickedly.

"That's not funny," she snapped. What was he doing here? This is my island, she thought. Can't I have ten minutes to myself without someone popping up? And after his surprise introduction of her at the meeting this morning, she didn't know if she wanted him here.

"Come on up here," he invited her, grabbing her hand and pulling her to her feet. They stood facing each other, her hand imprisoned in his. Tracy pulled away from him with a jerk.

"How did you know I was here?"

"I knew someone was here. I saw the footprints. You left an easy trail of breadcrumbs, you see." He began to laugh, and Tracy watched him impatiently.

"Well, you'd better head back," she counseled, "You're still wearing a suit, for heaven's sake. And your shoes are getting wet."

He looked down. "So they are." But he didn't move. He just stood there looking at her with that impenetrable look on his face as the ocean breezes wafted through her damp hair and made her shiver.

"You're cold," he said, and his hands were suddenly on her shoulders.

She regarded him solemnly. How could one man cause so many conflicting emotions in her? As much as she wanted to maintain an aura of control near him, she always felt—unraveled. It was a feeling she was learning to recognize and even to welcome, so she let him exercise his power over her.

"You really shouldn't run around like this. Someone might get the wrong idea."

"Run around like what?" she asked. "What do you mean by that?"

Just then, they were interrupted by a voice that called from the top of a small hill. "Wes! Wes, are you down there?"

He released her and spun around. "Who's there?" he called.

"It's John. You just got a phonecall from Paris. They want you to call back in fifteen minutes."

Wes tensed a little. "Okay, thanks!"

They stood apart and walked back up the incline as John retreated down the other side. Neither spoke, but their hands bumped occasionally as they trotted along. Something had changed between them: Wes had withdrawn into one of his sudden shells of silence, and there was nothing she could say to break it.

Canfield left her in the lobby after a brief, formal handshake. Tracy went back to her room wondering just what had happened. Sheila was there, talking to her children long distance. Tracy showered and changed into a Kelly-green sundress that was a vibrant contrast to her smooth shoulders and dark hair. They began serving drinks at seven, and she felt like she could use one. She went downstairs by herself and saw Jeff Conway and Stephen Marcus, who were sipping cocktails next to a sunny window.

"Hi, mind if I join you?"

"Have a seat, Tracy," they said cordially. They were relaxed after the day's events, and they were chatting leisurely about the publishing business and how it had changed in the past five years. Tracy listened intently, sipping a gin and tonic as she watched them. As Kippy had suggested, she was learning how to listen and absorb. There was no point in pretending she had something to say about what had happened five years ago. Five years ago, she had been a student, engaged to a Harvard law student, with no knowledge of publishing at all. But she soaked up their comments and observations like a sponge, and stored the information away for future reference.

The buffet opened at seven-thirty, and the hungry staff lined up to try the local cuisine, gossiping excitedly about the day's events. Tracy ate lightly, talking with Jeff and Stephen and Martha, but her mind was on Canfield the whole time. He appeared in the dining room after eight o'clock, still wearing his suit and tie. Everyone else had changed to less formal attire, and Tracy was surprised he had not. She stayed close to her group, laughing and talking about the local islands, trying to ignore the burning feelings his presence gen-

121

erated in her. Canfield stayed in a corner, talking to no one, surveying the scene. His eyes radiated a private excitement.

The next time she stole a glance at him, he was leading John Noble by the elbow, taking him to the far side of the room. His face was serious, and whatever he said made Noble's eyes widen with surprise. Then they were shaking hands enthusiastically, and Canfield said something else that caused the editor-in-chief to smile broadly. Tracy looked at Conway, who had also noticed the interchange, and he shrugged.

Then John Noble called for everyone's attention, and the room settled down as Canfield stepped in front of him. "I wish to announce that effective immediately, I am resigning from Franklin & Fields to move on to my own company," he began, but he had to stop as noisy whispers filled the room. He held up his hand for silence and continued. "I have enjoyed working with all of you, and wish you every success in the future. It has been a long-standing dream of mine to run my own firm, and I am grateful for the experience and support you have given me." His remarks were received with encouraging smiles and nods. "I also wish to announce at this time that Mr. Fields and the board of directors have appointed John Noble to be the new president of the company." This was greeted with surprised applause, and everyone pressed forward to shake hands with the two men and offer their congratulations.

Tracy shook hands with John, but found it impossible to get close to Canfield. He was surrounded by three layers of people, and suddenly she was too exhausted to make the effort. She edged her way to the door without being noticed and looked back at him. His dark head jerked around and he flashed her a brief, inscrutable smile before he was once again swamped with well-wishers. She might never see him again.

She slipped into bed as soon as she got to her room. But sleep was elusive as visions of Wes raced through her mind. He was no longer her boss. She saw him sitting across from her at the Four Seasons, saw him as he boarded Sam's plane and at the wheel of the Austin later. She lay on the firm mattress, letting the cooling breezes from the open window soothe her confusion. The sound of a calypso band drifted in from somewhere nearby, and she was roused by its lilting rhythms. She got up and walked restlessly to the window. The palm trees were lined up like dark statues by the side of the hotel, and she could hear the sound of the ocean as it lapped against the shore.

She took off her nightgown and fastened the sarong around her. Then she stepped quietly out of the room and locked the door behind her. She didn't want anyone to see her leave the hotel, so she went down the back stairs that led to a side entrance to the dining room. She opened the French doors and slipped out.

The night was enchantingly balmy, and a sparkling profusion of stars dotted the navy blue sky. She walked on the beach for a few minutes, letting the cool water wash over her feet. The cold, gritty sand squiggled up between her toes as she went in the same direction she had taken that afternoon.

The penetrating moonlight lit her path, and she passed the small slope that hid the hotel from view. She was just a few feet from the private place she'd found that afternoon, when she discerned the figure of a man standing about twenty feet in front of her. He stood motionless, watching her, and she hesitated for only a moment.

Silently, she glided up to him and murmured, "Hello again."

"I thought you'd come," he said. He was barefoot, the business suit exchanged for faded dungarees and a T-shirt. They faced each other as man and woman, all other roles stripped away.

Wordlessly, they began to walk again along the wet sand, their feet making small, crunching sounds that broke the silence. At last, they came upon a large boulder that was embedded in the sand, and they stopped, facing each other solemnly in the shadow.

"You're a very beautiful woman, Tracy," Wes said quietly.

She said nothing, her eyes shining like two golden jewels in the clear night. As she looked into his blue eyes, she saw that his face was etched with desire, and she wanted him suddenly, wanted him urgently, fiercely, with an ardor she did not quite understand. Her face lifted imperceptibly, and she felt his hands as they moved slowly, deliberately, from her shoulders down her bare arms to her hands. She could not remember just how it happened afterwards—but, somehow, they had stepped out of the real world. His mouth came down on hers with possessive finality. Without consciously knowing it, they had waited a long, long time for this moment, and now that it had finally come, it was irrevocable. They embraced it and relished its power as they held each other, trembling with desire.

They fell in slow motion, and then she was lying on her back, reaching out her arms to him, and he was straddling her on his knees, caressing her with tantalizing strokes that led lightly over her breasts and down her legs, leaving an unbearable tingling inside her thighs. She heard him moan slightly as he unhooked the single clasp that held the sarong, and it opened easily, expansively, revealing her naked body to him. He looked at her for a long moment, murmuring softly to her before he buried his face in her wild wavy hair, kissing her neck and then moving down to her breasts. Her eyes closed as she undulated beneath him, little sighs of pleasure escaping her lips. The scent of lemon blossoms wafted in from across the island, and the soft night was very still.

Tracy opened her eyes, drinking in the moonlight and the outline of her lover's body against the sky. She reached for him again, her fingers pushing his shirt up and over his head, her hands moving sensuously over his smooth, hard chest. His body was lean and compact, muscular without being bulky, and he moved with the grace of a panther. He stood up suddenly and stepped quickly out of his jeans, letting her see him fully unclothed. She gave a little gasp of delight when she saw that he wore no underwear at all, and as he knelt by her side, she reached up to hold his hard strength hungrily in her hands. It was silky and quivering with excitement, responding to every nuance of her touch. She felt the world turning on its axis as he covered her, pressing his long, hard body against her soft curves. When he entered her with one sure, powerful thrust, her head fell back and a moan of pure ecstasy was drawn from deep inside her. Waves of exquisite pleasure swept over them as he moved with a gentle rocking, building the rhythm relentlessly as he drove into her again and again. All time had stopped and they were together in a world that was only their need for each other and the fire of their passion.

Tracy was swept along on a tidal wave of ecstasy that could not have been halted for anything. At last, she was carried over the peak, and she lay trembling helplessly in his arms as he continued to kiss her throat and her breasts.

When at last she looked at his face, which was limpid with emotion in the pale light, she touched his cheek wonderingly and said in a broken whisper, "I don't know what happened."

He quieted her by holding her very close and rocking her soothingly in his arms, caressing her back and her arms. He rose above her again, and she could see the same sense of wondrous fulfillment that had possessed her etched on his features.

She slept for a while in his arms, and then they got up from the white sand, held each other silently for a small eternity, and walked slowly, closely, back to the hotel.

Chapter 10

THE RETURN TO THE OFFICE WAS A DISTINCT LETDOWN after the four eventful days in Bermuda. Tracy felt as if she had been away for weeks instead of days.

"Wow! Nice tan, Tracy," Dennis complimented her enthusiastically.

"Thanks, Dennis. Have you got a list of calls that came in while I was away?" Tracy's voice was dull.

He handed her the list and she scrutinized it quickly. "Anything else?"

"Oh, yes, there's one more."

She cringed. Not Steve Kramer again! He had tried to reach her three more times after his vitriolic phonecall, but she had instructed Dennis not to put his calls through. Even though there was nothing Kramer could do to her, she didn't want to subject herself to his anger.

"An agent by the name of Marie Somerville. She wants to set up a lunch," Dennis said.

Tracy sat back in her chair. "Okay, thanks."

Dennis went back to his cubicle, and she turned the swivel chair around to face the window. Thirty-eight stories below, the cars crawled along in the midmorning traffic, and the endless rows of windows in the buildings across the street revealed identical scenes of desks and offices and dark-suited men.

A dark-suited Wes Canfield was at this moment settling into his new office. It was only a short cab ride away, but Tracy felt far away from him today. His work would be difficult in the beginning, and Wes might be as unavailable to her now as he had been when he occupied an office two floors above her.

Tracy closed her eyes and remembered him as he had looked the first time she saw him. What would she have said then if anyone had told her that this dynamic man was to become her lover? How could she have imagined the way the muscles in his back rippled when he held her, or the shock of black hair that fell over his forehead in the heat of passion? The one thing that continued to thrill her every time she remembered it was the way his whole body trembled when he made love to her. The thought of his trembling left her weak with longing for another display of surrender. True, they had both been swayed by the moonlight and the heady unreality of the tropical setting. But their encounter had been inevitable. She could still smell the ocean breezes and the scent of lemon that had drifted across the island, and she could still hear the broken whispers of desire he had murmured in her ear.

A shattering scream brought Tracy back to reality.

"Oh, MY GOD!!!" Ken Maguire's cries echoed through the halls. Heads popped out of offices as he continued to give vent to his fury. "Oh, my Lord, I can't believe it! How could he?"

Tracy swirled around and saw John Noble rush past her door. A moment later, the door to Ken Maguire's office slammed shut. She saw Sheila trot by and called out, "What is it?" but Sheila shook her head helplessly. Well, they would find out soon enough. Ken was noted for his outbursts, but this one had a peculiarly genuine quality to it. Whatever it was, it made Tracy nervous.

She heard his door open, and the two men marched down the hall, Noble looking distressed and Maguire practically foaming at the mouth. He gave her a cold, angry stare as he passed, and she felt her heart jump with apprehension. Was she being accused of something? That's ridiculous, she told herself, and tried to brush off her fear as unwarranted and paranoid. She had never felt completely comfortable here, but that was no reason to feel responsible for everything that went wrong. Maguire tended to overreact to things. As she was trying to convince herself of this, Jeff Conway appeared in the doorway.

"There's a meeting of the entire editorial staff in twenty minutes. Whatever it is, it's important."

"What happened?"

"Who knows? But we'll find out soon enough."

"Ken seemed really upset."

"Well, don't worry about it."

Fat chance. It was already one of those days. Before, she could look to Wes Canfield for support, but now he was gone. She was on her own. The look Ken Maguire had given her as he stalked by her office was a knowing one, filled with out-and-out hatred. What could she possibly have done to earn such malice?

The conference room where they held their meetings seemed different without Canfield. John Noble now sat at the head of the table, and the empty seat to his right was reserved for the next editor-in-chief. Tracy hoped they would elevate one of the editors to the administrative position, but she could not guess who they might choose. She felt uneasy about the strong possibility that they would hire someone from outside the company. At least the people here were a known quantity. Her personal choice would have been Stephen Marcus, but she knew how unlikely that was. The man was a superb editor. The last thing he needed was a lot of paperwork and added responsibility.

Everyone turned as Ken Maguire entered the room. He was still very agitated, and Tracy realized with a shock that he had been crying. The room fell into an embarrassed silence, and Noble closed the door. Ken sat down noisily, pulled out a pack of cigarettes and tried to light one, cursing as his fingers fumbled with the match. Sheila extended her lighter and he leaned into it, nodding his thanks. Then the two of them turned and gazed at Tracy with animosity. She gazed back uncomfortably, and when at last they turned away, she shuddered.

The new president did not look happy. It was his first day in the new post, and already there was a major problem. He faced the group and cleared his throat.

"I'll get right to the point. Is everyone here familiar with Jack Wing, one of Ken's authors?"

Tracy had heard the name, but was afraid to ask any questions. Martha Hauptmann answered authoritatively.

"Of course. The author of *Year of the Dragon*. It's an excellent book, really excellent. We're hoping for a big paperback sale on that, aren't we?"

John nodded grimly. "That's right."

Ken was listening to all this impatiently. "It was stolen!" he broke in.

"Stolen? What do you mean, stolen?" Jeff Conway was equally impatient. He did not like Ken's theatrics.

"The film rights." Ken drew heavily on his cigarette and then put it out with shaking fingers.

"I don't understand," Stephen Marcus interjected quietly. "I assume the author controlled the film rights?"

"Yes."

"Then what happened? Who has them now?"

Ken's voice shook. "Carl Bendex."

Tracy gasped slightly, and everyone looked at her. She remembered that name, and she remembered Canfield's warning never to get mixed up with him.

John Noble asked, "Do you know him, Tracy?"

She was flustered. "Well, not personally. We just met once—I mean, he was with—"

"Stay away from him. That goes for everybody. He's unscrupulous. He makes his money by scouting out books he believes will have big movie sales. Then he buys them for ridiculously low prices before they become well known. Usually, he hits on an author who is new to the business, especially one without an agent. The author is thrilled to get a movie sale at all, and by the time anyone finds out about it, it's too late."

Conway gave a low whistle. "How much did Jack Wing sell for?"

Noble grimaced, and avoided the question. "We had no idea Bendex had the manuscript, and we have no idea how he got it. The author had no agent—it's a first novel—so Ken was trying to work out a movie deal with an agent in L.A. Wes Canfield had set something up before he left. This morning, the agent called and said he had got a producer to option the book for half a million dollars."

There was an excited buzz, and Conway muttered, "The book's a winner."

"But," Noble continued, "when Ken called the author to tell him the good news, he found that the man had already signed with Carl Bendex, for seventy-five hundred dollars."

There was a stunned silence in the room. Ken Maguire's head fell into his hands.

"But how did he know there was a big book here? And how did he get the manuscript?" Sheila asked.

"That," said John, "is the whole point. We don't know how, but there's only one possible explanation. Somebody in this company told him. For a price."

Ken Maguire's chest heaved as he added, "And now my author has been screwed. He feels sick about it, but it's too late. Too late."

Tracy's pulse quickened. They couldn't possibly think it was her. "But Ken," she said soothingly. "The book can still be a success. And the movie will sell more books, won't it?"

His head jerked up and he stared at her menacingly. "That's not the point," he hissed through clenched teeth. "My author has been cheated. This company was supposed to represent his best interests, and we failed. Whoever did this should be thrown in jail." His voice rose to a nasal pitch, and Noble put a hand on his arm to calm him down.

Tracy felt the familiar wrenching in her guts. He did blame her. That was the reason for the sudden hostility. They had never completely trusted her, and now they never would. They thought she was a thief, and there was nothing she could do about it.

Tracy sank back in her chair. Oh, no, she thought. Please, no. Not again. It's not fair. She didn't want them to see her distress. She was afraid they would misinterpret it as a sign of guilt. Even Stephen Marcus looked away from her politely. The pain in her stomach was becoming worse.

John Noble tactfully turned the meeting to another subject. "I am pleased to tell you all that a new editor-in-chief has been named. He is one of the most qualified men in the business, and we were lucky to get him."

"Who is it?" everyone clamored, but John laughed and said, "He should be here in just a few minutes. I believe he wants to make a dramatic entrance, so I'll wait and surprise you. If anyone has anything pressing to attend to, I can introduce you later."

Tracy opted for the latter choice. She had no desire to stay in the room full of suspicious eyes. For a brief second, she thought about resigning, but she realized just as quickly that that could be taken as an admission of guilt. It was an awful situation, but she would have to survive it somehow. As for now, she didn't feel like meeting the new boss. Not here, not now. She would meet him later, on her own turf. She turned toward the door.

"Hey, Tracy!" It was Jeff. "Where are you going? Stick around."

"Uh—I've got an important call to make," she hedged. She turned again to leave, but she bumped into a man who was now standing in the doorway. It was the new editor-in-chief, and she froze with fear at the sight of him. Her already knotted stomach contracted violently, and her palms began to moisten and grow cold. She tried to say something and couldn't as the man pushed past her and stood at the center of attention. Steve Kramer glowered at Tracy and turned to greet his new staff.

Chapter 11

"I GUESS IT'S ALL OVER FOR ME," TRACY SAID TO JOHN Noble.

He regarded the crestfallen young woman solemnly. It had been less than two months since she had burst into this office offering Jim Fleming to Wes Canfield.

"Don't be silly," he said smoothly. "There will be no personnel changes because of Steve Kramer's arrival. And Tracy, I like you and would like to see you do well here."

Tracy mustered a meager smile. She knew that everyone in the publishing business played musical jobs. A new editor-in-chief meant a new entourage. Maybe not this week or even this month, but soon. She looked out the window, and followed the straight path of Park Avenue down to the Pan Am building. Wes was there at the end of the street in his new office at One Park Avenue. Perhaps he would want to expand his editorial staff.

"Look, Tracy, Kramer is a fine editor with many years of experience. Don't forget, he was the one who got Fleming interested in doing a book in the first place. He paved the way for us. And it was F & F's money that bought that book, not Tracy Bouchard. I'd like you to try to get along with him."

John was being diplomatic. Jim Fleming had signed his contract and she was realistic enough to know that she was expendable. Fleming might have a contract, but she did not. She was skating on thin ice and she would have to take care of herself.

She left Noble's office and trotted obediently down to see Kramer, at Noble's polite direction. It was best to clear the air now, if she could. The door to his office was open, and she stood for a moment, watching him arrange some papers in a desk drawer. Clearing her throat slightly, she stepped inside and waited until he looked up.

When he saw who was standing there, he froze for a moment, and then sat back and stared at her frankly. It was the look of a challenger, of someone who has been beaten and is only waiting for the next round. "Sit down, Tracy," he said evenly.

She sat opposite him as she had so many times before and smiled ruefully. "This is where we left off, isn't it, Steve?"

He cut her off coldly. "Let me tell you something. My being here isn't a coincidence, and it isn't a miracle either. Franklin & Fields needed to polish its image and hang onto the Fleming book at the same time. There was only one way they could do that. They hired me to squelch the rumors of theft and to stop a possible lawsuit. In short, they threw me a bone—a big, fat bone—and I took it."

Tracy sat with her eyes downcast. The gravity of what he was saying sank into her deeply.

"I don't mind telling you that I wanted to let you go, but John Noble vetoed it. So I expect you to produce. You know next to nothing about editing books and there's only one way to learn—that's by doing."

"I was more than willing to do that when I was your assistant at Carey, but you never gave me the chance." Tracy bristled at this personal attack. Explaining the company's precarious position was one thing, but he didn't have to be vicious. "I did manage to learn a few things in spite of you, though."

Kramer pulled three manuscripts from the shelf and put them on the desk in front of her. "I want a full report on these by next week. Tell me what's wrong with them, what's good about them and which ones can make money. If I decide to buy one of them, I'll let you edit it."

She looked over the titles, and frowned.

"Not everything is the Fleming book, you know," he said.

"It can be!" She knew she was wrong, but she had an overwhelming desire to disagree with him.

"No, it can't be. Wise up. You still think you're pretty smart? Well, let's get one thing straight. John Noble notwithstanding, if you don't measure up here, out you go. As far as any books you want to buy, I'll decide what they're worth. And as for how you spend your time here, I'll be determining what's best for you and this company."

Tracy swallowed hard. The urge to bail out was strong. She could quit and go somewhere else. But if she did that, her reputation would always be tarnished. It would be like high school. No, she had to stay and see this through, no matter how difficult. She had to prove herself.

"Oh, and one more thing," he went on. "I don't want you going on more than one lunch a week."

Her mouth fell open. "But I'm already booked up for the next six weeks!"

"Then cancel."

This was too much. How could he expect her to get anywhere if he wasn't going to allow her to get close to the major sources? She had to see agents, and that was all there was to it. Perhaps some of them would come to her office instead of meeting her for lunch. But how could she cancel all of those appointments? She chose her words carefully.

"That wouldn't look good, Steve. How about if I spread them out more? Supposing we cut it down to say, two lunches a week and a breakfast? A lot of people like to talk business first thing in the morning."

Kramer sighed. "All right," he said. "You win. But remember, you're supposed to do more than eat. Use them to their best advantage."

"I know that, Steve. I have been working here as an editor for nearly two months."

They looked at each other for a minute, both sullen and resentful. There was nothing left to say. Tracy rose and left the room.

She met Ken Maguire on the way back to her office. He sneered as she passed him and her torment rose in a fresh wave. She sat down stormily at her desk and reached for the telephone, desperate to speak with Wes, who would understand and comfort her. But the phone rang, making her jump in her chair. It was Kramer.

"You forgot the manuscripts, Tracy."

"I'll send my assistant to pick them up," she answered stonily.

A few minutes later, Dennis appeared, carrying six manuscripts instead of three.

"What's all this?" she asked irritably.

"Mr. Kramer says half of these are mine."

"Oh. All right, then." She handed him half of the pile.

So Kramer was giving her assistant the same work he was giving her. She should have known. She scrutinized the three manuscripts and saw they were probably for the birds. Then she looked at Dennis, who was still standing in front of her.

"And Dennis."

"Yes?"

"If any of those are good and we buy them—they're yours."

His eyes lit up with excitement. "You mean it, Tracy?"

"Sure. You can only learn by doing."

He left happily and she watched him with mixed feelings. If Kramer had said that to her a few months ago, she wouldn't be here now. But he hadn't and she was.

Tracy worked listlessly for several hours, ordering in a sandwich for lunch. She took a few bites of her tuna on rye, but left most of it uneaten. Her mind kept replaying this terrible morning—so many things all at once. It was like being caught in a horror movie —only this was her life. By midafternoon, Tracy was ready to throw in the towel and leave early, pleading illness. She knew it would look horrible but she didn't care anymore.

"Excuse me, Tracy," Dennis was whispering to her from the doorway. "There's some guy on the phone. He won't give me his name. Says he's your lover."

"Well, that's a new one. Okay, Dennis, I'll take it." It has to be Wes, she thought. He must have heard about Kramer from the grapevine. There are no secrets in this business. She waved Dennis away and picked up the phone.

"Tracy Bouchard."

"Hi, Tracy."

The voice was not the one she expected to hear. "Tony? Is that you?"

"Why, how many lovers do you have?"

"How *are* you?"

"Just great, and loaded with some hot news."

"What news?" Tracy began to perk up.

"Marcel Aubert, that's what."

"Does he want to do a book?"

"I don't know, I never asked him. Max has been trying to get him on his client list for years, and he finally succeeded. Aubert came to a party at Max's last night. That in itself is something. The guy hardly ever sets foot outside his mansion. He's impossible to get to. He's on a plane right now to New York, and he'll be flying to Paris tonight."

"What a story he must have! Wasn't he married to whatshername—the actress who was killed in that horrible train accident? You know, that 1930s sex goddess?"

"Her and a few others. He was friends with Gable, Olivier, Leigh, Bacall and Bogart before they had that falling out. What he's been through is probably enough for *two* books."

Tracy's heart was racing. "God, I didn't even know he was alive. He hasn't done a picture in about ten years."

"Hold onto your hat, there's more." She could hear him rustling papers on his desk, three thousand miles away. "First of all, he's being honored by the American Film Institute at a banquet in four weeks. Second, and no one knows this but you, me and Max and the four walls until it's announced next week, he just signed a three-picture contract with Paramount. If a book by him comes out just as those films are released—"

Tracy was ecstatic. "It will be a smashing success! Oh, Tony, you're the greatest! What flight is he on?"

"Relax, Bouchard, I've got all the info right in front of me. He'll arrive at JFK at four-fifteen. His flight to Paris isn't until six, which gives you plenty of time to get to know him."

Tracy looked down at her watch. "I've got just enough time. I owe you one, Tony."

"We'll talk about that next time you're out here."

She grabbed her briefcase as they hung up, and hurried to the elevators, passing John Noble.

"Hey, what's all the rush?" he asked.

"Gotta catch a plane," she said as the elevator doors closed.

Chapter 12

WES CANFIELD ARRIVED AT THE FRANKLIN & FIELDS
building and went directly to his former office for a
meeting with John Noble. Margaret greeted him warmly and told him that John had been delayed a few minutes.

"I miss you, Margaret," Canfield told her. "My new
secretary doesn't hold a candle to you. Are you sure
I can't lure you away?"

Margaret smiled and shook her head firmly. "No,
thanks, Wes. I've been at Franklin & Fields since before you could read, and I don't want to leave now.
How about some coffee? It's about time for my second
cup."

"That would be terrific. I haven't had a good cup
of coffee since I left. How about parting with your
secret recipe?"

Margaret kept the president's office stocked with a
strong, French roast blend. "Not on your life, Wes.
How will I keep my job if I give away my trade secrets?" They laughed at this private joke, and she
moved off to the alcove that held the coffee brewer.

Margaret Layton did not need a coffee recipe to keep
her job. Her attention to detail was superb, and she
had integrity and absolute loyalty. Hard qualities to
find these days. Even in myself, Wes thought, as he
entered the room he had so recently vacated.

Although the decor had not changed, Noble had
added touches that made the office his own. The oak
desk held a green and gold Florentine desk set, and
pictures of John's wife and children in ornate gold
frames. The room had housed no such embellishments

when Canfield occupied it. Wes had little time for frills and froth.

The coffee Margaret brought was excellent, fixed just the way he liked it—dark, no sugar. As he sipped his coffee, Canfield reflected on the past few weeks. They had not been easy. All his life, he had worked to get to the top in publishing and now he was there, at the head of his company, Canfield Books. He had always been a winner, but now it was possible he could end up flat on his face.

Wes remembered the day he had come home from school with a second-place ribbon from the sailboat race. He had been about twelve and had only been sailing for a few months. He was bursting with pride, but his father had shrugged and said, "What's wrong with first place?" A good loser was still a loser, and he was expected, not required, to rise to the top. Even at the head of his own company, Wes lived in the shadow of his father, Werner Haas, a giant of the book publishing industry who had earned the absolute respect of his colleagues.

The Haas publishing tradition had started back in Germany with Canfield's grandfather, a brilliant, foresighted man who had had the rare talent of being able to pick out gifted writers with star-studded futures from scores of similar aspirants. His authors broke new ground in literature, making incomparable reputations for themselves and throwing their publisher into a spotlight that would shine for many years. Haas loved his work, and the environment that enabled him to flourish in it, but he was also a wise and perceptive man.

The climate was very bad for German Jews in the 1930s and Haas left Berlin in 1936. He took only his family, the savings that were left after the immigration officials and border guards had been paid off, and his reputation for being the most distinguished publisher in Europe.

America welcomed him eagerly, and he rebuilt his company with the same integrity and high standards that had made his name before the war. The only mark of his transition was a lingering bitterness about the religion he had never practiced. He had never thought of himself as a Jew, only as a German, but the Nazis thrust a new identity on him that he accepted only as he was forced to flee his home.

His son Werner watched all this closely. A teenager when they left Germany, he had not escaped the evils of Nazism, but he suppressed his memories and determined to make a new life for himself in America, just as his father was doing. The cries of *"Jude! Jude!"* became a thing of the past, and he strove to become an American, fully entrenched in the new life.

He enlisted in the U.S. army in 1941, as soon as he graduated from Yale, and was chosen to fly special missions into Germany. He knew the language and the terrain, and he was considered extremely valuable by the Allied Intelligence. Participating in the war against Germany gave him a grim satisfaction. At last, he could strike back against the country from which his proud family had run in desperation.

He was decorated upon his triumphant return to America in 1945, and his father welcomed him heartily. He entered the ranks of the renowned Haas editorial staff with a solid future ahead of him.

The year 1946 was a time for new growth and new plans. The younger Werner was anxious to settle down and to make permanent roots for himself. The war was over and he wanted to put all recriminations behind him. On an unusually balmy day in March, a young woman in a dove-gray suit walked into his office to apply for the post of secretary. She had the blond hair, blue eyes and fair complexion of a Dresden doll, and she glowed with youth and vitality. Her white-gloved hands were folded primly in her lap, but he could see the tall, lissome figure that was hidden underneath her proper clothing. Her name was Eleanor Canfield, and she lived with her parents on Staten Island.

Werner Haas watched Eleanor Canfield closely as he interviewed her. Her typing was excellent, she said, in a soft, well-bred voice, but her shorthand was a little rusty. If he would only be patient, she was sure she could bring it up to par in just a few weeks. In her eyes, he perceived the trusting innocence of a child, and yet he sensed that she could be womanly and warm and wise. Under the tailored felt hat with its jaunty feather, her round face was full of hope and a gentle, inbred dignity. Werner was fascinated by her. She represented all that America had to offer, all that Germany had denied him. Images of the unattainable pale young *fraüleins* who had snubbed him on the *Hardenburgstrasse* in Berlin before the war floated into his mind.

He glanced at his watch. It said 11:45. Did Miss Canfield wish to join him for lunch? She was surprised, but she accepted graciously. Six weeks later, they were married in the First Lutheran Church on Staten Island.

Eleanor Canfield was thoroughly American to Werner Haas, and her influence was welcomed with grateful pride. She became pregnant soon after they were married, and she insisted that their child should have an American name. They decided on Wesley for a boy and Wendy for a girl. In February of 1947, she gave birth to a healthy baby boy, and he was christened Wesley Canfield Haas.

Werner had his son's life planned. Wesley would go to prep school and then on to Yale. He would join the company, marry and produce a son, and prepare to take over the reins when the time came. The future was very bright for Wesley Canfield Haas.

Wes always knew that his father had high standards. His earliest memory was of running across the room in his overalls trying to catch a ball his father had thrown. He had picked it up and held it up triumphantly, but his father had smiled gravely and said with his cultured accent, "No, no, my boy. That is not good enough. Try again."

His mother was the warm haven into which he could always escape. She was always there to dry his tears, although he never cried after the age of seven; crying was met with stern disapproval from his father. But his mother always listened with genuine sympathy to his problems and fears.

One day, he was running too swiftly up a long staircase, and he tripped and fell. His father gave him a smack on the behind, and Wes straightened up quickly and kept on climbing, hiding the pain and shame he felt. Werner Haas did not consider himself to be a harsh or strict parent. He himself had been raised this way, and he felt it had given him structure and discipline, two qualities that had helped him all through his life. It was only natural for him to want to pass these excellent qualities along to his son.

There was a strange dichotomy in the Haas home, bred from a mixture of Werner's old-world discipline and Eleanor's more free and easy American ways. She was gentleness and patience itself to Wes, and he learned that even as he must always go to his father for approval, he could always go to his mother for love.

The household was organized around a clocklike regime. Werner arose at six A.M. on the dot, and left the house at 7:15. The moment he was gone, a subtle relaxation stole into the house that stayed until he returned in the evening. When Wes came home from school, his mother would be there waiting for him with a hug and a kiss. She loved him no matter what he did or didn't do. By the time his father got home, he would be playing happily in the kitchen as she made dinner. Werner would kiss his wife, sit down in his armchair, light his pipe and call his young son into the living room. After querying him about his day in school, he would pat him affectionately on the head and say, "That is fine, son. But tomorrow you must do even better."

The child did not fully perceive, as he struggled to grasp the paternal love that was dangled in front of him like a carrot, that his mother was being subjected to the same stern examination. Eleanor bore her husband's criticism, keeping silent when he berated her in front of guests, or when he made caustic remarks about her lack of neatness and order. When Wes was fourteen, she decided she had had enough, and she announced to her husband that she was leaving. He let her go peacefully, and he gave her and Wes everything they needed.

Wes was shaken by the divorce, feeling bitter and isolated, but gradually he began to flourish in the airy, sunny apartment they took in the city. His mother had no desire to remain in the large home in Ardsley she had shared with her husband. She took Wes on frequent outings in the city to museums and galleries, to concerts or the zoo, and on weekends they would drive to the beach. His mother's hair would fly behind her as they sped along the highway in her convertible. He saw she was happier, and after a while he understood why it had been necessary for her to leave. Their relationship opened like a flower that has been kept in the dark. Often, Wes and Eleanor would sit up late into the night, sharing their hopes and dreams.

But Wes never lost the fierce competitive drive that his father had instilled in him. He saw Werner frequently over the years, often going to his office after school, where he met the distinguished authors and editors associated with the Haas publishing empire. It was an exciting place and he absorbed a great deal of knowledge about the workings of the company. His father was always pleased to answer his questions and sometimes included the boy in dinners with business associates. Even before he entered college, Wes was a junior member of the publishing fraternity.

He decided to attend Columbia instead of Yale, ostensibly to be able to work part-time at the firm, which delighted his father, even though it was a deviation from The Plan. But Wes had been initiated into the art of love by a girl named Madelyn during his senior year in high school. She was an older woman, a junior at New York University. They met skating in Central Park and she took him back to her apartment near Washington Square and seduced him. His playful interest in girls turned into raw passion, and the pursuit of this deeply satisfying pleasure took precedence over nearly everything else. Wes knew he would meet more women in New York than tucked away at Yale.

He entered Columbia with a confidence that bordered on arrogance, and got straight As his first semester. His classes occupied a relatively small portion of his time, and he turned his priorities to other areas. He continued his pursuit of desirable and fascinating women, but found none who met his exacting standards. He was bored quickly, but there were always new pastures in which to roam. He became adept at rousing his lovers to a soaring response that matched his own desire.

But at the end of his third year, his lazy, self-indulgent lifestyle was shattered by a blow that would affect him for years. He returned to his apartment after spending the evening flirting and drinking at the West End bar to learn that his mother had been killed in a car accident. He was to go to his father's house immediately.

Numb with anguish, he caught the next train to Ardsley, and walked into his father's study at three o'clock in the morning. Werner was sitting in an armchair facing the fireplace, dressed in a pinstripe suit, his face a blank. He looked up as the young man burst into the room. "Your train was late," he said. "The funeral is tomorrow at four o'clock." That was all. Wes stiffened and went up to his old room to bear his grief alone. He sobbed into the pillow, not wanting his father to hear him, pounding the bed with angry, helpless fists.

As he stood by her graveside the next afternoon watching them lower her coffin into the ground, he felt that the sweetest, most unselfish love he had ever known was passing out of his life. Something snapped inside of him at that moment, something that had been straining and stretching for a long, long time. The instinct for competition and excellence that his father had pushed on him burst out of him like lava from a volcano.

If his father demanded excellence, then he was going to get it. An unconscious decision had registered in Wes's mind, and he pursued it with jetlike force. Although he was unaware of it at the time, he had developed the searing desire to achieve the ultimate. He would beat his father at his own game. He would surpass him and find a way to hurt him at the same time.

He graduated *summa cum laude* from Columbia, summered in Europe and returned to step neatly into the role that had been assigned to him. His first few years in his father's company went smoothly. Wes perfected his craft, sharpened his business sense and enjoyed the novelty of the experience. But something was happening inside the company, and Wes was quick to perceive it. They had been losing money at a very slow rate for several years, but now the loss was starting to escalate alarmingly. Although the management was able to cover the deficit with a steady income from its venerable backlist, it was harder and harder to keep up with the slick, new instant bestsellers that were coming out of younger, more aggressive houses.

Wesley Haas observed all this and went in to see his father. He came right to the point.

"Father, I think it's time to make some changes in policy."

Werner smiled. The young were always eager to make changes, but he believed that the old tried-and-true ways were best.

"What kinds of changes, Wes?"

"We've got to stop hiding our heads in the sand. We're going to have to start publishing some of the big, commercial books that bring in millions. If we have a few of those on board, we'll still be able to float the literary giants that get great reviews but don't make much money."

The indulgent smile faded. "No, Wes, that is not the way. We must never lower our standards. It is our responsibility to publish only the very best. We will leave second-rate material to those with second-rate minds."

"But we're losing money! How much longer can this go on?"

"If I have to take a loss, then I am prepared for that," Werner said staunchly.

"Times have changed, father. People want to read for pleasure. Even if it's only something they can read once on the beach and then throw away."

145

"I'm disappointed in you, son," Werner said gravely. "I thought you knew better than this."

But Wes was not deterred. "We don't have to lower our standards. Just change them. We have to give people what they want." His anger was rising like a flood.

His father regarded him stonily. Wes knew that his father would resist his ideas, but he also knew his ideas were sound. It was the wave of the future, and the older man refused to face facts.

"You must be patient," Werner said. "You still have much to learn. In the meantime, you must follow the guidelines of this company," he said with authority. This answer infuriated Wes.

"I don't want your guidelines!" he cried passionately. "And I don't want you!" He left the office in a state of uncontrolled rage, and the next morning, his terse letter of resignation rested on his father's desk.

The talented young man was out on the street, but not for long. Edgar Fields got wind of his availability and asked him to have lunch. Wes was eager to make it on his own, and he knew that Fields was getting old, still trying unsuccessfully to boost the fortunes of his ailing company. Franklin had been dead for years, and the company would probably need a new president before too long.

Before he officially accepted his new position as editorial director of Franklin & Fields, he did two very important things. First, he got Fields to agree that he would retire in two years, leaving the presidency open. And second, he dropped the name of Haas, the name that had both honored him and plagued him for years. His ultimate dream was to have his own firm with his own name on it, and he wanted that name to be Canfield.

It all came to pass just as he had planned it. Edgar Fields retired, and Wes, who had brought fresh blood and new life into the company, catapulting it into a prime position for the future, was appointed president. His vigor attracted some of the best people in the busi-

146

ness, and the company achieved a new status that put it in a class by itself.

Through his years at F&F, the vision of Canfield Books still floated enticingly before him, and now he had begun to realize his dream. In two days, he would fly to Paris to meet personally with the men who had changed his life. They were financiers, engineers of money, and the meeting in Paris was crucial to the success of his endeavor. His eyes glowed at the prospect, and he felt his heart race for a moment as the telephone rang.

He heard Margaret pick up the phone and say, "Mr. Noble's office." Then, as her tone grew more and more incredulous, he walked to the door of the office to see what was ruffling the usually unflappable Margaret.

"*Who?*" she was saying. "But that's impossible! I saw her only yesterday afternoon, and she was just—"

"Who is it?" he asked curiously.

"From *where?*" Margaret asked. "Paris, France?" She stopped, and looked at him beseechingly. Covering the mouthpiece, she said, "It's Tracy Bouchard. She's in Paris." She dropped the words like a small bomb, but Canfield just smiled and said, "I'll take it." He went back inside the office and closed the door.

He was close to laughter as he picked up the receiver. "Yes, operator, I'll accept the charges." He could hear the static as it crackled over the Atlantic Ocean, and he reflected briefly on how perfect her timing was. Whatever she was up to now, it was going to coincide perfectly with his plans. "Tracy? What the hell are you doing in Paris?" He listened to her excited explanation, and chuckled once or twice as he took in her story.

"No, I'm not surprised," he said to her anxious inquiry. "Just listen. You've gone this far and it sounds like you've got him. Aubert's a cagey fellow, and if he's put up with you this long, it means he's interested. Take him to dinner at Maxim's and keep on him." He paused as he looked at the calendar. "And Tracy. Don't come right back to New York. . . . No, I mean it. Stay there until Thursday and meet me at the Ritz Hotel. I have a meeting in Paris and I'll see you there. . . . Never you mind. It's business. And don't worry about the trip. I'll square it with John. How? I'll make a preemptive bid for the paperback rights. Your timing couldn't have been better. See you Thursday."

His face was shining with merriment as he hung up. He buzzed Margaret and she entered the room with a cautious air.

"Everything all right?" she asked.

"Yes, Margaret, just fine. Would you mind confirming my reservation at the Ritz Hotel starting Thursday?"

She hesitated for a moment and then asked, "For two?"

He eyed her shrewdly. "For two."

Chapter 13

LOOKING OUT THE WINDOW OF THE CONCORDE, HIS fingers resting comfortably around a martini glass, Wes Canfield took in the awesome sight of the curve of the earth. This commanding view of the planet seemed appropriate to him, because the next few days would determine the course his life would take from now on. All the years of striving and learning, working to build up a business that was not his own, receded into the past. He was about to meet with three powerful men, and he hoped this would be the last time he would have to rely on a power that was greater than his own. If they said yes, he would speed to the top of the mountain his father had always placed in front of him —reach the top and then cross over. And if they said no—but he wouldn't think about that. They couldn't say no. They had already agreed to a contract but his new plans required twice the amount of money they had originally agreed upon. He had gone over the details a million times, and he knew his proposition was sound. Still, those three men held his future in their hands, and he was impatient to wrest it from them.

He knew he had been called the "boy wonder" of publishing, and it made him nervous. Had his own record brought the title? Or was it the lingering stamp of his father's name? There was only one way to find out, and that was to make it or break it on his own.

It would be good to see Paris again. It was a city made for dreams. He looked out eagerly over the landscape as the plane descended through the clouds, catching a glimpse of the northern suburbs of Paris. The graceful jet headed onto the runway at Orly Airport, and the stewardess made announcements in French and English. As the plane headed toward the terminal, he was gripped by a momentary tension. This was it. He was about to turn the page on a new chapter in his life. His watch said ten o'clock, and he pulled out the timer and set it ahead five hours. There wasn't much time to freshen up. A limousine awaited him, and the chauffeur would collect his luggage and see him through customs.

The sounds and smells of Paris were cut off from him as he sat back in the soundproof car. The infinitesimal details of his plans were etched into his brain, but he went over them once again. The plan was as flawless as such a plan could be, but something could always go wrong. He ordered his thoughts meticulously, ready to present them in the most convincing manner. He was all salesman now, fired with the conviction and soundness of his ideas. There was no time to be nervous. Walking into this meeting would be like walking onstage at a Broadway opening. There was no room for mistakes. His rehearsal kept him preoccupied during the ride into town, and he was surprised when the car glided to a stop in front of the staid, elegant office of Duprès, Arnaud & St. Victoire.

"Nous sommes arrivés, monsieur," the driver said as he stilled the motor.

"Already? Yes, I suppose so."

"Shall I take your luggage to the hotel, *monsieur?"* the chauffeur asked in heavily accented English.

"Mais oui, merci," Wes answered as he collected his briefcase and straightened his tie.

The chauffeur opened the door for him and he stepped out, blocking the heady atmosphere of Paris from his senses. His mind was keenly tuned to the business at hand, and nothing would deter him from that purpose.

Inside the eighteenth-century building on the boulevard des Italiens, Wes stopped for a moment to get his bearings. Two marble columns supported an archway that led to a small reception area, and an executive assistant sat behind an antique desk. Wes approached the man and gave his name. He was greeted with formal cordiality and asked to wait on one of the marquise chairs. Presently, another man, dressed in a conservative Pierre Cardin suit, escorted Wes to the small, gilt-cage elevator. Then he was ushered into a plush suite decorated with lavish Louis XVI furnishings and shaded by tasseled, damask draperies. Two men sat at the polished rosewood table, and one stood leaning against the marble fireplace.

The escort withdrew silently, and Wes was left alone with the three men.

M. Duprès extended both his arms toward the visitor to welcome him. *"Bienvenue à Paris,"* he said. *"Nous sommes très contents de vous voir."*

Coffee and tea were summoned, brought forth on an antique silver service. The four men chatted politely as it was served, and at last they settled down to the business at hand.

Wes was ready—more than ready. He had several pages of neatly typed notes, along with charts and graphs that clarified his position. Over the next three hours, his vision and his belief in it became the center of attention, as he skillfully drew the three Frenchmen into his sphere. He outlined his goals and his means of attaining them so carefully and so convincingly, that before he was halfway through, he knew he would succeed. By the end of the afternoon, all of them were exhausted but satisfied. As the Parisian sun cast long shadows into the spacious room, the four of them shook hands heartily and ordered a round of cognac.

When the limousine came to pick up Wes, his mind was still racing with what he had accomplished that day. Now he knew, after all the years of doubt, that he had clout of his own. He wasn't just cresting the wave of his father's fame. And he knew this from the most indomitable, equalizing force of all—money. If three shrewd French investors were willing to bank that much money on him, he must be worth his salt. He sank back into the soft leather seat of the limousine, but he was too worked up to relax. It was something he had prepared for, in one way or another, for his whole life. Everything had crystallized in that moment, his moment to stand alone and shine. He closed his eyes in an effort to wind down, but facts and figures danced mercilessly in his mind. The long, black car headed down rue de la Paix. It was only a short distance to the Ritz Hotel, but he wanted to arrive in style.

Place Vendôme, with its imperiously elegant classical façade, looked exactly as he remembered it. He was ushered inside with cordial respect and was whisked up the elevator. A feeling of utter weariness was creeping over him. He had not slept well for the past two nights while preparing for this crucial encounter. He needed to stop the whirring and ticking of his brain. He stopped outside the door to his suite and rubbed his temples briefly.

Then he walked inside.

The sight that greeted him left him breathless. In one maddening second, he was drained of all exhaustion and refilled with a surge of uncontainable delight. Tracy Bouchard lay under the draped canopy of the elaborate duchess bed, stretched out like a lioness on the brocaded spread. She was breathing hard with excitement, and her eyes shone like rich topazes in the misty light. She was lying on one side, her hip curving provocatively, and the outlines of her slender, shapely legs were clearly visible under the scantily cut ivory negligée. Her long, graceful throat was bare, and his eyes moved from its soft contours to the tops of her breasts, which swelled seductively from the laced edges of her gown.

The alluring sight of her would normally fill him with pleasure, but today—today, of all days, her inviting presence was a source of passionate joy. She smiled —a coy, feline smile—and said softly, "Hi. Welcome to the Ritz."

He dropped his briefcase on the floor where he stood, and threw his coat over a chair. She watched his movements with veiled eyes as he walked over to the bed. The weary lines in his face were melting, and his sharp, blue eyes narrowed slightly, catching the glint of the last few rays of sun. Slowly, as they gazed intently into each other's eyes, the rest of the world fell away from them. There was only this time and place. They were in Paris, the city of love, and they welcomed the desire that washed over them.

He lay next to her on the huge bed, tracing a light, teasing line around the corners of her tiny smile. His finger moved on, stroking her cheek, her slightly up-turned chin and her eyelids, which fluttered to a close at his touch. Then, in an aching wish to prolong this moment, he continued his slow journey down her slender neck to the pulsing hollow in her throat and her bare, sloping shoulders. Her skin had been dusted with the barest sheen of glittery talcum, and she smelled faintly of musk. He slipped the negligée from her body.

His dark head leaned down and he kissed her very gently on the mouth. Then he repeated this tender, undemanding kiss again and again until she was reaching for him, curling her fingers around his neck to pull him in closer. He paused for a moment, looking down at her flushed, upturned face, and then he kissed her fully and deeply, cradling her head in his hands. She melted back into the satiny pillows, and he stood up, shedding his clothes quickly and letting them fall on the floor.

Tingling with anticipation, he covered her lush body with his own, leaving a sweet trail of kisses on her neck. His head moved down to one full, rounded breast, and he nuzzled it gently as he cupped it in his warm hand. The soft, pink nipple stiffened under his exquisitely gentle touch as he teased it awake with slow, tantalizing circles of his tongue. Her hands massaged his shoulders and buried themselves in his black hair, and his head moved to rouse her other breast. Then he was moving down again, leaving soft, lingering kisses on the gentle swell of her belly. Her golden brown eyes were only half-open, but she saw through the maze of her passion as his strong hands firmly parted her thighs and lifted them over his shoulders. Her breath was coming in short gasps and she watched

153

his dark head seek and then center on the soft inner flesh of her very core. His touch was so sure and so delicate she thought she would die with the pleasure of it, and her distracted whimpers became sensuous moans. He worked her slowly, at a deliberately leisurely pace that maddened her and thrilled her at the same time, until tears blurred her eyes and moistened her lashes.

When she felt she couldn't stand it for one more minute, he lifted his long, lean body and wrapped his muscular arms around her. Holding her very closely, with one hand under her shoulders and the other hand lifting her from underneath, he thrust himself inside of her, moving quickly and deeply with a powerful rhythm. Her hands stroked his broad back and moved down to caress the tight outlines of his narrow hips. His passion demanded her response as he drove swiftly and surely into her, manipulating her fragrant body into wild submission. He raised his head and looked at her face. Her hair was spread out like a fan in back of her head, the dusky light picking up the red and gold specks in it. He spoke the first words he had uttered since he entered the room. "Look at me." Her eyes fluttered open to find him watching her intently, his blue eyes shining like two sapphires, mirroring all the tender emotion he felt. His hand underneath her body tightened its grip, and she arched to meet his unrelenting thrusts, wrapping her silky thighs around him. Their frenzy peaked in a flowering explosion of feeling that left them both limp. Weakly, she let her legs loosen their hold from his body and slide down, resting against the hardness of his legs. When they had both caught their breath, he turned her head toward him and kissed her softly, not lifting his mouth from hers for an eternity.

At last they unwound, gently untangling arms and legs, and he fell into the profusion of pillows on the bed. *"Touché, ma chérie,"* he said, and they both laughed quietly in the darkened room. Outside, the silvery street lights dotted the blackness of the Parisian night.

Tracy reached over and turned on the light. They cuddled together in the small glow. "I think your meeting went well," she said.

His energy returned in a surge of enthusiasm, and he said, "Yes, it was better than I could have expected. I'm really in business now."

She could sense how much that meant to him, and she gave him a little squeeze, saying, "I'm glad."

"And I'm starving," he added. "Let's order up some food."

They consulted the menu, and then Wes dialed room service, placing the order in rapid, liquid French. Twenty minutes later there was a sharp knock on the door. Wes hopped up, threw on a robe and opened the door. Two congenial waiters entered, pushing an elaborate silver cart and ice bucket up to the edge of the bed at Wes's direction. Tracy pulled the sheet up to her shoulders and tried to look casual, but the two waiters were used to such scenes and had a delightfully Gallic acceptance of them. One of them uncorked the bottle of champagne with great ceremony, and the other one ladled the chartreuse sauce over the clams and checked to see that the medallions of veal would be kept warm. A small platter of fresh fruit and aromatic cheese was placed on the side. The waiters left after wishing the couple, *"bon appétit."* Wes lit the two candles and passed Tracy a napkin.

They ate sloppily, toasting each other with champagne throughout the langorous meal. When they had licked the last bits of cheese from their fingers, Tracy slithered out of bed. "I'm going to run a bath. Care to join me?" Grabbing her glass of champagne, she walked naked across the expansive suite and stepped into the spotless bathroom. He jumped up and followed her and soon they were sloshing around in the large, bubbly tub that sat squarely on four gold lion's feet.

"Now I'm going to wash you," Wes said imperiously, and Tracy squealed as he began to soap her shoulders and her breasts, lingering on their sensitive peaks. Then he made her stand up, and he rubbed the sudsy bar over her loins and down her long legs. Handing her

155

the soap, he said, "Now it's your turn." She repeated his teasing performance, asking him to turn around so she could explore the rippling muscles in his back. They downed the rest of the champagne and stepped out of the tub, wrapping themselves in fluffy bath towels before padding across the burgundy carpet to the bed. They fell on it together, nestling under the sheets. Tracy knew that the evening was far from over as he buried his face in her hair, kissing the side of her neck and nibbling lightly on her sensitive earlobe. Her passion mounted once again as she matched him touch for touch, her hands roaming hungrily over his lean body as they turned on their sides, arms and legs entwining as he pushed deeply into her. The flickering candlelight cast honey-colored shadows on their bodies as they moved together, and Tracy saw tiny, exploding stars behind her closed eyelids as the rush of feeling crested and then slowly ebbed.

They fell into a deeply relaxing sleep, her head resting on his chest, and woke to the sound of birds chirping and the pale morning sunlight that came streaming through the window. Wes ordered breakfast, and then he sat up and inspected the surroundings. The fairytale bed was situated against a flower-papered wall, and it was flanked by matching tables that were decorated with cubed parquetry and gilded bronze mounts. A heavy lacquered wardrobe with carved oval panels and a delicate writing table with cabriole legs stood against the opposite wall. Two bergère armchairs stood under the window, and a long-case clock made of tulipwood and kingwood stood in the corner. Wes looked around the room with satisfaction as Tracy stretched and yawned.

"You approve?" she said, snuggling close to burrow her nose into his shoulder.

He smiled. "The Ritz never fails to deliver. I believe some of these pieces may be signed originals."

"What would you like to do today?" she asked.

"That, Miss Bouchard, is up to you. This is your first trip to Paris?"

"Yes."

"Then you lead the way. But I'll give you a hint—the best way to see Paris is to walk."

She jumped up excitedly. "Then let's go! I didn't see much yesterday. It was crazy for me to be here at all, but I did have dinner with Aubert like you said. He wouldn't go to Maxim's, though. He didn't want anyone to see him."

He chuckled. "I take it Aubert is interested?"

She glowed. "Yes, thank goodness." Then she sighed. "I hope he makes this trip worthwhile. If he doesn't, I'll be in very hot water, your bid notwithstanding. As if I don't have enough to worry about." But she smiled, not wanting anything to spoil this day.

The city of Paris offers many delights to those who are willing to look for them. Tracy let the charm and power of the city seep into her as she explored it, and by the end of the day she was almost drunk with the floating, swirling fervor of it. London is the essence of civilized urbanity, and New York is ruthlessly stimulating in its frenetic movement. But Paris is like being drenched in a heady dose of French perfume.

She knew when they stepped into the silvery street outside the hotel that this was to be a whirlwind day, filled with wondrous sensations. The Place de l'Opéra, just down the rue de la Paix, opened into full view as they traversed the bustling square. The shopkeepers were busy arranging the day's wares, and Tracy's eyes opened wide with excitement at each new sight. The bakeries were filled with elaborate French pastries. The flower shops looked like an Impressionist painting, as if Monet himself had painted them. Wes left her for a moment to go inside and buy a long-stemmed pink rose. She cuddled up to him as he squeezed her, delighted with her happiness. Today the world was at their feet and no one could take it away from them. She breathed in the Parisian air, and tried to take it all in. So this is what it's all about, she thought. Everything seemed so extraordinary, and she was enraptured by every little thing. A master glassblower smiled at her from behind the sparkling window of his shop and winked as she watched him put the finishing touches on a beautiful swan. You like it, the craftsman seemed to say with his eyes, and Wes was inside buying it for her.

He was spoiling her, and she let him. She wanted the day to last forever. As they strolled along the left bank of the Seine, she caressed her nose with the long-stemmed rose, smiling at him from behind the velvety petals. They walked past artists and their easels, street vendors and bookstalls, and watched the boats gliding by on the river. As the medieval majesty of Notre-Dame rose before them, Tracy caught her breath. The famous church was more beautiful than she had ever imagined it to be.

As they walked around the Luxembourg Gardens, they spotted some children, dressed in their severe school uniforms, and stopped to watch them. Tracy laughed as they chanted the chorus of a rope-skipping song in their high, clear voices. Turning to Wes to catch his eye, she saw that he was already watching her. Arm in arm, they walked slowly along the quay, until they collapsed at a table inside a tiny, crowded bistro. Wes took her hand as they studied the scrawled blackboard menu, and they decided on wild mushrooms in cream sauce, roast duckling with olives and crushed pistachios, followed by black coffee laced with cognac. The oval mirrors reflected the beamed ceiling and stained glass, and other couples embraced in the flickering candlelight.

They spent the rest of the afternoon at the Louvre, concentrating on the Impressionist paintings at the end of the Tuileries Gardens. Here, the romance of nineteenth-century Paris came to life, adding to all the other layers of pure romance that Tracy had experienced that day.

They took a taxi back to the hotel to change for dinner, and Tracy dressed with great care in a deep crimson Chinese silk dress. The color of the dress heightened the color of her eyes and brought out the red and gold highlights in her glossy hair.

She marveled at the magical change that night brought to the city. The broad boulevards were aglow with red, orange and white lights, and all of the monuments blazed against the black sky.

Wes took her to Lasserre, the famous gastronomical landmark decorated in brocaded silks and Louis XVI originals. Tracy had never had such impeccable service or seen such a lavish presentation of a meal. Everything, from the Dresden china to the gold-edged crystal, was of the highest quality. The food represented French cuisine at its best. After much delightful indecision, they ordered melon in Spanish wine and a rack of lamb for two that was utterly tender and robustly flavored, accompanied by a vintage burgundy. Dessert was crêpes suzettes, flamed in their chafing dish by a waiter who enjoyed presenting the spectacle as much as Tracy and Wes enjoyed watching it.

Tracy reeled into the street after the extraordinary meal, leaning on Wes and sighing contentedly. She couldn't imagine what other delights he might have in store for her, but he hailed a taxi and they were whisked off to the Eiffel Tower. The elevator took them to the top, and the glittering spectacle of Paris lay before them. Wes stood in back of Tracy, his arms encircling her, his mouth pressing tiny kisses on the back of her neck. She spun around to face him and he gathered her against his powerful chest, kissing her deeply and longingly at the very top of the bejeweled city. She felt his ardor as she pressed against him, and her own response leaped into a flame of passion that could have only one end. Silently, they rode down to the street, where they jumped into a taxi and went back to their hotel. His fingers were at the buttons of her dress as soon as they closed the door to the room, and when it fell to the floor, he picked her up in his arms and carried her to the huge, canopied bed. He enveloped her soft, undulating body far into the night, and they did not fall into a deeply contented sleep until the first pale yellow streaks appeared in the sky.

Tracy awoke with her head on his pillow, and when she opened her eyes, she found him staring at her. They both smiled.

"I've already ordered a car," he said. "We'll have

some tea and croissants sent up, and then we're going to the Bois de Boulogne."

She snuggled up to him and yawned. "It sounds wonderful. Maybe we should take a picnic lunch with us."

He smiled. "I've already taken care of that. We can go horseback riding in the park, if you like, and we can walk around all the little pathways and look at the sky."

An hour later, they were sitting on a small hill in the huge and magical Parisian park, watching the horseback riders and bicyclists gliding by. The sunlight played through the leaves of the chestnut trees, creating dappled lights and shadows on the grass. Tracy stretched out with her head in his lap, and they began to talk about events in New York. Wes had heard about the *Year of the Dragon* theft and the rumors that surrounded her.

"I told you that Bendex was a shady character." He sighed. "This was bound to happen sooner or later."

"But it's still hard for me," she ventured shakily. "I—I still have so much to learn, and no one there is making it easier for me."

He made her sit up and looked at her steadily. Tracing a gentle line along the side of her cheek, he asked, "But why should they? Did you think it would be easy?"

She smiled shyly. "No. I didn't think about that at all. I just wanted to get out of the rut I was in."

"And you succeeded. Admirably. The rest will come. You'll be terrific. If I didn't think so, I wouldn't have hired you. Fleming or no Fleming."

"Really?"

He kissed the tip of her nose. "Really."

She flopped back on the grass and chewed on a blade of grass. "And what about you?" she asked. "I know so little about you. Except that you like pushy broads who barge into your office."

He laughed. "What would you like to know?"

"Well . . . about your family, your father." His

160

mouth tightened into a hard little line, and she murmured a soft "Ah-ha."

"Most people know about my father," he said. "And about why I left his company. It was a difference of opinion about the direction the company should take, and I felt I should not remain with a company whose policies I questioned." He recited this formally, rattling off the words without expression.

"You sound like a quote in *Publishers Weekly*," she observed quietly. "Do you talk to your father often?" she prodded.

There was a short silence, and then he answered, "I haven't talked to him in several years."

"I see," she said gingerly. She had found his weak spot. In a gentle voice, she asked, "What about your mother?"

He straightened suddenly, shifting around to face the hill. "She died when I was in college. In a car accident."

She was surprised, and saddened. "Oh, Wes, I'm so sorry. I didn't know."

He heaved a hard sigh, saying, "I know you didn't. I don't talk about it much."

"Were you close to her?"

"Yes. She's been dead more than ten years now and I still miss her. There's never been anyone else I could talk to the way I talked to her."

Tracy sat up and reached out to him, touching his cheek with her fingertips. Wes had not said many words, but he had revealed a great deal about himself. It was the first time he had shared his personal secrets with her, and she felt more connected to him than she ever had.

Wes took her hand in his and pressed her palm to his lips. "Oh, Tracy," he murmured. Then his arms were around her and he held her fiercely, crushing her to his chest so that there was no space between them. She held him as tightly as she could. After a few moments, he released her, and they both sank back onto the grass and watched the clouds drift by.

"Would you like some lunch, Wes?" she asked,

opening the basket they had brought. "Let's see what we've got here." She fished through the basket and produced a small, checkered cloth, a loaf of French bread, a small round of cheese, a container of pâté, some oranges and pears, two plump red tomatoes, a bunch of scallions and a bottle of red wine. Soon they were both munching on the simple, hearty fare. They talked about publishing, and he entertained her with some of his best stories. He mentioned names that were legendary, people she had often heard of but never met, and he talked about them casually, sometimes putting them in such an absurd light that she rolled on the grass in gleeful laughter.

After they had gobbled up the last of the lunch, they rented a rowboat on one of the waterways in the Bois. Tracy lay back luxuriously, letting him row as she gazed at the blue sky. An airplane flew by overhead, and she watched it with rapt attention, thinking of her father. Her conversation with him before she walked down the aisle in the Randolph home came back to her and she found herself telling Wes about her narrow escape from becoming Mrs. Robert Randolph III. He was fascinated by her flight from matronly splendor and interrupted her with question after question. As she spoke she began to see the dramatic, heroic side of her tale, and for the first time since it had happened, she felt proud and sure about what she had done.

"After I lived in New York for a while," she finished, "I stopped looking at what I knew I didn't want, and started concentrating on what I did want." She paused. "And here I am."

"And here you are," he repeated, lifting his hands from the oars and leaning forward to place them around her waist. She arched up to meet him, and they kissed lazily. They were like two kids sharing secrets, but with grown-up strings attached. The afternoon floated by dreamily, and at sunset, they stood on one of the bridges spanning the Seine. As the last fiery rays hung over the horizon, Tracy leaned her chin against her fist, and said, "Paris makes me hungry."

They both laughed, and Wes noted, "Well, if you're interested in food, this is the best place to be."

She agreed happily, and they walked along the river, passing Notre-Dame, which was lit up with ivory floodlights. By day, the magnificent cathedral was graceful and powerful, but by night, with its lacy flanks reflected in the flowing black water of the Seine, it seemed to be more a vision than a reality. It appeared to float serenely on the surface of the river, the many lights shimmering as bright patches against the dark night. They stopped in the lamplight to look at the lovely sight, and settled themselves on a bench to revel in the Parisian summer night. Tracy rested her head against his shoulder and closed her eyes.

"I had the hotel reserve two ballet tickets for tonight," he said. "I hope that appeals to you."

Her head shot up and she exclaimed ecstatically, "Oh! How did you ever know? I love ballet more than anything, next to flying!"

"Good. Then after dinner we will see the ballet, and after that . . . we will behave as the spirit moves us."

Tracy threw her arms out as if to embrace the city and then fell back against his chest with a small cry of utter satisfaction.

Over a savory meal of roast pork with onions and an endive and walnut salad in a well-hidden restaurant on the Ile St. Louis in the middle of the Seine, they talked reluctantly of departure from Paris. They agreed to leave the following evening, and Wes suggested that she have breakfast without him. He had some final papers to sign with his backers, and would have to go out at an early hour. But he would be back before lunch, and they would be able to spend the rest of the day together.

The next morning, Tracy was dimly aware of his early rising. He showered and dressed quickly, closing the door behind him with a soft click. She turned over and went back to sleep, reawakening at nine-thirty to order breakfast and take a bath. Then she ventured out into the street by herself, pressing her nose to the plate glass windows of the fancy shops, daydreaming about Wes. She had a sudden urge to give him something tangible, something to commemorate this unforgettable interlude. After browsing through several shops, she selected a silver and cut glass letter opener and had it giftwrapped. She knew it was something he could use every day, something that would always conjure her image in his thoughts.

As she walked into the hotel lobby, planning to slip him the gift during lunch, the man at the desk called her name.

"Mademoiselle Bouchard," he said politely. "There is a message for you."

He handed her a sealed envelope emblazoned with the hotel crest, and she slipped a fingernail underneath the flap and ripped it open as she rode upstairs in the elevator. Her eyes widened with shock and her vision blurred as she read the short note.

Tracy,

I'm in a terrible rush so I can't explain now, but something urgent has come up and I have to get out of here in a hurry. Paris with you was *très merveilleux,* and I'm sorry it has to end so abruptly. I'll call you in N.Y.

Love,
Wes

The note shook in her hand as she read it and re-read it, and she ran down the hall to her room, fumbling the key in the lock before swinging the door open. She couldn't believe he was gone. There had to be a mistake. She stepped inside and stopped. Her eyes traveled around the large, elegant room. The closet door was open, and a few hangers had been thrown onto the bed. The inside of the closet gave her irrefutable evidence. Only her clothes were hanging there. Everything of his was gone. She opened a bureau drawer and then another one, and finally had to admit to herself that it was really happening. She walked to the window and sighed heavily, looking down at the square. There must be a reasonable explanation, she thought. Probably something to do with his new business. She would have to try to understand. She was still holding the note in her hand and, after a moment's hesitation, she crumpled it into a tight wad and went over to the wastebasket. She tossed the note inside. There was a crumpled yellow ball in the bottom of the basket. She reached down and pulled it out, smoothing the single yellow sheet flat under her palm.

It was a telegram. From the United States. And her heart thudded with recognition as she saw who had sent it.

FROM

> TONY AMATO
> MAX ZWERDLOW ASSOCIATES
> 2700 SANTA ANNA ROAD
> BEL AIR, CALIFORNIA

TO

> WESLEY CANFIELD
> HOTEL RITZ
> 15 PLACE VENDOME
> PARIS, FRANCE

The message read:

> DEAR WES STOP AMBROSIA IN HOSPITAL
> STOP OVERDOSE OF DRUGS STOP ASKING
> FOR YOU STOP TONY

The telegram fell from her hands. So it wasn't a business problem. It was a woman. And not just any woman, but Ambrosia Jewell. "Wesley Canfield is my dearest friend." Ambrosia's words came back to Tracy in a taunting refrain. A feeling of betrayal swept over her, draining her of all the happiness she had enjoyed for the past two days.

How could she have been such a fool? Wes had been

using her, a handy body for an impromptu romp in Paris. He was riding high, and Tracy would do. But the minute another woman beckons, he's on the first plane back to the States.

The small package containing Wes's present lay next to her hand, and she picked it up and tore off the wrapping. She held the letter opener in her hand for a second, and then she threw it against the wall, watching it shatter.

The tears rolled down her face. The man she was crazy about was winging his way across the Atlantic to be with another woman, her job was on very shaky territory and she was sitting alone in a foreign hotel room. She stood up and started tossing her clothes into her suitcase, sliding toilet articles off the bathroom shelf with one sweep of her arm. She would be on the next plane to New York, whenever it was. Alone.

Chapter 14

TONY AMATO SAT BACK IN HIS FAVORITE ARMCHAIR, putting a frothy head on the Heineken he poured from its slender, green bottle into a chilled mug. He put his feet up, tired after a long day, and then the phone rang. He let it ring a few times, but couldn't let it go unanswered.

"Hey, Amato." Jack Davis sounded bored. "You better get over here and pick up your princess."

Tony reacted quickly. "Ambrosia?"

"Yeah." Tony could hear Davis taking a long swallow of something before continuing. "She's laid out stoned on my living room floor. I can't get her to move that cute little ass of hers."

Tony knew better than to call the police. He arrived with Dr. Lawrence Saunders, Hollywood's most discreet celebrity physician. As Ambrosia writhed and moaned on the hospital stretcher, Tony gripped her hand. She tried to call out a name.

Tony understood. "Relax, princess," he said. "I've already sent him a telegram. It may take a while, though. He was in Paris."

Her violet eyes flashed comprehension and then she fell limp. He was coming. She knew he would come.

The ambulance attendant leaned over to take her pulse, and Ambrosia thrashed weakly. Don't touch me, she tried to scream, but only a muffled groan emerged from her swollen lips.

All night, men had been touching her like hungry beasts in a jungle. She had been bound and gagged and taken into one of the lavish bedrooms of Jack Davis's opulent mansion. They threw her on the huge,

167

circular waterbed flanked by mirrors on three sides. Everywhere she looked, she could see herself and the men, their ghoulish faces and bloated bodies staring down at her.

Sounds of tearing cloth. Laughter. Her panties stuffed in her mouth. She was helpless, terrified. Poking. Slapping. Ropes tied her to the bed. Hands everywhere. Choking, she was choking. Then screaming—for air, for release, for rescue. Blackness. Everything quiet. Tony. Please, Tony, Wes. Coming. From Paris.

Ambrosia's eyes fluttered open. A man leaned over her. Her mouth opened to release the sickeningly familiar whitehot terror. "Relax, Ambrosia. It's just me. Dr. Saunders. We've had to pump your stomach. You were full of barbiturates. And you've been treated for superficial lacerations. But you're fine now. You'll be okay. Please try to rest."

Rest. Sleep. Home. The hills of Tennessee. Down into the past, drifting, dreaming her life like a Technicolor movie.

"Daddy?"

"Hush, Amby. You don't wanna wake yo' mama and yo' sisters."

He lays down beside the child. "Not even fourteen yet, and so purty. I'll bet all the fellas want to touch you here." He moves his hand to her leg and slides it firmly up over her belly to cup her breast. "You're sure growin', child."

She is not sure if she should protest as his huge frame shifts, and he straddles her leg. He begins to move rhythmically, rubbing against her leg until he holds her tighter and tighter, and then she feels something. Something she has only heard about, whispered in the alley behind the schoolhouse. The man jolts suddenly, and the child, too frightened to move, feels a sticky moisture under her body as he turns away from her.

"Good girl, Amby. We'll do this again real soon." He kisses her goodnight, a wet, sloppy kiss on the mouth. She knows he'll be back.

Night after night, week after week, it is always the

same thing. "If mama found out, I bet she'd be mad at you," he croons to her.

"But I don't want to, daddy," she whispers, and he silences her.

"Shhhhh, honey. Be a good girl now."

It continues for months, and then one evening, while everyone is away at the country store, Jake Joplin decides to teach his pretty daughter the ultimate fact of life.

She is astounded. It is the first time she has seen her father, or any man, naked and excited. His eyes are wild and his face is ruddy and splotched from drink. She backs away from him, but he catches her and holds her down. She smells the whiskey on his breath, and he almost loses his balance as he presses her down onto the bed. He leers at her as she fights him, and he tears the clothes from her with one huge paw. Suddenly, she understands. By sheer animal instinct, she knows what he wants from her, and she begins to scream with hysterical frenzy. She gasps in short, frantic wails as she feels a strange, repugnant hardness pushing between her legs.

And then a shriek from behind them cuts through the small room. Mama is home. The woman jumps and pulls at her husband before he can commit the incestuous act, and then Ambrosia is running. She runs and runs into the woods behind the house, and she collapses only when her trembling legs can no longer carry her.

Mama promises that daddy is gone for good this time. He will never be back to hurt her again. She remains fearful and withdrawn, starting at slight noises and screaming at loud ones, but after a while, the horrible memory ebbs and she begins to relax just a little. The local boys come buzzing around her, but she wants no part of them. They're all after one thing, she knows, and they're all sinful and evil. Her mama thinks it's just a phase, but Ambrosia knows she will never let one of those boys touch her.

Two years pass, and Ambrosia blossoms. Her striking beauty attracts the farmers' sons, but none of them bother to look at the terror that still rages behind those violet eyes. One of them proposes marriage to her on the porch swing, and she jumps up and runs inside, refusing to see him again. She becomes more and more reclusive, preferring the company of movie magazines and television shows to flesh and blood people. The faces of fashion models stick in her mind, and she learns to identify them and watch their progress. She collects the faces as a little girl collects dolls, and she stores all the pictures in the back of her closet until her mama complains and tells her to throw them out. But they are her idols, and she needs them. She knows they are like her: they are beautiful, but they are not real. People can look at them, but they can't touch them. They are on paper, and everyone looks at their pretty faces, not caring about what their names are or what they are like. If any of them carry shameful secrets like hers, no one can tell. Their beauty is a tool and a shield, and this is something she understands well.

And then, one day, her private nightmare becomes a reality. She is sweeping the porch when she sees the bulky form of her father heading down the road. But mama has promised her, and mama will protect her. She backs toward the door, calling for mama to come and drive her sharpest kitchen knife into his lying throat. Mama comes running out and she stops dead in her tracks when she sees him. Ambrosia looks at the happiness spreading over her mother's weary face, and knows she has been betrayed. She runs into the house, slamming the screen door behind her, as the frazzled, overworked woman rushes to her husband, wrapping her skinny arms around him and leading him inside.

Ambrosia's fear covers her and envelops her like a cloud. She hides in the attic until the house is quiet, and then she creeps into the kitchen. He has left his wallet on the table, stuffed with green paper money, and she hesitates for only a second. She knows where she can go, must go. To New York, where all the pretty models are, where all the glossy magazines are waiting. As the moon rises over the hills, she leaves the house and heads for the bus station. She is on her way to New York before anyone knows she is gone.

Although she has never been out of Tennessee, she feels a growing sense of relief as the distance between her and her father widens. She studies the guidebook she bought in the bus station and plans where to stay and how to begin her new life.

After arriving at Port Authority, she stuffs her clothes into a locker and dons her best dress. Then she goes immediately to Wilhelmina, one of the biggest modeling agencies in the country. She already knows about Wilhelmina from the clippings and articles in the fashion magazines she has left behind in the back of her closet at home.

She enters the plush reception area just as a trio of stunning women are leaving. They look at her smooth, unpainted face and her blue sailor dress, and smile condescendingly. But she is not discouraged. Her looks have fashioned her destiny so far, and she knows that they will carry her through.

The charming young man who usually sits behind the receptionist's desk is not there today. It is his job to make the girls who walk in feel beautiful and special from the moment they arrive. But he has called in sick on this day, and a typist has been asked to sit in at his desk.

Ambrosia asks timidly about a modeling job, and the typist examines her nails.

"Do you have any experience?" she asks.

"No."

"Do you have pictures?"

"Pictures?"

"Do you have a portfolio?"

"I—no. I thought—"

"Go see a good photographer and get some pictures taken. Then come back." She reaches into a drawer and pulls out a mimeographed sheet that lists the names of some photographers. "You can choose one of these."

Ambrosia backs away, intimidated, and heads back down in the elevator. She is pushing through the revolving door, when a man comes after her and grabs her arm, wrenching her around to face him.

She screams, and he steps back, surprised. He throws his arms up, showing he will not hurt her.

"Excuse me," he says hurriedly. "My name is Jerry Fenelon." He fishes for a card and produces one rapidly, offering it to her as he babbles on. "I saw you in the elevator and I wanted to meet you. I'm a photographer."

She studies the card and eyes him suspiciously. Is he for real, or some kind of crackpot?

"What's your name?" he asks, afraid she will run away.

"Ambrosia Joplin," she answers nervously.

"We'll change that," he mutters as he gazes into her violet eyes. Her bone structure is perfect. He can't wait to try her out in front of a camera. "Look," he says, "I'd like to take some pictures of you. My studio is right upstairs." Indecision and fear dart across her face, and he adds, "It's perfectly safe. My assistant will be there the whole time. She's a nice girl, a little older than you."

But this, after all, was what she had come for. If this man is a photographer, then she will have to overcome her anxiety and see what he can do for her. She nods shyly and he smiles with relief.

"Listen, Ambrosia. Are you with Wilhelmina? Is that where you were coming from?"

She looks embarrassed, and he puts two and two together. Here's this naïve young girl with a knockout face and a country accent, wearing a ridiculous dress and no makeup. She's probably been upstairs to Wilhelmina, and they've given her the brush. Well, it was their loss and his gain.

They go upstairs, and he positions her in front of the camera, focusing the strong lights on her ethereal face. As Ambrosia sits under the flashing lights, she knows it is going to happen for her. She poses effortlessly, using the artless innocence that marks her so unmistakably with unconscious ease. Jerry Fenelon takes her out for dinner that evening, and he explains some of

172

the ins and outs of the tough fashion business to her. Although she listens politely as she samples her first lobster Newburg, she does not let him penetrate her shell. Jerry puts her in a cab and hands the driver a bill, telling her to call him the next day.

Early the next morning, he sends Ambrosia's pictures to *Vogue,* and by the time she calls him, they have already seen the photos and flipped over them. She accepts this news calmly, as if she had always known it would happen. By afternoon, *Vogue* has hired Jerry Fenelon to do a cover photo of her.

The face of Ambrosia Jewell causes shock waves. Before long, her haunting, inscrutable beauty is a new standard. Hairdressers copy the sleek, definitive cut of her hair on dozens of eager customers, and her powerfully appealing yet enigmatic combination of exoticism and purity becomes an elusive ideal.

The photographers and editors soon learn the rules of the game with her. No one ever touches her, and she is treated with absolute respect. When one enthusiastic photographer tries to give her a hug from behind during an especially successful shooting, she shrieks in panic and runs out of the studio. She appears on dozens of covers across the country and in Europe, but she refuses to do lingerie spreads, and of course she never poses in the nude.

In a few months, she is contacted by Tony Amato and asked to come to Hollywood for a screen test. Although it is impossible to melt the ice that surrounds her innermost emotions, she is so breathtakingly vibrant on the screen that no one cares whether or not she can act. Tony gets her a small but noticeable feature part in a movie, and protects her from all the Hollywood dragons who try to come on to her.

The director of her first film gives her a quick kiss as she arrives on the set one morning. She bursts into tears and sits quaking in a chair, and Tony is summoned to calm her down. The director, Stan Geller, is intrigued rather than put off by her hysteria. He treats her with formal courtesy during the rest of the shooting, and by the time her scenes are finished, he has

173

fallen hopelessly and irrationally in love with her. On her last day on the set, he walks into her trailer and proposes to her.

She is incapable of giving him an answer, and for a while he takes this as a sign of encouragement. Ambrosia sends Tony to see him.

"Forget it, Stan," Tony says bluntly. "The girl has big problems."

"But I'm in love with her."

Tony grins sympathetically. "So are half the guys in the world, including me, but it's no use. She doesn't trust anyone in her bedroom."

"Look, I know she's uptight, but—"

"Uptight? This goes beyond uptight."

Stan Geller is not convinced. He is more determined than ever to win her heart. He keeps his distance, but he bombards her with a barrage of flowers, gifts, loving notes. But marriage is out of the question for Ambrosia Jewell. In the end, Stan sends her a final letter, in which he vows to wait for her, hoping against hope she will one day break out of her shell.

A year later, Max Zwerdlow throws a party to celebrate her first major role, and he invites Wes Canfield, who has expressed an interest in doing a beauty book with her. Tony briefs Wes in advance about Ambrosia's extreme shyness, warning him not to come on too strong. Canfield sits off by himself near the pool, waiting for the enigmatic lady to appear. When she arrives, escorted by Tony, he glances at her politely but does not make a move to meet her. Ambrosia is used to turning heads wherever she goes and cannot help but wonder about the quiet, handsome young man. She is immediately surrounded by the usual crowd of oglers and guys on the make, but she answers them in monosyllables. Tony keeps a close watch on her, as always, and she pushes demurely past her band of admirers to talk to him.

"Tony," she says, inclining her head so that her feathery, raven hair brushes his shoulder. "Who is the man by the pool?"

He smiles his charming, brotherly smile. "His name

is Wes Canfield. Why don't you go over and say hello to him?"

She hesitates. "Why don't you introduce me?"

"Okay, come on."

Wes stands up as they approach, and shakes her hand gravely. An hour later, they are still talking, and Tony discreetly keeps the other guests from straying out to bother them.

Wes draws her out slowly, asking her harmless little questions about her childhood and her hometown. Of course, these are loaded questions for her, but he asks them so gently and with such decency that she answers. Then she boldly asks him about *his* father. A tight little ripple crosses his face for an instant, but it is long enough for her to catch it.

"My father is Werner Haas," he says casually, intending to cover his initial reaction, but it is too late.

Her mouth curves in a tiny little Mona Lisa smile, and she says, "*The* Werner Haas? The great publishing genius?" His eyes crinkle in deference to her sudden insight, and before long, he has shared many of his frustrations and unresolved anger with her.

Ambrosia warms to this magnetic, sensitive man and tells him her whole story, quietly and without histrionics. His genuine sympathy and encouragement make her trust him with almost childlike dedication. She places her confidence in him, and he promises never to violate it. He becomes her big brother, a loyal and dependable shoulder on which she can always lean. She calls him whenever she feels low in spirit, which is often. Once, after receiving a guilt-ridden letter from her mother, she calls him in the middle of the night, and he soothes her jangled nerves until the sun comes up. One day she shows up in his office unannounced with a special request.

"I want you to promise me something," she asks seriously.

"What is it?"

"No, I want you to promise before I tell you. Just say yes," she pleads, her large, graceful eyes appealing to him.

He smiles. "All right. I promise."

"Good." She walks over to the window and looks down at the cars, crawling like ants down the avenue. Then she wheels and faces him. "If one day I should need you—if something terrible should happen to me —I want you to be there. I want to know there will be one person who won't take advantage of me, who will protect me, even if I can't protect myself."

He nods slowly and smiles. "You got it, kid," he says. Ambrosia beams at him, not the enigmatic smile she saves for the cameras, but an open admission of trust. She trusts Tony with her career, but she trusts Wes with her life. She runs to him and he puts his arms around her and his touch feels good, so good.

Ambrosia stops tossing and turning in her hospital bed. Wes is coming. He will make everything all right again. She is sure of it. The scene where she runs to him and he holds her in his arms plays over and over in her head until the projector stops whirring and the screen goes blank. Ambrosia sleeps peacefully, dreamlessly.

Wes Canfield stared straight ahead in the darkened cabin of the plane, wide awake. Images of Ambrosia and Tracy warred in his mind. He had not wanted to leave Tracy in Paris with just a note to explain his departure. She would be angry and upset, but she could take care of herself. No question about that. Ambrosia needed him. Surely, Tracy would undersand.

Ambrosia was the only person in the world who depended on him totally and he needed her dependency on him as much as he needed air or water or food. Her trust was as important to him in some ways as his company or Tracy. Wes didn't understand it completely, but he knew he couldn't sleep or rest until he reached Ambrosia's side.

Chapter 15

"WES CANFIELD, PLEASE. . . . I SEE. . . . WHEN DO YOU expect him? . . . Oh, well . . . no, no message." Tracy hung up the phone and sighed. She didn't like it at all. The plane ride back from Paris had been long and miserable, and she had returned to an empty, but obviously hostile office. The memos from Kramer attested to that. She was glad she had beaten everyone in this morning. She needed time to think, to adjust. If she closed her eyes, she might be back in Paris again, in Wes's arms. . . . She cut herself off and reached for the styrofoam cup of coffee that sat on the edge of the desk. Her fingers knocked against it and it fell, sending rivulets of brown liquid over the papers in front of her. She was snatching them away from the stream when Dennis Jordan walked in.

"Get me some paper towels, would you please?"

He came back with a stack and then took off his jacket. As he mopped at the floor, he said enthusiastically, "Boy, oh boy, Mr. Kramer went crazy last week when he heard about your trip." He smiled as though she had somehow triumphed again.

"Oh, really?" She tried to sound casual.

"Yeah, but it's okay. When he heard that Marcel Aubert actually called you on Friday, he cooled off real fast."

She jumped up. "Aubert called?"

"Sure. Everyone was talking about it." He winked. "I made sure they all knew."

"Oh, Dennis, you're a gem. What did he say?"

"He said he wants you to call Max Zwerdlow about your meeting in Paris. He also said something about

177

an awards ceremony, and he's sending you some stuff in the mail."

Well, she thought, with a surge of hope. I'm not finished here yet. Of course, she was still skating on thin ice. Kramer didn't want her around, and her little jaunt to Europe had been audacious, to say the least. But if she got Aubert. . . .

As she sat down and looked through her mail, the staff began to arrive for work, and Tracy overheard a few remarks that made her very uneasy. None of them were directed precisely at her, but she was still too nervous and insecure about her job to be sure. Then Sheila Zimmerman paraded by, talking loudly to Ken Maguire.

"Is our star pupil back?" she asked loudly. Seeing Tracy in her office, she marched in and said, "Soooo, how was Paris? God, what an expense account! I heard you're going to Pamplona for the bull festival. If you don't sign the matador up for a book, maybe you'd like to do the bull." She and Ken laughed boisterously at this, and Tracy grinned weakly. It was a dangerous joke, if it were a joke at all.

They left, and she sat down, fuming. She heard more laughter down the hall, and was considering sneaking off to the ladies' room when she perceived a sudden silence on the floor. Kramer must have just arrived, she realized with a slight shudder.

Steve Kramer wasted no time. Without even bothering to stop in his own office, he walked stiffly into hers and signaled for her to follow him to the nearest conference room. He threw his coat over a chair and motioned her into a seat.

She was in no mood for a lecture. He couldn't possibly say anything that she hadn't already imagined. As she sat waiting for him to begin, she calculated that she had been listening to him bawling her out for over a year and a half. Maybe she should just quit and relieve him of this last satisfaction. But then she thought of her rent, her shopping bills and all of her expenses. She didn't dare be glib with him. Well, then, she thought desperately, I just won't play. If it's a fight he wants, he won't get it from me.

He let the air out of his nostrils and moved into the line of fire.

"I really don't believe you, Bouchard. I know you're not stupid. But you sure are a pain in the ass. Just how did you expect to justify this little overseas adventure to Accounting?"

She said nothing. Obviously, he was prepared for a long speech, and she had no intention of interrupting.

"Let me ask you one question. Do you want to be an editor?"

She was silent.

"It doesn't happen overnight. You don't learn by making trips and spending money and going out to fancy lunches. You learn by doing the hard stuff. Going over tedious manuscripts line by line. Writing boring reports. Reading piles of crap until you find something good."

He paused again, waiting for a response, but she was absolutely quiet.

"When you get back from L.A., I want you doing some serious work around here. I'm assigning you six books that the others don't have time for—"

He went on talking, but all she heard was that she was going to L.A. That meant she had a chance. She still had a job, and they still needed her on the Fleming book. Why else would they send her back to L.A.? She listened as he finished talking, and then she spoke quietly.

"All right, Steve. I understand. I—I'm sorry about running off last week, but I didn't expect to actually go to France with him. It happened so fast, and we were getting along so well. He hardly ever talks to anybody, and he was talking a mile a minute to me. I really surprised him by showing up at the airport. It seemed like it was worth a shot. Not only that, but he's a good friend of Jim Fleming's." She winced slightly as she said that, but it was still a strong point. She hurried on. "If the company does his book and makes a lot of money from it, then this trip will have been a very

179

worthwhile investment, don't you think? And it looks like it may work out. He called my office on Friday, and he wants me to call his agent."

Kramer threw down the pencil he had been drumming on the table and she relaxed. The small gesture spelled defeat. She had won and he had lost. The victory did not fill her with elation—merely a sense of relief that Round Two had been passed without bloodshed. And she had no desire ever to see Round Three. But Kramer was up and slugging.

He nodded quickly and said, "So, Tracy, let's put all our cards on the table. Fleming likes you. We need you on that book because of that. Right now, that's your ticket to stay here, but remember one thing. One more false move on your part and you're out on your ass."

She was trembling inside, fighting to keep from shaking, and she hoped he was finished. But there was one more item on the agenda.

"Fleming called me last week. He wants you to come out to L.A. and help him with the book. John and I will put together some notes, and we'll go over them with you before you leave. I also want you to do some research on Fleming. Find out as much as you can about him before you meet him again. You shouldn't have to ask him too many questions that you don't already know the answers to."

He was jealous. He was trying to hide it, but she could see it in the rapid tics in his face, and she could hear it in the slight tremor that colored his voice. He wanted desperately to be the one to handle this book, but he had to settle for the sidelines. He had no choice but to send her out to the coast as Fleming had requested.

"I know what you're thinking, Bouchard, so let's get one thing straight. You might win most valuable player of the year award, but that doesn't guarantee that you'll stay on the team. This book won't last forever, you know. There *is* life after Jim Fleming. Sooner or later, you're going to have to pull some weight around here." He stared at her for a minute and then said, "So Fleming likes you. My hands are tied. I know it. I admit it.

But I didn't have to like it. And I don't have to like you."

She was very near to breaking down, but she still didn't want a fight. He had shot his arrows; now, maybe he would settle for a truce.

"No, Steve," she said softly. "You don't have to like me. But you could anyway. You used to. And as long as we have to work here together, I think it's worth a try."

His eyebrow arched suddenly, and the simple but definitive gesture reminded her of Canfield. He had encouraged her to stay in Paris, told her she wouldn't get in trouble. She tried to blink back the tears as she thought of him, wondering where he was and why he had left her, but she knew she couldn't mention him now. Even though he had made a bid for the paperback rights to the Aubert book, she had acted on her own responsibility and didn't want to be bailed out of mischief like a child. And if she didn't come through with the Aubert book, Wes's offer would be useless.

"Okay, Tracy," Kramer said. "That's all." Tracy looked down to hide the tears that welled in her eyes. It was an ambiguous answer, but she was satisfied. She knew she had gained some time. And that was all she needed.

Chapter 16

The announcer's voice brought Tony Amato out
of his reverie. He had been thinking about the first time
he took this flight, a long time ago, with a one-way
ticket.

Tony was far from the neighborhood in Brooklyn
where he grew up, but the old place was still close to
his heart. He tried to stop in for a visit when he was in
New York. It kept him in touch with some important
things—things that were easily forgotten in California.
The old neighborhood had sheltered him and taught
him how to survive. It was the kind of place where
you knew everyone and everyone knew you. You belonged just because you were there. People looked out
for each other. His talent for looking out for people,
especially women, had taken him a long way in California. But if it hadn't been for the neighborhood,
he wouldn't be standing in the airport waiting for
Tracy Bouchard.

He had always been a popular kid, making friends
easily. His charm and sincerity endeared him to the
girls, and his prowess in sports and fairness gained
him respect from other boys, even the older guys.
Whenever he played ball in the park, there were always three or four girls watching him from behind the
plate, waiting to talk to him or hand him a bat.

"Hey, lover boy! Hey, Amato!" John Catania, the
pitcher, would kid him and throw a few mock punches.
"You wanna play with the girls or you wanna play
ball?"

"Both," Tony would say. "I wanna do both." And he did.

He treated girls with the utmost respect, as befitted his Italian upbringing, and they trusted him with sweet abandon. Tony understood something that many of his teammates never would: sex was a pleasure to be shared with a woman. A woman was a flower to be cherished, not a toy to be used and then tossed aside.

Girls never had to worry about Tony respecting them. They always knew his feelings were genuine. When he said, "I love you" to a girl, he meant it. Of course, he said it to all the girls, but he meant it each and every time. He moved among women like a happy butterfly.

Tony's destiny was set on an irrevocable course soon after he graduated from high school. He was walking home, past the mom-and-pop grocery stores, the barber shops where the old men played cards, the knots of kids hanging out on the street corners, when he saw a maze of lights and a group of people gathered at the corner. Workmen were affixing large, glaring round lights to the tops of the old brownstones, and the side street had been blocked off by the police. A long line of trucks, vans and trailers stood at the intersection, and thick cables and wires were looped in bunches around them. Tony walked up to the nearest onlooker and asked, "What's going on?"

"They're making a movie," the man replied.

Although Manhattan streets were often used as film locations, Tony and his friends rarely ventured over the Brooklyn Bridge into that maze of big money and high stakes. Brooklyn was Tony's territory, his turf, and movie crews were seldom seen on the old, time-worn streets. As he watched the men set up their equipment, there was a feeling of having been chosen. His own little street where he had lived, shopped, worked and played would be transported onto the silver screen.

He stood transfixed as the hours passed and the faces in the crowd changed. As hungry as he was, he was too excited to leave, and he watched as the familiar street became a movie set. He was awed by the way

183

the workers created magic out of pavement and concrete, and he became enchanted as the mechanics behind the magic were revealed.

Finally, the director arrived and the shooting began. He motioned for the powerful lights to be switched on, and Tony tingled with excitement as the night was lit up, transforming the block into another world, a fantasy world. As the camera was rolled into position, the crowd became unruly, and it was hard for the crew to keep them from getting onto the set.

After one take was ruined by a man who walked into the frame to get to his house, the director yelled at the crowd. This only caused them to become less cooperative. The more he pleaded with them to move back, the more they taunted him, until Tony decided to intervene.

The director watched in appreciation as the young boy used all of his charm and street tactics to keep the onlookers at bay, even the local girls who wanted a glimpse of the handsome star.

When they were ready to shoot another take, the crowd was at a peak of excitement. There was a hush as the director called for "Action!", and just as the camera started to roll, two toddlers ran out into the street, knocking over the police barrier. In a flash, Tony scooped them up and delivered them back to their mothers, and the director threw him a grateful glance. The teen-aged girls began to chant and giggle, trying to catch the attention of the leading man, and again Tony charmed them into silence. When the shot was finished, Hal Sterling, the director, walked over to Tony Amato and slapped him on the back.

"Listen, kid," he said. "You stick around for the night and take care of the people like you're doing, and I'll give you fifty bucks for the night's work."

"You got a deal." Tony smiled.

The shooting continued on into the night, and Tony kept monitoring the crowd, collecting as many admiring girls as the leading man. The crew broke for dinner, and many of them sat down to gulp down sandwiches and cups of hot coffee. They still had to shoot another exterior night scene, and they had come to rely on Tony, who was making their job easier than usual.

They finally quit at four o'clock in the morning, and as they began to pack up their gear and load the trucks, the director walked over to Tony and handed him a one hundred dollar bill.

"Thanks, kid," he said. "You've been a big help."

"My pleasure, Mr. Sterling," Tony answered. They shook hands and Sterling turned to go. Tony called him back.

"What can I do for you, Tony?"

"Let me come and work for you full-time. I can do a lot of things. You won't be sorry."

Hal Sterling laughed. "Yeah, okay, kid. But I work in California. You come out there and I'll give you a job." He turned away, figuring he would never see the kid again.

He was wrong. Tony went home and thought seriously about what he had just seen. He had loved every minute of it. He didn't know if Hal Sterling would really give him a job, but even if he didn't, somebody else would. He *had* been a big help, and he knew it. It was worth a shot. It was definitely worth a shot. If he wanted to work in movies, then he wasn't going to get anywhere sitting on his bed in Brooklyn. He would have to go to where the jobs were, and that meant Hollywood. He smiled to himself. Somehow, he didn't feel like just another star-struck kid going out to make it in the movies. He knew what he was good at. With some of the money he had saved up, he bought a one-way ticket to Los Angeles and appeared at the entrance to Universal Studios asking for Hal Sterling.

The director had spent a long day shooting and looked up to see a vaguely familiar form running toward him.

Recognition spread across his face, coupled with disbelief. But he had given his word.

Tony had a job.

He moved into a small place near the ocean. When he got his first paycheck he made the down payment on a second-hand Chevy. He bought some new clothes, and quickly met and surrounded himself with his usual retinue of beautiful girls.

Hal Sterling was never sorry he had hired Tony Amato. Tony was a fast learner and a good worker. He did everything with good will and an openness that enabled him to absorb information like a sponge. He was especially good with women, knowing how to make them relax on the set and how to get their best camera angles. At the end of a year, Tony was a comer with a reputation for getting difficult jobs done.

Max Zwerdlow first noticed him during the shooting of *September's Dream*. He had come to check out a starlet named Dorene Redding. Zwerdlow stood quietly off to the side, watching as she blew take after take of a particularly difficult scene. After the eighth attempt was scrapped, she collapsed in tears and ran off the set. Tony Amato immediately dropped the script he was holding and ran over to comfort her. Zwerdlow observed with interest as the young man put his arm around her in a brotherly fashion, told her a joke or two to make her laugh, and lifted her drooping chin with one finger to give her encouragement. Then he escorted her back to the scene like a perfect gentleman and sat next to her, talking reassuringly until the shot was set up. Take nine was a success.

The next time he saw Tony was at the opening of *September's Dream*. It was a night that none of them were ever to forget. Although her performance had been good, the starlet was hysterical with fear, and seemed on the point of a nervous breakdown. Tony knew that she had spent the previous evening with Armand Axelrod, a notorious film critic, and it wasn't hard to figure out what had happened. Axelrod was a brilliant writer with an acid pen, and he was not above rating the performance of rising actresses according to their sexual, instead of their artistic, abilities. Dorene had fallen into his trap but had escaped at the last moment. Now he was threatening her with a hatchet job.

Tony knew that Axelrod's review would not carry

as much weight as Dorene thought. The truth was that bad reviews did not have all that much to do with the box-office success of a movie. But a good review certainly didn't hurt, and it was almost impossible not to take the bad ones personally. Dorene was as sensitive as anyone else, and she had a right to fair treatment. This blackmailing business enraged Tony, and it had been going on far too long. He decided that it was time to put a stop to it.

Zwerdlow listened as Tony put his arms around Dorene and talked soothingly "Calm down, sweetheart. I'll fix everything."

"No, Tony, you can't fix this. It will take more than a hug and a kiss and a few nice words."

He looked down at her and smiled—confidently. "If I promise you that Axelrod will write the best review imaginable, will you calm down?"

"But how? He threatened to—"

"Shhhhh." Tony gave her a squeeze. "I give you my word that he won't. You'll get a great review and you'll be a big star. I'll tell folks I knew the great Dorene Redding."

"But, Tony," she protested

He let her go and walked out to his car. Max Zwerdlow watched him with interest.

Tony drove over to the *L.A. Times* building and walked up the back stairs. Looking through the glass partition at the news room, he saw Axelrod seated at a desk, pounding away on a typewriter. The man continued typing furiously for several minutes, and then he got up and tossed the pages he had just written into a bin on the editor's desk.

"There you are, Charley. That's for the first edition."

"What's it on?"

"*September's Dream,* or should I say nightmare?" He laughed as he left by the front exit.

Tony waited a minute and then strolled casually into the large room. The two reporters still pounding out late night copy paid no attention to him as he headed over to where Axelrod had deposited his review.

He stared down at the article in the bin and made a face as he read it. Looking around to make sure he wasn't noticed, he picked up the paper from the bin, and crumbled it and tossed it in a wastebasket. Sitting at an abandoned desk, he fed a piece of paper into the typewriter. Ten minutes later, he pulled it out, waited for his chance, and dropped it into the same bin. Smiling victoriously, he sauntered out the front door.

The next morning, he got a call from Max Zwerdlow.

"I won't ask you how you did it," Zwerdlow began, "but I just read Axelrod's rave review of Dorene Redding."

Tony knew something was up, and he waited eagerly at the other end.

"Come up to my office and pick up a contract. I'll pay you the usual percentage if you sign her, and you'll have yourself a job."

That same afternoon, Dorene Redding signed with Max Zwerdlow Associates, and word got around that a hot young agent was looking for clients. New talent flocked to him, and as time progressed, he found that all of his clients were women.

He began looking around for new ground to conquer, and he was intrigued by the dazzling photographs of Ambrosia Jewell. She had a reputation of being very hard to get, but that had never stopped Tony. He called her and convinced her to come out for a screen test, and he sweet-talked her into staying around. Ambrosia trusted him, and knew he was the best possible movie agent for her.

Producers learned that whenever they needed a terrific new face, they had only to call Tony Amato, and he would line someone up. Zwerdlow trusted him with the jobs that were too sensitive for anyone else to handle. That was how he had first been assigned to welcome Tracy Bouchard and show her the ropes. Now the assignment was pure pleasure.

As he sauntered over to the arrivals area, he remembered something and smiled. Hastily, he buttoned his shirt and slipped his gold neck-chains into his pocket.

Chapter 17

As she came into the terminal, Tracy spotted Tony's smiling face and pushed through the crowd to put her arms around him.

As his strong arms went around her, she could feel every muscle in her body relax.

"Ummmmm. You know something, Tony Amato?"

He kissed her on the forehead and she looked up at him with a big smile.

"You feel very good."

"It's California, not me. Why don't you just move out here, then you can be as laid back as you want?"

"I couldn't survive in this kind of environment. Besides, I'm a devout New Yorker. I read the *Times* religiously every Sunday, and I need the city as a constant reminder that there's a better life somewhere else."

He laughed as they made their way over to the moving ramp that led to the baggage claim area.

"You know something, Tracy? You're a lot different from anyone I know."

"You mean, from any girl you know."

"Maybe, but I'm not so sure you operate on luck anymore."

Tracy was a little taken aback by this last statement.

"What do you mean?"

"You had one bad break that you turned into a positive thing. Steve Kramer fired you. Unjustly maybe, but he did fire you."

"I don't believe this. Is everything I do transmitted to the world?"

"Huh? Oh, no, this isn't Hollywood gossip. I got all my facts from the horse's mouth."

Her face plainly showed betrayal, but he quickly reassured her that he was on her side.

"Hey, easy does it, Bouchard. What are you trying to do, give me the evil eye? Where do you think Kramer got the tip on the Fleming book, anyway?"

She was perplexed.

"Kramer wasn't the first to try for the Fleming book. Lots of other publishers have tried, including your former boss, but Kramer got lucky. I met him at one of Zwerdlow's parties. Fleming was there, and I introduced them. It was all timing. Jim had slowed down to three shows a week, and had already entertained the idea of doing his memoirs. Kramer was just in the right place at the right time, but that didn't mean he had him. Zwerdlow was thinking of approaching Franklin & Fields long before Tracy Bouchard and Steve Kramer battled it out on the east coast."

Tracy couldn't believe what she was hearing. "Do you mean to tell me that I had nothing to do with Zwerdlow going for the F & F deal?"

"Not exactly. Jim wasn't going to contract for the book until after the season ended. You just sped things up." Tony smiled at her in a congratulatory way. "Jim really likes you. You two hit it off so well that he went for a contract hook, line and sinker."

And then it struck her. In the eyes of Tony and everyone out here in Hollywood, she was not a thief. It was all coming together. Max Zwerdlow had hoped Wes Canfield would do the Fleming book all along. If she had never been born, Steve Kramer still would not have got Fleming. And there was one more important fact. Wes Canfield would never have got credit for it if he had left F & F before Fleming announced his intentions. And in a way, she was instrumental in Steve Kramer's coming to F & F. She thought of asking Tony to explain this to Kramer, but then decided not to involve Tony in her problems. Besides, she figured, Kramer would never believe him. Better to wait for a more appropriate time.

Tony pulled up to the curb and she stared at his car. As he got out to open the door, she couldn't help but smile at his mannerisms. He fit into this world so easily. "New car?" she asked.

"Oh, this," he said, with a wave of his hand. "It's an Alfa Romeo. One of my clients had no need of it after she got divorced, so she gave it to me as a present. Said it reminded her of her husband too much, so I did her a favor and took it off her hands."

"You're too much, Tony." Tracy laughed.

She slid into the red leather bucket seat. Even as the car idled, she could feel the power of Tony's new toy. That's what it's all about, she thought. Power. At least here it's in a pretty package. Tracy settled back to enjoy the ride.

"Is Jim expecting me this afternoon?"

"No. He'll be taping at four. You'll see him this evening, and afterwards you and I can have dinner at Ma Maison. So, where would you like to go this afternoon? The beach, Disneyland—"

"The taping, let's go see the taping. I'd like to get an idea of how he works. It will help me when I talk to him tonight. I don't want to pump him with questions I can have answered by seeing him in action."

They headed onto the freeway for a short distance and then turned onto an exit. Tracy tried to get her bearings, but it was difficult to adjust to L.A. The six-lane highway was striking to her, especially as she recalled the usual traffic jams on Fifth Avenue. He turned onto a side road and then into downtown Burbank.

One more turn and they were at the studio. A huge line of people stood outside waiting to be let in. As they walked by, Tracy felt Tony's strong arm around her waist. He escorted her to a side door, where a guard waved them inside. They went up a stairway and through a double door into the huge studio. Tracy smiled in anticipation. The bright lights were electrifying as technicians and men with clipboards and earphones scurried back and forth in preparation for the taping.

Tony called one of the men over.

"Mike, this is Tracy Bouchard. She's the editor for Jim's book."

He took her hand with interest.

"Well," he said, "this is where we've been taping for twenty-two years."

Mike's been a writer for the show on and off over the years."

Tracy listened as Mike explained how the show was produced. The writers got to the studio at nine A.M. Over coffee and Danish they read the morning newspapers and weekly magazines. The monologue was put together before lunch at one, and was always on Fleming's desk by three P.M.

"Come on," Tony said as he hurried her over to a group of first row seats directly across from Fleming's desk on the set. She couldn't have been more than fourteen feet from it. Meanwhile, the audience was being escorted in, and Tony began pointing out some of the other men on the set.

"That's Mort Baily."

"The producer?"

Tony nodded. "You'll see him call most of the shots from the sidelines. The gentleman to his left is Hank Granley."

She watched as Hank yelled some orders out across the floor. He nodded to Tony and then went back to work.

"Fleming really runs the show, though. Under his desk is a button that controls a camera always focused on his face. Whenever anyone does anything that is too outrageous, or if they begin upstaging Jim, he'll push the button for a closeup. Then he'll make a face or gesture of some sort to control the audience and keep control of the show."

"Where is he now?"

"Across the street in a private office. He never mingles with anyone before the show starts. The whole thing is spontaneous. Each guest has a private dressing room backstage. And you can bet that each one is nervous as all hell. This is good publicity for them.

That's why they only get paid scale for being on the show."

Tracy took it all in. She scrutinized the layout and began thinking about what she would say to her author when her turn came that evening. Tony pointed out some of the other features, especially the lack of any applause sign.

"He doesn't need one. It's hard enough trying to quiet them down."

Just before four, a man appeared in front of the audience to warm them up. The three large cameras were rolled into place. "One minute to take," Mort Baily called. Tension peaked when the countdown from ten began. At the count of one, the lights brightened up the entire studio, a drum roll sounded and the theme song blared out. The *Jim Fleming Show* was beginning.

As the familiar song excited the already animated audience, Tracy could feel the electricity. Then Jim Fleming popped through the curtain and there was pandemonium for at least two minutes. She watched him soak it all in. He was wearing a handsome, light blue suit with a soft tie and shoes that could not be more than a week old.

The music stopped, but the audience continued. Then the traditional pot of coffee was wheeled out and he poured himself a cup. As he sipped, the audience responded with the usual, "SALUDE."

"You're a lively group tonight."

Again, they went wild with whistles and yelps. He cut them off with a conductor's finale swing. There was a hush. He was every inch in control, and he waited as silence prevailed.

Tracy didn't laugh at his jokes. She was too intent on interpreting his every move, and she watched as he timed his jokes to get the highest possible reaction from the audience. It was as though they all knew him personally, as though they were a professional audience rehearsed in the tradition of the show. They knew just how to respond to his every whim. He commanded them and they followed, like a general with his army.

Each night of the week for twenty-two years, he had shown up on this stage doing the same thing. And they always loved him. He conducted his audience and they played like a seasoned orchestra.

Tracy noticed that Mort Baily never cracked a smile. He was intent on seeing that the monologue was presented without a flaw. On the sidelines, only seven feet from Fleming's desk, sat three men who also didn't smile. They took notes. One had on a set of earphones with a mouthpiece, and he was looking up at the back of the set. Tracy turned around to look, and saw someone in a glass booth perched above the audience in the back. For the people who worked here, this was serious business, and the taping was critical. The monologue ended to applause and music, and Jim broke for a commercial.

All of a sudden, the tension subsided and Jim walked calmly over to his desk. Mort said a few words to him, and he took a sip of coffee as the band went into a short number. The cameras swung around to cover both sides of his desk, and Tracy noticed the camera that was focused on Jim's face. She knew he had pressed the button under his desk as a frontal view of his face appeared on the monitor over her head. Then he sat back, everyone cleared the area, and the band continued.

"Four, three, two, one," Mort signaled him to start as the music died out and the audience responded with enthusiastic applause.

Jim announced his first guest, and Alan Alda came out from behind a curtain and walked onto the stage. They shook hands and Alda sat on the chair to Fleming's right.

He was practiced and charming as he discussed his new movie, and Fleming had just the right amount of control as he led Alda on, allowing him free reign when he was rolling. When there was slack, Jim came up with a joke or a comment to keep the tempo moving. Tracy noticed a man on the side holding up a sign that said, "Commercial." Tracy watched as Jim turned to Mort for advice. "No commercial" was the silent command. The conversation was too good to interrupt. Finally, the sign was held up again and Fleming had to break the action. "We'll be right back," he said, and applause followed as the band struck up a tune.

Fleming pulled a phone from under the desk and looked up at the booth in back as he talked. Then he turned to Alda and told him something before getting back on the phone to assure whomever was on the other end that the problem would be taken care of.

Back on the air again, the conversation resumed. Fleming was the ideal straight man. Most of the time, he was not looking at the actor but at the audience, to see if they were responding well. The audience was his barometer, and he read them flawlessly. There was no clipboard full of questions so he would know what to ask. It was all spontaneous. After each funny line or quip, Tracy saw that he would look at the producer for assurance that the technical end was running smoothly.

The band was phenomenal, improvising whenever Jim needed them to. When he and Alda got up to dance a corny duet, the band responded with "Swanee River," and they danced off into a commercial. Tracy could tell he was having a good time, because after the break they were still dancing.

They walked back and Alda moved over to make room for the next guest. Makeup people came on to touch up both stars and then the countdown began again.

Tony watched Tracy as she took it all in.

"What do you think so far?"

"Electrifying," was all she could get in over the noise of the applause and the band.

The next guest was Garson Murphy, the outspoken critic. Only today, he wasn't too outspoken. Instead of the usual six minutes, they broke for a commercial after only two minutes in order to cut Murphy's time.

"He's not cutting it," Tony explained. "If one of Jim's guests bombs, they use some jokes, and go to a fast commercial break. He'll be off in another few minutes, and they'll fill time with one of Jim's routines.

Tracy understood the show now. Boredom was the first deadly sin, but Fleming knew how to catch it before it started. He sized up the audience and played with them, sometimes at the expense of the guest. Murphy was off on a bad tangent, going on and on about his first job. It got so bad that Jim signaled the closeup camera and pretended to be falling asleep. Murphy got the message, but the men on the sidelines held up the sign, and they went to a commercial break again.

"That's it for him. He blew it."

"Jim certainly knows how to handle it, though. I thought he was quite funny."

She watched as a conference started around the desk. The men on the side came up to confer with Jim and Mort, who was yelling something above the roar of the band. Garson Murphy looked depressed as they asked him to move over, but then Fleming said something to him and he brightened up like a light. So did everyone else. Alda said something to him and then the countdown began. They all scurried back to their places while Fleming put on a ventriloquist's dummy mask and sat on the lap of a giant mannequin, controlling it from the seated position.

Tracy couldn't help but roar with laughter. After a while, she couldn't tell which was the dummy and which was the real person.

When the routine was over, and they broke for a commercial, Fleming kept the audience entertained until he was told he had fifteen seconds to air time. He didn't hurry, but was only halfway out of the suit when the ten second countdown began. By the count of three, he had disengaged himself and walked slowly back to his desk, sitting down just as the cameras rolled.

Then he brightened up the place with one of his famous smiles, as though he had been sitting at his desk all that time. The audience applauded his keen sense of timing, and Tracy realized that a lot of the applause she heard him get at home when she watched the show was for being able to get from the breaks back into the show without losing that all-important sense of timing. He was master of this show, and the audience loved him for it.

Tony looked at Tracy, whose face registered a new respect for this extraordinary man. Jim Fleming was in a class by himself. There were no retakes and nothing was rehearsed.

The next and final guest was an author. The man's book was on Fleming's desk and it had been well-thumbed. Fleming didn't interview an author without reading his or her book and he spoke knowledgeably, as though he had read more than one book on the subject. The author appeared a little nervous, and Fleming helped him along gently. After the writer came up with a good one-liner, Mort Baily put up his hand, signaling a cut to commercial.

The writer took some hard swallows of water as Fleming talked on the phone. Mort came over to confer with the other producers, and it was decided to let the author go the last three minutes of the show as best he could. If there were any problems, Fleming would cover. Sure enough, Fleming bailed the author out of a tough spot, and finished the time slot with a good plug for the book. Tracy could see that the author was grateful, and as the band played out the credits, she found herself applauding wildly.

When things quieted down, and the audience filed out slowly, straining for a last-minute look at their hero, Tony called to the stage.

Fleming came over and Tracy smiled and shook his hand.

"Well, how did you like my show?"

"It was a thrill seeing you in action. Your timing is extraordinary. I think we should try to work that same kind of rhythm into the book."

"Well, I'll tell you what," Fleming suggested. "Ride back home with me and we'll work in my study."

She looked at Tony to check with him.

"Fine," Tony said, turning to Tracy. "What time will you be finished?"

Fleming smiled. "You can pick her up around eight. That should give us enough time."

Tracy was higher than a kite as she and Fleming walked out a side door to a waiting limousine. He was all charm, pointing out the sights, and making subtle jokes.

"That's Bob Hope's house," he said, and then added dryly, "and that's the Hope tennis courts next to the Hope swimming pool. And right outside the gate to his drive—those are the Hope garbage pails. And that's Bob Hope." Tracy laughed until she realized that it was Hope.

Fleming waved as they passed by, and Hope looked up and acknowledged him.

"He's not always a private man. Likes to give the tour buses that come around a show for their money once in a while. A few weeks ago, he was out in the middle of the road looking for a golf ball. The tour bus came by right on time and a bunch of tourists watched as Bob hit the ball back over the wall onto his front lawn."

"How about you, are you private?"

"Totally. Laura and I like it that way. When I first got started in show business, she promised to marry me only if I gave my word she would never be forced into the limelight. The last thing she wants is to be known as Mrs. Jim Fleming. So we're quite private, and to tell you the truth, I love it that way."

Tracy was already beginning to see the makings of two books. Fleming had two sides to his life—public and private. Just how much he was willing to reveal would determine the feasibility of a second book, but she would respect his feelings, whatever he decided.

"I guess a lot of readers would be interested in my life as a father and husband?"

Tracy nodded.

"I think I'm one of the few talk show hosts to beat my own television record by twenty-six years of marriage. My kids are less private than I am, though. They love the publicity. But someone is always asking which will last longer, the Fleming show or the Fleming marriage."

Tracy already understood the answer. Here was a man who could have any woman in the world, but who had given all of his allegiance, respect and love to his wife. His married life and his family were his firm grip on reality. She saw this in his eyes as he spoke about Laura, his wife.

"Laura writes a few jokes a week for me. She especially likes to do the political spots."

He continued to talk about his views and she realized that behind the neutral façade on TV was a man with a keen mind for public issues. There was the private Fleming, the public Fleming and the politician in Fleming.

"Have you ever thought about running for public office?" she asked.

He laughed and answered her question half-seriously. "Only if I can still do my show three times a week. If it interfered with my show business life, I wouldn't be able to do it."

He went on about the politicians he knew as the car turned into a modest side road.

A large but unimposing house stood solidly behind a group of pines, and the limousine pulled up and stopped. Fleming jumped out and opened the door for her himself.

"Come on in," he said. "I'll introduce you to the family."

They walked inside, and it looked like any comfortable, well-heeled family home, except that it was much larger. There were the requisite tennis courts and a pool in the back and a screening room, but otherwise, it was a very welcoming, warm house, and Tracy felt completely at ease.

A smiling, slightly plump woman greeted them in the den, and Fleming put his arm around her. "This is my wife, Laura," he said warmly. "And this is my editor, Tracy Bouchard."

Laura Fleming, dressed in a pair of jeans and a T-shirt, offered Tracy a cold drink. Her bright smile flashed often, lighting up her pleasant face, and Tracy liked her at once.

"Where are the girls?" Fleming asked her.

"Out running," she answered, and shook her head.

"Do you jog?" Laura asked Tracy.

"Once in a while."

"I don't understand it. But Jim and the kids love it." Laura shrugged. "I'll leave you two alone now," she said, "but let me know if you need anything."

Tracy and Fleming walked into his private study, and he turned on a recorder to tape her comments on the book. For two hours, Tracy worked with him, using the notes that Kramer and Noble had given her. Any time it was possible to give credit to Steve Kramer, she did so, hoping that Fleming would eventually mention it to the new editor-in-chief. Maybe that would soften him up a little. Tracy and Fleming worked with speed and efficiency for what seemed like only minutes to Tracy. But when the doorbell rang, she looked up at the clock and realized it was Tony who had come to take her to dinner.

Before she left, Jim Fleming gave her a hearty bear hug and a friendly kiss, and then she and Tony were driving back down the private road.

Tony looked at her face. Her expression was one of sheer exhilaration.

"You did good, huh, Bouchard?"

She let out a happy sigh. "Yeah." Then she laughed outright. "I'll say! He's got a private side that's absolutely delightful. He's so witty, so intelligent. In a way, he reminds me of Wes Can—" She caught herself abruptly, but Tony smiled knowingly. She wondered if Tony knew she had been in that room at the Ritz Hotel in Paris when he sent that telegram about Ambrosia. Should she bring it up? No, if he wanted to tell her anything, he would. The thought of Wes threw her for a moment, but she resolved to put him out of her mind. She had just spent a memorable two hours with one of the greatest entertainers in the world. She was doing fine without Wes Canfield. So why did she wish he were here right now?

As Tony pulled into the parking lot across the street from Ma Maison, she saw rows of expensive sports cars and vintage autos that looked as if they had been transported from a movie set. The Ma Maison sign dominated the façade of the outwardly unimpressive building, but she knew that the appearance was misleading. Inside, some of the biggest stars and wealthiest people in the country were breaking bread. She was going to have a memorable evening and no one, not even the mercurial Wes Canfield, was going to put a damper on her spirits. She linked her arm through Tony's and gave him her best smile as they headed through the crowded parking lot.

Chapter 18

TRACY LOOKED AROUND AS SHE SQUEEZED BETWEEN A Rolls Royce and a Ferrari. "My God," she said, "there must be over a million dollars worth of cars here."

"I wouldn't doubt it. The first time I ever came here, it was in a '67 Chevy. They wouldn't even let me in the parking lot," he joked.

Tony put his hand on her back, escorting her to the door. They were led to a well-placed table in the garden, and Tony seated himself facing away from the dining area. Tracy wondered if he did that in order to avoid interruptions from acquaintances, or if he simply wanted to give her a tourist's-eye view of some of the patrons. There was indeed a lot to look at. She was careful not to stare, but glanced here and there while Tony politely pretended not to see what she was doing. At last, he smiled and pointed discreetly to Tracy's left, as Gregory Peck and an unknown companion made their way to a corner table.

She laughed weakly, admitting her curiosity.

"It's okay, baby. I was like that the first time I was here. You don't have to pretend to be cool in front of old Tony."

"Thanks, Tony," Tracy said sheepishly. "I may take a peek now and then, but I'm listening to you."

Tony turned the conversation to Jim Fleming. "I was surprised when Jim asked you to come out to his house. He rarely invites anyone there."

"I know," Tracy replied. "I felt very comfortable there. Jim and Laura are warm and easygoing. They have a great relationship. I'm thinking of asking Jim to do a second book about how he's managed to maintain such a strong family life in spite of being one of the biggest stars in Hollywood."

Tony whistled softly. "I don't know if he'd go for anything like that. He works hard at keeping a low profile. He rarely goes to parties. Once in a while, he'll show up at Max's but it's usually to meet someone, like he met you the last time you were out here. He's cordial to everyone, but he doesn't invite hangers-on. Some of them do that—they need it—but Jim doesn't."

"I didn't mention it because my thinking isn't quite clear on it. I wouldn't want the book to be a Jim-Fleming-tells-all but, well, maybe a personal testimony to the success of his private life."

Tony cocked his head, looking at her with admiration. "Not a bad idea, Bouchard. But I still don't know. Jim surrounds himself with that big house and all that land. He keeps his activities private and secluded; takes his vacations in unusual, out-of-the-way places. Even with the best of intentions, a book like that could backfire on him. Let's face it, you're having a field day catching glimpses of the heavies in this place. Can you imagine how far Fleming would get if he walked one block on Fifth Avenue?"

"He'd be swamped."

"The price one pays for stardom." He shrugged.

Tracy looked at Tony, bemused. He certainly had the mechanics of this town under control. Nothing seemed to surprise him, and celebrities didn't impress him one way or the other. He was immune to them. He judged them in the same manner that he would judge a new sports car. If they cost a lot, they had better perform well. Tony had changed slightly from the last time she had seen him, or maybe she was the one who had changed. But something was different. She had walked in with the ghost of Canfield over her shoulder, and maybe it showed. But something else seemed to be bothering Tony as well.

There was a pause in the conversation, and she felt a surge of gratitude and affection for him. Gently reaching out to take his hand, she whispered, "Is something wrong?"

His large, brown eyes looked frankly into hers. "Well, there is something, but I took care of it. Just a little problem with one of my girls."

"Your girls?" Tracy asked demurely.

"Yeah, my girls."

"Funny way to refer to clients who pay your rent."

"How did you know I was talking about a client?" he said coyly, and she dropped the whole subject with a laugh. But there was still something on both of their minds, even though they carried on with pleasant small talk. His mute preoccupation cropped up again as they ordered coffee, and she saw that his eyes roamed around the room apprehensively.

The meal ended quietly and Tony signed the American Express receipt. Tracy stood up, preparing to leave. Then her mouth dropped open in horror and surprise as she stared into the equally shocked face of Wes Canfield. He recovered his composure and walked over to greet her. All the hurt and anger she had felt in Paris welled up in her.

"Well," she said stormily, "where's Ambrosia? Still in the hospital?"

"I can't believe you're out here, but I guess the Fleming book brought you."

"You guess?" she cut in sharply. "And did you guess how I felt in Paris last week?"

"Tracy, I'm sorry about running off. I thought you'd understand."

"Well, you're wrong, Canfield. Dead wrong. And why haven't you called me in New York? Just what is going on here? Never mind. Don't answer that. You just wanted to get your hands on the Fleming book and the Aubert book and it didn't matter whom you stepped on to get them. Unfortunately, it was me."

"You know that's not true," Canfield said in a furious whisper. "Tracy, I—." He stopped short. "It was an emergency. I had to leave Paris immediately."

"I know all about your emergency." Tracy felt like hitting him. "You could have waited for me. A few hours couldn't have made a difference."

"You're wrong," he said impatiently. "And you have

no business asking about that, especially here. It's a very private matter."

A waiter carrying a large, round tray dodged them smoothly, and Wes almost bumped into Tony, who was standing quietly to one side.

"And what the hell are you doing with him?" he demanded.

Tony put a constraining hand on Canfield's shoulder. "Why don't you calm down, Wes?"

"Why don't you mind your own business, Amato?" Canfield glowered at Tracy, who looked at him with growing desperation. Canfield caught her expression, turned on his heel and stalked away. Tracy stood helplessly clutching her bag and let out a sound of pure frustration. Then she turned and followed Tony out of the restaurant, ignoring the stares and the trail of measured whispers.

When the attendant brought Tony's Alfa to the door, she opened the door herself, got in and slammed it hard. Tony slid behind the wheel and drove off without a word.

"Sorry about that," she said after a few minutes. "I didn't mean to cause a scene." Tracy let out a heavy sigh.

He gave her one of his trademark grins. "Don't worry about it. Happens all the time."

She realized this was true, and she sank back uncomfortably. The last thing she wanted was to be a tidbit in somebody's gossip column. Tony chattered away about Max and his girls, and the cool evening breeze wafted through the open windows of the freewheeling sports car. Tracy settled back and closed her eyes, letting the anger flow out of her into the wind. It was impossible to stay upset in Tony's company. Tracy welcomed the calm that descended upon her. It was the first time she had relaxed since Paris. Unpleasant as the incident had been, she was glad she had let Canfield know how hurt and angry she was.

Tony drove directly to his house, and they pulled up in his driveway before she knew it. He jumped out of the car and hurried around to open the door for her, helping her out slowly and gently. His touch was intimate and suggestive, and she realized that he meant to seduce her, Canfield or no Canfield. Well, she wasn't going to let Wes Canfield spoil her evening. If he wanted to play nursemaid to Ambrosia Jewell, that was his business. She had her own life to live. As Tony put his arm around her and guided her into the house, she leaned against him and gave him a little squeeze. Tony walked her straight to the back of the house to the open patio directly outside his bedroom. He slid the double doors back, and motioned her outside.

"Take your clothes off. I'll be with you in a moment. I have to make a quick phonecall."

She was startled for a moment, and then she realized he was talking about the Jacuzzi on the patio. He activated the dials on the side of the whirlpool bath and disappeared inside the house. The night sky twinkled with stars, and the palm trees and tall cypresses stood out in graceful silhouettes among the mass of shrubbery that shaded the patio from view. Everything was absolutely peaceful and quiet, and Tracy hesitated for only a second. She shed her green linen dress, and stepped out of her lacy white teddy and high-heeled sandals.

Three tiled steps led down into the circle of swirling water, and she breathed a long sigh of relief as the hot, soothing waves enveloped her body. She sank into the pulsing water and closed her eyes. Several rooms away, she could hear Tony's voice as he carried on a short, intense conversation, and after a brief interval, she heard his footsteps as he padded to the back of the house. She smiled up at him as he crossed the patio, enjoying the sight of his slender body, so dark and inviting.

They floated side by side in the darkness for a few minutes. Only the gentle bubbling of the water broke the absolute stillness of the night. At last, Tony lifted one muscular arm and placed it lazily around her shoulders, drawing her close to his side. Their bare bodies touched silkily in the flowing water, and she let her head fall onto his shoulder, the dark, glossy waves spilling onto his chest. His hand began to massage her shoulder gently, and when she responded with a small, contented sigh, he turned her around and kneaded the upper part of her back.

"Why do you always know how to take such good care of me?" she murmured. This was his specialty, he told her. She should leave everything to Uncle Tony. His capable hands slid down to clasp her firm waist as he crouched over her, planting tiny kisses on the back of her neck. He continued holding her around the middle as her legs floated out in front of her, gently swaying in the moving water. She leaned against him, and she could feel his hardness growing as he pressed against the small of her back. Her hands reached down through the hot whirlpool to grasp his strong legs, and she stroked the muscular torso and all the masculine lines of him as he enclosed her in his long arms, exploring the deep valley between her breasts and flicking his fingers across her delicate nipples.

Then he centered himself against the back of the tub, and stretched his legs out underneath hers. The two pairs of legs locked and opened under the swirling water as he lifted her hips and placed her directly above him, positioning her carefully before lowering her onto his waiting body. He continued to move her hips up and down, the muscles in his arms rippling with the effort, and she swayed limply and helplessly in the water, anchored only by the strong thrusts that rooted him inside of her. He clasped her close as he perceived her mounting excitement, but he could not see her eyes open for a long moment as she gazed up at the stars with unmistakable wistfulness. Despite Tony's skillful ministrations, she could not shake the memory of two sharp, blue eyes from her mind, and even when her passion crested in dutiful response to Tony's expert maneuvers, she drifted back to reality with the lingering pain of Wes Canfield's broken promise planted firmly in her heart.

Chapter 19

THE TELEPHONE IN TONY AMATO'S HOUSE RANG AT nine o'clock the next morning, and Tracy answered it sleepily on the fourth ring. Tony had told her he had a five A.M. shooting, so she wasn't surprised to see that his side of the bed was empty.

"Hello," she said brightly, trying to disguise the sleep in her voice.

"Good morning," a smooth, husky voice answered, and Tracy realized with a start that it was Heather Gentree.

"Oh, hello—I—Tony isn't here right now, but—"

"I wasn't calling for Tony. I was calling you." The woman's radar was incredible. Tracy said nothing as Heather continued. "My chauffeur will be around in half an hour to pick you up and bring you over here. Have you had breakfast yet?"

"Well, no, I—"

"Good, we'll have breakfast on the terrace." She hung up the phone with a gentle click.

Tracy sat up in bed. That was no invitation; that was a command. Talk about the prerogatives of power! She scrambled out of bed and dressed quickly in yesterday's clothes, thankful that Tony had considerately hung her dress in the closet. He did so many little things that reflected his appreciation and understanding of women, and she couldn't help but feel grateful. She would never be in love with him, and he knew that without her telling him. He didn't care; he was happy to enjoy her company whenever she might be available, and he would never resent her moods or preoccupations. He was a rare friend.

The doorbell rang, and she forgot about Tony as she went to answer it. A uniformed chauffeur was standing on the porch. "Miss Bouchard?"

"Yes."

"This way, please." He led her outside to a stunning pre-1930 "Silver Ghost" Rolls Royce.

"It's like something out of *The Great Gatsby!*" she exclaimed, and the man smiled graciously as he helped her inside.

She settled against the plush, white leather seat and watched with interest as he started the vehicle and steered it onto the main road. She was seated high above the rest of the traffic in the sleek, jaunty vehicle, and she enjoyed the feeling as it rolled along. It was like being Queen for a Day, Tracy giggled to herself.

The chauffeur drove north into the most secluded residential part of Bel Air, and they passed palatial mansions, each more impressive than the one before. Some were in the Spanish style, with white stucco and red-tiled roofs; a few were traditionally colonial; some were starkly modern and one was a concoction of bubblegum-pink domes and towers.

The vintage automobile turned up a steep path that wound to the top of a grassy hill. A wrought iron gate flanked by lanterns and twin cypress trees stood at the end of the road, and a small booth that held a uniformed guard and an intercom system stood at one side. The guard stepped out, waved at the driver and then back inside the booth to activate the mechanism that opened the spiked gate. The doors swung forward noiselessly, and the car passed inside, winding up a smaller dirt road that was completely surrounded by a profusion of bright California shrubbery and flowers. At last, they came to the very pinnacle of the incline, and the road stopped at a wide expanse of lush, green grass. Several yards away from the end of the dirt path stood an imposing, gleaming white mansion with six Doric columns and two smaller porticos at each end. The dirt path changed to light gravel, and the deluxe vehicle crunched slowly up alongside the house. The scene reminded Tracy of a southern plantation, and it was not hard to imagine Scarlett O'Hara herself bursting out the front door. She stifled a giggle as the chauffeur led her to the nearest portico and rang the bell. A youthful butler opened the door and invited her inside as the chauffeur disappeared around the side of the house.

She followed the butler into the large, circular front hall, shining with polished wood. An ornate staircase wound its way to an upper level, but the butler led her down the hall and to the left, through a lavishly appointed parlor decorated in navy and sky-blue. The sun shone brilliantly through the tall colonial windows, casting glittering rays on the Chinese porcelain lamps. Several large oil paintings hung on the walls, and although some of them looked fleetingly familiar, Tracy barely had time to look at them as she trotted through an archway into another room, this one done in gilt and white, with touches of rose silk brocade and rosewood. She was going too fast to take everything in, but she caught flashes of a Viennese crystal chandelier, a row of family portraits and huge vases of freshly cut flowers. She was marched through room after dazzling room, and a parade of soft velvets, richly oiled woods, carefully papered walls, brilliantly crafted furniture, valuable paintings, sculptures and artifacts, and rare Indian cottons and Oriental weaves flew by as she walked.

Finally, they came to a rectangular terrace that was completely enclosed in spotless glass. Artfully arranged flowers and plants were organized into little islands, and a forest green carpet wove its way around them, cut precisely to fit the spaces. A circle of natural wicker and white satin chairs and couches stood in the center of the garden, surrounding a small, bubbling pool and three white marble tables. Heather Gentree was stretched out on one of the couches, her feet resting on a tiny embroidered footstool, her arm looped over the back. She was dressed in a white caftan with a heavy gold necklace and pearl teardrop earrings.

"Good morning," she said cheerfully, and she simultaneously nodded for Tracy to approach and for the butler to take his leave. He bowed and strode off in the other direction, and Tracy advanced into the circle of green and white.

"Good morning," she said, a little out of breath from her hike through the mansion. Tracy sank into a satin armchair.

"How nice to see you, my dear," Heather said coolly.

"I'm glad you invited me," Tracy replied. "You certainly have a lovely home."

"Thank you," Heather said perfunctorily. "Ah, here's the tea."

The butler had returned, wheeling a silver cart that held two covered plates, teacups, grapefruit halves and an English bone china teapot. He positioned the cart at Heather Gentree's right, placed the plates and grapefruit dishes on two of the marble tables and poured the tea ceremoniously.

"Thank you, Malcolm," Heather said, as the man bowed out of the room. She turned to her guest. "Sugar or milk?"

"No, thank you. Just lemon."

Tracy sipped her tea and examined the contents of her plate. It contained a delicate watercress omelette and two thin slices of Danish ham. The grapefruit half had been neatly sectioned, and she started on it with relish. Her evening with Tony had left her hungry. She watched as the older woman used a tiny, antique spoon to measure a pinch of sugar substitute into her tea, and Heather explained obligingly.

"It dates back to the thirteenth century. Court of Philip of Burgundy."

"It should be in a museum."

"Perhaps." The violet eyes crinkled. "But I get a sense of historic pleasure in using it here." Then, without pausing for a breath, she asked, "Are you comfortable in your new job?"

"Excuse me?"

Heather repeated the question and Tracy shrugged noncommittally.

"Sure. I love books, and I'm learning more every

211

day. And I've got one of the most exciting books around to work on right now."

"Ah, yes. Is Jim cooperating with you?"

Tracy wondered what Heather was driving at and answered as diplomatically as she could. "He's a pleasure to work with." She began to feel the conversation was taking on the aura of a third-degree interrogation. "He's an extraordinary man."

"How so?"

"Well, he really opens up when he's not on camera, and his mind is quick and flexible. He's committed to doing a good job on the book, and that's important." Heather's eyes studied her for a moment, and then Tracy turned the conversation around with a question of her own. "What were you doing with Carl Bendex that day I ran into you at the Four Seasons?"

Heather didn't flinch. "What do you know about Carl Bendex?" Her eyes bored into Tracy's as she sipped her tea calmly.

"He's a thief," Tracy said indignantly. "He bought the film rights for one of our books and undercut the unsuspecting author by almost half a million."

Heather smiled politely. "That half-million," she said, "was mine."

"It was?" Tracy was dumbfounded. "Yours? So you were the other buyer?"

Heather put her teacup down and faced Tracy squarely. "Carl Bendex is producing a film that should have belonged to me. I tried to buy back the rights, but Bendex refused, even when I offered him an exorbitant sum. And this kind of thing will keep happening until we uncover his silent partner. Somehow, Bendex always manages to know when a book with excellent dramatic possibilities is available. For all I know, he might have a string of spies planted in every publishing firm in New York. But I won't put up with these shenanigans in my company."

Tracy was shocked. "Your company?"

"Of course. I own a controlling interest in Franklin & Fields. It was something I more or less inherited from another deal that went sour, but nevertheless, it's mine."

"In that case, you're—well, that makes you my—"

"Boss. Yes, it does, doesn't it?" Heather chuckled. "But don't worry, my dear. I don't concern myself with day-to-day operations at F & F."

Tracy put down her fork. What did Heather want from her? Why had she been summoned for this royal audience? There was no reason for Heather to be telling her this unless . . . Tracy's stomach began to knot. To cover her fear and pain, she returned to the safer topic of Heather's involvement with F & F. "So, when you were trying to buy the film rights to *Year of the Dragon,* you were actually buying—"

"My own property, so to speak. It's a bit more complicated than that. My dear, I'm in the movie business, and anything that will further the success of my production company interests me. When F & F was offered to me, I bought it for the sole purpose of being able to get first crack at good potential film properties. I was planning to pay fairly for them, of course. It's not an uncommon strategy, and Franklin & Fields produces a lot of books that would make good movies. But Bendex has somehow infiltrated my domain."

And you think I'm the one who is feeding Bendex information at F & F, Tracy thought to herself. She wanted to ask Heather outright, but simply did not have the nerve. What would she do if Heather said yes? But, then, Heather Gentree was shrewd enough not to reveal her strategy. Even if she did ask, she wouldn't get a straight answer. Tracy pushed her plate away.

"Why, Tracy, you haven't finished your omelette. Is there something wrong? Something else I can get you?"

"No, no thank you. I've just had enough to eat. I'm not a big breakfast eater. It's quite delicious, though."

In the worst way, Tracy wanted to be out of there, back in the security of Tony's house, Tony's arms, anything to take away the awful fear in her gut. But Heather asked politely about her family and schooling, and Tracy, taking small sips of tea to brace herself, answered the questions.

Heather's interest seemed genuine enough. Maybe I'm making too much of this, Tracy thought. She seems to really like me. Nevertheless, Tracy was grateful when Malcolm announced Heather's next guest. Now that was power. Everyone came to Heather Gentree, she went to no one.

Tracy was shown through the house once more and helped into the silver Rolls Royce. She might have felt like a Queen for a Day on her way here, but now she felt like a wretched parlormaid who had been dismissed because the silver was missing. She rubbed her aching stomach. Please, let the thief be found, she prayed.

Chapter 20

Dear Tracy,

I'm sorry I missed you before you left for New
York, but the shooting lasted until two A.M. Good
news, though. I'll be in New York in a couple of
months or so. Then it will be your turn to show
me a good time. I heard this morning that Jim
Fleming has to come to New York some time
soon, and I thought you'd like to know. I'm sure
he'll be around to meet the crew at Franklin &
Fields. It was great seeing you again. Be good.

Love,
Tony

TRACY SAT AT HER DESK IN FRONT OF THE STACK OF
mail that had accumulated during her absence. She had
sorted through it and found Tony's note, opening it
before tackling the rest. The office was quiet, Tracy
the only staff member at her desk so early. Ah, Tony,
she sighed. Such a sweet, sweet man. But not *the* man.

Her trip to California had been sobering—the terrible fight with Wes, the breakfast with Heather Gentree. At least she had learned from Tony that F & F
would have got the Fleming book with or without her,
because Max Zwerdlow wanted it that way. But not
everyone knew that. Especially not her colleagues here.
Things may have turned out all right with the Fleming
book, but the way in which she had aided its acquisition left her vulnerable. She was under suspicion in the
matter of *Year of the Dragon,* and would remain so
until the culprit was found.

The only way she could swim against the tide was to work her tail off. And she would do that, work harder than she had ever worked in her life. Burying herself in her work would keep her mind off Wes, too. He wasn't the only man in the world. There would be others. Somewhere. Sometime.

By the time Tracy finished going through the mail, the office had begun to bustle. She heard the click of typewriters and the slamming of desk drawers as the editorial assistants arrived. The phones began to ring and Tracy knew the day had officially begun.

Dennis popped in to welcome her back. "Great to see you Tracy," he said cheerfully. "How come you're so early today?"

"Turning over a new leaf," Tracy said dryly. "Don't be surprised to find me here every morning."

Dennis raised his hands in mock horror and backed out the door. "I don't know what the world is coming to. Editors arriving before assistants. Unheard of!"

Tracy chuckled at his antics and turned to the stack of manuscripts that had been dropped on her desk. Dig we must, she thought, and picked up the box on top of the pile. She read ten pages and knew it was hopeless and put the box on the "to be rejected" shelf. The next two suffered the same fate. Dennis would return them with appropriate polite notes.

Enough of this for now. Tracy stretched her arms over her head and sighed. She reached for a yellow legal pad and was making a list of people she had to phone when Steve Kramer walked in.

He seemed genuinely surprised to find her at work so early, and she was equally surprised to see him. She remembered several mornings at Carey when he hadn't shown up until lunchtime. He wasted no time on preliminaries and asked, "Did he like our ideas?" Not a hello, not a good morning, just business.

"He loved your idea about dividing the chapters like acts in a play, and he's also amenable to getting old correspondence from the network files. He's written about a hundred more pages, but he's still a little nervous about it. I have the new section here and I

216

think it's terrific, but you and John can make a final decision on that."

"Good." Kramer remained cool and listened to her without betraying any emotion.

She gave him a few notes on the estimated length of the book and its tentative completion date. He still did not comment in any way. Tracy wished she could tell him the truth about Zwerdlow's decision to sell the Fleming book to F & F. She wanted to point out that he would never have been hired for his new job if the circumstances of the acquisition hadn't drawn attention to him. But she kept quiet. He would never believe her. Tracy consoled herself with the knowledge that the truth would be revealed eventually. It had to be.

"Do you have reports on the manuscripts I gave you before you left for L.A.?" He was outwardly casual, but couldn't hide his surprise when she handed him the memos. She had stayed awake on the red-eye flight from the coast, laboring over the dreary chore in the dim light to make sure it was completed in time.

Tucking the reports under his arm, he faced her and said, "Good. As you can see, you've got a few more to work on here. A few months of doing this, and you'll be able to spot a winner in your sleep."

"A winner? In the slush pile?"

"Yes, a winner. You've heard of Beverly Hawkins?"

Tracy nodded reluctantly, waiting for the onslaught.

"Her book was pulled out of the slush pile by an editor. It was on the bottom of a stack as high as the one on your desk. Now she's the biggest popular history writer in the country."

He looked at her pompously and she knew a lecture was coming.

"Two rooms down the hall is the biggest collection of unsolicited manuscripts in the city. This company has an obligation to review them, and I respect that obligation. Sitting in that room right now could be the next Hemingway or Mailer or Oates, but they won't be discovered unless we all pitch in once in a while and go through the pile. The assistants can't handle all of it. There's simply too much. They come in at a rate of a hundred a week. From now on, I want you to oversee the slush pile. Make sure that everything is read and that rejection letters are written and manuscripts returned to the authors with our thanks. I also want to see a full report of all the manuscripts you receive from agents, and a detailed memo on anything you want to buy before you present it at an editorial meeting."

She nodded congenially. "Okay, Steve, I'll have a complete report on these by Wednesday."

He stared at her with disbelief. "I didn't say to kill yourself. A week will be fine."

But she had them ready on Wednesday, as she had promised. It took her two late evenings and a severe curtailment of sleep, but the look on his face when she strolled in on Wednesday and plopped them on his desk made it all worthwhile. He didn't say a word, and she knew this was only the beginning. She had decided to match him point for point at whatever he might try. His demands on her had been tough, but she was determined to meet them all. He didn't want to read her reports any more than she wanted to write them, but she would ask him about them, and seek his advice. After a while she hoped the extra burdens would become an albatross to him, and he would back off.

But her new dedication to her job awakened a dormant force in her. She began to change, imperceptibly at first, as she threw herself into her work, and her devotion reached a new and fruitful plateau. There was a feeling of satisfaction and achievement in completing the routine tasks that had been assigned to her, and when the more pleasurable aspects of her job presented themselves, she turned to them with real joy. It wasn't unusual to find her burning the midnight oil at home or sitting up late in her office after the janitors had packed up and gone home.

Her reports became razor sharp and deadly accurate, and agents who submitted to her found their manuscripts read and returned within a week. When an agent finally sent her a book she really liked, she wrote a detailed, convincing report on it and sent it to Steve Kramer immediately.

"Not bad," he mumbled judiciously. "Not bad. *The New Hollywood.* He tapped the manuscript and looked up. "Do you have an exclusive look at this, or is it a multiple submission?"

She faltered. "I—I don't know."

As it turned out, the agent had sent the book to several other companies, and Tracy was outbid before she had a chance to get an offer together. "This will teach you to hustle the agent into giving you an exclusive look," Steve said later. "We can't spend two or three weeks getting our figures together just to find out we're competing with five other places. Find this out from now on. They don't always tell you."

Tracy was disappointed, but she resolved to be more alert next time. Sure enough, an agent called and told her about a book on Japan that sounded good, and she coaxed the man into letting her see it before anyone else. He agreed on the condition that she would read it within a week, and she did. She had her report to Kramer finished in three days and it went before the editorial board immediately. Everyone liked it, and Tracy was heartened. She was told to try and get the book for ten thousand dollars.

"It's a promising project," Kramer explained to her as he stood in the doorway of the conference room. "Japan is in the media a lot these days, and since it's the author's first book, he shouldn't expect a miracle. If the guy were better known, we'd pay at least twice as much, but all things considered, you should see if they'll settle for ten." He turned to talk to Stephen Marcus, and Tracy was left to ponder his words by herself. There was only one way to find out if the agent would go for it, and that was to ask.

She decided to get it over with right away, and she walked directly to her office and started dialing the phone. Despite Kramer's rationale, she had a suspicion that her offer was not going to be high enough, and that she was about to lose another book.

"Hold it, Bouchard." Jeff Conway's voice startled

her into dialing the wrong digit, and the receiver clattered into the cradle. "Have you ever done this before?"

She thought back to the day she had offered Max Zwerdlow one and a half million dollars for the Fleming book. "Well, no—uh, not really."

He closed the door and sat down, swinging his legs up onto her desk. "Okay, listen to me. We'll practice a few times and then you'll do it for real."

She smiled gratefully and nodded.

He clapped his hands together authoritatively, and asked, "Your ceiling is ten grand, right?" She nodded. "Okay, let's see. The book is about Japan, which is getting to be a hot topic. So don't talk about money at all. Focus on the inexperience of the author and on what a great job we'll do with it. Of course, the bottom line is always money, but not if you get to it last. Keep talking about everything else until he gets excited, and then hit him with the offer. He might go for it right up front. An offer is an offer. Just don't get too excited. If he can tell you're hot to trot, he'll aim for a higher price."

She nodded again, trying to take in everything Jeff was telling her. Suddenly, the whole thing seemed extremely complicated. She was supposed to act excited, but not too excited. She was supposed to focus on the negative points while pointing out what a great job she would do with the book. She wiped her palms on her lap, and then stopped abruptly when she saw Conway was watching. "Well," she said uncertainly, "I think I've got it."

"Like hell. Let's try it, you and me. You be you, and I'll be the agent."

"Okay," she said weakly.

"Who is the agent, anyway?"

"Joe Shane."

"Good. He's no pushover, but he's not a monster either. You can handle him."

Her confidence was beginning to assert itself. "I know I can."

"Great, let's start. Ring!"

They launched into an enactment of the imminent conversation, and Tracy found that everything she had been learning recently helped enormously. She realized that she actually knew what she was talking about, and she managed to corner Conway on a few points.

"That was good, Tracy," he said after they had pretended to hang up. "But next time, save your best arguments until the end. Now let's try it again." They ran through it a few more times, and then Tracy announced, "That's it. It's now or never." He sat back and watched as she picked up the phone.

"Joe Shane, please." Conway winked at her and she took a deep breath. "Hi, Joe. It's Tracy Bouchard. . . . Yes, I did, and that's why I'm calling. Well, we think it's a promising idea, and we've got some solid ideas on how it should be done. Of course, it's a little risky, since the author hasn't established himself yet as an authority on the subject, but we think that with our promotion and distribution, it will have a good chance." She paused as the agent answered her, and then she continued. "Yes, I know that Japan has been getting a lot of attention, but who knows if it will last? By the time the book comes out a year or so from now, interest may have waned. I understand that India is the next big topic. . . . Well, our interest is solid but cautious. We'd like to make you an offer of five thousand dollars." Conway's face tightened with expectation as he watched her. Her lips clamped together tensely as she listened to the argument on the other end. Obviously, the agent was telling her why the book was worth a lot more, and he was probably right. Tracy waited patiently, inserting a cool "Mm-hmm" every now and then, and she took up her end of the conversation smoothly, as if she had not been interrupted. "Of course, money is an important factor. We want to do the book right, which means a lot of color photos and prints and other expensive items. We feel it should be done lavishly or not at all. We're prepared to make a substantial investment in it, and we hope the author will respect our commitment to the book despite his strong interest in money." She sat back as the agent countered, and at last she heaved a long sigh. "Well, Joe," she said reluctantly, "I do see your point. And we'll stretch as far as we can reasonably afford to go. So I'll go up to seven thousand, five hundred dollars, but that's it." Conway sat up and listened with interest. If she could get away with only seven thousand, five hundred dollars, it would be a steal. Apparently, the agent was saying as much on his end. Suddenly, Tracy stood up, and she threw the pen she had been jiggling nervously onto the desk. She cut the agent short as she said firmly, "Okay. Eight thousand, five hundred dollars, and that's my final offer. My hands are tied. I'm already over my limit, but I think I can get it through. I'll bring it up at the meeting this afternoon, and I promise to call you as soon as I know for sure. But I *think* they'll go for it. Everyone here is excited about the book, so I think I can swing it. Will you let me try for the eight thousand, five hundred dollars?" There was a short pause. "Good. I'll get back to you this afternoon. She hung up and Conway jumped up and grabbed her hand, shaking it enthusiastically.

"That was terrific!" he shouted.

"I still have to negotiate the rest of it," she reminded him, "but I'm over the hump. And I have the rest of the day to practice. I can't call him back until after our imaginary meeting this afternoon." She giggled happily, and he opened the door.

"Congratulations," he said warmly.

She waltzed down the hall to Kramer's office and told him she had just bought the book for eight thousand, five hundred dollars.

Kramer looked up with surprise. "Eighty-five hundred? And Joe Shane was the agent? Good work, Tracy."

"Thanks, Steve." Tracy beamed. She had done good work and Kramer had acknowledged it. This was a banner day. She fairly skipped back to her office, stopping along the way to pick up a new pile of unsolicited manuscripts.

Tracy had learned to accommodate the task with

uncommon efficiency. She had devised a system that organized the endless stream of manuscripts into six major groups. Each group was represented by its own standard rejection letter, and the six letters were fairly long and quite helpful. The poetry letter included a list of small journals and quarterlies that the author could try; the autobiography letter explained why the lives of ordinary people did not always share universal meaning; and the special topics letter pointed out sensibly that despite the author's passion, not many people were likely to buy books on marigolds or flintlock rifles. The other three letters addressed themselves to novels, since most of the slush pile was fiction. They dealt with common problem areas in novels, and managed to sound fairly specific.

She also had the reading down to a science. After the first two or three pages, she skipped to the middle, scanning it briefly. Then she would skip to the end. If at any time the manuscript failed to hold her interest, she would give up on it immediately. Her reports to Kramer became crisp and uniform, a whole week's reading summarized on two or three pages, as most of the submissions required only a line or two of explanation.

During the next several weeks, Tracy successfully negotiated the contract for a promising first novel. She and Dennis whittled the slush pile job down to a speedy mass production system that took less and less of their time, but she continued to stick to the task faithfully. Her days took on a pleasant routine and she worked hard from day to day, without undue ambition. Her hostilities and penchant for rebellion subsided.

She found an ally in Jeff Conway, who treated her like a favorite younger sister. Jeff had confided to her that he was tired of always being a wise guy. He found it refreshing and a great relief to shed his hustler image and find someone who looked up to him and relied on his expertise. As their friendship grew, Tracy saw the benevolent side of Jeff expand. And she had someone she could trust with her questions without feeling ignorant or vulnerable.

Stephen Marcus always had a friendly word for her, and she respected him enormously. So did everyone else, of course, so her attitude was not remarkable. Ken and Shiela ignored her the way they ignored everyone else. They were too busy with the mutual admiration society they had formed to pay much attention to anyone else in the company. Martha Hauptmann remained friendly and concerned, offering advice and asking Tracy's opinion now and then. She sometimes gave Tracy promising manuscripts she didn't have time for, but so far none of them had panned out for Tracy.

Tracy worked diligently, finding pleasure in the work for its own sake, and one rainy afternoon an unexpected plum fell into her lap. She was going mechanically through the slush pile with her usual dizzying speed, when she came across a manuscript that caught her eye. It was called *Louisiana Legacy,* and it was the true story of a southern belle, Georgina Montague, who had been a spy for the Confederate government during the Civil War. The book traced Georgina's illustrious family to Belinda Caruthers, a prominent Manhattan socialite living on Sutton Place, only about ten blocks from the Franklin & Fields building. It was nonfiction, but it read like a novel, and Tracy found herself enthralled after the first few pages. She kept on reading, and she didn't stop until she had finished it. It seemed too good to be true. She checked the author's name and address, and learned from the cover letter that the book had been written by one Maxine Wilkins, a housewife in Iowa who had never written a word before. She had done meticulous research, and had traveled to New Orleans to authenticate her claims about the Montague family.

Tracy finished reading at six-thirty, and was startled by a knock on her door. It was Steve Kramer. For the first time in weeks, she had not delivered the slush pile reports to him, and he wondered what had held her up.

"How are things going with you?" he asked, surprisingly amiable.

She blinked and said nothing, pointing dramatically to the manuscript in front of her.

"Any good?"

"It's fabulous. It's called *Louisiana Legacy,* and I can't put it down. Needs a little work, but I love it. I think we may have a winner here."

She found that he was genuinely pleased. "Who's the agent?"

"No agent. It was written by a housewife out in Iowa. It's her first book."

"Slush pile?"

She nodded wordlessly, and he was quiet for a moment.

She looked at him. "After forty-three autobiographies, seventy-two poetry collections, eight novels about the life of a dog, twelve *Jaws* rip-offs and two hundred and twenty supremely boring and badly-written novels, I think I've found something." She waved the manuscript in the air and he took it from her, examining it closely.

"Not bad," he muttered as he flipped the pages. "Looks like it's nicely written."

"It is."

"Needs some editing, no doubt. Probably cut it down to—" He stopped short. "Belinda Caruthers!" He turned to the end of the book and read rapidly, his eyes widening. "Well, I'll be damned." Throwing the manuscript down on the desk, he asked, "Do you know who Belinda Caruthers is?"

"She's some sort of jet-setter?"

"That, my dear, is an understatement. She is only the greatest party-giver since Elsa Maxwell. The White House uses her as a consultant when they entertain. If she gets involved in the publication of this book—"

Tracy interrupted him eagerly. "It will become a social event!"

They stared at each other excitedly, and Tracy was elated. At last, they had something they could share. A truce could finally be declared.

"Let me read it tonight," he said. "If it's as good as you say it is, we'll make an offer on it right away. You can skip the report on this one."

Tracy bought the book on Friday even though she had some trouble convincing John Noble. He wanted concrete proof of the author's credentials and the book's authenticity, and he also wanted a firm commitment from Belinda Caruthers. But Tracy was afraid to alert the author to the book's dynamic possibilities, worrying that the woman would take the book elsewhere to stimulate competition. And Belinda Caruthers was cagey, refusing to make any commitment until she was sure that the book was of high quality, and that the publisher would give it full support. Tracy presented these arguments lucidly and with great conviction, and Steve Kramer backed her up all the way. Finally, Noble agreed to let her have the book, as long as she could get it cheap.

She did.

Maxine Wilkins was thrilled, and Tracy patiently explained to her what the next steps would be. "After the book is edited, we'll see what kind of excitement we can drum up. A lot of that will depend on how much Belinda Caruthers is willing to cooperate. If there's enough interest in the book before it is actually published, we'll have an auction for the paperback rights." The author was confused, and Tracy elaborated, "We will publish the book in hardcover, but we don't publish paperback books. Instead, we sell the privilege to another company that does. We will send the manuscript to all of the paperback houses, and we will let them bid against each other for the right to reprint the book as a paperback. The one that offers the most money gets the book. We will retain half of that amount, and you will get the other half. Sometimes, these auctions can run into very high figures, and you might find that we owe you a lot of money."

Maxine Wilkins agreed to everything readily, and Tracy edited the book in record time. Before she was finished, she asked opinions and advice of everyone in

226

the company, and her thoroughness had a good effect. Soon, everyone at Franklin & Fields knew about *Louisiana Legacy,* and everyone was interested in its progress.

One of the key people involved was Katie Molloy in the publicity department, who had to gauge just how much attention the book could get and whether or not they could count on Belinda Caruthers to help them. She and Tracy had several strategy meetings in Katie's colorful office. Katie was short and plump, with a mop of curly, brown hair, and she brought effervescent enthusiasm along with careful experience to her job. They decided they would send Belinda a B.O.M.—a set of first galleys cut and bound like a book with a paper cover—so it would look more official. It was also Katie's job to arrange television and radio appearances for the author, and for Belinda, if she were agreeable.

Tracy and Katie spent a lot of time together, and they became good friends. One evening, they were sitting on the floor admiring the view from Tracy's window and drinking Sambucca, when Katie discovered one of Tracy's sore spots.

"John Noble is a good administrator," Katie was saying, "but he's not as dynamic as Wes Canfield was." Tracy shifted uncomfortably, and tried to look unconcerned. No one at F & F knew about her involvement with Canfield, and she wanted to keep it that way. Katie was a friend, but this was too juicy a morsel of gossip to reveal. "Of course," Katie went on, "Canfield isn't doing so well himself these days."

"Oh, really?"

"I hear he's been working twenty hours a day, but he's not cutting it. Apparently, his financial backers would rather take a loss that they can write off than risk a lot of money up front on a book."

"I never thought of him as a tax write-off." Tracy laughed nervously. "He said in Paris that the backers were very enthusiastic, but I—"

Katie sat up sharply, comprehension flooding her face. "That's right!" she exclaimed. "You were in Paris the same time he was!" Tracy squirmed and Katie smiled knowingly. "Okay, you don't have to say anything. I think I get the picture. You like him."

Tracy sighed. "I did."

"Oh, I see. And now?"

"Now—I really don't care how he makes out. It's not my affair."

"Have you talked to him?"

"Not lately. How do you know all this about him?"

"From his new secretary. She used to work in our department."

"Well, she ought to keep her mouth shut," Tracy reflected with some anger.

Katie chuckled, patting her friend on the shoulder. "Ah, Bouchard, I think you do care."

"Let's just say I'm curious. What else did the blabbermouth say?"

Katie moved in closer. "Well, the problem is money—what else? He simply can't pay for the big books, and he keeps losing them. He tried to get *Year of the Dragon* from us, and Noble did everything he could to get him the book, but in the end, Canfield couldn't come up with the money. His backers are too conservative. They don't understand the book business, and he's stuck without a strong lead title for his debut."

"So what is his lead title?"

"That's just it. He doesn't have one yet. He doesn't have anything that will get any real attention. If he doesn't get something by the end of the year, he may well be out of business."

Tracy listened with half an ear as Katie chattered on. She thought about Paris, and the things he had confided to her about his hopes and dreams. What would happen to him if his venture failed? Of course, he could always get another job, work for another company. But that wasn't what he wanted. He had a driving need to succeed on his own level, by his own standards, and she understood this more than she liked to admit—because she had the same kind of personal drive. Deep down, she knew it was one of the things that had drawn them together.

But there was no point in dwelling on that now. He had too much on his mind to bother with her. That much was clear. One of the things on his mind had to be Ambrosia Jewell, and Tracy wanted no part of his part-time affection.

Chapter 21

Mrs. Maxine Wilkins
282 South Fork Road
Des Moines, Iowa 54880

Dear Maxine,

I can't tell you how pleased I am with the final revisions of LOUISIANA LEGACY. It's going to be a great book, and we're planning a major ad campaign for it. Belinda Caruthers is excited about it too, because she mentioned it to someone at a party recently, and it got written up in the next day's society column. There is little doubt now that she will be involved in the promotion, and we will probably auction the book before publication. Our hope is that Belinda will throw one of her famous parties in honor of the book, and if so, we hope you will be able to come. We are all anxious to meet you, and Katie Molloy, the publicist working on the book, wants to line up some TV spots for you. She says that the *Today Show* is interested. Of course, they will have to see the book first, but it looks good. I understand about your wanting some time off. You deserve it. Have a wonderful time with your family, and I'll be in close touch.

Cordially,
Tracy Bouchard

"TRACY?"

"Yes, Dennis?"

"This just came for you by messenger." He handed her a small, sealed envelope with her name on it.

"Thanks. Here's something for you." She gave him a memo that had been sent to her. "You might like to read this. It explains some of the changes in the editorial policy this year." She wanted him to have all the training she had never got from Kramer. Fresh out of college, Dennis had been her first choice as an assistant because of his bright, eager-beaver attitude, and he repaid her generosity with a loyalty beyond question. Sometimes, he seemed like an adoring puppy dog, but he worked hard and had good ideas. He was thrilled just to be near the Fleming book, and he had treated the recent correspondence with Marcel Aubert with reverence. Tracy was anxious to give him every opportunity, and gave him interesting chores that would provide useful experience, or delegated some of her growing workload to him. He accepted these offerings gratefully, applying himself diligently and learning as much as he could.

Tracy was now very busy, and her work had grown in importance. Kramer had finally thrown in the towel about making her read the slush pile, but she kept a sharp lookout for promising books among the reports written by the assistants. She knew there might be another *Louisiana Legacy* tucked away somewhere, and she didn't want to miss it if it did materialize.

She had earned a place for herself as an accepted member of the team. The cold glances and unspoken suspicion had stopped, except for occasional pointed references to *Year of the Dragon* from Sheila or Ken. Tracy still cringed every time the book was mentioned, but she learned to brush it aside. There was nothing else she could do, and to try and discuss it would only bring more attention to the one subject she dearly wanted to bury. For all she knew, Ken or Sheila could be the thief, and their antics were a way of covering up.

So she learned that hard work and less talk were really her best allies, and she moved along at a steady pace. Three more books had been added to her list— an Oriental cookbook by a famous Japanese chef, a long novel about an Irish family and another novel about the life of a ballerina.

Tracy tore open the envelope Dennis had handed her and took out a small, folded note and a ticket. The ticket was for a private box at the ballet that evening. The hand-written note contained a single line. "See you there, love." There was no signature, and she checked the envelope and the other side of the note, but there wasn't a clue.

Tracy fingered the ticket. No, it couldn't be. He wouldn't have the nerve. If Wes Canfield wanted to see her, he could pick up the telephone and apologize for his inexcusable behavior. Tracy's heart began to beat rapidly and she grasped the ticket at each end, starting to tear it in two. Then she stopped. Katie had told her Wes was cutting the week short to attend a meeting with his backers' representatives in Montreal. He wasn't even in town. Tracy let the ticket slip through her fingers and stared at it as it lay on the top of her desk.

Well, maybe she did have a secret admirer. She was genuinely intrigued. Since returning from California, she had done virtually nothing but work. She had gone out to visit Kippy a couple of times on the weekend, but otherwise her social life had come to a standstill. Could it be the agent she had bought the ballerina novel from? Maybe he was more interested in her than he had let on. Or Jeff Conway, trying to slip out of his big brother role?

There was only one way to find out. Tracy glanced at her watch. It was nearly five o'clock. She'd run home and change before hopping a cab down to Lincoln Center. The idea of a surprise escort amused her more and more, and she left her office in high spirits, planning a light meal and a bath before dressing for the ballet.

It had been a long time since Tracy had been home this early. This is like a marvelous, unexpected vacation, she thought. She soaked luxuriously in a hot tub scented with Coriandre, pondering the identity of her mystery companion and debating what to wear. The secrecy of the occasion seemed to demand a lavish presentation, and she decided on a pink-and-lavender-splashed Luciano Soprani dress she had bought on sale at the Lina Lee Boutique in Beverly Hills. It had seemed an extravagant purchase at the time, but now she was glad she had indulged herself. The dress had a simple, sleeveless bodice that sank into a deep, graceful oval, and the purple, wide-sashed waist gave way to a flowing tulle skirt that fell slightly below her knees. When Tracy was growing up, it was called ballerina length. Her sisters had worn dresses like this to their proms. And now this up-dated version was the perfect dress to wear for the phantom of the ballet. Let's hope he doesn't look like Lon Chaney, she thought, giggling.

After her bath, Tracy slipped into pale lavender, lacy tap pants and a matching camisole. The feel of the elegant garments against her supple, perfumed skin sent small shivers of delight through her. She applied a pale pink foundation and heightened it with wine-colored eye shadow, blusher and lipstick. The effect was dramatic, yet warm and inviting. Then she bent over at the waist and brushed her long hair up from the nape of the neck. When she stood up, it was full and shining, framing her face like a soft mane. She stepped carefully into her dress and high-heeled lavender sandals and surveyed the results in her full-length mirror. Whoever joins me in the box will be pleasantly surprised, she thought.

The cab sped downtown, and her excitement mounted. It was only the beginning of the evening and she could hardly contain herself. When she handed the gold ticket to the caped usher inside the Metropolitan Opera House, she looked for a familiar face. But the crowd streamed inside, and no one stopped to greet her.

Tracy had never been in a parterre box before. The exclusive boxes were on the first level above the orchestra, and they were enclosed on three sides. She reached the designated box by walking down a carpeted hallway and finding a door with a corresponding number. An usher opened the door for her, and she found herself in a small anteroom where she was able to hang up her shawl and fix her hair before sitting down. The box itself contained two comfortable gilt chairs that faced the stage. It was separated from its neighbors by a partition, making Tracy feel as if she were at a private performance. The American Ballet Theater would be dancing just for her and her mystery companion.

Checking her watch, she saw that it was ten minutes to eight. Her mystery escort still had not arrived and she began to feel nervous, watching the door every few minutes to see if it would open. She was still alone when the famous snowflake chandeliers began to rise slowly to the gold-encrusted ceiling of the theater. She anxiously smoothed her dress and glanced back at the door one last time before the lights dimmed. Disappointed, she sat back to watch the ballet.

The conductor entered and took a bow, and the audience applauded. As he raised his baton to begin, the door behind Tracy opened noiselessly and a man slipped into the parterre box. As he took the seat next to her, she turned and stared at him.

It was Wes. He nodded slightly, smiling with an air of cool confidence. She was furious. How dare he? Did he think he could command her to appear at his whim? He disappeared for weeks at a time, courted his precious Ambrosia, and then he expected her to jump as soon as he snapped his fingers. Besides, he was supposed to be in Montreal. He moved his chair closer to hers, and she turned away as the music started and the curtain rose. The stage was bathed in blue light, and two dancers swayed together as the music swelled to a crescendo. Tracy kept her eyes glued to the stage.

More dancers twirled onto the stage, and the music surged around their sinuous movements. Tracy was concentrating on the maneuvers of the prima ballerina when she felt his hand grasp her knee. What on earth did he think he was doing? She tried to move her leg away, but he held her firmly, tightening his grip. Fighting him would only increase his determination, so she sat motionless, staring straight ahead. Her eyes widened as Wes slid his hand very slowly under the gently flowing skirt, stroking the bare skin under the soft fabric ever so lightly.

She turned to him, hissing in a sharp whisper. "Stop it! What do you think you're doing?"

He didn't answer, but continued his maddening journey up her leg. She didn't want to make any noise or create a scene, and tried to turn away from him again. If she jumped up or pushed him away, it would only draw attention to them. His hand began to rub softly, tickling the underside of her knee, and she found to her horror that she was responding. Her eyes closed as his hand stole its way up her inner thigh, and her hands gripped the side of the chair as she fought to maintain control. The strokes against the silky flesh were long and tender, and she began to rock with a slight, involuntary movement as her lips parted, letting her breath come in small, inaudible gasps.

The stage lights darkened, leaving them in deep shadow, and the sonorous music swept over her. His hand had moved to the very top of her leg, and she parted her thighs slightly to give him room. He teased her for a moment, flicking his hand across to the other thigh and then back again, and she let out a brief, soft, "Oh!" "Shhh!" he murmured sharply, letting his hand settle lightly between her legs. His finger rotated almost imperceptibly, but its effect was like lightning. Tracy lost all sense of time and place as she opened to him, and he continued the tiny, maddening strokes until she thought she would break apart.

The ballet came to a sudden end, and he withdrew his hand abruptly, applauding politely as the dancers took curtain calls and the conductor left the pit. She was out of breath and limp with desire. The house lights came up as people all around them stood up to stretch during the intermission.

Wes took her hand. "Come on," he said quietly. His face was full of urgency, and she did not stop to argue. They left the parterre box rapidly, and walked down the red-carpeted stairway to the entrance to the theater. They swung through the revolving door, walked quickly across the plaza, and he opened the door of the nearest waiting cab. Tracy almost fell inside, and he slammed the door and gave the driver his address. She leaned against him, her hands aggressively gripping his thighs, rubbing his chest, and pulling his head down to meet hers. They kissed, fiercely and longingly, as the cab sped uptown, and they did not stop or exchange a single word until the cab stopped in front of Wes's building. He threw the driver a bill, and they jumped out of the taxi and ran inside. They stood impatiently in the elevator, surrounded by other tenants, but as the doors opened on the eighteenth floor, Wes grabbed her hand and led her briskly down the hall to his apartment.

She did not get more than a glimpse of the interior in the dim light, but followed him breathlessly down the hall to his bedroom. At last, they stopped rushing, and as Wes turned on the lamp next to the bed, Tracy finally spoke.

"What are you doing to me?" she demanded weakly.

"Loving you," he answered, and she was too surprised to speak. He walked to her and began to undress her like a child. Her passion returned at his touch, and she helped him along as he let her dress drop to the floor and reached for the lacy underwear he had touched only minutes before. She fell back onto the bed, the curves of her body glimmering in the lamplight, and he stepped out of his own clothes. Then they were together, tracing slow, sensual lines across each other's flesh, their mouths meeting again and again with increasing abandon, and their responses lost in a tide of swiftly growing fever. Tracy's mouth sought every inch of his hard, lean body, and she saw that his blue eyes followed her movements with candid enjoyment. She felt like a lioness and she wanted the feeling to last forever. She abandoned herself to the gigantic wave of feeling in her, and wondered how she could have gone so long without his fiery touch.

He rose suddenly and pinned her shoulders to the bed, leaving a trail of long, teasing kisses on her neck. Her sloping breasts strained upwards to meet him, and he complied willingly, nuzzling the soft contours of each one. His lips traveled down the length of her body, and then he turned her over and worked his way back up again, moving with a slow, deliberate pace that left her dizzy and whimpering for him to continue. She could no longer bear his torturous attentions and swung around to face him, her golden eyes wild with passionate determination. She pulled his body over hers, but he only dove down again, swinging his legs around and burying his head between her thighs. They devoured each other until she was shaken by tight, clenching waves, and then at last he was inside of her, his body filling hers even before she had stopped trembling.

Tracy felt like a small boat in a fantastic storm—tossing and rolling in the waves under a magnificent sky of many colors. She lost all sense of where her tingling body ended and his began. They melted together to become a single entity, moving with a timeless rhythm that lifted them into another dimension. When their imaginary boat finally capsized, leaving them in a warm, suddenly calm sea, she opened her eyes to find that tears had left their marks on her cheeks. His face was pressed close to hers, mingling his tears with her own. They lay silently for several minutes, exchanging little kisses and small caresses, and then their desire claimed them again. He did not tease her this time. They joined firmly and slowly as she lay on one side with a leg thrown over him. Tracy gazed into the startling blueness of his eyes and saw her passion reflected in them.

Their tender exchange lasted far into the night, until they lay utterly spent in each other's arms. Tracy fell into a light doze, her body curled into an arc, her head resting lightly against his shoulder. She could not tell if a minute or an hour had passed, but a rousing sensation was calling her from deep in the blackness of sleep, and she responded to it naturally, moving slightly as it grew stronger. It might have been a pleasant dream or it might have been reality, until the firm thrust of his body opened her eyes, expanding her and demanding release once again. She reacted with a

237

startled cry of pleasure as his arms went around her from behind, holding her closely against him. One strong hand lingered on her torso, and the other one moved down to awaken her most sensitive spot as he continued to rock back and forth. Once again, they were lost in a dream world, peaking sleepily and languidly before falling back down from the clouds. Tracy turned and cuddled against him, her arm spanning his supple chest, and he reached over and turned out the light.

Chapter 22

THE SMELL OF FRESHLY BREWED COFFEE AWAKENED her from the most peaceful sleep she had had in months. She could hear Wes out in the kitchen cooking up something that crackled occasionally, sending tantalizing aromas drifting down the hall to the bedroom. She sniffed expectantly and sat up against the pillows, looking around the room. It was obviously a man's room, but it had many small, personal touches that made it uniquely his.

The room was carpeted in rich chocolate brown, and the down comforter was covered with stark, geometric brown and tan stripes. Hazy light filtered through the ivory-colored drapes that covered the entire wall to her left. On the night table, there was a small statue of Isis, the Egyptian goddess of fertility. Isis shared the table with a carved ivory unicorn. Photographs of turn-of-the-century New York lined one wall, and a large, potted fern stood in a brass vase in the corner. A framed black and white photo of Wes and his mother stood on the dresser, watching over the room.

She was still rubbing the sleep from her eyes when he walked in carrying a tray loaded with dishes.

"Breakfast is served, mademoiselle," he announced cheerfully.

She looked at him and began to giggle, falling back against the pillows.

"What, may I ask, is so funny?" he demanded.

"You. That outfit," she said, pointing.

He was wearing a pair of cut-off sweat pants and an old rugby shirt. "What's wrong with it?"

"Nothing," she said, sobering. "I guess I've just never seen you like this."

"It's what I wear around the house sometimes. But I assure you, it was designed by Christian Dior."

"Oh, I knew it looked familiar. Actually, it looks kind of sexy."

"Good," he said with mock arrogance, putting the tray, with its covered plates, down on the bed.

"Scrambled eggs, Italian sausages and scones."

"Sounds delicious."

He walked over to the window and pulled the drapery cord, saying, "Let's have a little sunlight."

Tracy peered towards the window and gasped aloud at the overwhelming view. They were on Central Park West and Seventieth Street, and an ocean of autumn colors was stretched out below them. It created a wonderfully peaceful feeling, as if they were floating high above a forest. The sounds of the city were masked from that height, and the only noise came from an occasional gust of wind.

"Oh, Wes," Tracy exclaimed. "What a stunning view. You can watch the seasons change from your own room. It must be wonderful to wake up and look out at the park every morning."

"I'd rather wake up and look at you," he said, moving back to the bed and taking her in his arms. "I missed you, Tracy. And I'm very sorry about what happened in Paris and California. I. . . ."

Tracy put a finger to his lips. "Let's not talk about it. It's in the past." She leaned in and kissed him deeply.

"Okay," he murmured. "What shall we talk about?"

"Business." Tracy sat up, reached for the plates on the tray and removed their covers, the pungent aroma of the sausage tickling her nose. She handed one of the plates to Wes.

Wes laughed and shook his head. "You don't fool around, Bouchard. That's why I like you."

Tracy brought him up to date on her progress at F & F.

"So it sounds like you're doing okay," he said.

"You sound so off-hand about it."

"It's just that I always had confidence in you. You know how to get what you want."

Tracy turned away slightly, but he caught her look of self-satisfaction. "But I'm afraid modesty was never one of your virtues," he added dryly.

"No," she admitted. "Or patience. Speaking of which, I'm anxious to hear how it's going with you."

"Not well," he answered candidly. "My backers seem to be more interested in me as a tax write-off than as a source of profit. I've given up trying to understand it. I've got too much else on my mind."

"I'm surprised," she answered truthfully. "I remember how enthusiastic they were in Paris."

"I know," he sighed, "but they don't understand the ins and outs of this business. They don't understand the kinds of risks you have to take. I've tried to explain it a million times in a million ways but they don't—or won't—get it."

She studied him for a moment with sympathetic eyes, wondering what to say. He caught her gaze, and smiled ruefully.

"All I need is one really strong book," he said, punching the mattress in frustration. "But if I can't pay for them, I can't get them. I've lost two already that I should have had, but my backers wouldn't authorize the large advances. At the last minute, I had to back out, and if this goes on much longer, it will be all over. I didn't foresee, this happening when we signed the contract."

"I can't believe it."

"It's true. I'm a potential tax gain. Frankly, I don't think they care. They dole out a certain amount to invest in me, and if it doesn't work out this way, they make it work out another way. Even the unsold books sitting in a warehouse can be used as a deduction after I'm out of business."

She took his hand and held it between both her own. "Something will come up," she said softly. "You'll think of something." He turned sideways, resting his head in her lap, and she wound his black curls around

241

her fingers. "You know, the book I found in the slush pile is going to be auctioned soon."

"Louisiana Legacy?"

"Why don't you call in early and see if you can't get a fast look at it?"

He sat up, interested. "Why don't you send me a copy?"

"But it's not ready yet."

"I don't care. Let me see what you've got."

"All right, I will," she agreed, pulling him back down to her lap. "I'll bring a copy down to you on Monday." She knew that was unnecessary. All she had to do was call a messenger. But it was an excuse to see him again.

"No, I won't be in all next week. But send it down, and they'll forward it to me."

"Where are you going?"

"Montreal. I'm going to plead once again for more money. My backers have representatives there. I was supposed to go yesterday morning, but they called and changed it, so I'm leaving this afternoon."

"Today?" She tried to hide her dismay. "Then you're going to throw me out, I see."

He reached up and kissed her. "Stay as long as you like. Just make sure the door is locked before you leave."

"When will you be coming back?"

"Well, I'm not sure. It will depend on their response."

She pouted a little. "Oh."

"Hey, now," he chided her. "Trust me. I'm in the middle of a business crisis. If this doesn't work out, I may be looking for handouts on the street."

She saw he was serious, and she tried to take his mind off of it by changing the subject. "You're still remembered fondly at Franklin & Fields. Your name came up during the editorial meeting last week. We were talking about *Year of the Dragon,* and Ken Maguire said he wished you had got it in the auction."

"Oh, did he? Dear old Ken."

Tracy looked away. "I'm positive he still thinks I'm

242

the person who smuggled the book out of the company. And, of course, his friend Sheila thinks so, too." She sighed. "It's hard putting up with that all the time."

He turned her face to his and planted a kiss on her nose. "Don't let them get to you. I could tell you stories about them that would make them blush."

She jumped on him at once, demanding, "Oh, tell me everything!"

He chuckled and put his arm around her. "Well, Ken is probably just jealous of you. He tried to do what you did, with much less success. He worked at Hennessey House before I hired him, and their top author is Jane Sheraton. He came to see me, swearing that he could bring her over to F & F if I hired him, and of course I was interested."

"So what happened?"

"Jane Sheraton wasn't interested, and she was shocked he had used her name so freely. Hennessey House fired him, and he came whining to me."

"So why did you hire him?"

He shrugged. "He's a good editor. He just tried a little too hard, and it backfired. I understand why *they* had to fire him, but that didn't mean *I* had to punish him."

"I had no idea," she said slowly, absorbing this new piece of information. "What a relief. Now tell me something nasty about Sheila."

He grinned. "That's not hard to do. Sheila was sleeping with half the staff at her last job, and she got caught screwing the publicity director's husband. The woman threw a tray of hors d'oeuvre at her."

"My God! Where were they?"

"At a party in the woman's house."

"You mean they were having an affair right there in her home, under her nose, in the middle of a party?"

"On top of all the guests' coats on the bed. It was wonderful."

"You were there?"

"Oh, yes. It created quite a stir."

"Then why did you hire *her*?"

"Same reason—she's a good editor. And I believe in

243

a little notoriety. Anyway, I knew I wasn't interested in her, and Ken Maguire is gay, Conway hadn't been hired yet, Steve Marcus is a family man and John Noble is happily married. So I knew she would have thin pickings under our roof."

Tracy laughed ecstatically. "I never knew this. Tell me about someone else. Kramer! What about Kramer?"

"I don't know him. You worked with him."

She sighed. "I guess he's okay, really. I just wish he'd believe that about me. And I hope one day they discover who the spy is."

"Don't worry so much about Kramer. You're doing fine. Just get me that manuscript of *Louisiana Legacy,* and maybe I'll be doing as well."

He took off the rugby shirt and threw it on the bed. She watched the muscles ripple in his arms and a wave of longing swept over her. She wanted him more than she had ever wanted anything in her life. But one obstacle stood between them. "Wes," she said hesitantly, "I know I said we shouldn't talk about it, but I have to ask."

"What?" he asked, his eyes boring through her.

She took a deep breath. "Ambrosia."

He sat down next to her and looked at her seriously. "She's a very sensitive woman, and there's nothing for you to be upset about."

A look of regret crossed her face. "But are you involved with her?" It cost Tracy something to have to ask that, and she felt a small knot of desperation growing inside of her.

He didn't answer for a moment. "We're friends," he said at last. "Very good friends." Then he stood up again. "And that's the end of that subject."

She was hurt. It was hardly a satisfactory answer. Before she could stop herself, she blurted out. "Okay, I won't ask. But don't ask me about Tony, either."

He stopped for a split second, a glint of curiosity in his eye. "I'm not asking," he said. He slipped out of the cut-offs and walked naked from the room.

The little knot of desperation grew as she stared

out the window at the peaceful view. Why did she always jump in and ruin everything? Why couldn't she be patient? He would have told her about Ambrosia when he was ready. Wes returned from the bathroom, freshly shaven and with a towel knotted around his waist. She watched him sadly as he packed a leather suitcase, organizing ties and belts and socks, feeling that he was slipping away from her, and not knowing how to draw him back. He seemed unaware of her as he dressed and prepared for his important trip. Neither of them spoke, and he was ready to leave before she knew it.

Now he looked like the Wes Canfield she had first met—a handsome, dynamic businessman in a trim, gray, pinstripe suit. She held out her arms and he sat on the edge of the bed. Tracy held him close and kissed him goodby.

"Good luck," she whispered into his ear.

He kissed her again. "Thanks. I'll call you when I get back." He picked up the suitcase and turned to leave.

"Wes?" Her voice sounded weak, but she had to know. "Why did you send me that ballet ticket?"

He smiled carelessly and shrugged. "I don't know. Maybe I wanted to see you." He blew her a kiss and was gone. She heard the click of the front door as he left.

Tracy leaned her head against the pillows, feeling the absolute silence envelop her. Wes was gone and she was back at Square One. She lay in the bed for a long while, the sheets fragrant with the special smell of their lovemaking. And now she was alone. She had no idea when—or if—she would see him again.

She forced herself to get out of bed and took a long, hot shower. The smell of his aftershave lingered in the bathroom, and even the soap and scalding water could not wash the smell of him from her body and her mind. Wrapping herself in a towel, she returned to the bedroom, feeling strange and restless. She wanted to stay in his bedroom, as if by staying she could make everything right.

Clutching the towel to her, she walked to the closet and opened the door. Instead of the answers she sought, she found only a neat row of tailored suits and crisp shirts. She reached out to touch one of the shirts. The material stung her like dry ice and she pulled her hand away. She slammed the door shut and reached for her dress, flung carelessly over a chair, a bitter reminder of the evening that had begun so sweetly. Tracy grabbed her shawl and purse and hurried out, closing the door firmly behind her.

Chapter 23

"WES CANFIELD, PLEASE." THE RECEIVER FELT COLD in her hands. "I see. He wasn't in last week, either. Doesn't he ever come into the office?" Tracy waited impatiently as the receptionist coolly brushed off her inquiry. "But it's been over two weeks. . . . Yes, I even tried his home. . . . Well, do you know if he got the manuscript I sent him? *Louisiana Legacy?* . . . You *mailed* it to him? Where? . . . Oh, I see. No, there's no message. Just tell him not to bother calling me, wherever he is. . . . That's Bouchard . . . B-o-u-c-h—" She slammed down the phone. "Son-of-a——"

Her phone rang again. "Tracy Bouchard," she barked.

"Tracy? It's Tony."

"Tony! How are you? God, it's good to hear from you. When are you coming to New York?"

Then she screamed and threw down the phone. Tony was standing in the doorway holding Dennis's extension.

"How about lunch?" he said. "My treat."

She ran to him and gave him a huge hug, and he gave her a long kiss. As she clung to him, Sheila Zimmerman passed by, staring intrusively and with frank appraisal at Tony. Tracy caught her eye and Sheila moved on reluctantly.

"So," he said, "this is where you work." He looked over her shoulder to the window. "Nice view."

The memory of the view from Canfield's bedroom window sprang uninvited into her mind, and she shook it away. "How long will you be here?"

"Only until tomorrow. But my business is finished, and I've got the day and the evening free."

"Great. I can't have lunch—I've got an appointment I can't put off. But how about dinner and a night on the town?"

He kissed her again. "It's a deal." Tony's eyes lit up. "Wait a minute. I just had a terrific idea. I'll pick you up here about six, okay?" He was grinning like the Cheshire cat.

"What are you cooking up, Amato?"

"You'll see, lovely lady. You'll see. Six o'clock. Don't make me wait, beautiful." Tony sauntered out of her office.

At the dot of six, Tracy emerged from the F & F building to find Tony standing at the curb, leaning up against a fire-engine-red Mustang. He opened the passenger door ceremoniously.

"Where did this come from?" Tracy asked as she slid into the snow white bucket seat.

"Rent-a-wheels, babe." Tony revved the engine and pulled into the traffic on Park Avenue.

"So where are we going?"

"You'll see." Tony maneuvered his way through the rush hour traffic to the FDR Drive and crossed the Manhattan Bridge into Brooklyn. Once over the bridge, Tracy didn't have the faintest idea where they were as Tony wove his way in and out of a maze of highways and access roads. About thirty minutes later, he parked the Mustang in front of an unassuming building, hardly distinguishable from the other buildings on the residential street. A small sign in the window said "Angelo's."

Tony held the door and she entered a dimly-lit room with bare plank floors. The square tables were covered with plain white cloths and the paneled walls were covered with dozens and dozens of framed pictures. Tracy recognized the Pope, the Kennedy brothers and the old Brooklyn Dodgers. The others showed local teams and social organizations.

"I know it doesn't look like much, babe, but it's the best food in Brooklyn."

A waiter wearing black trousers, a white shirt and a black bow tie approached them. "Two, sir?"

"Hey, Jimmy, don't you recognize me?" Tony clapped the man on the shoulder.

"Tony, Tony Amato. You haven't been around in ages. Where you been keeping yourself? Hey, Angelo," he called over his shoulder, "look who's here."

"You're looking good, Jimmy. Place hasn't changed."

"Hey, Tony, why change a good thing, right? I got a nice quiet table over here in the corner for you and the lady."

When they were seated, a short, husky man wiping his hands on his white apron came through the swinging doors that led to the kitchen. Tony rose and shook his hand vigorously. "Tracy, this is Angelo Bruno. Angelo, Tracy Bouchard."

Angelo extended his hand to her. "Tony Amato always brings a beautiful lady into my place, but you are one of the most beautiful, Miss Bouchard."

"Why thank you, Mr. Bruno." Tracy smiled at his gallantry.

"Angelo, please. Everybody calls me Angelo."

"Angelo, then."

"Long time, Tony," Angelo said, turning back to Tony. "Still out there with all the movie stars? I bet this beautiful lady is one of them, right?"

"No, Tracy's a friend, not a client. She's an editor with Franklin & Fields."

"Oh," Angelo said, nodding his head sagely. "So, what can I get you to eat tonight? I got some nice striped bass today. How about it? In a light tomato sauce? Maybe some mozzarella in carrozza to start?"

Tony smiled. "Angelo, we're in your hands."

"This is fantastic, Tony." Tracy settled back in her chair. "I feel so comfortable here."

"Yeah, they really make you feel at home."

"So what are you doing out in California? Why didn't you stay here?"

Tony reached for her hand. "Tracy, I was eighteen years old when Hal Sterling shot that picture on my street. All my life, I'd lived thirty minutes from Manhattan. I'd been there twice. Sure, it's great here. They love you, they take care of you, but there's nowhere to go. What was a kid like me going to do? I'd been out of school for a couple of months. I was living at home, hustling this and that. I saw a ticket out of here and I took it."

"Excuse me, Tony. Compliments of Angelo." Jimmy stood by the table holding a tray with two stemmed glasses and a thin, green bottle shaped like a fish. "Our best verdicchio. Enjoy."

Tony thanked the waiter and poured a glass of the pale white wine for both of them. *"Salud,"* he toasted. They clinked glasses and drank.

"Mmm. This is excellent. Light and dry." Tracy raised her glass again. "Here's to Angelo and Brooklyn and Tony Amato, one of Brooklyn's finest products. It's great to see you, Tony."

Tony leaned in and kissed her lightly on the lips.

"Uh, excuse me, Tony," Jimmy said sheepishly, placing a platter in the middle of the table.

"That smells divine." Tracy admired the two golden brown squares on the platter. "What is it?"

"That's your mozzarella in carrozza, miss," Jimmy explained. "It means cheese in a carriage. You put the mozzarella between two slices of bread, dip it in batter and deep-fry it. Angelo makes the best. Enjoy. But watch out, it's hot."

Tracy cut a small piece and blew on it to cool it off. Biting into it she found the combination of textures irresistible. The cheese was soft and chewy, the coating crisp and crunchy.

Throughout the rest of the delicious meal, Tony answered Tracy's questions about growing up in Brooklyn, explaining the people in the pictures. Tracy was particularly fascinated with the way everyone had a nickname. Their waiter, Jimmy, was known as Jimmy the Jump because he liked to jump off his front stoop when he was a kid. He never walked down the steps, so he became known as Jimmy the Jump. He hadn't jumped off a stoop in forty years but the nickname stuck.

By the time they were sipping espresso and small glasses of Sambucca, Tracy's mind was clicking away.

"Could I interest you in writing a book, Tony? The old Brooklyn neighborhood through the eyes of someone who left it but still loves it. I think it would be terrific."

Tony shook his head emphatically. "Not me, Tracy. I'm no writer. And who's interested in these old stories? I'm a different guy now."

"You don't have to write. You could just talk into a tape recorder." Tony was silent, staring down at the table. Tracy had the feeling she'd touched on a sore spot and changed the subject. "Well, if you change your mind, let me know. So, enough of Brooklyn. What's going on in California?"

Tony brightened. "Things are great. Ambrosia's finally up and around. She went out for the first time, since her, uh, accident. I ran into her and Wes Canfield at the Polo Lounge and she looked terrific. He's always great medicine for whatever ails her."

Tracy's face contorted and her heart began to pound. Tony read her reaction and frowned slightly. "I guess I said the wrong thing. Sorry, Tracy."

"Look, Tony," she said flatly. "What's with Wes and Ambrosia anyway? I want the story straight." Her voice was flinty.

"I thought the two of you finished each other off back in L.A.," he said quietly.

"Not quite."

"Well, that's not the issue. Ambrosia is not the issue, either. She's a very fragile person and she needs a lot of support. Believe me, Canfield is her friend, her good friend. And that's all."

She smiled sadly. "Nice try, Tony, but I can hardly believe their liaison is so sweetly platonic."

"Well, it is. Don't be a jealous type, Tracy. It doesn't become you."

Damn that Canfield! What a slippery, two-faced charmer he was! Twice he had disappeared and ended up with Ambrosia, and twice she had been hurt and humiliated. No matter how much he meant to her, she was undoubtedly of secondary importance to him. Somehow, she would have to find a way to blot him out of her thoughts.

"I can't help it, Tony. It hurts."

"I know, babe. Uncle Tony knows all about it." He put his arm around her and gave her a gentle hug.

On the way back to Manhattan, Tony was silent, leaving Tracy to her own thoughts. Canfield was out in California with Ambrosia when he had told her he would be in Montreal. Tears gathered in her eyes and slipped down her cheeks. How foolish she had been. She had been calling his office and waiting for him and all the while he was out on the coast, not thinking of her at all. Not only that but she'd given him an early look at *Louisiana Legacy* and he hadn't even had the professional courtesy to respond. She was doing him an enormous favor. How could he treat her like this after the magical night they had spent together? Naïve, she thought; that's what I am: dumb and naïve.

Then Tracy broke completely, and the tears spilled rapidly. Hard, gasping sobs rocked her whole body. Tony pulled the car to the shoulder of the road and reached across to hold her, stroking her hair as she cried. When she was still he took out his handkerchief and wiped her face gently. He put the white square over her nose. "Blow," he ordered.

Tracy laughed like a little girl and did as she was told.

"All better?"

"Yes," she sniffed. "Thanks, Tony."

When they reached Tracy's apartment building, Tony walked her to the elevator. "Get a good night's sleep, babe. You need it."

She put her arms around him, holding him close, feeling the comforting warmth of his body. "You're the best, Tony."

"You're not so bad yourself, Bouchard." With that, he planted a tender kiss on her forehead and moved across the lobby, the heels of his shoes making tiny clicking noises that broke the late night silence.

Tracy let herself into her apartment, but didn't turn

on the lights. Drained and exhausted, she removed her clothes and put on her nightgown. After splashing her face with cool water she curled up on the window seat, watching the river. The Hudson was an eerie grayish green, lit by high-intensity lamps that lined the promenade. Tracy was hypnotized by the sight of it, moving, moving, never stopping. It's not the end of the world, she told herself. I still have my work. There will be other men. Her eyelids began to droop and she leaned back against the wall. The next thing she knew, it was beginning to get light. Tracy stretched her stiff limbs and fell into bed for a few more hours of sleep before work.

"Tracy?" Dennis's voice was excited. "Jim Fleming is on line thirty-four."

"Thank you, Dennis." She took a long breath and picked up the phone. "Jim?"

"Hello, Tracy."

"Hi! It's nice to hear from you. What's up?"

"I'm going to be in town for a few days next week, and I'd like to stop by and see you."

"That's great! When will you be arriving?" Her mind began to race as he told her of his arrangements. Jim Fleming would be coming to Franklin & Fields, and she would get a chance to show off her good work. What would Canfield—She stopped herself and concentrated on Fleming. "Yes, I'm sure we'll have a meeting here to discuss the book. . . . Good. I'll talk to Steve, and I'll get back to you. Is there anything I can set up for you before you come? . . . Fine, then I'll look forward to seeing you next week. Goodby."

She hung up in a daze. Jim Fleming would be coming right here, to her very office! She burst out of her office and ran down the hall to see Kramer.

"Steve?" she said, knocking on his open door.

He looked up. "Well?"

"Fleming is coming here."

His eyes lit up like two lanterns. "Here? When?"

"Next week. He wants to spend the day working on

the second half of the book, and he wants to meet with the marketing and promotion people."

"I should hope so. Advance sales for the book are terrific."

"How many so far?"

"I just looked at the sales reports this morning. It's over six figures, I can tell you that."

She was stunned. The book was already a bestseller, and it wasn't even published yet, absolute proof that her first book was going to be a smashing success.

Tracy was walking on air as she returned to her office. Jim Fleming's trust and confidence made her feel wonderful, and his call had already softened the sharpest edges of the pain she had been confronting. She had done well with Jim Fleming, even if she had been a gullible fool with Canfield. But as the thrill of the impending visit settled into her, making her tingle with pride and excitement, she knew that a much deeper emotion, one that had been forged from her most vulnerable yearnings, was still lying in wait.

Chapter 24

Dear Tracy,

I hope you're feeling better than you were the other night. It broke my heart to see you unhappy, but if I know you, you won't be down for long. Don't worry, everything will work out fine. I never say that unless I know it's true. You're a terrific lady, and you'll always have my best affection.

Love,
Tony

TRACY READ TONY'S LETTER WITH A TWINGE OF SADness. The man who had been her lover was now just her friend. He had taken on his new role spontaneously, in response to her need. Her feelings for Canfield had been too raw and too strong to hide. She knew that her eyes had flashed and her face had flushed every time his name was mentioned, and Tony was too keenly sensitive to the needs and desires of women not to notice.

There was still no word from Canfield. She *had* to give him up, put him out of her life. However, it was one thing to make that decision and quite another to carry it out. A hundred times a day, involuntary thoughts of him crept into her mind and, relentlessly, she tried to push them out. The silence was the hardest thing to bear. If she had known for sure that he was back in town and avoiding her, or out in L.A. shacked up with Ambrosia Jewell, she would have had tangible fuel for her anger. But there was nothing at all to go on, and the days dragged by as she forced herself not to speculate.

Tracy knew she was attractive, and she enjoyed her good looks. But Ambrosia Jewell's beauty was powerful enough to crush the hopes of any competitor. Tracy couldn't help but compare herself to the famous model, sneaking looks at the magazine covers that bore the glossy image of the legendary face. It was not a happy time for her.

She buried herself in her work with renewed zeal, hoping it would keep her mind from straying to Canfield. There was certainly enough to do. She was now as busy as every other editor in the company, and the days did not seem long enough to accommodate her schedule. She had bought a string of books, she had developed good relationships with agents and she had earned some measure of respect within the company.

If there were still people who doubted her integrity, they were too polite to mention it, but she knew her trial period was not quite over. Dennis gave her wonderful support, and she allowed him free reign on two of her smaller books. This was met with raised eyebrows and a lecture from Kramer, and it had a curious effect on the other assistants. Before they had been resentful and jealous of her, but now they wanted a chance to work for her in the hope that some of her generosity and success would rub off on them. She and Dennis often worked late together, and sometimes she would take him out for a quick hamburger after hours. Occasionally, someone would comment or raise an eyebrow, but Tracy wisely ignored it and went on with her work. Dennis was far too excited about his work to take much notice. It was actually kind of funny. If only the gossips knew about her and Wes Canfield. That would give them something to whisper about. But, she reminded herself again and again, there was no longer anything between Canfield and herself.

As she was checking over the style sheet for her Japanese cookbook, the door burst open and Dennis rushed inside.

"He's here!" he announced dramatically.

"Okay, take it easy. He won't run away."

Smiling brightly, Tracy walked down the hall and saw Jim Fleming talking to John Noble when she rounded the corner. Fleming's eyes lit up when he saw her.

"Well," he said warmly, "here's my editor."

"Hi," she said happily. "Welcome to New York." He leaned over as she took his hand, giving her a kiss on the cheek.

"You mean welcome *back* to New York. Don't forget, I began my career here as an announcer on a quiz show."

She laughed. "That's right."

Steve Kramer rounded the bend, and the first thing he noticed was the obvious rapport between Tracy and Fleming. Fleming recognized him, and extended a had. "Steve, how are you?"

Kramer was delighted. "Just fine, and you?"

Fleming looked around for a moment, and he nodded approvingly. "I'm in good hands, I can see that. Between you and Tracy and John, I might come out of this looking like a writer."

"Don't worry about that," Steve said hastily. "I've read the first half of your manuscript. Tracy only needed to do some light editing. But her initial hunch was correct—you're a master of the pen as well as the tongue."

"Careful, Steve. Flattery will get you everywhere."

Tracy saw Dennis hovering in the hall behind them, holding a manuscript. They were blocking traffic and he was too shy to push his way through, so he turned around and headed back to his desk.

"Come back here, Dennis Jordan!" Tracy commanded. Dennis jumped three feet in the air. The manuscript flew out of his hands, but he caught it. Everyone laughed as Tracy pulled him into the group.

Jim Fleming shook his hand and said, "So you're the face behind the voice that puts me on hold?" Dennis grinned to beat the band, his head bobbing up and down like an eager puppy. If he'd had a tail, it would have been wagging furiously. Tracy was delighted by his excitement.

The group went down to the large conference room, where coffee and pastries had been set up for the many people who would attend the meeting. All the editors, the sales manager, the marketing director, the subsidiary rights staff, the art director and several publicity and advertising people, including Katie Molloy, were expected. Tracy stayed close to her author, introducing him proudly to everyone, marveling at the way he found something special and personal to say to each individual.

When everyone had arrived, John Noble seated Fleming next to Tracy near the head of the conference table, and the room quieted down. "On behalf of the entire company, I'd like to welcome Jim Fleming. And may I say that this is one of the most exciting books this company has published in its forty-eight years in business. I'd like to begin with our marketing strategy, then move on to publicity.

The meeting progressed smoothly. The publicity discussion was the most colorful part of the conference, as key media targets were pinpointed, and special plans were announced. "Every major city will have posters of Mr. Fleming holding his book on buses and subways and key transfer points of public transportation," Katie Molloy said proudly. "And we've scheduled over three hours worth of thirty-second spots on the three major networks."

Fleming stood up to add, "My network has agreed that I can plug the book on my show, as long as we make it a part of the regular format. They've consented to a feature spot during the first week that the book is out, in which someone will interview me, for a change. And they are amenable to commercials for it both before and after the show is aired."

"Those will start two weeks before publication," Katie said. "That should create a lot of anticipation and excitement."

"Actually," Fleming broke in, "I've told my writers to have one good joke about the book in every monologue. And they're working on a sketch for my ventriloquist routine. The 'dummy'—that's me—will poke fun at the book while the 'ventriloquist' defends it. The idea here is to soften and temper the massive publicity with humor and with a frank acknowledgment that we are indeed hard-selling."

This was met with a burst of laughter and approval from the staff. They all knew how skillfully Fleming would be able to handle the selling of himself, especially when his best talents were put to use.

"The build-up will be tremendous," Steve Kramer enthused.

John Noble stood up. "Why don't you give us the latest figures on advance sales, Steve?"

Kramer gathered together a mass of computer print-out sheets, and consulted notes he had calculated on a pad. "As of this morning, we have exactly—" He paused, and there was an expectant hush. "One hundred twenty-six thousand, four hundred and thirty-two advance orders for Mr. Fleming's book." Applause and excitement followed, and Steve held up a hand to continue. "Most of these, of course, come from the large chains and outlets. As we discussed earlier, we'll be hitting the smaller, individual markets soon."

"Thank you, Steve," Noble said. "Well, I think I can safely say that we have the support of the entire house on this project."

Everyone laughed, and Jim Fleming beamed. The meeting ended officially when John Noble uncorked a bottle of champagne and poured Jim Fleming the first glass. Everyone had a glass of champagne, and merry toasts were proposed as the group loosened up and became even livelier. Steve Kramer edged his way over to Fleming, whose arm was around Tracy.

"I'm glad things are going so well," he said.

Jim Fleming looked at Kramer and then at Tracy. "So am I," he said. "Tracy did a wonderful job, and you were a great help, Steve. Tracy told me about many of your suggestions, and as you'll see, we incorporated many of them into the book."

Tracy looked at the floor and Kramer's face glowed.

259

"Just doing my job," he said modestly. He was called away by the art director, and Fleming winked at Tracy.

The morning fled by as the staff drank champagne and talked about the book. Everyone wanted a few minutes of conversation with Jim Fleming, and he managed to oblige them all with tact and skill. As noon approached, Tracy realized suddenly that she had nothing to do for lunch. She had left the day open for Fleming, but he had begged off with an obligatory lunch with one of his show's sponsors. She walked over to Katie Molloy and tapped her friend on the shoulder.

"You'll never believe this, but I'm looking for a lunch date. Are you free?"

Katie laughed. "As a matter of fact, yes. Where would you like to go?"

Tracy closed her eyes and threw her head back. "Some place fancy," she said ardently. "I'm in such a good mood."

"I can see that." Katie giggled. "I'm feeling pretty happy myself. Don't overdo it, Bouchard. You can always get smashed at lunch."

"True, true. I know—let's go to Giambelli's and have pasta. To hell with calories!"

"To hell with calories!" Katie agreed, and they clinked glasses and drank.

Half an hour later, they were seated in the small, elegant Italian restaurant, sipping white wine. "I'm so glad you were free," Katie said. "I'll be able to tell folks I knew you when."

"Oh, come on."

"No, I mean it. Do you know my phone hasn't stopped ringing all week?"

"Well, Jim Fleming is no small item."

"Fleming? Who's talking about Fleming? Let's face it, he doesn't need little old me. I'm talking about *Louisiana Legacy*. It's turning into pretty hot stuff."

"My God, I'd forgotten all about it this week. I was so excited about Jim Fleming's visit that I didn't think of anything else."

"Well, I've got some interesting news for you."

"When it rains, it pours."

"In torrents." Katie signaled the waiter, who poured them each another glass of wine. "Guess what Belinda Caruthers has been doing all week?"

Tracy shrugged.

"She's been calling up all of her friends and telling them that a book about her family is being published, and that it's going to be a bestseller. And some of her friends have called me."

"So?"

"So!? Don't you know who her friends are? I've had a call from Truman Capote and another one from Ethel Kennedy."

Tracy's heart began to race. "What did they say?"

"They want to see the book and maybe give us some quotes for the jacket."

"That's fantastic!"

"Right."

"Well, take a look at this. It was delivered by messenger this morning." Katie handed Tracy a cream-colored envelope that had been neatly slit by a letter opener. It contained a beautifully engraved invitation that was bordered in gold.

Tracy read it out loud. "Belinda Caruthers requests the honor of your presence at a gala in celebration of *Louisiana Legacy,* to be published in June by Franklin & Fields. Sixty-six Sutton Place, December 2nd, nine o'clock P.M. Black Tie."

"I'm sure you got one too, but you weren't in your office all morning," Katie said.

"And a lot of other people at F & F," Tracy added.

"You're right. It should be quite a party. She's flying Jean-Jean Fouchet up from New Orleans to do the food, and she ordered three hundred magnolia blossoms for decorations."

"I can't believe it." Tracy's head was spinning, and she didn't know if it was from the wine or the news she was hearing. A painting on the wall across from her began to dip and sway, and she said, "Oh, dear. I think we'd better order now."

They signaled the waiter and Tracy indulged in a savory bowl of minestrone followed by a large plate of linguini with fresh basil sauce. The steaming dishes of hearty Italian fare were especially appealing after all the wine they had drunk, and they dug in with relish.

Tracy's head began to clear a little as she got food into her stomach, and she settled back against the plush banquette contentedly. "What a perfect day," she murmured.

"Well, I hate to ruin your perfect day, but I've got some great gossip. Have you heard the latest about Canfield's new company?"

Tracy was instantly alert. "No, what?" she said.

Katie leaned forward. "It's about to go under. One Park Avenue is trembling on the brink."

"You're kidding."

"I'm not. He's stalled his spring catalogue in the hope that he can get a terrific lead book. But it's unlikely that he'll find one."

Tracy was silent, but the giddiness that had been so pleasant only moments before faded, and a slight feeling of nausea took its place.

"Look," Katie said, putting her fork down, "I don't know what's going on between you two, but I do know one thing. He can use all the help and support he can get right now. He's almost finished."

Tracy closed her eyes for a second and remembered firmly that Wes Canfield was no longer in her life. His problems were not her business. He had hurt her, lied to her, and left her cold. "As far as I'm concerned," she said, her voice tinged with anger, "he's already finished."

"He's hurting, Tracy," Katie said very quietly. "Why don't you call him?"

Tracy looked down at the table. "I have called him," she whispered, on the verge of tears. "Either he's never there or he refuses to talk to me."

"But Tracy," Katie pleaded, "that doesn't make sense."

"I know."

Katie was stymied, and there was nothing she could say. She looked at her friend sympathetically.

"Maybe he'll bid for *Louisiana Legacy*," Tracy said.

"And maybe he'll get it, if he can pay for it." She knew how cold and hard-hearted she sounded, but she didn't care. A book like *Louisiana Legacy* could save Canfield's company. Deep down, Tracy hoped and prayed he would manage it. She didn't want him to drown, no matter how he had treated her. She still cared about him and wanted him to succeed. And there was one more aspect. If he bought the book they would have a reason to communicate with each other, and maybe there would still be a chance for them. The truth was etched all over Tracy's face. She didn't have to say a word to Katie.

"Come on, Tracy, I think it's time to get back to the office," Katie said gently.

Katie insisted on picking up the tab and they left the restaurant. In silence, they returned to the Franklin & Fields building.

Chapter 25

"THIS AUCTION COULD GO ON FOR A LONG TIME." JOHN Noble addressed the small group that had gathered in Tracy's office. "When we auctioned *Year of the Dragon,* the last bid came in at nine-fifteen at night. I have a feeling this one is going to be just as long."

Tracy swallowed and sat down at her desk. Mention of *Year of the Dragon* still made her uncomfortable, and she asked the others to leave, pleading pressing work. She breathed easier after they left.

It promised to be an exciting day. The subsidiary rights director, who was to conduct the auction, was anticipating full interest, and the book could go for a very high price indeed. Steve Kramer ran into her office with good news written all over his face, and Tracy looked up expectantly.

"What is it, Steve? You look like you just won the sweepstakes."

"Wes Canfield just called in with a fifty thousand dollar bid. We're using it as a floor, and he's got topping privileges for seven percent."

Tracy's face widened with surprise. "Where was he calling from?" she asked faintly.

"Why, from his office. You know, he's right down on Park Avenue." Kramer looked puzzled.

"I know," she breathed.

"Well, I just wanted to let you know. I've got to run now. We'll keep you informed."

"Thanks." He left, and she grappled desperately with the confused sea of emotions that swept over her. She was glad and angry and hurt and relieved and anxious all at the same time. This isn't doing me any good, Tracy thought impatiently. She had an obligation to her author who was waiting on tenterhooks out in Iowa. She flipped through the cards on her Rolodex, and dialed Maxine Wilkins.

"Hello, Maxine? I have good news."

"Already?"

"Already. We've had a first offer of fifty thousand dollars, and we've given the bidder a seven percent topping privilege."

"Oh! What does that mean?"

Tracy explained. "It means that we'll continuue the auction until we reach the highest bid. Then we'll call the company with the topping privilege. If they want, they can buy the book for the highest bid *plus* seven percent. If they don't want to buy it, the book goes to the other company."

"I see." Maxine was fluttering. "Well, keep me posted. This is all new to me, Tracy, but I'm learning fast."

"Don't worry, Maxine. We're off to a great start, and it looks like it's going to be a long day."

"I'm so thrilled I don't know what to do."

"Don't do anything. Go out to a movie. Go shopping. I'll call you later."

"Okay, I'll try. Thanks a million."

"My pleasure. Goodby."

"Goodby, Tracy."

Tracy picked up a manuscript and tried to read but ended up doodling wiry designs on her notepad. She was so preoccupied she jumped when the phone rang. Dennis buzzed her.

"Yes, Dennis?"

"Wes Canfield is on line thirty-three."

So. He was finally calling. Now that he wanted something from her, he was suddenly available. But it was too late. She had nothing to say to him. He had hurt her too badly.

"Tracy?" Dennis was waiting.

"Yes, Dennis," she answered dully. "Tell him I'm not here."

"Are you sure? He's—"

"I'm sure. And you don't know when I'll be back." She watched the button on the phone as the light went off, and she had to stifle an impulse to pick up the receiver and say, "I didn't mean it! I'm here!" It gave her absolutely no feeling of satisfaction to treat him as he had treated her. This wasn't the way she wanted it.

"Mr. Canfield?" a young woman said hesitantly from the doorway.

He flinched, as if he had been wrested from a trance.

"It's the subsidiary rights director at Franklin & Fields."

He hesitated and then picked up the receiver. "Marion? It's Wes." His face was tense as he listened. "Yes," he said, and he looked down at some figures he had scribbled. "Fine. Thanks for keeping in touch."

He hung up slowly, and then he wrote down the new figure, crossing out the old one. The bidding was now up to two hundred and fifty thousand dollars.

"Mary?"

The secretary returned.

"If any calls come in from Paris or Montreal, put them through immediately. No matter what I'm doing."

She nodded wordlessly and left.

He heaved a shaky sigh and shook his head. Looking down again at the latest figure, his three hundred thousand seemed small and insignificant. He had worked and cajoled to the limit to get it, and now it didn't matter. Damn, he thought hopelessly. They'll top that by four o'clock. He sat back heavily in his chair and stared blankly out the window. He remained that way until after one o'clock and the phone never rang in all that time.

"Hey, Tracy." Conway strolled into her office. "How about lunch today?"

"No, thanks, I'm eating in. I'm too nervous to leave the building. I don't want to miss any news about the auction."

"What's it up to?"

"Five-fifty and rising steadily."

"Sounds like a possible—"

"Don't say it, Jeff. It's bad luck to second guess these things. Let's just wait and see, okay?"

"Whatever you say. But I promise you'll be flying before it's over."

"Well, in the meantime, I'm not leaving this room. Care to join me for lunch? I'm calling the coffee shop and ordering in."

"Sure, I'll be right back. Order me a BLT, French fries and a Coke, will you?"

She watched him disappear and called the coffee shop. He returned just as the food was arriving. Conway reached into his pocket, but Tracy stopped him.

"My treat."

"Thanks. I owe you one."

She grinned. That was Conway. His mind was in constant calculation, keeping small favors in mind for the day when he could return them. He had helped her edit *Louisiana Legacy,* and she had given him full support on the books he had wanted to buy. Whenever Ken and Sheila turned on her, he was there to offer a line of defense. Her fragile position in the company had gradually strengthened, and now all she needed was the exposure of one underhanded crook to release her completely from suspicion.

She thought carefully about each one of her co-workers. She pictured each face and imagined each one meeting secretly with Carl Bendex in some dark hotel room handing over *Year of the Dragon.* First, there were the assistants. She eliminated them quickly, one by one. It was unlikely that any of them would have the nerve to do something like that. Of course, she wanted the culprit to be either Sheila or Ken himself, but that was wishful thinking.

Conway's voice brought her back to earth. "Hey," he said. "You look like you're in a trance. Want to share it?"

She stared at him and wondered if he could be the one. She hoped he wasn't. "Well," she said hesitatingly, and then she made a fast decision. "Let me ask you something."

"Shoot."

She got up and closed the door.

"It's a secret?" he asked hopefully.

"I just don't want to share this with the immediate world."

He put down his sandwich and waited.

"What are your thoughts on the manuscript theft?"

His eyebrows met in a frown. "You mean, do I think you took it?"

She nodded.

"Let me put it this way," he said slowly, calculating how to phrase it.

"Just give it to me straight. Do you think I took that manuscript?"

"Do you think I took it?" he shot back, and she relaxed a little. "Look, Tracy. Any one of us could have done it. I'm not saying you aren't a likely suspect, but so are we all. If Carl Bendex offered me fifteen percent of a movie just for handing him a manuscript—" He never finished the sentence, and he didn't have to. She knew what he was driving at.

"Do you mean to tell me that—"

"I don't mean to tell you anything. Do you have any idea what fifteen percent of ten million dollars is?"

She was flabbergasted.

"Oh, come on, Bouchard. You're in the big league now. Hell, what about the reprint auction that's going on right now?"

"What about it?"

"F & F paid a few thousand for that book, and now it's selling to paper for over half a million. Fifteen percent of a movie, and you could retire for life. So why the hell should this spy even give a damn about being caught? It's underhanded, but not technically illegal."

"I never thought of it that way."

"Well, maybe you didn't, but someone else did."

"Then you don't think it was me?"

Conway laughed crudely. "I just don't care. It doesn't affect me one way or the other. If one of my authors is dumb enough to sell out at a low price, then that's his problem. What's it to me? I'm not on commission."

"Please, Jeff. Tell me if you think it was me."

"Does it really matter?"

"To me it does."

There was a knock on the door and Tracy called, "Come in!"

"It's up to six hundred and fifty thousand," Dennis announced grandly. "Steve just told me to tell you."

"Well," Conway said as he got up from his chair, "it looks like a big day for you and your author. Call me if you go over a million."

"Sure," Tracy answered. "You'll be the first to know."

They left the room and Tracy got up and closed the door. She sat down at her desk and buried her head in her hands. Whoever this spy was, she hoped he would show his face soon. She couldn't take much more of this fence-sitting. Suddenly, she wanted to talk to Kippy, needed to hear her calm, gentle voice. She picked up the phone to dial Connecticut.

"Mr. Canfield?"

He swung the swivel chair around to face his secretary.

"It's Paris calling," she whispered, and she left quietly, closing the door behind her.

He composed himself and picked up the phone, knowing that his transatlantic performance would have to be razor sharp and letter perfect. They simply had to be made to understand how crucial this book was. He knew that if they balked now, he would have to call them again later. It could be as late as four o'clock in the morning their time, and that was a hell of a time to ask someone for an extra half a million dollars.

He spoke forcefully and succinctly, and as the conversation ended, he thanked the man on the other end and jotted down the final offering. They had budged, but not by much.

He now had six hundred and fifty thousand dollars

to work with, and he looked at his watch. Two-thirty. There was time to call the bank, but it would be a futile effort and he knew it. Even with a bank loan, he could still be shy by as much as two hundred thousand. He opened his drawer and reviewed the figures on *Louisiana Legacy*. It had already been optioned by Heather Gentree, and the movie was sure to be a huge success. He smiled as he thought about it. By the time the book had left the bestseller list, the movie would be released, shooting the book up the list all over again. Angry tears of frustration came to his blue eyes for an instant as he thought about the loss of such a lucrative property. Then his face turned into a stony blank and he stared again at the street below.

The phone kept ringing, and Tracy realized that Dennis was not at his desk. She picked it up quickly and straightened when she learned who was calling. "Oh, Mrs. Caruthers! . . . Yes, thank you, it's going well. . . . Seven hundred thousand. . . . Yes, I believe that will probably be the final offer. . . . Well, it's been slow since five-thirty. Most of the competition has dropped out. . . . Oh, yes, they were beautiful. I received it last week. . . . I will, and thank you again."

Well, that was interesting. Belinda Caruthers was certainly taking *Louisiana Legacy* seriously. This was a day she would not soon forget, and it wasn't over yet. She got up and walked down the hall to the drinking fountain. Half the offices were already empty. Tracy wasn't going to wait around by her phone anymore. She decided to head down one floor to the sub rights director's office to hear the latest news. As she was standing by the elevator, Steve Kramer came out of his office and joined her.

"Hi," he said congenially. "Heading down to get it from the horse's mouth?"

She nodded. "I think it's all over. Seven hundred thousand."

"And Canfield still has topping privileges."

The mention of his name unnerved her. Please, God, let him get the book, she prayed silently.

The elevator doors opened, and John Noble walked out. His face was shining with anticipation. "Have you heard?" he asked breathlessly.

"Heard what?" Tracy and Steve asked at the same time.

"A last minute bid came in. It's all over except for the topping privileges."

Tracy took a breath and held it.

"The final bid is eight hundred thousand dollars."

"Yes, operator, thank you. Yes, I know the time it is there. Would you put the call through for me, please?" He waited as the clicks and buzzes hummed across the overseas connection, and the call was answered after many rings. His mind switched to French as he apologized for the lateness of the hour and for calling the man at his home. This time he did not have the forcefulness and the persuasive energy that had worked before. This time he was desperate, he was on the brink of collapse, and he was sure that a pleading note was present in his voice. The polite, clipped French on the other end was adamant. He tried another angle, throwing in every last ounce of confidence and strength that he could muster. But it was no use. The answer was an irrevocable no, and he hung up in a state between fury and tears.

It was all over. The sensation of failure was utterly foreign to him, and it almost made him sick. He staggered to a cabinet in the corner of his office and opened the bottom drawer. There was a bottle of bourbon inside, and he took it out, fumbling with the cap. His hand was actually shaking, as he lifted the bottle directly to his mouth for a long swig. He was about to take another drink when he realized what he was doing. He was sitting on the floor of his office drinking liquor straight from the bottle. I'm not that ruined, he thought fiercely, and he put the bottle back in the drawer. The drink had steadied him and he stood up, brushing the lint from his suit.

A new thought entered his mind and it grew in his head like a helium balloon that would not explode, but only rose gracefully in the air. He returned to his chair, bracing himself for what he was about to do. Again, he hesitated. It had been years, but he still remembered the number.

The phone rang several times, and he was about to give up when someone answered. He waited for a few seconds before responding. "Is he still in?" he asked. "No, that's fine, I'll wait. . . . Yes, tell him—" he hesitated for a second and then said, "tell him—it's his son. . . ."

Chapter 26

WES CANFIELD STOOD IN THE ELEVATOR AND HAPPILY watched the numbers light up one by one as they approached the familiar floor. It was just like old times. As the elevator came to a halt, the doors opened onto a pleasantly familiar sight. The receptionist sat at the curved desk, and she smiled amiably.

"Good morning, Mr. Canfield. Welcome back."

"Good morning, Liz. Is John in yet?"

"I haven't seen him, but why don't you head down to his office and wait inside? I'm sure he won't mind."

"Thanks," he said, "but I think I'll go downstairs and say hello to everyone."

He rode down one flight and started to walk towards the editors' offices when he was grabbed from behind.

"Well, congratulations!"

"Thanks, Jeff." They shook hands heartily.

"Hey!" Sheila came running over to give him a hug. "I heard about your big success last night. That's terrific!"

"Word travels fast," he said dryly. Shaking loose from Jeff and Sheila, he headed around the corner and ran into Ken Maguire.

"Nice going, Wes," Ken called out.

"Thanks."

He looked down the hall to where Dennis Jordan sat, and their eyes met. Dennis turned his head sharply to look into Tracy's office and then pulled back without looking up. Canfield's eyebrows went up and he blew out a long breath. He marched straight into her office and stood in front of her. Her head was bent as she read a memo, and her glossy hair with its hints of red and gold fell luxuriously onto her shoulders. He had forgotten just how beautiful she was.

She looked up and he saw that her face was a cold mask.

"Hi," he said. "Is it safe to come in?"

"Not without an invitation. Do you have an appointment?"

"No."

"Then get the hell out."

"Easy there," he said mildly. "I didn't come here to fight. I came to—"

"What are you doing in my office, Wes Canfield?"

He gazed at her impatiently and then slammed the door shut. Walking up close to her, he stood with his hands on his hips and looked down at her. "Shut up, Bouchard, and listen to me. For the last four weeks, I have been on the verge of bankruptcy and I was going out of my mind trying to keep my company alive. Last night, I called my father, and he agreed to lend me the money I need—"

She cut him off, her eyes shooting darts at him. "Just get the hell out of here! Why don't you move your damn company to Los Angeles, so you can be closer to your precious Ambrosia? Now get out."

His face flushed with fury. "You spoiled little jealous brat. All you can think about is yourself. You've been that way ever since I've met you." He turned on his heel and strode to the door, flinging it open. "It doesn't become you, Tracy. When are you going to learn that?"

Tears stung her eyes as she watched him leave. For weeks, she had endured the excruciating silence, and now he burst into her office and expected her to act as if nothing had happened. He had his nerve. She brushed the tears from her eyes and shook her head with determination. How dare he march in here and expect her to pick up where they left off? How could he be so cruel and insensitive?

The phone rang, and she picked it up before Dennis could answer it, grateful for something to do.

"Tracy Bouchard."

"Hi, sweetie. It's Tony. What's the matter, have you been crying?"

She had to smile at his ever-sensitive antenna. "Nothing important," she said.

"I don't believe that for a minute, but I won't pursue it unless you want to. I'm just calling to congratulate you. It looks like your success has rubbed off on me."

"What do you mean?"

"One of my clients just signed to play the lead in the movie version of *Louisiana Legacy*."

"Tony! That's great! Who is it? Anyone I know?"

"Ambrosia Jewell."

Tracy almost cursed. The last person she wanted to hear about was this woman whose name kept cropping up at every turn. But Tony went on enthusiastically.

"Stan Geller is directing it. He's crazy about Ambrosia, and she trusts him enough to work with him."

Tracy sighed in exasperation. She decided to ask him point-blank what she feared. "Tell me something, Tony. Did Wes Canfield have anything to do with her landing that part? You already told me he was in L.A. just a couple of weeks ago."

Tony was silent for a minute, and then he said, "Tracy, I already explained about that. Ambrosia— well, she doesn't trust many people, but she trusts Canfield. It's a very delicate situation."

"So I gather," Tracy said sarcastically.

"You're in love with him, aren't you?"

"Don't be silly."

"You are." He paused. "Look, I'll be seeing you next week at the Belinda Caruthers party. I'm invited and so is Heather Gentree, so you'll get to see her, too. I'll talk to you then about this. This isn't the time. Meanwhile, why don't you try to work out your differences with the guy? I understand he was almost broke before he got this book. So ease up. I've got to go now, but I'll see you next week, okay?"

"Okay," she said shyly. His smooth voice had quelled her anxiety for the moment, and she suddenly felt hopeful again, although she couldn't imagine why.

She hung up the phone and spent the rest of the

morning trying to give a name to her jumbled feelings. Yes, she was in love with Canfield. There was no point in denying it. But what could that lead to? More disappointment and loneliness? Tracy was not a glutton for punishment, but Tony had cut through her layers of defense to put his finger on the crux of the issue. She was in love with the man.

Wes Canfield was in no mood to socialize after his encounter with Tracy, and he decided to wait in John Noble's office. He sat at his old desk, toying with a letter opener and reminiscing about the first time he had seen Tracy. It had been right here in this room. A smile spread involuntarily across his face as he recalled how arrogant and cocksure she had been. And he remembered the way her beautiful long legs had swung back and forth over the side of the desk as she talked to Max Zwerdlow.

He was deep in thought when the phone rang. He waited for Margaret to answer it, but she was not at her desk. After a moment's hesitation, he decided to answer it himself.

"Hello?"

"John? Listen, your check is in the mail. I like the way you and I work together. Let me know when you've got something else that's hot."

Canfield recognized the gravelly voice, and he covered his profound surprise by clearing his throat. When the man at the other end finished, he rallied and thought fast. "Don't worry, Bendex," he said softly into the phone. "Our deal's still on."

Chapter 27

IT HAD BEEN RAINING ALL DAY, AND TO MAKE MATTERS worse, the weather report predicted that it would freeze over by evening. Tracy stood at the window of her apartment gazing out moodily at the rainwashed view. Ice was already beginning to form on the glass, and she drew designs on the pane with her finger. Her heart fluttered a little as she thought about Belinda Caruthers's gala celebration, which was now only hours away. She had prepared carefully for it, combing the shops on upper Madison Avenue for two full afternoons, getting an up-to-the-minute trim on her hair, and indulging in both a manicure and a pedicure. She had even had a facial at Orlane, and her skin was fresh and dewy. Her dress hung on a velvet hanger in front of her closet, over the new pair of Ferragamo shoes. Her shopping had been tinged with a driving need to have everything absolutely perfect. Wes would undoubtedly be there, and she didn't want the slightest flaw to mar her appearance.

She sighed unhappily as she thought about him. He had looked so handsome, so full of life, when he walked into her office the week before. And Katie had filled her in on the rest of his story. Not only had he reconciled with his father, but Werner Haas had stipulated only one condition on which he would lend his son the money. Wes had to agree to eventually merge the two companies, so that the Haas legacy would be able to continue after Werner's death. Wes had accepted the condition readily. Haas and Canfield. She played with the sound of it for a minute, knowing that one day it would be a catch phrase in book publishing. But it was not her affair. Tonight, her head would be held high.

For tonight was her night, as much as it was Belinda Caruthers's and Maxine Wilkins's. She had discovered *Louisiana Legacy;* she was the one who had nurtured it and convinced everyone in the company to support its growth. Tonight would be a far cry from the Zwerdlow party she had attended in the spring. Then she had been awkward, trying too hard. She had learned a lot since then. And she deserved to enjoy herself tonight. She would take her place in the limelight—Wes Canfield or no Wes Canfield.

She went into the bathroom and filled the tub with hot water and Chanel bath oil. Disrobing quickly and pinning her hair on top of her head, she sank into the foamy water and relaxed, letting her mind drift aimlessly as she played with the bubbles. Then she crawled into bed for a nap before it was time to dress for the party.

The alarm woke her harshly, and she groped to turn it off. The room was dark and the windows were caked with ice. She had ordered a taxi and it would be here in an hour. She turned on the light and got out of bed, stretching and doing a few quick exercises to get her circulation moving. Then she went into the bathroom and dusted herself lavishly with bath powder, adding generous amounts of perfume at pulse points all over her body. She applied her makeup carefully, brushing gold and tan eye shadow onto her eyelids and outlining her eyes with thick, smoky brown pencil. Several layers of mascara brought out the full, luminous shape of her eyes, and a powdery blush heightened her cheekbones and contoured her jawline. Next she brushed her wavy hair, pinning it behind one ear with a gilt-trimmed ivory comb.

Now it was time to gingerly don the new clothes she had bought, and she took two thin, flat boxes from her top drawer. The first one contained the sheer cotton eyelet underwear she had bought at Montanapoleone, and she stepped into it lightly. Then came the pair of sheer silk stockings that felt smooth and luxurious against her legs. The stunning evening gown slid over her head and fell into place with a soft billow as she tied the rope belt around her waist. It was made of a shimmery golden beige chiffon that matched her tawny coloring. The softly draped bodice plunged to the waist in the back. Finally, she stepped into the matching high-heeled slingback shoes and surveyed herself in the mirror. She had forgotten the jewelry. There was no need for ornament at the neckline, but she looped gold bracelets onto her arms and put dangling gold earrings in her ears. Now she was ready. She had chosen wisely. The result was superb.

The intercom rang and she grabbed her evening bag. Throwing a brown velvet cloak over her shoulders, she ran out to the lobby, where the doorman helped her into the waiting taxi. The cab moved slowly through the cold, wet streets, finally turning to go through Central Park. Small icicles hung from the bare trees, and the lights of the East Side came into view as they emerged on Fifth Avenue. The streets were practically deserted, Tracy observed as they continued across town and neared the East River. Then they were heading downtown again, and as the cab passed under the Queensboro Bridge, she saw the neat row of townhouses that faced the water. They pulled to a stop in front of Belinda Caruthers's Sutton Place townhouse, a turn-of-the-century building of classical elegance.

Tracy paid the fare and stepped out carefully into the street, lifting her long gown above her ankles. The sidewalk was make of red brick instead of concrete, and old-fashioned gas lamps lined the street. She slipped through the wrought iron gate and stood between the fragrant spruces that stood on either side of the painted oak door. It was opened almost immediately by a uniformed butler, who took her velvet cloak, and ushered her through a large foyer into a carpeted hall. She traveled the length of the hallway that was lighted by brass sconces on the walls, and stood at the edge of a spacious, brilliantly lit drawing room. Her eyes roamed over the Gothic windows, the Oriental carpets, and the magnificent double chandeliers before she walked down the three steps that led inside. People were milling around, the women in colorful evening gowns, and the men in tuxedos. The furniture was covered in forest green velvet, and the green was picked up in the many lush plants that adorned the room. A tall woman draped in a flowing black and white gown spotted her and broke away from a small group to meet her.

"Good evening," she said, an extravagant southern accent marking her throaty voice. "I'm Belinda Caruthers. So nice to have you."

"Good evening," Tracy said. "I'm Tracy Bouchard."

"Tracy, darling!" Belinda kissed the air on both sides of her face. "How wonderful to meet you at last. I'm so delighted you could come." She took Tracy's arm and escorted her into the room. "Let me introduce you to some lovely people who have been dying to meet you. Roslyn and Jonathan Wakefield, this is Tracy Bouchard, the editor of *Louisiana Legacy*."

Tracy shook hands with them, and they greeted her with interest. "I hope the book will be a great success," the woman said.

"Of course, it will!" Belinda said gaily. "And I couldn't let it be published without christening it with a party!" She laughed heartily, and the others couldn't help but join in. Belinda had an infectious enthusiasm and Tracy liked her at once. It was obviously an important occasion for the lively hostess, whose romantic family had been honored in *Louisiana Legacy*. "You must excuse me, darlings," Belinda said. "I must show Tracy around." Tracy was introduced to the Ostermans, the Vanderpools and the Lombards, and was just meeting Chester Haywood, the famous banker, when the high-pitched voice of a tiny, wiry woman in a purple gown with a purple turban called out the hostess's name above the buzz of the crowd.

"Oh, Belinda! Belinda!"

Chester Haywood turned away, a resigned smile on his face, and Tracy watched as the woman careened into the room. "Oh, Belinda. I simply can't believe what happened. Those people from Kentucky are so awful. Do you know what they said about Godfrey's new yacht?" She babbled on as Belinda tried to calm her, and she caught Tracy's eye.

"Oh!" she said. "Who is this?"

"Tracy Bouchard, this is Trudy Tuller. Tracy is the editor of the book, Trudy."

"You don't say!" Trudy dragged her new find into a corner and regaled her with the story of her own family, whose fortune had been made in the fish canning industry. Tracy endured the incessant chatter for fifteen minutes, until a familiar voice pulled her away.

"Hey, Tracy!" It was Jeff Conway. "Say, you look sensational." He led her away, and Tracy mumbled a hasty excuse to the manic woman, who immediately latched onto Martha Hauptmann to continue her tirade.

Tracy giggled and they made a beeline for the spiral staircase in the back of the room.

"Thanks, Jeff, you just saved my ears. I owe you one."

"Don't mention it. I knew you were in trouble when I overheard her talking about sardine breeding."

Tracy admired his tuxedo and realized that it was probably brand new. He confirmed her thought.

"I bought this outfit especially for this affair," he confided. "Damn thing set me back a couple hundred bucks."

"I guess this is one party where you can tell a book by its cover," she said, indicating her own special outfit.

He laughed. "Isn't this the most outrageous house you've ever seen?"

She remembered Zwerdlow's house, and Fleming's, and especially Gentree's. "It's very unusual, especially for New York. It seems specifically designed for big parties."

"It is," he said. "There are small alcoves upstairs for people who want to talk in private, and there are bars on both floors."

They talked for a while until Jeff saw a controversial congressman come in, and he began to edge away.

"Excuse me," he said, "but I'd love to do a celebrity book of my own. And my subject just walked in."

"Go ahead," she said. "Good luck." He sprinted off, and Tracy saw Belinda heading her way with a small, modestly attired woman on her arm.

"Tracy, my dear. I have the honor of introducing you to a wonderful lady. It's about time y'all met. Tracy, this is Maxine Wilkins."

Tracy's face lit up and she gave Maxine an impulsive hug. "Oh, Maxine, it's so nice to meet you."

"At last!" Maxine cried, and they laughed happily.

Tracy talked to her author for several minutes, and they discussed the promotion tour that had been planned. Maxine was nervous about the grueling trip, and Tracy promised to talk to Katie Molloy about it.

"I don't want to be away from my family for too long," Maxine explained, and Tracy sympathized.

"Perhaps they could meet you at the end, and you could turn it into a vacation," she suggested.

"Oh, I never thought of that."

They went on to talk about her next book, and Tracy said she had been thinking about a western saga. They were discussing the possibility of a Civil War novel when a pair of strong arms wrapped around Tracy from behind.

"How's my favorite editor?" a husky voice said, and she turned around and fell into Tony's arms. "Tony! How great to see you!" She introduced him to Maxine and some of the editors, as Sheila stalked over to where they were standing.

Tracy introduced them. "Sheila Zimmerman—Tony Amato."

"How are you?" Sheila asked coyly, nuzzling up to him. "So you're from Hollywood. I bet you've got a hundred great stories hidden away in that good-looking head of yours."

He blinked and smiled innocently.

"Oh, come on," she insisted, "don't you represent a lot of movie stars? I'd like to talk to you about that—"

Tracy and Maxine moved away and Tony shrugged

helplessly, a wide grin on his face. Sheila continued to purr and coo, while Tracy and Maxine picked up their conversation. At last, Belinda took Maxine away to meet more people, and Tracy wandered amiably from guest to guest, exchanging pleasantries. She was just stepping away from the bar with a fresh drink when her eyes zeroed in on a familiar face.

"Tracy?" The immaculately groomed woman greeted her hesitantly.

Tracy's eyes widened in surprise. "Mrs. Randolph, how are you?"

"I'm very well, thank you."

Mr. Randolph joined his wife and he was equally startled to see her. "Well, look who's here," he ventured. "How have you been?"

"I'm fine, Mr. Randolph. Uh—how is Robert?"

"He's doing well. He's married now, you know."

"No, I didn't," she said, realizing with light-headed certainty that she had put Robert and her flight from the wedding behind her.

"Yes, he and his wife live in Connecticut not far from us, and he's a partner with Randolph & Winchester."

"That's wonderful. I'm so glad to hear he's happy."

"And how are you keeping busy these days?" Mrs. Randolph inquired.

"I'm an editor at Franklin & Fields."

"Oh, how nice."

"She's being modest," came Belinda's voice from behind. "Tracy is one of our V.I.P.s here tonight. It was she who discovered and edited Maxine's book." She looked at them curiously. "I see you're already acquainted?"

Mrs. Randolph cleared her throat, and her husband said, "Well, yes. Tracy and Robert went to school together."

"Oh, I see," Belinda answered, and then it came to her. She had once been invited to an elaborate wedding at the Randolph's, but the bride had changed her mind at the last minute. Now she knew where she had seen Tracy's face before, and she chuckled quietly to

283

herself. "I'm going to have to steal Tracy away from you right now," she announced. "Maxine is about to be toasted. Do join us." She knew they wouldn't as she took Tracy's arm and led her away.

The F & F people had gathered in a chattering group at the opposite end of the room and they greeted Tracy with exuberant cries of welcome. Tracy smiled triumphantly as they all lifted their glasses, and John Noble drew Maxine into the center of the circle.

"To Maxine Wilkins and the great success of *Louisiana Legacy*," he said formally.

"And to the movie!" Steve Kramer added gaily.

"Hear, hear!" they all shouted, and the glasses were emptied swiftly.

"I understand Stan Geller will be directing the movie," Kramer said with interest.

"He should be here later," Belinda said. "I'll introduce you. And a very good friend of mine, Heather Gentree, will be with him."

"She's producing the movie, isn't she?" Sheila asked, edging closer to Tony.

"Oh, yes," Maxine put in. "She said she might bring the leading lady of the movie."

Tracy turned to Tony to see if this was true, and he nodded.

"They should be arriving at any time," he said.

Maxine continued feelingly. "Heather Gentree is a very interesting woman. And a very generous one, too. It's a lucky thing that she called right after Tracy bought the book, or I might have been cheated out of a lot of money." She sipped her drink and went on. "Of course, I got myself an agent right away, and he handled the negotiations. But right after that, I got a call from a horrible man named Carl Bendex who made an offer that was so low I'm ashamed to tell you. . . ."

Her voice trailed off as she perceived the silence that had overtaken the group. Tracy's heart dropped into her stomach and she stood frozen with horror and fear. She knew what they were all thinking. They thought she was the one in cahoots with Bendex, and she wanted to scream out her unspeakable frustration. They thought she was the spy! How could they think she would cheat her own author, or be unscrupulous enough to undermine her own book? She opened her mouth and tried to say something, but she could only stutter helplessly. Everyone was looking at her, and Maxine's face was clearly puzzled.

It was Stephen Marcus who broke the awful silence, and slowly, painfully, the conversation picked up again. Tracy didn't move, her eyes glued to the ground. She felt sick and she wondered how she could escape gracefully.

Tony saw her dilemma, and he tried to elbow his way over to her. But John Noble already had his hand on her arm, and he pulled her off to a corner near the entrance. His face was stern and he let out a long breath, his mouth compressed into a tight line.

"Okay, Tracy, this is it." His words stung her.

"It was one thing the way you got the Fleming book," he said quietly. "I never said anything about your tactics, but you put us into a tricky spot. We had to hire Kramer to stave off a lawsuit. There's no telling what might have happened."

She was speechless. His words pierced her already shattered composure, and her mouth felt suddenly dry. She had promised herself that she would never cry in a professional situation, but there was nothing she could do to stop the tears that were gathering in her eyes. Her anguish overwhelmed her, and she bent her head and clenched her teeth to hold back the sobs.

"It was a messy deal," he went on, "but I figured we could salvage it by hiring Steve. Then, on almost the same day that he was hired, *Year of the Dragon* was ripped off. And now it seems that another book was almost doomed to the same fate. That book was yours. Kramer was the only person who even knew about it until after it was signed. Now, I'm not accusing you of anything, but perhaps it would be best if you quietly resigned."

She refused to look up, and the tears were dripping freely onto the top of her gown. This was the most humiliating moment of her life, and her face burned with fury and embarrassment. She sensed other people watching them, and she lifted her chin slightly. Ken and Sheila was staring at them with frank interest, and she saw the Randolphs at the other end of the room. Then, through the blur of her tears, she discerned a tall, dark figure standing in front of her and her eyes came into focus.

It was Wes Canfield, and the exquisitely carved face of Ambrosia Jewell was next to him, her tiny hand clutching his arm. Tracy's misery was complete, and she knew that she couldn't stay there and face them. A feeling of nausea overcame her and the lights and colors in the room began to spin. She uttered a sharp, desperate cry.

Canfield's face was contorted with anger. "You son-of-a-bitch," he whispered fiercely.

Tracy's legs finally moved, and she bolted out the door and out to the street, not knowing what she was doing. She did not see Canfield's fist lash out and strike Noble in the jaw.

Noble was sent sprawling across Belinda Caruthers's drawing room floor. He looked up at his former boss with a stunned expression on his face. Canfield stood over him, pointing an accusing finger.

"You filthy bastard. You sold out your own company. I was in your office last week waiting for you, remember? Well, your phone rang and I picked it up. I forgot to give you the message," Canfield said with venom. "Carl Bendex was calling. He wanted you to know that *Year of the Dragon* is going just fine, and he's looking forward to seeing anything else that's hot. Pretty convenient," he spat out, "but you're not going to lay the rap on Tracy." He looked down at Noble with disgust. "And I trusted you," Wes went on sadly. "I even recommended you for my job." He turned to look for Tracy, and Heather Gentree walked calmly over to them. She stood over John Noble, who was still lying on the floor. "Don't bother to show up for work tomorrow, John," she said smoothly. "If I find you in my building—in *any* of my buildings—I'll have the security guard throw you out the window." She turned away imperiously, the matter irrevocably decided.

Canfield looked around, but Tracy was nowhere in sight. "Where's Tracy?" he asked Heather.

She inclined her head and lowered her voice. "She ran out before you hit John." Her eyes met his. "Tony ran after her."

Chapter 28

TRACY RAN INTO THE FREEZING NIGHT, FEELING NUMB and hysterical at the same time. The cold air brought her to her senses and she ran onto York Avenue, where she hailed a passing taxi and gave the driver her address. As she sat back against the seat, the tears started to flow again. Her career in publishing was over.

The cab pulled up in front of her building, and she threw the driver a bill, saying, "Keep the change." She ran into the lobby and rang for the elevator, just as the doorman shouted, "Hey, mister! You can't go up unannounced!" The elevator arrived and she stepped in and pressed the button for her floor, when a hand reached inside and stopped the doors from closing. Tony Amato stood there, out of breath and panting. She fell into his arms as they rode up, her words punctuating her shaky sobs. "Oh, Tony, it was so humiliating. The things he said to me!"

"I know, babe, I was there, but it's all over now."

"I'll never be able to show my face there again, and I'll never get another job."

He took the keys from her and opened the door to her apartment, taking her in his arms again and leading her to the couch. He left the door standing open.

"Shhhh. That's not true, and I'll tell you why if you'll just stop crying."

Slowly her sobs halted, but she listened with no hope of comfort.

Tony began to talk softly, his smooth, sure voice winding a spell around her. He explained everything to her. "Noble used you," he said simply, "but Wes found out." She fell against him with enormous relief, and he kissed her forehead as he continued. "And this is the time to tell you about Ambrosia. It's very private, but I think you need to know. But, Tracy, this is between you and me and Wes." And he recounted the whole story of Ambrosia's background, explaining the complexity of her fragile condition and her relationship with Canfield.

Tracy's eyes filled with tears again, but they were tears of relief. She nestled gratefully into Tony's arms and he stroked her hair and whispered little words of comfort. Neither of them noticed a lone man with dark, curly hair standing in the doorway. He stared at them, sad comprehension flooding his face.

"Oh, Tony," she breathed softly. "I don't know what I would do without you." Tony kissed her cheek, and as her head turned, she caught sight of Wes. She called out to him, but he dashed into the elevator and the doors slammed shut. She jammed her finger on the down button, but it was too late. He was gone. She turned desperately back to Tony, and he gathered her close again, lifting her chin to look at her.

"Don't worry about that," he said soothingly. "You can explain it to him."

"He won't ever want to see me again," she cried.

"Yes, he will. I'll take care of it."

"No, Tony. This is one thing you can't fix. You don't know. . . ."

He gave her a little squeeze and smiled his gallant smile. "Trust me," he said teasingly.

She shook her head and he took her hand and led her back into her apartment. All at once, she was exhausted.

"Now I want you to listen to me," he said with authority. "Get a good night's sleep. Don't think about this any more tonight. Tomorrow everything will look different, and you'll know what to do."

She stood there like a limp doll, and he pushed her gently towards her bed. "Go on," he said. "I'm going to leave and let you sleep. You need it. Can I get you anything?"

289

She shook her head weakly, and he kissed her lightly on the mouth. "Okay, then go to sleep. Promise?"

She nodded dumbly, and he blew her another kiss and slipped out the door. She was too drained to disobey him. Shedding her dress and all the fancy trimmings, she climbed into bed and fell into a restless sleep.

Chapter 29

IT WAS A LITTLE PAST ELEVEN A.M. WHEN TRACY finally arrived at the office the next day. The sun had come out, melting the ice from the previous night, and there were no clouds in the bright, pale blue sky. The temperature had risen to over forty degrees, and she couldn't help but feel light-hearted. The ride up in the elevator felt strange because of the lateness of her arrival, and she smiled as she remembered the first time she had ever been in it. It was ironic that everything had happened as a result of that one day.

When she reached her office a message was waiting for her on Dennis's desk. He handed it to her and she read it aloud.

" 'Heather Gentree's office called. Be at the Four Seasons for lunch at one o'clock.' Thanks," she said. "Is there anything else?"

He pointed to her office and she looked at the door and then back at him.

"Go take a look," he said mysteriously.

She opened her office door with a hesitant grin on her face, and saw a huge bouquet of flowers sitting on her desk. "Oh, how beautiful! Who sent them?" The profusion of color dominated the room, and she admired the lush arrangement as she looked for a card. She found one, tucked in between a daisy and a rose, and opened it eagerly. The note read: *Congratulations on Louisiana Legacy.* Steve, Jeff, Ken, Sheila, Stephen and Martha. Happy tears blurred her eyes as she realized just how much this offering meant, and all that it represented. Now she was truly one of them, a member of a team that welcomed her whole-heartedly. She sniffed the fragrant bouquet, touching the petals lovingly and wondering how to thank them.

The mild weather had had such a positive effect on her spirits that she felt buoyant and fresh, as if nothing could possibly go wrong. But there was one thing left to do, and she decided to take care of it at once. Quickly dialing the number at One Park Avenue, she sat back and thought about what she would say to him. But after several rings, she was informed that he would not be in the office all day. She sighed and stood up, not wanting to let anything spoil her happy mood. He would turn up. She walked down the hall to Steve Kramer's office.

"Well," he said when he saw her, his face lighting with a smile. "So how are you doing, Tracy?"

"Just great, Steve. I—I wanted to thank you for the—"

"Don't mention it. It was Jeff's idea. We all want you to know that we're behind you. I guess you heard by now that John Noble was the one who—"

Now she interrupted him. "I know," she said quietly. "Tony Amato told me." They looked at each other, confronting the unpleasant truth, and then she smiled sadly. "At least it's all over," she said.

"Yes. The matter is closed. The feeling of immense relief and joy swept over her again. It was like flying, like being at the controls of a small plane that soars high into the sky.

She went back to her office and fiddled half-heartedly with some paperwork until twelve-thirty, and then she went to carefully comb her hair and fix her make-up. She wanted to look A-1 for Heather Gentree, especially after last night's scene.

The day was so beautiful that she walked to the restaurant, and the short stroll put a fresh glow into her cheeks. She remembered the very first time she had been to the Four Seasons and she smiled ruefully as she recalled how nervous and jumpy she had been with Wes. She hadn't known then that she would fall in love with him. She could admit that to herself now, that she loved him, and the terrible uncertainty of the situation didn't bother her. Nothing can possibly bother me today, she thought exultantly, as she crossed the street and headed to the door of the restaurant.

She climbed the now-familiar stairs and was shown quickly to Heather Gentree's usual table by the fountain. Heather hadn't arrived yet, so she sat down and ordered a drink, looking around the room as she waited. She knew many of the people there, and they exchanged friendly glances and nods as she caught their eyes. She was so busy enjoying her own thoughts that she did not notice the tall, dark man standing over her. At first she thought it was the waiter, and was about to order another drink when she looked up and saw that it was Wes Canfield.

Too surprised to speak, she sat there gaping as he took the opposite seat and crooked a finger at a passing waiter. "Martini, please. Very dry."

"Hi," she said faintly.

"Is that all you can say? 'Hi'?"

"I wanted to explain about last night," she went on, trying to regain her composure.

"Forget it. Tony called me this morning. I think we're all squared away."

"I see." She lapsed into silence again, and then she remembered Heather Gentree. "Where's Heather?" she asked.

"Heather? Oh, she's not coming."

"She's not?"

"No."

"I tried to call you this morning," she ventured, "but you weren't in."

"I was with my father."

Happiness spread over her face, and he watched her carefully. "I'm so glad," she said. "And I'm so sorry about last week in the office," she continued in a rush. "I was—"

"That's all right. I deserved it."

Her confidence and spunk started to return. "True," she said dryly, and he smiled broadly.

She looked down at the table, and rubbed a fingernail self-consciously along the linen cloth. "Uh—Wes?"

"Yes?"

"Uh—what are you doing here?"

"I'm glad you brought that up. I have a proposition for you."

"Oh?"

"Yes. I think we should get married. A sharing of the profits, you might say."

"What?"

"You heard me," he said, somewhat miffed.

"You can't just—you can't just waltz in here and ask me to marry you!"

"Why not?"

"Well—because—because, that's why," she sputtered.

"I don't see why not," he said unreasonably.

"Is this what you call a proposal?" she asked acidly.

His eyebrow arched and he looked at her cynically. "It's the best you can expect from me."

She was incensed. "Oh, really?" she asked heatedly, standing up and throwing her napkin on the table. "Well, this is the best you can expect from me!" And with that, she turned and flounced away, her chin up and her shoulders thrown back. It was her intention to make a grand, lofty exit, but she was greatly surprised when she felt a strong hand on her shoulder, forcing her to stop in the middle of the floor.

Wes was standing over her and his blue eyes caressed her intently for a moment before his other hand went around her waist. She felt her fury melting as he drew her close, and before she knew what was happening, he bent his dark head and kissed her for a long, full, intense minute. She was oblivious to the patrons and staff, who were watching them with unbridled curiosity. His mouth lifted from hers, and she clung to him, too overwhelmed by her own passion and love for him to let go. Then his cheek was against hers, and he was whispering in her ear.

"Don't you know that I always loved you?" he murmured distractedly. "Ever since that first day when you came barging into my office. I won't let you go, so you might as well say yes."

294

Her eyes closed for an instant, as the words she had despaired of ever hearing from him sank in and took root. When she opened her eyes, they were covered by a thin haze of happy tears. "You're impossible," she whispered. "But I love you, too. So I guess I'll just have to put up with you."

He kissed her again, slowly and tenderly, and then he put a strong arm around her and led her out of the room and down the stairs.

"Where are we going?" she demanded.

"Home," he said.

You Have a Rendezvous with Richard Gallen Books...

EVERY MONTH!

Visit worlds of romance and passion in the distant past and the exciting present, words of danger and desire, intrigue and ecstasy—in breathtaking novels from romantic fiction's finest writers.

Now you can order the Richard Gallen books you might have missed!

These great contemporary romances...

Continued next page

Dear Reader:

Would you take a few moments to fill out this questionnaire and mail it to:

Richard Gallen Books/Questionnaire
8-10 West 36th St., New York, N.Y. 10018

1. What rating would you give *Trade Secrets?*
   ☐ excellent ☐ very good ☐ fair ☐ poor
2. What prompted you to buy this book? ☐ title
   ☐ front cover ☐ back cover ☐ friend's recommendation ☐ other (please specify) _____
3. Check off the elements you liked best:
   ☐ hero ☐ heroine ☐ other characters ☐ story
   ☐ setting ☐ ending ☐ love scenes
4. Were the love scenes ☐ too explicit
   ☐ not explicit enough ☐ just right
5. Any additional comments about the book?

   _____

6. Would you recommend this book to friends?
   ☐ yes ☐ no
7. Have you read other Richard Gallen
   romances? ☐ yes ☐ no
8. Do you plan to buy other Richard Gallen
   romances? ☐ yes ☐ no
9. What kind of romances do you enjoy reading?
   ☐ historical romance ☐ contemporary romance
   ☐ Regency romance ☐ light modern romance
   ☐ Gothic romance
10. Please check your general age group:
    ☐ under 25 ☐ 25-35 ☐ 35-45 ☐ 45-55 ☐ over 55
11. If you would like to receive a romance
    newsletter please fill in your name and
    address:

    _____
    _____
    _____